Indian Hill

INDIAN HILL

Mark Tufo

Electronic Edition
Copyright 2012 Mark Tufo
Discover other titles by Mark Tufo
Visit us at marktufo.com
and http://zombiefallout.blogspot.com/ home of future webisodes
and find me on FACEBOOK

Editing by:
Teri Gibson
teri@editingfairy.com

Cover Art:
Dean Harkness

Dedication: To my wife who did more work getting this book out to the public than I did. Thank you for your hard work! I love you and appreciate all of your hard work on this new endeavor we find ourselves immersed in!

To the men and women of the armed forces and uniformed services, a thank you to each and every one of you for the sacrifices you endure for our continued safety.

To my loyal readers and fans, I know I've been promising this story for about 4 months now and I truly am sorry for stringing everyone along, I hope that the hard work that was poured into this story delivers and that you can once again reconnect with our wayward hero.

And so it begins...

Chapter 1 – Mike Journal Entry One

Our ship was close to landing on home, sweet home after what seemed like weeks of traveling. Beth had completely withdrawn from me as if I were the monster, instead of the supreme commander whom she actually spent more time conversing with than me during the entire voyage home. With some perverse satisfaction, I watched them talk, knowing full well he saw her only as his next meal, or some form of entertainment, and then a meal.

Deb retreated into herself wholly. I think that Beth's presence and my indifference had something to do with it. But I wasn't completely self-centered. I knew the main cause of it was the realization of the horror she had just escaped. And, probably, the comprehension of the wide-scale horror that was yet to come. The few hours that I had to adjust to this semblance of "freedom" were truly liberating. I knew it wasn't over but no longer did the lives of these women depend solely on me, or so I hoped.

The Genogerians and Progerians were coming; of that, there was no doubt. When? Well, that was a good question. I knew deep down that running and hiding was not an option; oh, but how I yearned for that avenue. I wanted to see my folks; yes, even my mother. I wanted to eat dinner at my sister's, I wanted to play Risk with my brothers, I wanted to drink beer with my friends. I wanted to do what every "normal" young male wants to do. But I knew those things weren't going to happen. Not any time soon.

I wasn't sure if years of psychotherapy would ever get me back to "normal." All my early years of the pampered

American life had left me completely unprepared for the ordeal I had just endured. The thoughts that allowed me to survive were becoming vastly distant as I stole a glance at Beth. She saw me eye her but paid no attention whatsoever. Unbeknownst to me, however, Deb had also seen it, and that just seemed to twist the knife in her heart a little bit more.

What a great love triangle we were. More like three non-parallel lines, from my perspective. Deb wanted me, I wanted Beth, and Beth wanted nothing to do with any of us. She saw the girls and me as the beasts, incognizant that the creature she kept talking to, the supreme commander, was the real beast and the sole reason for our predicament. Sometimes, the more education you receive, the less smart you are.

Indian Hill's peaceful slopes beckoned me. Could I find some sort of "peace" there? The place where I did so much exploration not only physically, but spiritually as well? Paul, Dennis and I dropped acid for the first time up there, making the place that much more surreal, like it needed any help. We had actually spent hours up in the "Hobbit Tree" looking over the vast expanse of greenery that was Walpole.

Surveying Indian's Pond to the left, the train tracks where we almost met our untimely demises; and even further, the Stop and Shop roof, which was sort of the start of it all. Oh, how I longed for simpler times. My gut was roiling with emotion; my fight or flight reflex was in overdrive. But there was no one to fight and nowhere to run--what a fucking dilemma. Deb began to weep silently as we approached Earth. Her shoulders shuddered as she attempted to quell her emotions. Was she relieved to be getting away from this whole mess? Or just to be getting home? My guess was a little bit of both.

Beth's eyes gleamed; I knew that look, she was excited. There would be no way she could ever understand what the rest of us went through. She looked like a kid who had just spent the day at Disneyland and was now headed to Disneyworld. The other girls' responses varied as well: from full on, open-throttled weeping to the "whooping" of over-excited, drunken sorority girls. Sororities, fraternities... Shit! College! Would I be going back? I wanted to but I doubted it. I'm not sure that I'd ever be able to sit still for that long again. What employment could I get with my newfound skills? Cab driver? Maybe. Maybe I could join the mixed martial arts circuit. Naw, that wouldn't work; I'd never be able to stop myself.

Well, I figured realistically, I probably only had about a month or so left .The Genogerians weren't going to sit tight for long, not while their supreme commander was being held captive. For now, Earth awaited and I definitely wanted to reacquaint myself with her. I knew she, at least, would welcome me.

"General Burkhalter?" I asked incredulously. It seemed odd to me that a general would put himself out just to greet me.

"Come; let's get off this ship. If we stay on it too long, the scientists might just dissect us along with it. They've been chomping at the bit to get a hold of this thing. I think they were more pissed at the sick staff sergeant than at you and your crew." the general said as he surveyed his surroundings.

"I appreciate you greeting us, General."

"It's the least I could do. Especially since we need to take these necessary precautions," he said, pointing to his haz-mat suit.

"I understand, General, it's just difficult. We've been confined for so long, that being able to see freedom and not embrace it is a little bittersweet."

"And now it is my turn to understand. We will do all in our power to make this, hopefully short, stay as enjoyable as possible. But you do realize we are going to have to debrief you until your throat is raw? We need to know as much as we can about this new foe, and we don't have very long to get it."

"One thing first, General, before we get this whole

show on the road."

"Name it, son."

"Pizza."

"Done."

When we reached the makeshift hospital, pizzas of all sizes and toppings awaited our diligent ministrations. Ah! To be back home… The food was great, the service impeccable. Even better than a five star resort. Well, almost. The doctors watched our every move. I'm not sure if they were disappointed that we didn't sprout wings or third eyes, but they monitored us twenty-four/seven while we were in their custody.

"How are things going, Mike?"

"Great, General, but we sure were hoping we'd be out of here by now. Ten solid days in quarantine and not one of us has developed any strange rashes or bumps." I sounded a little peeved, although I tried not to convey that over my voice; but restraint was not my strong point.

"Mike, I came here on a serious note."

"What, General? Did one of our lab reports come back bad?" Not that I was really worried about it, but the general was concerned.

"No, no. All of your tests came back remarkably well. The whole lot of you are in perfect health."

"Will that bring a better price at the auction block?" That should have gotten some response from the general, but he did nothing. Now, he did have me concerned. "Spill it, General; this is worse than knowing."

"Your mother has passed away."

"What? When? Just now? I've got to go!" I said as I headed towards the door.

"You know as well as I do, Mike, that you cannot leave just yet. That armed guard will riddle you with bullets before he lets you break the seal on this place."

"What happened?" I asked as I slowly turned back towards him.

"It was a few months after your disappearance; she

had a stroke. She never fully recovered from it and deteriorated fast."

"Was it because of me?"

"Part of it, maybe, the stress and all surrounding your disappearance."

"And because the government didn't 'fess up to what was really going on!" I said heatedly.

"Mike, we had to look for the common good. If we told even one woman to ease her fears, we would have panicked millions. And do you really think that the truth was any better than the scenarios she was imagining?"

"How long did she live after the stroke?"

"About a month and a half. She was apparently trying to hold on until she could see you one last time."

That stung. My mother and I weren't exactly close but still, it was a fundamental loss, one that could never be replaced. It was another tragedy that I would carry with me. Unfortunately, it would not be my last.

My mother had gotten sick and passed; all while I was struggling to survive on an alien vessel. No, the truth would not have done her any good. More than likely, it would have hastened the effects of her stroke. I still had a difficult time wrapping my mind around the fact that I had been on that ship for almost a year and a half. Eighteen months of my life was stolen from me and I would never be able to get it back. I always wondered what went through those innocent men's minds who were wrongly convicted of a crime and then sent to prison. What must they think after five or ten years of incarceration when a new piece of evidence comes to light that sets them free? The chunk of their lives that was taken from them can never, ever be replaced. Mine was only a small taste, but even a small taste can be sour on the lips.

"General, don't get me wrong. You and your staff have been nothing short of magnanimous. They have taken care of our every need. But I really have to know when we will be free to go. None of us has displayed any traces of anything. I have told and retold my experience to you and the president. Hell, I even brought their commander back. I'm just sick and tired of being cooped up, and now I would just like to go back to Walpole and visit with my family. Do they know I'm back?"

"As for the first question, just four more days, Mike. The medical staff will feel much more comfortable with four more days. Then I promise you a direct flight to any destination that you desire."

"To be honest, General, I'd rather have a car. Kind of sick of flying too."

"Understood. How about a Humvee?"

"You're going to give me a Humvee?"

"I cleared it with the president this morning. He felt it was the least we could do."

"Awesome! I want the one with the hard plastic shell on the back."

"Done. And as for your family, they have no idea that you're back. We couldn't tell them. They'd be up here breaking in doors and that just wouldn't do anybody any good."

"Got any idea where they are, General?"

"Well, after your mother passed, your dad took it pretty hard. He holed himself up in his Searsport cabin."

"My dad is in Searsport? Hell, that's only a few hours south of here."

"Your brother, Ronny and his wife Nancy, are still in Walpole. Your brother, Gary took the loss of your mother pretty hard, took him a few months to go through the mourning process. He and Ronny have put all their energy into their paving company. Your brother, Glenn, moved back to West Roxbury after the funeral. He actually works from time to time with the paving crew. But mostly, he repairs small aircraft at one of the local airports. Your sister is still living in Connecticut, but travels up to Maine every other weekend to check on your dad. Your mother's death hit him a lot harder than anyone really anticipated."

"What are the odds that this weekend would be that weekend, General?"

"It appears, Mike, that luck favors you because this is one of her scheduled arrivals. Would you like me to notify them of your imminent visit?"

"No, General; I'd just rather show up."

"Mike, about the Humvee."

"Oh, you want it back already?"

"Not quite. At least, not the Hummer."

"Then what, General?"

"We would, or rather, I would like to have the person driving the Humvee back."

"General, I don't want a driver." And then my not-so-fast brain finally caught up with me. "You want me back? What the hell do you want me back for?"

"Son, I've been watching you for ten straight days. I've listened to your story probably a hundred times. I've interviewed every one of these girls at least twice. I want you in my service. You are exactly the kind of man that we are going to need in the coming months. You, and thousands like you."

"General, I'm not cut out for the military life, I'm sure that you have a dossier full of my pre-alien days. I wasn't quite on the straight and narrow."

"Son, those events in no shape, way, or form have anything to do with the person that you are now."

"General, I just don't play well with others. I have a real authority issue."

"If I make you an officer and accountable only to me?"

"General, I just don't…"

"No, don't answer now. Why don't you get out of here this weekend, go see you family and friends, drive around this country? And then in a week or two, give me your answer. But please just promise me that you will at least consider it."

"Don't worry, General I will, at the very least,

consider it, and often. What branch would I be in?"

"Why, Army of course."

I laughed. "General, my dad and my brother were both Marines. I'd never live it down if I came home in Army duds."

"Son, if you join up, I'll give you any uniform you want."

"Thank you, sir. I've got more on my plate now than I could possibly even begin to finish. And I suddenly found myself very tired. Please excuse me, General, I think I'm going to take a nap."

"Very well, I'll see you in three days. I've been called back to Washington. And it's not very wise to keep the president waiting."

"General?"

"Yes, Mike."

"What have you done with the commander?"

"Ah! See? If you were in uniform I could disclose that information to you. But civilians cannot be privy to those details." I thought he was kidding until he walked through the sealed outer chamber.

"Son of a bitch," I mumbled as I laughed and headed for my bunk.

The four days came and went without much incident. Tanya developed a small sneeze that almost shut down the state, but it ended up she was just allergic to some of the detergent that was being used on the hypo-allergenic pillows. Kind of ironic, I thought. Beth hadn't said more than two words to me since we landed. She pretty much kept to her side of the quarantine wing. Deb had become increasingly morose and sullen the longer we were cooped up.

I avoided everyone like they had the plague. The general did not make it back from Washington before the doctors finally cleared us. The women all hopped into one of the troop transports. They were shuttling them down to the Bangor Airport so they could go home or wherever they desired. A few of them were actually going to the Bahamas on the U.S. government dime. Why not? Might as well enjoy it while it was free. And true to his word, the general gave me a Humvee with the hard plastic shell, and also another little gift. A USMC officer's uniform with captain's bars lay on the passenger seat. I was still sitting on the fence with that whole question but it sure was an impressive looking uniform. I barely set foot into my new vehicle when the troop transport truck came to a grinding halt. Beth jumped off the back and ran straight towards me.

"Mike, wait a second!" she yelled with her arms outstretched. I waited patiently. She had just doubled the number of words she had spoken to me since we got back to Earth. I was too curious to do anything but wait and see what she wanted. I did, however, notice Deb sticking her head out to see what was going on.

"Wait, Mike. I just have to get this out before you leave," she said with a little bit of laborious breathing.

"I'm listening," I said coolly. I'd been waiting for two weeks for her to say something. I wasn't about to now let her know that my heart was somewhere in my throat, and jumping around like a frog on crack.

"I know I've been distant to you. I know that everything you did out there was for us. I---I'm just having a difficult time handling the images of what you did up there with the person I fell in love with."

"Do you think it was easy for me? Killing those men?"

"No, no! I'm not saying that!"

"Would you rather it were me on the wrong end of one of those swords?"

"No, God, no!" She screamed. "You're not being fair."

"Beth, what the fuck is fair? Certainly nothing that happened up there."

"I know, I know."

"I did what I had to. To get us out of there, I did what I had to." My voice level dropped in half. I had no desire to yell at her. "And I am going to keep doing what I have to do."

"What does that mean?" she asked as she looked at me with pleading eyes.

"The general asked me to join the Marines, and I am going to." It was that simple and easy. I was well aware that I had to continue the fight; the day was far from won, and I would do what I had to.

"How could you? How can you? Haven't you seen enough death for a thousand life times?" Disgust crossed her face.

"Beth, they're coming." I pointed skyward. "They're coming whether we want them to or not. And now it's time for me to pay them back for all the kindness that they bestowed upon us."

"You're not the man that I fell in love with."

"No, I'm not. How could I be? I don't know what you went through up there, but I can guarantee it wasn't anything like what I went through. I was forced to kill other human beings for the entertainment of aliens. Do you know what that did to my moral conscience? Not only was I being torn up physically in those bouts but also spiritually. Do you know how many times I almost laid down my arms so that I could just have it end?"

"Then why didn't you?" she shot back.

"Because of you!!" I yelled. She stepped back from the sheer force of my voice. "When it all comes down to it, I did it for you, Beth." She was crying; I was crying; it was not a pretty sight. Half the base was watching. Some Marine I'd make.

"I still love you, Mike, but I'm going to need some time, to get over all of this."

"I understand. Are you going back home or are you going back to school? " I asked.

"I'm going home now; if I do go back to school, it won't be in Colorado."

That hurt for me, was the first time I truly felt that

nothing was ever going to be the same. No more wake and bakes with Saturday morning wrestling, no more parties on the quad, no more concerts at Red Rocks. Life had forever been altered and, at age twenty-two, I felt cheated--cheated out of those things that were rightfully mine.

"I'll give you all the time you're going to need. If and when you can forgive me, I'll be waiting for you. But if we do start over, I want you to know what happened on that ship." Now it was her turn to look hurt. "When I thought that I wasn't going to make it, I sought comfort in the arms of another." She did not seem nearly as surprised as I anticipated. Hurt, but not surprised.

"Debbie, right?" she guessed as she looked down at her shoes.

"How?"

"I see the way she looks at you, when you're not looking. I see the pain in her eyes. I see the way she eyes me when she thinks I'm not looking. That what-does-she-have-that-I-don't-have? look. I can't blame you, with the hell you were put through. That's not what has me at odds , though, Mike." She spoke tenderly, and caressed my face with both of her hands. "It was the brutality you unleashed, the savagery in your eyes. They are indelibly burned into my brain. I don't know if I'll ever be able to look at you without bringing up those images. It's as if there is a devil living inside of you. Most of the time, you have control of him, but on those occasions when he breaks free, he wreaks havoc on everyone around you."

"That's not fair, Beth." I pleaded.

"No, it's not; like you said, nothing that happened to us up there was fair. I just need some time, Mike. I need some time to reflect on all that has happened to me, to you and ultimately to us. I wish I could say that everything was going to turn out alright, but I just don't know." She moved in closer and gave me a hug, the likes of which I never wanted to be released from. A tidal wave of emotion flooded through our bodies. Had we not been in a public place, we may have taken great strides in improving our strained relationship. The hug ended oh, so shortly. She got up on her tiptoes and kissed my lips. I flushed, it was the most intimate kiss I had received since leaving this planet.

"Goodbye, Mike," she said as she pulled away. That goodbye sounded so final, I didn't know how to respond. I wasn't prepared for this. I would much rather have been facing an enemy in the ring, at least there I knew where I stood. This was horrible; it was an unseen wound, but it struck deeper than anything I had encountered thus far. I thought my heart would rip in two. My head felt like I was burning a fever and I couldn't think straight. Do I run after her? Do I stand here like a fool? Do I get in my car and drive?

"Beth?" She turned. "Goodbye." A small smile flitted across her face replaced by deep sorrow. I wasn't one hundred percent sure, but I thought that she had already made up her mind. I cried for the first two hours of my drive. Luckily, not many people live that far north in Maine, because I'm sure that I was all over the road.

I finally came to grips with the levity of my situation and the last hour went a lot smoother, especially after I found a liquor store. I was halfway through my third beer when I started down the turn-off to my father's cabin. I had the windows down on the Hummer; the crisp winter air was invigorating. The only sound I heard was that of the crunching ice under my tires. I slowed to a crawl when I entered my dad's driveway. Off to my right was Mann's pond, completely frozen solid at this time of year. I noticed one solitary figure gliding along on the pond. I couldn't be sure from the distance, but in this remote of a location, at this time of year, it could only be one person.

My father stopped his precision glide to look over the pond at the vehicle intruding on his land. I'm sure the sight of any military vehicle was not welcome, especially after the runaround the family received concerning my whereabouts. He slowly skated closer to the edge of the pond, perhaps to verbally accost the intruder. At the previous stop, I changed out of my civvies and donned the Marine Corps uniform. The general knew I would take the commission and it seemed he also knew my size perfectly. I had to admit, I cut a pretty good figure with it on. I stopped the Hummer on the driveway, my father now within thirty yards, and at the edge of the pond. I knew at this distance there would be no way he could tell who I was. Especially, since the last time I saw him, I was twenty pounds lighter with long hair and more than likely wearing an Ozzy Osbourne T-shirt.

    At one hundred and eighty pounds, with short hair and in an officer's uniform, it might as well have been Halloween. I began the descent down to the banks of the pond, while my father just stood there, most likely still not recognizing me. He looked warily at me under the assumption that I would be bringing him bad news about his son. And, to be honest, he didn't look like he could handle it. This once virile man had been reduced to a shell of his former self. The stress and loss of the past year and a half had visibly taken their toll. Now, I wondered if I had the right person. From a distance, he looked like the man I called "father," but as I approached, I saw how reality had ravaged him. Tears were welling up in his eyes. Recognition was becoming evident on his face; but he wouldn't let his guard down until he was completely sure. The pain of false hope would be almost too much to bear. I was now within fifteen feet.

    "Mike?" he said, almost as a whisper, so unsure of his sight and mind. "Mike? Is that you?"

    "It's me, Dad." The voice sealed the deal. He might not have been able to trust his eyes, but his ears certified what his mind longed to hear. He fell to one knee, crying, his face buried in his gloves. Sobs racked his body. I ran the rest of the way.

    "Dad! It's me!" I hugged him as hard as I could; then eased off, afraid that I might break him in two. He grabbed my arm with his. I think he had to touch me just to make sure.

"Is that really you?" He didn't let me answer. "Your mom…" And he started sobbing anew.

"I know, Dad, I know. I'm sorry that I couldn't be here for you and the family." My sister had been watching the whole event unfold from the large picture window that overlooked the pond. She came running out of the cabin, not knowing who I was or why I was there.

"Dad!" she screamed. "Are you alright?" I stood up and turned towards her with my father still clutching my arm, not wanting to let go. She had been running at a full sprint and suddenly stopped dead in her tracks as if she'd just seen a ghost. And who knows? Perhaps she had.

"Mike, is that you?" She seemed more unwilling to accept my appearance than our dad. Perhaps she had already made peace with my passing. My dad had still not been able to let go of me and was more than eager to accept my return. My sister couldn't move, she was rooted to the spot. She just shook her head back and forth.

"It can't be you. We buried you." The general didn't tell me that little nugget of information. I guess it's kind of tough to tell someone he is dead and buried, when he's standing right in front of you.

"It's me, sis." She approached cautiously. This was, of course, Stephen King territory and who knows? Maybe I was about to change into a clown outfit and chase her up to the cabin door. But nothing like that happened. I had to physically extricate myself from my dad's clutch as I slowly approached my sister. Her head shaking intensified. I grabbed her and laid on one of those bear hugs until she stopped shaking. My dad had come ashore, skates and all. We embraced as one huge mass of family; hell, we even walked up to the cabin that way. It would have made a pretty funny video. Nobody dared let go, lest the dream end. None of us were quite ready to wake up just yet.

"How? How did this happen?" My sister was at a loss for words, which, up until this moment, was something I had never encountered. Oh well, I had seen some pretty strange things this year. Why stop now?

"In due time, sis. But for now, I just want to sit here and soak up this moment."

Anxiety always made my dad cook. He must have been one anxious puppy, because we ate like kings: corn on the cob, mashed potatoes, pork roast, all topped off with pecan pie. I hadn't eaten this well since before leaving Earth. We ate and my dad just stared at my sister and me like the Mad Hatter. My sister was happy I was home, but she knew something was amiss. "It was in my eyes," she told me later. I wasn't sure just how much of my story I wanted to share with my father. I didn't know if he could take it, number one; and number two, at this point I didn't really think he'd care. He was just happy I was home.

I called my brother, Ron, after dinner, who first thought I was playing a practical joke, a sick practical joke. That was, of course, until I reminded him that he still owed me one hundred eighteen and one half beers from our bets on the 1982 baseball season. It was our inside joke, nobody knew the final tally except us; so by process of elimination, it had to be me.

We talked for an hour. He wanted to know my plans because he was coming up first thing in the morning. I told him fine as long as he brought beer. After the phone call, my sister, father and I sat around the table until midnight, talking about the old times. More than once, my dad had to wipe a tear away from his eyes and he would discreetly leave to use the bathroom.

"He didn't take Mom's death all that well," my sister reflected on the obvious.

"How long has he been like this?" I asked with concern in my voice.

"This is one of his good days. Most of the time, I have to remind him to eat. But now that you're back, I hope he'll snap out of it. I come up here every other weekend just to keep tabs on him. I've asked him over and over again to come live with us. But he says this place gives him peace."

"What about Ronny and Gary, do they come up?"

"Every so often, Nancy comes up with the kids on the weekends that I don't come up. Thank God for that, because I just can't get up here anymore than I already do."

"Does he go back to Massachusetts at all?"

"He goes every once in a while just to see Mom's and your graves." She looked at me sideways, maybe to see my response at that one. I didn't have one for her. "He spends the night at Ron and Nancy's and then heads back up here. I make sure those are the weekends I come up, because that's when he's at his worst."

"My wake wasn't an open coffin was it?" I laughed as my sister punched my arm.

"God no! I think we would have known something was wrong. Although whoever it was, I'm sure they would have been better looking." I grabbed my sister's head and put her in a headlock.

"You better be nice to me," she mumbled from underneath my grasp. "You know I can still kick your ass." I let go and put my hands in the air, as if in compliance. "What happened Mike?"

"How much do you want to know?" I sat back down. It seemed appropriate for the mood that was rapidly approaching.

"All of it. The government told us there was a terrorist attack on Red Rocks and they were only able to partially identify remains, using DNA tests. They sent what we thought was your body two months after your disappearance. Obviously, it was a sealed coffin. We had a ceremony and we buried you. Although I don't think dad ever thought you were truly gone." She put her hands in her face as she wept. I caressed her shoulder to comfort her as best I could.

"I'm sorry that you went through that, but I wouldn't wish what happened to me on anyone. You might want to refill that glass of wine before I begin. I'm going to need your mind open for this little tale." And for the next five hours, I related everything that happened to me during the past eighteen months or so.

She killed her bottle of wine and began on my stash of beers. Ronny had better get up here early with those replacements, I thought to myself. My sister could have caught flies the way her mouth hung open. If she hadn't been looking directly at me, I doubt that she would have believed me. As it was, I think she was having great difficulty coming to terms with the whole thing. My sister was a person who believed everything has a place and there's a place for everything. But there was no shelf big enough for this whopper.

"When?" she asked, taking a big drag of beer to get her mouth parts wet again. She had completely dried them out while her mouth gaped open. "How long do you think that we have before they come... here?" She swallowed another big swig. That was a hard piece to get down the gullet in one swallow.

"Three weeks, a month. Two months at best." Her eyes grew to the size of saucers.

"What time did Ronny say he was getting here?" She got up and went to the fridge after discovering that our alcohol supply was running dangerously low, which had to be remedied under these conditions. I laughed.

"Sis, I don't think you need any more anyway."

"Where should we go? What should we do?" my sister said anxiously. I could tell that she was nervous because she began to clean absent-mindedly.

"First off, you can sit down. Nothing's going to happen tonight." I crossed my fingers behind my back. She threw her hand towel into the sink and plopped back down with an audible sigh. "My advice would be to stay away from all large urban centers; that's where they are going to make their presence known."

"Are they planning to wipe us out?" she asked almost like a five year old asking if she could stay up late, quivering lip and all.

"Worse, sis. Much worse; they plan to enslave us." She almost fell out of her seat.

"What are we going to do?"

"All that we can. We live, we fight. I'm not going down like a sheep. I've seen these bastards; they have no regard for our lives whatsoever. They'd just as soon eat us as pet us." My sister was shivering visibly. "I don't mean to scare you, but this is going to happen whether you want it to or not."

"Why isn't the president doing something about it? Why haven't we been told anything?"

"He is doing things. But he can't tell the general population just yet. What do you think would happen? There'd be mass hysteria, rioting, looting and worse. And just at a time when we need the entire country locked together, we would be tearing each other apart. That's just what the Progerians want. Although, to be honest with you, I don't think they are all that concerned about us as a species anyway. But who knows? Maybe that hole we ripped in their side might just make them think things over for a bit. My sister and I just sat there, both deep in our own separate but reflective thoughts. We both turned to watch as the sun began its ascent over the pond.

Ronny must have slept for an hour before he hopped in the car. I blurrily watched as his little red Beemer screamed up Dad's dirt drive. Fifty years old and he still drove like he was seventeen! No wonder he had totaled so many of his cars. I walked out onto the porch to greet him; the winter air was electrifying. My mind went from dullness to crispness in mere seconds. I was tired and wired all at the same time. My body was ready for sleep but my mind could go on forever, or so it seemed.

Ronny slipped while getting out of the car, barely catching himself. He looked like something out of a Three Stooges matinee. Legs going a mile a minute, but getting no traction. If he actually got some tread, I thought, he probably couldn't stop until he was halfway through the side of the house.

"Mike, just because you're back, does that mean that I still owe you the beer? You know there is a statute of limitations on all debts, public and private."

"Have you been thinking up that excuse the entire time you spent driving up here?" I shouted from the porch.

"Well, yeah," he said. He had finally made progress with his battle for footing and joined Lyn and me on the porch. I soon found myself in a bear hug that threatened to break bones. "God, I missed you," he said, muffled because his mouth was buried in my sweater. He proceeded to wipe away a tear. "So what was it, community service?" he asked, trying to lighten the moment.

"Yeah, something like that. I'll tell you all about it, provided that you have enough beer to wet my whistle."

"Mike, I'm paying my debt in full, plus some extra."

"What the hell are you talking about?"

"I bought five cases, two Buds, two Coors and a Labatts blue."

"Are you kidding me? I said, truly shocked. We never actually paid up on our debts,

"Yeah, well this time was a little different. Most people don't come back from the dead."

"True." I wasn't going to argue; I just wanted the beer, and knowing Ronny, I knew it would be cold, not because he bought it that way, but because he was too cheap to fix the heater in his car.

"Dennis will be up later. I called him the minute I got off the phone with you."

"Awesome, I can't wait to see him. What about Paulie? Any news from him?" Ron's face turned serious.

"Mike, he pretty much went underground after you disappeared."

"Underground?"

"Yeah, radical, militia type. Last I heard, he was training up in the mountains of Colorado."

"That doesn't sound like Paul at all."

"Yeah, well there's other things going on too. When Dennis comes up here we need to talk."

"That's a definite." I gave my brother another big hug, and drained the beer I had just opened. "Ron, we'll talk more but Lyn and I have been up all night and I was up all the night before. I'm pretty much done for now. How long 'til Dennis gets here?"

"He said he'd be up here around noon. So probably oneish or two."

"Even better." I said stifling a yawn. "Wake me then."

Dennis arrived around three that afternoon, but they didn't wake me. Apparently, I looked like I needed more sleep. What roused me were the smells wafting from the kitchen. My dad was well into preparing day two's feast. And if I wasn't mistaken, I smelled turkey and his world-renowned stuffing. I was tempted to run down the stairs and dig in when I realized that I was crying. I wouldn't have even noticed had I not watched a teardrop hit my father's wooden floor. Even then, I thought it may have been sleep drool. I wiped my mouth with the back of my hand. It came back dry. Not until I wiped my eye with my finger did I realize from where the offending liquid was leaking. Moments passed before recognition dawned.

I had been dreaming about the ship, although I suppose that would be considered a nightmare. I had been reliving the death of Carol, the cruelty of her death would never leave me. I was crying for what had happened and for what was to come. This feast I was about to enjoy, would it be a short-lived moment in the coming months, years, forever? I didn't know. Did any of them down those stairs know? Could they know? Could I tell them? I went to hell and back and for what? To tell everybody that we were going back to hell? The feast wasn't smelling so good now. I began to turn tail and just lay back in bed, when my sister opened the door.

"I thought I heard you moving around in here," she said as she peeked her head around the door.

"What do you have, bat ears?"

"Come on; dinner is almost ready. And Dennis and Ronny are like two little kids waiting for Santa Claus."

"I'm not sure if I'm ready for this." And then her words hit home.

"You don't have a choice." She wasn't trying to be condescending or mean, she was just trying to tell me like it was. She was right, of course. I had no choice; none of us had a choice in this matter. We would live and we would die, how we chose to do both was completely up to us, or was it? She had steeled my resolve.

"Just give me a sec." She walked back downstairs fully cognizant that the sec I needed was to hide the obvious on my face. I made a big production about going to the bathroom and washing up, but she knew the only thing I was washing away was the evidence of tears from my face. I walked down the stairs, and my sister was right, they both looked like they had just seen the Easter Bunny and Santa Claus walking hand in hand down the stairs. Wags nearly fell over trying to untangle himself from his chair.

"I seem to be having that effect on people today," I grinned.

"Dude! It's so awesome to see you!!" he shouted. "You look ripped. You been working out?" he said as he grabbed me and gave me a hug that rivaled Ronny's earlier one. I hugged him back. This was doing wonders for my soul, but it was murder on my spleen.

"Dude, let me go before you bust something," I said breathlessly.

"Oh man! It's so good to see you. After we buried you, I didn't think I'd ever smile again."

"Well, that shit-eating grin you've got going on now should make up for any lost smile time you had coming." He hugged me again, and this time, came bearing gifts... A cold Budweiser, just what the doctor ordered.

"Dude! Where have you been?" Dennis asked in amazement, not sure if I was, in fact, truly there.

"Bud, we'll talk about that after dinner. That smells way to good to mess up with the story I'm going to relate." I walked over to the stove where my father was stirring some mashed potatoes.

"Dad, that smells awesome."

"How you doing, Butch?" my dad said, using my nickname as a youth. "Did you sleep good?"

"Yeah, Dad, I really did." As I hugged him, I looked over his shoulder right at my sister. Our eyes met; she knew the truth, but had no desire to shatter Dad's illusions. Dinner was unbelievable. I still think of that meal from time to time, especially in the cold nights when I get to hunker down to another MRE. For those of you not in the know, that is a Meal Ready To Eat. We in the know affectionately like to call them Meals Rarely Edible. Nothing like processed pork to get you through the dead of night. Umm, umm, good.

Chapter 2 – Mike Journal Entry Two

We sat and drank and laughed. It was the best I'd felt in a long, long time. I was able, for the time being, to put my considerable burden to rest. I didn't go into as finite detail as I had the night before with my sister, but they got the general idea. And I was still hoarse from talking for over two hours. I wanted to move on to lighter subjects but someone always had another question. I felt bad they had to endure what they went through, not even a clue as to how I had supposedly died. Nobody bought the terrorist bomb theory, there had just been too many witnesses.

Although the government had done its best to discredit them as drug-taking hippies, those who did not want to believe the truth had a viable option with the government account of events. But a growing majority were aware of the truth, especially when news of similar events in China and Russia leaked out. It was just too difficult to hide events of such magnitudes. China's government owns the media and even they couldn't suppress it.

"Did you know the Giants won the Super Bowl?" Dennis piped into my head.

"What?" I asked incredulously. I had drifted so far into my own thoughts I didn't even hear what he said.

"I said the Giants beat the Raiders in the Super Bowl. In overtime, no less."

"Oh come on. You've got to be kidding me," I moaned. "My favorite team goes to the Super Bowl and wins in overtime while I'm stuck up in an alien vessel? That's just my luck."

"Yeah, you should go again next year. I'd really love to see them in the bowl again." He got up and ran because he knew I was going to lay the smack down on him as soon as I caught him. While he was running, he had the presence of mind to add in one final tidbit. "Yeah, it was a barn burner, thirty-five to thirty-two. One of the best games ever."

"Fuck you," I said as I closed the distance. He headed out the door and towards the small body of water. If he got there, I'd never catch him. I was always faster, sprint wise, but I swear he could dodge a bullet. If he ever got on the ice, all the foot speed in the world wouldn't do me any good. I was tempted to tackle him, but I had no desire to wrestle in a briar patch. He made it to the ice and waited for my arrival. I came to a skidding halt at the edge.

"Man, I missed you so much. I almost didn't watch the game because you weren't there. As it was, I just about cried during every intermission."

"I'm sorry, that you and my family had to go through that."

"No, I'm sorry that you had to go through that."

"Fuckin' Giants! I can't believe they won the Super Bowl without me here."

"I taped it!"

"What are the odds that you have that tape?"

"Pretty friggin' good."

"Man, I knew I liked you for some reason."

"I wanted to kind of lure you out of the house."

"For what, Wags?" I knew it couldn't be good. But it wasn't all bad.

"Paul has some pretty heavy stuff going down."

"How's he doing?"

"Man, you wouldn't recognize him if you passed him in the street."

"How so?" I asked cautiously.

"He's gone underground. He started something like the United Earth Corps, or something along those lines."

"He did what?"

"Yeah, his hair is as short as yours and he's running some sort of commando unit out in Colorado."

"Are you serious? The last I saw Paul he was smoking a bong on the twelfth floor lounge."

"Dude, I'm as serious as a heart attack. And he is extremely well funded."

"How well funded?"

"I don't know exactly; but he has lots of weapons and he's doing some serious construction."

"Alright, but why is he doing this?"

"He never believed the government's byline, so he did some investigating. He actually was able to get a few photos of the ship that took you, as well as the mother ship. It didn't take a rocket scientist to figure out what was going on from there. He's fortifying Indian Hill."

"What!? Why!?"

"He says his inside source said a storm is coming and the homeowner hasn't even put tape on the windows yet. He doesn't want to be caught off guard."

"So why the Indian Hill thing? Why not just stay out in Colorado?"

"My guess is he wants to get out from under the watchful eye that's funding him."

"So is it someone from the government?"

"I don't know, man, he's pretty tight-lipped about the whole thing. He gives me a set of orders every week, and miraculously, the money comes in and I do what I'm told."

"So you have no idea where or who the mystery funds come from?"

"Mike! Mike!" my sister yelled from the porch. But in the dead of winter and on a frozen pond, she would have been able to whisper and we would have heard her.

"What is it, mouth?" I yelled back just to let her get an idea of how loud she really was. She eased off the decibels a bit.

"You have a phone call." I began to walk back up to

the cabin. "It's General Burkhalter." I stopped dead in my tracks.

"What's the matter, Talbot?" Dennis asked as he came up alongside me and handed me a beer.

"When the hell did you snag these?" I asked incredulously. "Oh well, doesn't matter, I have a good idea who our mysterious funding man is."

"Huh?" Now Dennis just stared at my back as I walked up to the cabin.

"General! How are you?"

"How's the uniform fit?"

"How do you know that I tried it on?" I asked, now more than a little pissed that I was being watched.

"Relax, I'm not having you tailed and I don't have a satellite watching your every move. I just know the type of person you are. I know that you feel compelled to do the right thing." I relaxed a bit but I wasn't too happy that this man already had a bead on me.

"It fits fine, General."

"Good, now I want you to enjoy this time with your family. But I'm going to need you in Washington by Wednesday."

"General, I haven't agreed to anything."

"Say around eight a.m."

"General, are you not listening?"

"I'll have a car here Tuesday night."

"No, I'd rather drive myself down."

"Fine, son. I'll have my lieutenant program your navigational system with the directions."

"That Hummer has a navigation system?"

"Yeah, and a homing beacon."

"You're a piece of work, General."

"Thank you, son. See you Wednesday."

I hung up the phone and finished my beer. Something told me it was going to be a long time before I got to enjoy these again.

Dennis had finished his cigarette and came back in the cabin, his nose as red as Rudolph's.

"Cold out there, bud?"

"Yeah, just a little bit." he said sarcastically.

"Everything alright?"

"Just dandy. Hey bud, when do you talk to Paul next?"

"Thursday."

"Do me a favor?"

"Yeah, anything."

"Don't tell him I'm here just yet. I think I'm going to make a surprise visit this week."

"Oh man, you're going to make me sit on the best news we've had in almost two years? Alright, man, but you owe me for this."

"No problem; let me buy you a beer," I said as I headed for the fridge.

Chapter 3 - Mother Ship

Senior Helmsguardsman Borlock was an enormous being for a Progerian. He was considered a gargantuan and was even bigger than most Genogerians. His physical might and prowess had guaranteed him success in the military field. He was scared of nothing, and battle didn't faze him in the least. But he was apprehensive to say the least about his meeting with the interim supreme commander. Kuvlar was not a Progerian to be trifled with. He was a big male of the species but nowhere near the stature of Borlock. Kuvlar was a Progerian of action; he did not threaten, he had no need. Without a doubt, Kuvlar was the next in line for the position; the puny hu-man had merely sped up the process. Where the original SC was more a visionary and liked to think out every problem, Kuvlar acted first and thought about it later, if at all.

At times, Kuvlar's lack of prudence had landed him in trouble but he had not risen to his current status by being afraid. And now Borlock had a one-on-one meeting with the interim supreme commander to tell him just how much damage the hu-man vessel had done. It would not go well, this was the biggest military blow the Progerians had ever suffered at least since the five hundred year war with the Stryver's. But never once, while they were on a conquering mission, had they suffered anything even remotely similar to this and from worlds far more advanced than these hu-mans.

"Supreme Commander, Senior Helmsguardsman Borlock reporting."

The ISC did not waste time. "What is the status of my ship and when can we launch?"

Alright, so much for pleasantries. "Sir, the hu-man weapon did much more damage than we had originally estimated." Borlock could tell that the ISC was upset; his mouth hung open an inch or two and saliva poured out the right side of his maw.

"I want numbers, Borlock, I want times. I want this planet under our control. But the one thing I don't want, Borlock, is your opinions. Understand?" the ISC said with quiet control. Borlock's shortened tail flicked in response to the tension. He couldn't remember being reprimanded like that since he was a child and his father scolded him for eating the family pet.

"Sir, we lost four hundred and ninety-eight ships. Most were cruiser class or freighters; but we also lost seventy-four fighters and four Battle Master Class ships." Borlock attempted unsuccessfully to stop the incessant flicking of his tail.

"What does that leave us for our attack?" The ISC already knew but he wanted to make absolutely sure that Borlock did, too. If he couldn't be trusted to know his ship, he was useless; except, of course, for the battle arena and, the ISC thought, he'd make for some fine entertainment. Borlock sensed a mood change in the ISC and he didn't like it, not one bit.

"Sir, we still have two hundred and twenty-six fighters but only one Battle Master Class ship left. The one that wasn't damaged was in dry dock, being repaired from our last encounter with the Stryders. And that ship will be down for at least another month, even with crews working around the clock. The fighters alone will not be enough to subdue this planet, we will need to launch ground forces also." The ISC already knew this fact too, and he had no desire to hear it from his subordinate.

"And the damage to the launch bay is another thing, sir." Borlock couldn't wait to get out of there; he worried the more he talked, the closer he approached an execution.

"There's more!?" The ISC said as his jaw opened just a little wider.

"Sir, the residual radiation from the weapon is making work on the launch bay difficult and, in some places, impossible." Go on, the ISC motioned with his hand. "In some places, the surface temperature is too hot to even approach. My senior staff feels that it could be up to another week before the temperatures are reduced to a working level; and even then, the shifts will have to be shortened. The radiation is also making my men sick, sir. Anyone exposed to it for more than two hours usually does not wake up for his next shift."

"Then get some Genogerians in there to do the brunt of the work. I want launch capability in a week."

"Sir, we can't even get to some spots in a week."

"I suggest you get it done, Borlock, I don't care how. Or even how many men die. I will not go down in history as the first Genogerian to lose a conquest venture. Understood?!"

Borlock understood; either ships were flying in a week or he was dead. His first stop was to the Genogerians' quarters, where he picked up some "volunteers."

Chapter 4 – Mike Journal Entry Three

I left Maine early Monday morning. I wanted to go visit my mother's grave, say my goodbyes and make peace with her. I also was very interested in checking out Indian Hill. I would make sure to get clear of the Hummer first, though. I had no desire to let the general know where I was going. If Paul didn't want him to know what was going on, that was good enough reason for me.

It was a lonely, quiet drive down to Massachusetts, especially after the festivities of the previous weekend. And, to add insult to injury, I had to drive from rest stop to rest stop, to purge my irritated bowels. I just wasn't used to beer anymore and my body protested vehemently over my excessive liberations. I hit the Mass Line two hours and six stops later than I should have. It would be late afternoon before I even got into Walpole.

When I finally entered Walpole, I headed straight for my mother's site. I was unsure what I would do once I got there, but it was something I felt that I needed to do.

"Hi, Mom. How you doing?" That's a stupid question, dumb ass, I thought to myself and how crazy does this look? I'm not talking to anybody. Still, I felt she was listening.

"I'm sorry I wasn't there to say my goodbyes. I'm sure by now, you know my reasons why. Did God give you any clue as to how this all turns out?" I waited, expecting some sort of sign or omen, but was only answered with the cry of a distant crow. If it had been closer, I might have taken that for my ominous sign. Thank God, for small miracles.

"Mom, I'm sorry for the way we ended. I wish now that I could go back and change that. Hell, I wish I could go back and change a lot of things, but the universe just doesn't work that way. Mom, is God angry with me?" Another crow, or possibly the same one, flew a lot closer and cawed, then flew away. That could be just close enough to be accepted as my answer. Isn't that sacrilegious? I thought. Superstition in a Catholic graveyard. Stop being silly. Goosebumps ran down the length of my arms. The temperature seemed to drop another ten degrees. "Mom? Is that you?" Was she embracing me in death; something we were never able to achieve in life?

Now, I was really freaking myself out. Still comfort is comfort. But was she telling me that everything would be alright? Or to be strong for what comes next? "Mom, I miss you so much." As I wiped the tears that began to flow, a car passed on the right and I turned so as not to let my anguish show. But of all places you should be able to cry, wasn't this one of them? Damn male pride. I placed the flower I brought with me on the grass next to the headstone and walked back towards my Hummer. The day was growing shorter but my list of things to do wasn't. The temperature warmed back up to a balmy twenty-eight or twenty-nine degrees as I approached the car. It had to be in my head, didn't it? I stopped before I entered. "Goodbye, Mom," I whispered over my shoulder.

I tried every avenue I knew to get up into Indian Hill, but bogus construction crews were strategically placed at every possible entry way. I used Dennis' name in vain.

After a few curious looks at me, they all denied any knowledge of Dennis Wagner. I thought to use the path we had discovered so many years ago, but if I knew about it, so did Dennis and, in turn, so did these "construction men." I had no desire to become a casualty of friendly fire.

I did a slow loop of my old stomping grounds, just for nostalgia. It's amazing how much things changed. Whoever said, "You can never go home" was right. That might be one of the saddest phrases you can ever hear. There was Cap's field, where we played baseball. And the Aggie field, where we played football. Cobbs' pond, where we played hockey; Dennis' house, where we had so many parties. It was up for sale. Lori's house, the first girl I ever kissed. This was almost unbearably tough, not so much that I could never do those things again, but because I was afraid no one would ever do those things again.

After I'd had enough of this self-inflicted torture, I headed for the local sporting goods store. I had an idea. I made my transaction and looked for the local Stop and Shop. I parked in the back and made my way up the drainpipe. I figured I would have a good view of the goings on up at Indian Hill, especially since there would be no tree cover to obstruct my view. I unpacked my new purchase and took a look through my binoculars.

I honestly didn't see too much activity up there. I spied the occasional person walking around, but most of the construction must have been behind Indian Hill itself, and from this vantage point, I'd never see it. I was half tempted to leave when my binocular view became totally obstructed. I was about to bitch about what a crappy pair of one hundred and fifty dollar binoculars I bought.

"What you looking at, son?" I almost jumped out of my skin. The exhaust fans on the roof had completely hidden the approach of this person.

"Who the hell are you!" was all I could stammer out, my heart still slamming in my chest. He appeared to be in his mid-forties, built like truck. A squashed nose told me that he was used to taking a punch; and judging by the size of him, he could also deliver a good one.

"No, son, you have it wrong. I ask the questions and then I decide if I beat you to a pulp or if I let Chaz, over there, do it." So intent was I on the man in front of me, I completely missed his even bigger partner approaching from my blind side. I was beginning to wonder how bad the jump off this roof would be. Would I be able to get up and drive away? Or would they climb down and finish me off? My brain was spinning for an answer to appease them, but lying was out of the question. I was driving a military issue vehicle, I had a high tech pair of binoculars and I was looking straight at the area they were assigned to protect.

"Dennis Wagner," I said, spitting out the first thing that seemed to make any sense.

"Excuse me?" Chaz said.

"I'm friends with Dennis Wagner."

"Yeah, and I'm doing some ice fishing up here." Squash nose said sarcastically as he stepped closer.

"I was just with him, he's the one that told me about this place."

"Then why aren't you with him?" Chaz threw in.

"Because he's still at my father's cabin." Chaz had had just about enough and was

getting ready to lay the hurt on, when old Squash nose held up his hand.

"And just where is your dad's cabin?"

"Maine," I answered.

"What's your name, son?"

"Mike, Mike Talbot."

"You're Mike Talbot? Shit, piss and vinegar!"

"What is it, George?" Yeah, that name fits, I thought to myself.

"This is the guy that disappeared last year," George said elatedly.

"Get out of here!" Chaz said.

"Yeah, he's the reason we're doing all this." And then Squash nose, I mean, George, turned to me. "What are you doing with the Hummer?"

"It was a gift," I answered; my heart had finally begun its descent out of my throat.

"Hell, if you are who you say you are, why didn't you just try to go up there?" Chaz said as he pointed to the hill.

"I tried, but the men on the streets wouldn't even listen when I said Dennis' name."

"Do you want to go up there now?" George asked.

I was always accused of talking before my brain fully engaged. "No, I have to get to Washington first thing in the morning so I should be heading out." That raised both of their eyebrows, but at least they didn't try to throw me off the roof. I climbed back down the way I had come. Both still eyed me warily, wondering if they'd made a mistake. I didn't hang around long enough to let them reconsider their choice.

My stomach had finally calmed down from the beer and I figured I could drive the majority of the way to D.C. before I took a siesta. But I was going to look for a good place. It was on the government dime and I figured they owed me at least that much.

The drive was fairly unremarkable except for the over abundance of cars nestled along the Eastern seaboard. However, I didn't see that little inconvenience changing today, at least. An icy wind cut across my exposed face.

The Pentagon? The general wanted me to go into the Pentagon? What was I really expecting? He said Washington, I guess I was figuring, I don't know what I was thinking, but that building was almost as intimidating as that ship I had been on for so many months. I pulled my Hummer up to the main gate, I figured there was no way I would get through. I didn't even put the uniform on yet. I didn't want the general to feel that he knew me completely. The staff sergeant at the gate stooped down to take a precursory glance at me, saluted and waved me through. He looked a little disapprovingly at my two-day stubble but still showed the respect that the rank I had been given rated.

"Uh, Staff Sergeant, which way do I go?"

"Follow your navigational system. You'll notice, sir, that it has been scaled down to only show the Pentagon area in detail. Follow it, sir, and you'll be just fine."

I thought about telling him that I'd never be "fine" again but he didn't really seem the type to care. I looked down at my Nav-Gat system and noticed it was an aerial view of the Pentagon and the outlying parking lot. My route was marked out in yellow on the map and my car position was in red. But what they failed to tell me was that I would get so absorbed in the little plasma screen that I forgot to watch out for the minor details like parked cars and pedestrians. I think I pissed off half of the chiefs-of-staff. Oh well, that's what they get for inviting me here.

My entry point was on the far side from where I drove in. I parked the Hummer in a brigadier general's spot; I didn't think that he would be too pleased. I was now wishing that I had maybe donned the uniform. I would have been hard pressed to stand out anymore than I did right now. Here I was, a twenty-two-year-old kid with a scraggly beard, blue jeans and a Widespread Panic T-shirt, heading into the military capital of the world. I could have built a car out of all the brass that was walking around here. Captains were a dime a dozen, basically just high ranking coffee-fetchers. I was going to have to talk to the general about my rank; I wasn't getting coffee for anybody. I didn't even like the stuff.

"Ah, Mike, how was your drive?" The general put on a jovial façade as he put his arm around my shoulder. But I think I caught him off guard coming here all disheveled and in civvies. "Come on; the president is waiting."

"Whoa, whoa," I stopped. "The president? You didn't say anything about the president being here."

"Why? Would you have dressed more appropriately?"

"I might have."

He laughed. "Don't worry; the president doesn't look too much better than you. We had to go pick him up off his ranch; he was fixing one of the cattle fences."

"The President of the United States was fixing his cattle fence? Doesn't he have people that do that kind of thing for him?"

"Sure he does, but he says it relaxes him. Son, he's the president. If he wants to knock those fences down, who's going to tell him he can't?"

"Good point." I felt better about meeting the president but my stomach was still tied up in knots. We walked into a huge conference room that must have held half of all the generals in the armed forces. And there sat the president, directly in the middle of them. All of them jockeyed for position, to have their ideas heard.

"Welcome to political hell," the general mumbled. Everyone stopped talking, almost on cue. The president turned to see what had taken the pressure off him.

"Mike Talbot, I presume." The president knew my name!

"Uh, yes sir."

"Call me Jack."

"Ah yes, Mr. Pres... I mean Jack."

"Gentlemen, I truly want to hear all of your ideas and opinions, but my very distinguished guest here has finally arrived and I wish to speak privately with him. I value all of your opinions; so if you could all please draft up your proposals in triplicate and have them on the secretary general's desk by nine o'clock tomorrow, I will personally make sure he goes through all of them. Now if you could please excuse me."

The generals shuffled out the door as fast as their feet would take them. General Burkhalter shut the door when the last of them left.

"Well, looks like I've killed two birds with one stone."

"Sir?" General Burkhalter asked.

"Well, all of those generals will be so busy tonight drafting proposals that none of them will dare come back here tonight and waste any more valuable time. And all day tomorrow, the secretary general will be reading said proposals. That man has been so far up my ass, he knows what I had for dinner every morning." I couldn't help it; I snorted out laughter.

"You think that's funny, Mr. Talbot?" the president asked.

"Ah, yes sir, I do."

"That's good! I like people that actually say what

they are thinking. If you stay in this town long enough, you'll realize that that is a rare thing indeed. The general showed me the tape of your debriefing. I would imagine that you are beginning to tire of telling the tale."

"A little bit, sir. I'm getting to the point where I wish I could just get on with my life and put this behind me."

"You know that that isn't going to happen."

"Yes sir, I realized that a long time ago. You can never go home, even if home is planet Earth."

"What's that?"

"Nothing, sir, just reflecting."

"Have you made up your mind on the general's and my decision to have you commissioned into the service?"

"I have, sir, but just one question."

"Shoot, son."

"I'm not going to have to get coffee, am I?"

"What?" the president asked with a sidelong glance.

"Mr. President, there is so much brass in this building that captains are relegated to gophers. If I were to accept the commission, I have no desire to be a glorified secretary." The president laughed.

"That's funny, I never noticed before, but I guess you're right. No, that would never happen, and anyway, you would be reporting directly to General Burkhalter here and nobody else. He reports directly to me and nobody else."

"Then I accept the commission, sir."

"Good; then let's get started. General , if you could please dim the lights." The general dimmed the lights as the president started the DVD in the corner of the conference room. It was difficult to tell exactly what we were looking at on the TV screen. It was mostly darkness punctuated with bright bursts of light. I was about to ask what we were watching when the image cleared up dramatically.

"This footage was taken from our deep space probe, Orion," the general noted. He didn't have to clarify what we were looking at. Chills ran up my spine as I glanced at the ship that held me captive for over eighteen months. The general continued, "We have reason to believe that they will complete their repairs much sooner than we had anticipated."

"What kind of time frame are we looking at, General?" the president asked as if this were the first time he had viewed this tape. Could that be possible? Why on Earth would they have waited for me?

"It's hard to say, sir. It would appear that they have the technology and the motivation, considering that we have their supreme commander, to have the repairs done in a matter of weeks. But they honestly appear to be dragging their feet."

"Reinforcements," I muttered.

"Excuse me?" the president asked.

"Reinforcements, sir. They are waiting for another mother ship before they launch an invasion."

"Whatever would give you that idea, Captain?" the president asked as he wiped his glasses.

"Sir, during my stay on the ship I was informed that the Progerians have been attacking planets around the universe for thousands of years. We're probably one of the first races they have encountered that has given them pause to reconsider their efforts. Or quite possibly, they have radioed for help because they no longer have a supreme commander, and just don't know what to do."

"That makes no sense," the general said. "They must have some sort of contingency plan in effect if and when their supreme commander dies."

"Maybe this is it, sir," I suggested.

"So they just sit there like ducks in a puddle?" the general asked.

"Well, first off, General, it's a very large puddle and I am under the impression that they will never allow one of our ships to leave Earth's orbit, much less get inside their mother ship again. What say you, Captain?" the president intoned.

"I agree with both of you. They are just sitting there, and I wish that we had some sort of long-range strike capabilities. But they'll never let us launch an attack. They may be without leadership, but they certainly aren't helpless."

"So now what?" the president asked his general.

"We wait, sir. We wait and we prepare. We pull back all of the military we can and we defend our shores as best we can."

"General, you know how I feel about pulling back our troops. It will destabilize the world to near anarchic conditions."

"And you know how I feel, Mr. President."

"Yes, and I fully empathize with your patriotism, but this is now a global conflict, not solely an American one," the president chimed in.

"Sir, if America is attacked and we fall, there will be nobody on this planet who could stand up to these invaders."

"General, if we abandon our posts worldwide, there won't be anything worth defending." The president was beginning to raise his voice. Apparently, they had been round and round on this topic before. I wanted to quell things before this turned into a shouting match.

"Mr. President, General Burkhalter, please!" I yelled, definitely louder than my station warranted. "I will be as honest with you both as possible. I do not believe that anything we do now will stop or even diminish their initial assault. You've seen their ships and their weaponry. Our best course of action will be to evacuate the largest cities worldwide and hide."

"You would have us stick our head in the sand, and just hide?!" the general asked incredulously.

"Yes, sir, I would. That would be our best defense. We wait until they are done 'beating us down and sapping our will' then we come out from hiding and strike with everything we've got."

"I don't agree, Captain." the general said in an attempt to browbeat me. "We will need to stop them before they ever get a toe hold on planet Earth."

"I'm sorry, Captain Talbot, but I have to agree with

the general on this one. And what do we tell the citizens of the world as we evacuate them?" the president asked.

"The truth, sir. I think it might be getting to the point where we have no choice in the matter."

"No, we always have a choice, and to paraphrase, I don't think they can handle the truth."

"See sir? That's where I think you have it wrong." The general looked up at me as if I were performing hari cari. "People, when pushed to extremes, can do amazing things. And no matter what you decide here today, they are going to find out. Whether it's this week or the next, by our media or by the alien gunships." I was hot, and I definitely didn't want to start cussing at the president of the United States so I went over to the water cooler to calm down a bit.

"Captain, we appreciate your candor, but if you could please excuse us, the general and I have some logistics we need to work out."

"Certainly, sir."

"Captain," the general motioned. "Wait for me in the officers' lounge."

"Yes, sir." I walked out the door, careful to make sure that I didn't slam it and show my true feelings.

43

Chapter 5

"Definitely outspoken, isn't he, general?"

"That he is, Mr. President, but you've got to remember he's been through a lot and he knows this enemy better than anyone on the planet. He's even killed a dozen or so of them."

"And what of his plan?"

"I've got to admit, General, it has merit. We know technologically and logistically they have a huge edge over us. But I strongly feel that they will be like cockroaches; once they get on the planet we'll never be able to get them off. No, it's better to never let them footfall on this planet." But all the while, the general was thinking of how he could hedge his bets with Paul's militia.

Chapter 6 – Mike's Journal Entry Four

I watched all of "Cops" and was halfway through the news, when the general finished his meeting.

"So how was that for fun, Captain?"

"I had more fun on the enemy ship," I answered.

"Just remember, this is Washington and very rarely do things go the way you want them to."

"General, I don't think the course of action you are heading towards is the correct one."

"Well, son, I have an entire staff of generals who believe otherwise."

"Sir, and just how many of those generals have actually even seen our enemy?"

"I see where you're going, Captain," the general said sternly. "But we made up our minds a long time ago on this matter and we are not about to change course now."

"Sort of like the Titanic?" I muttered. The general chose to ignore my bait.

"Captain, I need you to get on a plane in two hours."

"To where, sir?"

"Colorado, Captain. I need you to look in on a side project of mine." Ah! So my hunch had been right.

"And what about my Hummer, sir? I was beginning to grow very attached to it."

"Don't worry about that, Captain; you'll be flying on a Galaxy C-42. You can take it with you."

"Rank has its privileges. Are you coming, sir?"

"No, I've got to play the political game for a few more days, and then we have to start the evacuation of some of our major cities."

"You're going to tell them the truth?"

"Not exactly; we're going to blame it on terrorists and backpack nukes. But as long as the civilians get out, that's all we're trying to do. Well, that and we're going to house our military in the cities, so when they come, we'll be ready and waiting."

"Sir, I just don't think that is such a good idea."

"Captain, the matter is closed. Let's go get some lunch and then we can get you and your Hummer on that plane."

The lunch itself was fairly uneventful but surprisingly edible. I was under the impression that we would be served "shit on a shingle" as my father used to affectionately call the slop he was served during his time in the corps. The general came with me to the military airport but said very little beyond the pleasantries. He appeared deep in thought and would only speak to tell me left or right as the case may be.

"Are you alright, sir?"

"What? I'm sorry did you say something?" I guess the general hadn't finished with his thoughts yet.

"I asked if you were alright, sir."

"I'm fine," the general replied. But he looked like he had something more on his mind. And I was right. "I hope that we have made the right decision," he continued. "I just don't know if there is a correct one to make." I had no answers for him, but I don't think that he was looking for one anyway. He seemed to be voicing his concerns more than anything. But, for everything I thought was right, there was the equal wrong.

"What do you think, Captain?" He turned, finally focusing on me instead of that thousand-yard stare he had going on.

"Sir, you know where I stand on this."

"I know, I know. I want to hear it again."

"Sir, the Progerians' standard operating procedure is to come down here with guns a-blazing. They will want to crush our military and a few major cities just to prove who is in control. They want to sap the will out of us before they move in for the occupation and eventual colonization. We will basically be there cattle, their dogs and their slaves."

"That will only happen if they break through our lines of defense," the general interjected. He seemed a little perturbed. I don't think that he was used to being contradicted by someone of such junior rank.

"General, you asked me for my opinion." That seemed to ease him down a bit.

"Continue, Captain," he said as he settled back in his seat.

"With all due respect, sir, we got extremely lucky by being able to get that nuclear weapon aboard their mother ship. And I agree it did some serious damage. But the fact remains, and so does the ship. We threw our hardest punch at them while they weren't even looking; and they are still up and swinging. If we go toe to toe with them, we will lose." The general, once again, began to let his emotions bleed through, but thought better of it.

"Our best bet, sir, is to let them believe that we have been knocked out for the ten count. Let everybody in the stands go home. Then we get up and mount an attack when they are at their most vulnerable, after they are completely comfortable on this planet."

"What you're saying, Captain, is that we should just open the gates and allow them in?"

"Sir, in a way, yes."

"We'll just let those 'things' crawl all over our planet? It could be months before they relax their military grip."

"That's a possibility, sir."

"We could be wiped out in that time period. Are you willing to take that risk? You said yourself you would rather go out fighting than become their evening meal. How, Captain, would we launch a full-scale invasion after they're here? We'd have no means of communication that they wouldn't have already tapped into. And where would we hide this onslaught? I'm sure they'll have surveillance craft circling the globe for months just looking for stockpiles.

"After our little stunt with the shuttlecraft, they may not deem us a race worth retaining, they just might want to obliterate us. If your dog bites, you shoot him. That's my biggest concern." The general had valid points and I could see the reasoning behind them, but in my gut, I felt that the joint chiefs-of-staff had erred. I believed they were taking a big step against mankind's very existence.

"If we do not take action, the population of the world will give up even quicker. They will wonder what has happened to their respective militaries. They will be thinking, 'If they don't fight, then we won't fight'."

"But sir, the other side of that is equally as devastating. If they see the military taken out in a stroke, they will believe that they have no chance to stand up and fight either."

"Hence my dilemma, Captain. But this is where you and a few of your friends come in."

"How so, sir?"

"The president may or may not know about this. Either way, he hasn't said anything. For almost a year now, I have been in the process of funding a militia."

"Paul, sir?"

"Well, well, Captain, you certainly are full of surprises! Anyway I want you attached to his unit. I have no desire to see you wiped out in a stroke, as you call it."

"But, sir?"

"No buts, Captain. If this really goes down as you think it will, I want men of your caliber waiting in the wings to rectify the wrongs that will have been committed."

"We're the back-up plan, sir?"

"Yes, and a very well funded back-up plan. I know Paul has something in the works now. He wants to get out from under our scrutiny, and I'm going to allow him that illusion."

"Well, sir, now it's my turn to be surprised. How did you know?"

"I have my ways."

"You have a plant!"

"How I know is not important. I have actually made every attempt to know as little about his operation as possible. The less I know, the less I can tell anybody else. Yes, even the enemy, if it comes to that. My only dealings with Paul are financial. The occasional hard to find military equipment, as well as keeping all the federal bulldogs off his back. The FBI and the ATF are all over his training area, just waiting for a screw-up so they can shut that place down."

"Sir, how can you possibly keep them at bay?"

"Well, I'll be honest with you, son. The president is a very powerful man but he is not the most powerful. I have connections in this town and around the world that could make the president quiver in his boots, if he knew. I have given my assurances to these 'connections' that what is happening in the mountains of Colorado is of vital national and global security. The rest, well, the rest takes care of itself."

"How many men does he have up there, General?"

"It's somewhere in the neighborhood of two thousand."

"Two thousand!" I exclaimed as I swerved the vehicle. I was thinking somewhere perhaps in the fifties or maybe a hundred. Definitely not two thousand."

"Yeah, I thought it was pretty impressive myself."

I boarded the plane still half in a daze. Paul had never struck me as the type to lead that many men and, I guess, women. He had always been a charmer and very charismatic. Thinking about it, I guess those are traits that you want to have to pull off this kind of thing. I was just always so used to seeing it done on a much smaller scale. Normally, he pulled out his best stuff to get Suzy Rotten Crotch back to his apartment so that he could, once again, rub my nose in how many women he had scored with. He sometimes had a hard time tracking exactly how many girls he'd seduced. I could count all my conquests on one hand and still have some fingers left over.

I had known Paul almost seven years, lived with him for almost a year, and still, could not figure out how he did it. He was so good with the women. They were drawn to him like puppies to milk; it was pretty impressive to watch.

I drifted in and out of sleep on the flight. It was by no means crowded, but lacking the protective shell that commercial planes had, it was a very loud ride. Of the fifteen or twenty odd military personnel on board, most looked like they were going to Colorado for a little R and R on the slopes. There were some upper brass but, for the most part, they were lance corporals and corporals, probably all headed to Aspen for some skiing. Good for them, I thought, they might as well enjoy it while they can.

The plane landed right outside of Colorado Springs at the Air Force Academy. I decided that the pilot of this plane could use a few more classes while he was here. He bounced the plane off the runway four times before he got it right. If there had been ice, we would still be trying to stop. I was allowed to unload my Hummer first which more than pissed off one colonel.

"That general and his lackeys, always trying to show his superiority with special privileges and all," the colonel said, a trifle too loud. My guess was he wanted to be heard. Fine I'd call his bluff.

"Did you say something, sir?" I asked as I turned towards him.

"No, nothing, Captain. I was just commenting on the weather."

"Beautiful day, isn't it sir?" I answered with a smile. I would have to remember this colonel's name, he had no balls.

"Yes, quite," he replied as he turned away to shun any further conversation. We both knew he had backed down, and now he wanted to save as much face as possible to his friends.

My Hummer had been off-loaded and I was about to make the three-hour trek when I noticed the corporal and a couple of his friends heading towards the bus depot.

"Corporal! Hey Corporal!" I shouted.

"Yes sir!" he said as he came running towards me. I imagined that he assumed I had some unenviable task for him to perform and, more than likely, was trying to come up with all sorts of explanations as to why he couldn't.

"Corporal, where are you headed?"

"Winter Park, sir. My friends and I are going to meet our girlfriends and do some skiing at Corporal Biddington's fiancée's cabin."

"Very nice, grab your gear."

"Sir, I'm on leave, sir."

"Corporal, get your friends and your gear and let's go."

"Sir?"

"Corporal, I'm headed that way too. You can either wait two hours for the bus and then take a six-hour trip on said bus or you can all pile in here and be there in three hours."

"Alright, sir!" The corporal was obviously pleased not to have to waste the majority of the day on a crowded bus. "Guys! Grab my stuff! Let's go!" The other corporals were just as surprised, but they knew a good thing when they saw it.

The trip went by a lot faster with the laughter and conversation. And it was a great relief not to have to be introspective for the rest of the day. The corporals said their thanks and crawled out into the waiting arms of their girlfriends. I envied them that. They would be spending this cold winter night in the arms of the ones they loved. I would have to work on that, if and when I got the chance.

The rest of the drive was solemn. I began to do what I had so valiantly tried to avoid. I began thinking about all those poor souls whose lives I cut short. I don't know if I was being selfish, but I kept coming back to one thought, better them than me. I had been in my dress alphas the whole trip, but decided it would be prudent to get into my BDU's (battle dress uniform) before I arrived at the training facility. I would stick out like sore thumb, if not. From the general's briefing, it was my contention that a regular military presence might not be welcomed with open arms. I stopped at a gas station along the way to do the change. When I came out of the men's room, I saw two men poking around my Hummer.

"Can I help you, gentlemen?" I tried my best to quell the anger that was burning inside of me. One of them was on a cell phone reporting to who knows who?

"Yeah, you can help us by leaving us the hell alone," the bigger man said as the smaller man cut short his conversation and approached from the other side of the vehicle.

"Sir, I don't even know who you are." Although I had a very good idea of what he was talking about.

"Don't be playing stupid with us, soldier boy. We know you've been spying on us from the very git-go," the smaller one said as he spat a wad of tobacco onto my tire.

Now I was pissed. I charged the big one before he could even put his hands up to defend himself. I drove him so hard into the ground I knocked the wind out of him. He would be out of commission for a couple of minutes at least. The smaller man was looking a little worried but he was prepared.

"You can't do that! You're an Army officer." He hoped his words would stop me.

"Wrong, fucker, I *can* do it and I'm a Marine officer." His eyes went wider, if that were possible. "I'm going to give you one shot. You pick up that foul shit you spat on my tire or I'm going to make you clean it up." I'll give him credit; he actually thought about it for a second before he sealed his fate.

"Fuck you, GI Joe!"

"Fine, have it your way." He stood his ground, I

kicked him square in the balls, and then, while he was down, I wiped off my tire with his shirt. At least, he didn't protest. The big man was starting to get up and prep himself for round two. I figured it would be a good idea to make my escape before any of his buddies came out of the store. I contemplated resting for the night in Vail, but I was sure that the entire town would be under surveillance, and a Marine Hummer was a pretty obvious target in a city of Beemers and Benzes.

I was also not thrilled about entering Paul's encampment in the twilight; I didn't want to get shot by a zealot. My other option was to go to Grand Junction for the night and make my entrance in the morning. But, having no desire to drive anymore, I figured I'd take my chances with Paul's men. I turned on the Nav-Gat system to find the route up into the encampment and was amazed at the details, even for off-roading. It showed old railroad tracks, small streams; I bet if I wanted it to, it would show me individual blades of grass. I overlaid the topographical map onto my route to see exactly what kind of off-roading I would be doing. I prided myself on being able to drive almost anything on the road, but off-road? Well, let's just say, my experience was lacking.

The route looked fairly moderate, but nothing the Hummer couldn't handle. Paul had to be trucking supplies up here to feed his army so this should be nothing for a Hummer. But off-roading at dusk wasn't calming my nerves. I should have expected it but I guess I just didn't believe Paul was that organized. I drove straight into a checkpoint. And it was strategically placed around a bend, so that you couldn't see it from a distance and by the time you did, you had nowhere to turn around. I was hoping they hadn't received any reports from their comrades whom I encountered earlier. I had to admit these three men were much more polished and professional than their fellow compatriots. But they still didn't conceal their disdain for my uniform very well.

"Well, Captain, what can we do for you?" A sergeant came up to my window while the other two loosely leveled their weapons in my general direction. Not totally threatening, but certainly capable of being brought up and fired in a split second. The Hummer can do a lot of things, but speed is not one of them. If they opened fire, I was a goner.

"Well, Sergeant, I have a message for Mr. Ginson, from General Burkhalter."

"First off, Captain, it's General Ginson. And secondly, we have no scheduled visits from any messenger of General Burkhalter."

"Sergeant, I don't have time to debate the matter with you. Call your general and have me authorized to pass." The sergeant wasn't thrilled with being ordered around but he had sense enough not to interfere with matters he wasn't one hundred percent in control of.

"Private, get on the horn to the colonel and check this out."

"Right away, Sergeant." The private went into the hut and the third guardsman readied his weapon, now that he didn't have back-up.

"Sergeant, the colonel says let him up," the private yelled from the booth.

"Stand down your weapon, Lance Corporal Conner," the sergeant said as he waved me through.

"Have a good evening, Sergeant." I said as I drove through. I couldn't tell for sure because of the encroaching darkness, but I think he gave me the finger. It's gotta suck to be on guard duty, in the dead of winter on the side of a mountain.

I drove the rest of the mile and a half very slowly; the sheer drop visible on my side had me sweating rivulets. My knuckles were white on the steering wheel. I had completely shut off my radio for fear of distractions. If I rolled off, they wouldn't find me until spring, and that's if they even bothered to look. I somehow felt that wouldn't be on the top of their priority list.

I was about to pull over and take a breather when I

topped the last rise. I came out onto a flat expanse in front of me, which appeared to be the main encampment. Marking lights were on the roadway(?) pathway(?) That, at least, let me know in which direction I needed to travel. I hadn't gone more than a hundred yards when I came to my second checkpoint. I was waved to a stop and this time, a lieutenant hopped into my passenger seat.

"Welcome to Camp Talbot, Captain. I will escort you directly to the command tent."

Camp Talbot, huh? That had a nice ring. I wonder what this lieutenant would think if I told him I was the namesake for this place. Most likely, he wouldn't believe me. The lieutenant made small talk the remainder of the way, which suited me. I had nothing to say to him. He guided me to the tent and hopped out.

"Have a good evening, Captain; it was a pleasure talking to you." And that's about what he did, talk to me.

"Sir, Lieutenant Benson reporting. I have brought our guest, sir."

"Very well, Lieutenant." I had half expected to see Paul but it appeared that his executive officer was going to perform as message receiver. I got out of the Hummer and approached the colonel.

"Well, what's your message, Captain? I don't have all day," he said, before looking up at the sky. "Or night for that matter," he added.

"With all due respect, sir, this message is for General Ginson's ears only."

"Captain," the colonel began, visibly starting to get perturbed. "Let me assure you that whatever you tell the general will be relayed to me in a matter of seconds; so let's just avoid the extra steps and be done with it."

"Again, sir, I have very explicit orders."

"Damn your 'very explicit orders'!" The colonel was not used to having his demands ignored.

"What is all this noise about, Colonel?" said Paul, stepping from behind one of the partitions in the tent. Damn, he looked fit; nothing like the college roommate I remembered. His face was chiseled, he didn't appear to have an ounce of fat on him. But the most noticeable difference was the character of his face. It was obvious to see that Paul was a commander of men. Confidence oozed out of him.

"Sir, I didn't mean to disturb you. General Burkhalter has sent another lackey with a message."

"Why didn't he just radio it in?"

"I don't know, sir, but this captain," he started. His disdain was visible, "will not tell me, the lowly colonel."

"It's alright, Colonel," Paul said as he placed his hand on the colonel's shoulder. "We shall find out what this important message is together. Captain, come in all the way so that we may hear your message clearly since you have traveled such a great distance to announce it in person."

I stepped all the way into the tent and stood directly under the light that hung in the center. Paul turned white as a sheet and had to grab hold of the table the colonel had been working on. The colonel turned to brace his leader. "Sir, are you alright? Sir?" The general shrugged him off.

"Mike, is that you?"

"In the flesh, Paul." The colonel didn't know what was going on but the informality was making him flustered.

"How is this possible?" Paul asked as he rounded the table to completely embrace me in a bear hug, which I gladly reciprocated. "We---I thought you were dead. I attended your funeral."

"How was it?"

"Not bad, not enough beer though." Ah, that's the Paul I knew.

"You might want to let me go now; you don't want the men thinking anything about this." Paul let go, tears streaming down his face.

"Oh man, it's so good to see you, you need to tell me what has been going on for all this time."

"And you the same for me, bud. But first, man, I'm hungry and thirsty."

"Colonel, this is Mike Talbot, this is the man that is responsible for all this."

"Captain, it is an honor and a pleasure to meet you. But I thought you were dead."

"In a manner of speaking I was, Colonel, and as soon as I am finished eating, I will lay out my entire story for you. And do not be alarmed, but the need for this camp is even more dire than any of you could have expected."

That allayed the colonel's fears. When he realized I was alive, his first impression implied that the need for this camp was completely useless. Relief flooded over his face. "You don't play much poker, do you ,Colonel?"

"Huh?" the colonel replied.

"The colonel's good at a lot of things but hiding his emotions isn't one of them," Paul said as he realized what was going through the colonel's mind. We laughed, ate and drank for hours. The colonel remarked how he had never seen the general so happy since… well, since ever. And that got us laughing all over again. I tried to give Paul the story somewhere in between the debriefing, full-length version and the condensed, story-telling version. We all watched the sun come up over the horizon by the time I had recounted the whole thing. Paul could do little more than stare at me in amazement. He was as impressed with my new growth as I was with his.

"So the Army right now has this Progerian in custody?" I nodded in agreement. "Funny, General Burkhalter never mentioned anything about that little fact. I'll have to let him know what I think the next time I talk to him."

"He probably didn't tell you, because then you'd ferret out of him that I was back; and I very much think that he wanted me to surprise the hell out of you."

"Well, that you did, Mike, that you did. So you're a Marine Corps officer now?"

"That does seem to be the case."

"Where do they have you going after your visit

here?"

"Well that's just it, General, I'm staying here."

"Are you another one of Burkhalter's plants?"

"No, I think he already has that avenue covered."

"Yeah, I know. I've been feeding one of my newer captains disinformation since he got here. So what gives? Why is the good general allowing you to attach to my 'militia'?"

"Well, I think he was telling it to me straight, Paul. He doesn't think that the entire combined military force has a chance of stopping the Progerians. We are his back-up plan and he wants the best on the bench, at least for now."

"Interesting, I was always under the impression that we were just some sort of plaything for the general and when he got tired of playing with us, he would discard us to the wings and the waiting arms of the FBI."

"So that's the whole reason behind the Indian Hill project?"

"How much do you know about that and who else knows?" Paul asked as the color drained out of his face.

"Relax, my friend, Dennis came up to Maine while I was visiting my father and sister." Paul was relieved but still not happy that Dennis had talked.

"Paul, come on, man, he told me, nobody else, just me. And I sure didn't

tell Burkhalter. I trusted enough in you for you to have your reasons to keep it secret. Now, trust in Dennis to do his part." Paul relaxed a little more, but I knew the next time he talked to Dennis, a decent tongue lashing was going to be attached. "Paul, he's got that place locked down better than the security here. I even tried the Stop and Shop roof to get a look with some binoculars and almost got my head bashed in for my efforts."

"Well, not to change the subject too radically, but how is your family doing? I'm sorry about your mom. I wanted to go to the services, but I had some things here that I had to take care of."

"Lyndsey's great; she goes up to Maine every other weekend to spend some time with my dad. Ronny's the same old Ronny, working his ass off. My dad has slipped a bit, my mom's passing took him hard. I don't know, I guess you just get so used to one way of living that when it's taken away from you, you become lost. And to be honest, Paul, that's how I feel about the whole planet. We're a few months away from possibly losing everything we know."

"That's why we're here, bud," he replied as he placed an arm over my shoulder. It was going to take more than that to wring the chill from my bones.

"When are you planning on moving these people to the new station?"

"Well, we already started, we want it to look more like attrition than total abandonment. We were going to take our time and possibly have it done in six months and just make it look like nobody believed in the 'cause' and it fizzled out. That way, no suspicion would be aroused. But your story kind of puts a wrench in that scenario. We'll have to do some mass moving in the next week or two. I definitely don't want to be caught out here in the middle of nowhere with our pants down."

"Is the Hill going to be able to house that many people?"

"This times two is the design, plus two year's worth of rations."

"That had to have taken some serious green."

"I think the project is somewhere up in the billion range."

"How is the general allocating that kind of money?"

"Beats me how he's doing it, he's pretty tight-lipped about the whole thing. I would imagine it has something to do with plausible deniability. Colonel, could you see about finding Captain Talbot here some suitable quarters?" Paul turned back to me. "Hey Mike, why don't you go get a few hours of shut eye and then I'll show you around the place. You might be more than a little surprised."

I was attempting to stifle a yawn before I answered. "That sounds good to me, but don't let me sleep past noon or I'll never get to sleep tonight."

"Don't worry, with all the noise we have going on up here, you'll be lucky to make it past nine."

"Great," I muttered sarcastically. "Just try to keep me as far away from the firing range as possible."

"Will do," Paul smiled. "Bud, I can't tell you how much good seeing you has done for me."

"Yeah, it feels pretty good for me too, my friend." I headed out the door to check out my new digs. My new quarters were nothing if not sparse; and it appeared to me that it had been vacated only moments before by some now greatly disgruntled lieutenants. An Army standard issue cot dominated the room. I almost laughed when Colonel Salazar asked if these quarters would be sufficient. I wanted to tell him that my alien abductors had put me up in what was equivalent to the Ritz, at least, comparatively speaking. But I refrained. It was going to be hard enough getting along around here, especially when the henchmen from out of town returned to tell their tale. Well, at least the cot was off the cold, ice-packed ground. That gave me a little comfort but right now, I was pretty sure that I would have been able to sleep on that too.

I awoke possibly a few hours later to the rumblings of a low flying jet. This thing flew so low it nearly uprooted my tent in the after wake. The jet passing by was closely followed by the shouts and curses of all the people it had disturbed. I walked out of my tent and tried to stretch my way to wakefulness. I asked the first passer by what the hell was going on.

"They like to let us know every once in a while that they are still watching," the private said as he shuffled on by, bearing his load of what appeared to be munitions. I strolled on up to the command tent, where Paul and the colonel and a few of his other staff officers were discussing tactics. All conversation ceased as the other officers noticed the Marine insignia on my uniform.

"It's alright, gentlemen; we can talk in front of him," Paul said to cut through the silence.

"But sir," one of the captains spoke out, "he's regular military. He's exactly what we're trying to keep our secrets from." Paul looked squarely at me.

"Captain, are your orders to report directly to me?"

"No, General, they are not," I answered much to the amazement of Paul's staff. I continued. "My orders are to report directly to General Burkhalter." A couple of the junior officers looked like they were getting ready to throw me out of the command tent.

"Relax," Paul said as he commanded everyone to sit back down. "If you gentlemen had been scrutinizing his uniform more closely, and looking past his Marine emblems, you may have noticed his name tag. The officers turned in unison. Recognition dawned on most of their faces. A few, however, were not able to piece the puzzle together quite so quickly. I remembered who those men were; they might just be a little too dim to be leading men into battle.

"Captain Talbot, what an honor to meet you" said one of the first officers who had risen to throw me on my keester. I shook his hand; it felt like granite. This man had spent more than one summer out in the sun. "Captain Dusty Davidson, at your service."

"Pleasure's all mine, Captain."
"Good afternoon, General."
"Good afternoon, Captain."

"Why was that recon plane flying so low?" I asked no one in particular. Captain Davidson spoke up.

"Ever since we hid everything under our camo netting, they've been flying lower and lower to try to get some good pictures of our encampment, but what they don't know..." The captain turned to Paul to make sure that it was alright to release this information. Paul nodded his consent. "Well, what they don't know is that we're tapped into their radar systems down in Colorado Springs. We know the second their planes leave the runway."

"What about the satellites?"

"Well, this special camo netting completely throws those cameras off. It's infrared and radar scattering. They can't tell if there is a mouse or a division under these things. And for those times when we do training out in the open, we know the fly-overs of every possible spy sat in orbit."

"Does that leave much time to do anything?"

"It gives us roughly half an hour, each hour, to be safe. But there have been times when we had to be out longer; so we've devised a system for that also. We try to use it sparingly because we don't want them to catch on. But when we're out there with our pants down, and have something we definitely don't want Big Brother to see, we can send a micro-burst of highly ionized particles into the satellite that completely scrambles the onboard computer. The machine has to reset and, by the time it boots back up, it's long gone."

"You guys developed that?"

"Don't be so amazed, Captain. There are a lot of very smart people on this project who are not happy with the way the U.S. is preparing for this war. They want to be as prepared as possible to save their families, their lives, and their country."

"No, you misunderstood me, General. I wasn't in astonishment that this organization developed it, I'm in astonishment that anybody developed it. If the military knew, they'd be on you like flies on a shit storm." I realized my error when most everyone at the table looked at me. It suddenly dawned on me that I was that very military. "Present company excluded." The men relaxed after my joke.

I stood up. I knew the majority of these men still did not trust me and would not speak their minds while I was present. I did not want to disrupt their proceedings.

"General, if you could have one of your privates show me the way to the mess tent, I would greatly appreciate it."

"Sure thing, Captain, and when we are done here, I

will join you for some of our fine cuisine. After that, I would like to show you around."

"That would be great, General. Gentlemen, it was a pleasure meeting you." A few nodded their courteous greetings; but most just stared at me, waiting for my graceful exit.

The militia adopted the old rule of two hots, meaning two hot meals a day. Lunchtime wasn't included. But they had a huge variety of MRE's. Even inedible food was better than no food. And, to be honest, it was actually pretty good. I was halfway through my meal, attempting to open my tube of peanut butter, when Paul joined me.

"So how goes the war council?" I asked as I looked up from my task at hand. From the look on Paul's face, it didn't appear that all had gone well.

"Not as good as I would have liked," he said as he plopped himself down on the chair opposite me. "I hoped that your return would spark more of a fire in their eyes. But instead, it has aroused more suspicion than anything else."

"Suspicion?!" I half yelled as a stream of peanut butter nearly made its way across the table.

"Yeah, are you familiar with the Helen of Troy story?"

"You're comparing me to a woman?"

"You know what I mean; why are you busting my balls?"

"I'm sorry, bud, I know the story. The Trojans fought for years and years to get her back and, when they finally succeeded, they figured she was a spy."

"Exactly."

"Why would I spy for the government? I already told you they sent me here."

"It's not the government, that they are concerned about."

"Then who is it?" Then it hit me like a ton of bricks. "Aw, Paul no way! I hate those bastards and what they did! I told you about everything that happened. Why would I possibly spy for them?" I was now shouting and most of the people at the chow hall tried their best to ignore my outburst.

"Mike, try to settle down. I don't for a minute believe that you are working for them," Paul said as he pointed skyward.

"But?" I was on the verge of shouting again.

"But some of my officers think that your 'fantastic escape' and your timely arrival are just too coincidental."

"Coincidental? Bud, I know I'm not the sharpest tack on the board, but could you please clarify this for me?"

"Why? Because we are about to start our migration in earnest to the Indian Hill bunker and an invasion seems imminent."

"Paul, you know how crazy that sounds? I'm the one that told you of the impending invasion; and, if anything, I've provided you and your men some crucial preparation time."

"Mike, I know that and you know that, but my officers are going to need a little more time and a little more convincing. They have suggested everything from detaining you to letting you go. But both of those have their inherent problems."

"Such as?" I seethed.

"Well, if you are a spy," he started as I began to rise. "Mike, please sit down. This is not my line of reasoning." I sat, but my muscles were on full alert. I was tensed to strike but I wasn't sure in which direction I should go. I hadn't been this riled up since the battles. Paul continued talking but it took me half a beat to catch up. "…And you left you could tell the aliens exactly where we were going, and if we detained you they might have some sort of way of tracking you."

"What? Like a friggin' Lojack?" I sputtered.

"Yeah, pretty much like that." Paul was trying to lay on the charm, but I was far beyond that. "If you would submit to an MRI, my men would go a lot further into accepting you as one of their own."

"A MRI? Aren't you in charge here, Paul? Can't you

make them see the error that they are making here?"

"I'm definitely in charge, Mike, but I don't MAKE them do anything. They do it because they feel that I'm right. If I go against them on this, I might lose some of their trust. And I just won't take that chance."

"What if I refuse?"

"Well then, my friend, you put me in a precarious position. Do I forcibly make you do it and lose the best friendship I have ever or will ever have? Or do I betray the trust of the men and women that have come to serve under me and jeopardize the very mission which I am attempting to accomplish?"

"Well then, what if I just leave?"

"I don't think you'll make it."

"Is that a threat, Paul?"

"No, of course not, Mike, but there are officers under my command who feel very strongly about your presence here."

"Can't you control your men?" I shouted. The mess hall was rapidly vacating as our argument heated up.

"I can, but I don't have them on a leash!" Paul shouted to match my own. "Mike, I'm telling you that if you leave here under these circumstances, you are jeopardizing your life at your own risk."

"This is beautiful! I battle my way off a hostile ship full of aliens to give Earth all the information about the aliens that I can; just so I can be treated like some kind of virus! Fuck you, Paul! You and your officers! I'm out of here! And if any of your lackeys tries to stop me, I'll take them out, no questions asked." I rose and headed for the door when I heard the distinctive cocking of a pistol.

"I'm sorry, Mike, I can't let you leave. Not like this."

"Fuck you, Paul… Shoot me in the back if you have to; I'm out of here." I heard the firing mechanism hit true and the warm sensation spread across my lower back. He shot me! My best friend shot me! I felt my cheek slam onto the turf. That's gonna leave a mark, I thought to myself, and, like the movies, I faded to black.

Chapter 7

"Hello, Deb? It's me, Beth."

"Beth? Why are you calling me? Do you realize how late it is?"

"I'm sorry, Deb I... I just needed to talk to someone... someone who has experienced what we've been through. And I'm worried."

Deb sat up in bed, wiping the weariness from her eyes; she hadn't really been sleeping. Truth be told, she hadn't slept much since her return to Earth. It was partly because of the nightmares but mostly because of her concern for the man she loved.

"Worried about what, Beth?"

"I haven't heard from Mike since we've been back."

Deb's interest was piqued. She also hadn't heard from him since the return, but she figured it was because he made the decision to be with Beth. "What do you mean you haven't heard from him? I thought he was with you."

"Oh God!" Deb could tell that Beth was crying on the other end of the line.

"What is it, Beth?"

"I thought he was with you!" she fairly wailed. "Beth, I thought he was with you." Deb also became misty-eyed, more from relief than worry, at this point though.

"I love him so much and I treated him so badly. I just wanted to let him know how I truly feel. I hoped and prayed that, by now, he would have found a way to forgive me and at least give me a call."

Now anxiety welled up in Deb in the same way that relief had flooded her moments earlier. Since he wasn't with Beth and he wasn't here, where the hell was he? Deb's myriad thoughts were shattered.

"Deb, can I come see you?" It sounded more like a

little girl begging to go to McDonalds than a full-grown woman. But Deb barely noticed; she nodded in agreement before realizing that Beth couldn't see her.

"Sure, Beth. When?"
"Now."
"Now? Ah… sure."
"I'll be there in twenty minutes."
"I'll put the coffee on. Bye."
"Bye."

Chapter 8

"General Burkhalter please, this is Captain Moiraine, clearance code Alpha Omega Foxtrot 227."

"Right away, Captain," the drone-like voice said at the other end of the line. After what seemed an interminable amount of time, the captain heard sheets ruffle and the unmistakable, gruff voice of the general.

"Uh, hello? What is it, Moiraine?"

"Sir, I'm sorry to disturb you at this hour, but something is wrong up here."

"Is there any chance, Captain, that you could be a little more descriptive?"

"Sir, Mike's arrival at camp set off some serious fireworks among the higher echelon here; and now he's missing."

"Missing? How so, Captain? I gave you strict orders to keep a very watchful eye on that young man."

"Sir, I understand that, but my comings and goings in this camp are tightly monitored. I did my best."

"Apparently, Captain, your best wasn't good enough. Have you talked to General Ginson?"

"Sir, they won't let me within one hundred feet of his command tent."

"Captain, you find out what happened to that man by any means possible or I'll have a division of Marines up there within the hour. Do you understand me!?" The captain could feel the rage steaming over the phone line.

"Sir, yes, sir!" The other side of the line went dead with what seemed more like a clap than a click. But the end of the phone conversation was only the beginning of the captain's problems. How was he going to get to Paul to discuss this matter without letting Paul on to him? That problem, however, was solved easily enough when the captain's tent flaps burst open and three heavily armed guards strode in.

"Captain, please unholster your weapon and place it on your bunk."

"What is the meaning of this?" the captain shouted.

"Sir, please unholster your weapon and place it on the bunk gently or we will use force." The two flanking guards stepped forward as if in preparation to enforce those words. The captain unholstered his weapon, barely able to control the anger inside of him.

"Again, what is the meaning of this?" the captain inquired, now physically shaking with rage.

"Sir, we detected unauthorized transmissions emanating from your tent."

"Unauthorized transmissions? I was making a call."

"Nevertheless, sir, all transmissions must be cleared through headquarters. General Ginson wishes to talk to you now, sir."

Well, at least some good may come of this, he figured. Now, at least, he could go to the source and try to locate the whereabouts of Captain Talbot. The guards completely encircled the captain and marched him unceremoniously to the general's tent.

"Ah, Captain, what a pleasure it is to see you," a weary-eyed Paul said.

"I'm not sure I had much of a choice, General," the captain said as he gestured to the guards flanking him.

"Ah yes, Sergeant, please take you and your men outside; there are a few matters I would like to discuss with the captain."

"As you wish, General." The sergeant and the guards retreated from the spacious command tent, but the captain was fully aware that they would still be able to hear the conversation, and were only a heartbeat away in the event they were needed.

"Is there any reason, General, why I cannot make a phone call to a relative without prior approval?"

"I did not realize, Captain, that you were in any way related to General Burkhalter."

The captain's face fell. "Captain, if anyone ever asks you to play poker, you should politely decline. Now your mind is reeling. How could they know? Is my tent bugged? Was someone listening outside? No, it's none of those things. We've known all along that you're a plant, Captain." The captain's face slipped even further, if that was possible.

"Then why would you let me stay, General?"

"It's better to have a spy that we know than one which we may not know about. And besides, knowing who you were and who you reported to, allowed us to handcraft the information that we wanted you to send.

"What now, General?"

"Well, we could have you shot as a spy." Sweat poured off the captain's forehead. "But don't worry, Captain. We're not quite that uncivilized. We are, however, Captain, using you as a little insurance policy until my next phase of planning is successfully launched.

"What?! I'm an officer in the United States Army! I will not be treated like this!"

"Enough, Captain!" Paul's voice raised noticeably. The sergeant poked his head in to make sure that everything was alright. "Everything is fine Sergeant," Paul said as he waved off the guard dogs. "Relax; we have every intention of letting you go once your purposes here are served."

"General, if you know about my conversation, than you must know what General Burkhalter said."

"I'm fully aware, Captain." Paul answered as he pushed "play" on a small tape-recording device, which the captain failed to notice on his initial entry.

"I'll have a division of Marines up there within the hour," the general's voice said, remarkably clear over the small device. The captain looked up.

"We are able to intercept satellite calls, Captain."

"So you have all of my calls on tape?"

"Why, of course! How else could we make sure that

you were reporting exactly what we wanted you to report?"

"And what of Captain Talbot, General?"

"That is a matter, which is none of your concern."

"General, may I comment on the obvious? Captain Talbot is also an officer in the United States military as well as being your best friend; and the reason for which you have set up this entire operation."

"Captain, do not lecture me! I do not recognize the authority of the United Sates military; and, as for my best friend, that man no longer exists."

"General, what are you saying?"

"I am saying that it is no concern of yours."

"And what of the Marines that will inevitably be here?"

"Let them come, for they will find an enormous surprise. Sergeant, take this man out of my tent and keep him restricted to his tent under guard. And, Sergeant, send in Colonel Salazar after you post a sentry."

"As you wish, General. Captain, please come with me."

"This isn't the end of it, General! You'll pay for your insolence!"

"Sergeant, remove him immediately before I do something which I might regret."

The sergeant wrested the captain out of the headquarters and back to his tent.

"Well, how did that go, General?"

"About as well as could be expected, Frank."

"Paul, you look tired. Why don't you catch a few z's? I'll take care of anything pressing."

"Frank, I'd love to, but we've got entirely too much work to do. We're going to have some guests soon and I want to be prepared for them."

"Guests, General?"

"Marines, Captain, probably somewhere in the neighborhood of five thousand or so." Frank nearly fell over, were it not for the chair that saved at least some of his dignity.

"What's the matter, my friend? Don't you think we can take care of a few of the best that the United States government can throw at us?"

"Uh, sir, I'm confident that we could take care of twice that number, on the ground."

"But? Come on, Colonel; you can be frank with me, no pun intended."

"Sir, you know as well as I do they aren't coming up here without some sort of air support. We just don't have the weaponry to handle that right now. Or at least the training on them."

"That's why we are going to blind them."

"Sir?"

"Colonel, get the satellite jammers up and running, full power."

"Full power? General, you know as well as I do that if those jammers run too hot, they'll knock the satellites out."

"That's the idea, Frank. I've got a huge surprise for our guests and I don't want them to have any clue as to what it might be. And as soon as you have that completed, get the rest of the staff in here. We have a lot of groundwork to complete and not much time to do it in."

Chapter 9 - CIA Headquarters

"General Burkhalter, what a pleasant surprise it is to have you here."

"Oh come now, Doctor; you know I can't stay away from our prize captive. How is the commander doing?"

"Quite well, General. We gave him a computerized chess game three days ago and he is already at a grandmaster level."

"What's his record?"

"Sir, he hasn't lost."

"He's playing at a grandmaster level and he hasn't dropped a game?"

"Sir, he is an amazing specimen, I would have to rate his IQ equivalency somewhere in the two hundred and thirty to two hundred and fifty range."

"So, he has brains to match all that brawn? What are we in for?" The general shuddered, he hadn't been this scared since he was a boot lieutenant in the jungles of Vietnam.

"Doctor, do you think perhaps only the supreme commander is this smart?"

"Sir, I've been talking to him, and, on his home planet, they play a game similar to chess but much more involved. They use something along the lines of sixty-four pieces that move inter-dimensionally. He rates himself as somewhat of a middling player at that game. Sir, he claims his strong point is what we call diplomacy."

"How are his spirits?"

"Sir, he, for lack of a better term, is as cool as a cucumber. And completely confident that his stay here will be a very short term event."

The general shuddered again although this was because of a physical reason than mental; his cell phone went off.

"Excuse me, Doctor. I have to take this call."

"Sure thing, General. I'll be down the hall if you need me. There was something unusual in his blood sample that I wanted to go over again."

"What do you mean 'the Captain missed his check-in time'?!" The general was severely pissed off.

"Sir," the major's voice sounded more like a little boy being berated for drawing on the living room wall. "Sir, since your last communication with the captain, all radio and satellite transmissions from the Mount have gone completely blank. And one more thing, sir."

"Well, what is it, Major? I don't have all day."

"Sir, all of our satellites over the Mount have gone dark."

"Dark? How is that possible?"

"Sir, it's some sort of high-powered, jamming device."

"Can't we switch to a different frequency?"

"Sir, by dark, I mean completely burnt. The signal was so strong, it appears that the internal circuitry has been fried."

"Fried? How long 'til it can be repaired?"

"Sir, it's irreparable."

"Oh, this is great! I've got two captains missing and a rebel general running around with a small army on American soil. Just great! Major, can you divert some satellites to that location?"

"Sir, the signal is still emanating; we would just cook those too."

"What about an air strike?"

"Sir?"

"An air strike, Major. I'm sure you've heard of those."

"Sir, our planes would be flying blind too."

"Major, get me Camp Pendleton and Twenty Nine Palms on the horn as quick as you can."

"Right away, sir."

The general turned back around to look through the two-way glass at their new prisoner, the commander, who was peering straight at the general with what appeared to be a huge, man-eating grin. The general turned away; things were already bad enough without having to wonder what that beast was thinking. The general barely had time to collect his thoughts when his phone rang again.

"Sir, this is Major Hadley. I have General Weston from Camp Pendleton and General Trent from Twenty Nine Palms on conference call."

"Thank you, Major. Generals, I don't have time for niceties. How fast can you mobilize a division and have them up in Vail?"

"General, this is General Trent; I don't have anywhere near a division here. Most of my troops are located at the DMZ in North Korea. But I could have twenty-five hundred men, one hundred tanks and ten Apache helicopters there by seventeen hundred hours tomorrow."

"General, this is General Weston; I can have four thousand men, fifty tanks and five Harriers there by the same time." God, I love the Marines, the general thought to himself. You never get the usual bullshit when you deal with them. They cut right to the chase and they don't ask useless questions.

"General, what can we expect upon arrival? And what kind of force are we returning?" asked General Weston.

"Gentlemen, you will be facing an enemy about half your number, they are however, highly trained and supplied. They are motivated."

"Sir, is this some sort of breakaway unit from the Army? It sounds too big to be some sort of militia," said General Trent.

"It's more of a rogue force, General. I'm not sure if they are ready to trade bullets with you just yet, but they are hostile. I'm hoping that just the mere show of force will end this little standoff. Gentlemen, let me know when you are a few hours away from the rendezvous site. I will tell you how to proceed from there."

"Very well, General." General Trent hung up.

"Very well, sir." General Weston did the same.

Chapter 10

Beth drove up the long drive to Deb's house or rather, Deb's parents' house. Deb had grown somewhat phobic of venturing outdoors and, although she was in counseling, she had foregone going back to school just yet. She found some comfort, not much, but some, by going home. Her parents had been more than happy to oblige, especially after her long absence and feared death. Beth took a deep breath and was about to push the doorbell, when the door swung open.

"Hello Beth, come on in."

"Mrs. Carmody?"

"Yes dear," a rotund little woman said. She appeared to be a young version of Mrs. Clause with one noticeable difference: she wasn't nearly as cheery. But Beth didn't need to ponder the reason for that now. Her daughter had been missing for a year and a half; and, now that she was back, she had withdrawn into a near cocoon state. "Deb will be down in a minute, she's getting ready. She doesn't get many guests these days. Do you know Deb from school?" Beth became silent, lapsing into her own thoughts for a moment. "Don't worry dear, I'd recognize that stare anywhere. Would you like some tea?"

"That would be great, Mrs. Carmody," Beth answered. She found herself taking to the woman immediately. Perhaps, she felt that with the love and support that this woman could offer, Deb would be on her feet in a relatively short time. "Maybe I should stay here too."

"Did you say something, dear?" Mrs. Carmody shouted from the kitchen.

Did I say that out loud? Beth thought. "Nothing, just thinking out loud, apparently," she answered.

"Sugar?"

"Huh? Oh, sure, one spoonful." Mrs. Carmody

returned with two steaming cups of tea, when Deb started down the stairs.

Beth thought, Deb was, for lack of a better word, gaunt. She looked like she had lost fifteen pounds from her already petite frame. Her eyes were bloodshot and puffy. It didn't look like she had slept a wink since she'd been back. Well, it's not like I've slept well either, Beth thought to herself. as she rose to greet her... What? Certainly not "friend," but more than an acquaintance. "Comrade"? Naw, that sounded too Russian. "Fellow survivor", she guessed, would have to do. Beth didn't know if she should help Deb down the stairs or not. God, she looked rough.

"Hi Beth, how have you been?" The first thing that came to Beth's mind was, better than you, but luckily, this time, she didn't think it out loud.

"I've been better," she answered more diplomatically.

"Well, as you can see, so have I," Deb answered sardonically.

"I'll leave you girls alone," Mrs. Carmody said with concern laced throughout her voice. A very quick glance towards Beth hinted that if she, in any way, upset her daughter, she would have to deal with her.

Beth did the first thing that came to her mind: she hugged Deb. It was more instinctual than anything else. At first, Deb resisted, but eventually, the stiffening lessened and she actually embraced her back.

"Oh God, Beth," Deb sobbed into Beth's shoulder. "I haven't slept or eaten in weeks. The nightmares are the worst. When I was on the ship, everything was so clear. Do what you have to do, just survive. Yes, I was scared, for my very life. But I wasn't panicked. Now I feel like I'm fighting to save my soul. I feel like I've worn it thin. I don't feel like I have anything left in me. And the man that could take me out of this stupor is nowhere to be found." Deb sat down on the sofa with her face cupped in her hands. Beth sat down next to her and put her arm around Deb's back. "I haven't been out of the house since our escape. The news media was camped on our lawn for a week before they realized I wasn't coming out to give them a story."

"I know. They followed me around for a while too. I've been trying so hard to pretend that none of this happened, to go back to a normal life, if there is such a thing. I haven't given myself a free moment to dwell on it, I'm so afraid of what might happen."

"Look at me, Beth; this is what would happen."

"Oh, Deb. I'm so sorry." And she once again embraced Deb.

"So you haven't heard from Mike either?" Beth noticed a hint of a weary happiness in her statement.

"No, I had at least hoped that you had." But that wasn't true and they both knew it. "I just want to know that he's safe." And whom he's with. "I treated him so badly, after all he did for all of us, I just want to let him know how I feel," Beth said with remorse.

"He loves you. Still."

"I don't know, Deb." Beth replied but in her heart, hope surged. Do you really think so? she wanted to scream to the world. "He loves you too."

"But not in the soul mate way he feels about you. We shared something, something terrible. And in that terribleness we comforted each other. But everything he did, he did for you. If not for you, I think he would have just laid down and died, instead of taking all those lives."

Could that be true? Please don't let it be. Beth didn't think that she could bear the thought of all those people dying on her behalf.

"Beth, don't blame yourself. Those people would have died either way and so would have the rest of us, either at the hands of that mad man or suffer a slow death as prisoners on an alien ship." They both shuddered. "Mike saved you, he saved me, a dozen other girls and possibly our very planet; and he did it for you. His love for you was so strong, he overcame odds that Vegas wouldn't even touch."

"Girls, can I get you anything?" Mrs. Carmody

stepped into the room to see how things were going, and was actually relieved to see her daughter crying; at least it was an emotion. It was far better than the thousand-yard stare she had transfixed on her face for the past few weeks.

Chapter 11

"General Burkhalter, we are exactly two hours from our rendezvous point with 'Little Rock'." This was the code name assigned to the mission. "We are awaiting your instructions before we proceed."

"General Weston, you're three hours ahead of schedule," a weary Burkhalter noted. "But not unexpected from you and your troops. I want you to proceed with caution, General. I want this matter dealt with as quietly as possible but, if you are fired upon, I want you to return fire in kind. But let me be clear, General, I do not want an escalation. If you are fired upon by small arms I want you to return small arms fire. Don't bring the A-1 Abrams into the fray just yet. Let them see them and maybe they'll decide to back down. I want this over as quickly as possible and I want two of our own returned as well."

"Sir, I'm not following you. We have personnel in there?"

"Yes, one undercover... A Captain Moraine, and a Captain Talbot whose whereabouts has not been known for over forty-eight hours. General Weston, I want them alive."

"Sir, understood. Over and out."

"General Burkhalter?"

"What is it, Lieutenant? Can't you see that I'm a little busy here."

"Sir, I think you're about to become a lot busier."

"What is it, Lieutenant?" The general was in no mood for verbal jousting with a boot lieutenant.

"Sir, the mother ship is lit up like a Christmas tree on the infrared."

That grabbed the general's attention like jumping into a cold mountain stream on a hot summer day. The general nearly ran across the control room, temporarily incognizant of all military decorum. But it went completely unnoticed. Everyone's gaze was transfixed on the computer screen that was monitoring the mother ship's orbit.

"Lieutenant, switch to visual mode."

"Yes, sir." The lieutenant no sooner switched to visual mode when a complete and utter, uneasy silence filled the room. Thousands of small craft were exiting the ship. It looked more like a mass exodus of bees from a hive. Unfortunately, however, it appeared to be a swarm of killer bees, all headed for planet Earth. They stretched for thousands of miles. The lieutenant felt that the sheer weight of this offensive would push the Earth out of its orbit to go veering off into some equally unlucky mass. A radar operator wept openly; most though, were either too stunned or too lodged in disbelief to show much of any emotion.

"So this is how it ends," the general said, more to himself than to any one in particular. " I always figured it'd be the Chinese. Lieutenant! Get the president on the phone. Lieutenant!" The lieutenant snapped around.

"Sir?!" The glaze that had begun to form around his eyes like that of a condemned man being led to the electric chair briefly vanished.

"Get the president on the line, and then go to DefCon 5."

"Sir, only the president can give the order for DefCon 5," the lieutenant sputtered.

"I really don't think the president is going to mind this one time, Lieutenant; and I don't want to waste another five minutes waiting for the answer I already know is coming." And somehow, Lieutenant, I don't think that any mistake I make tonight will be noticed at all tomorrow. But the general merely thought the latter; he had no desire to send his entire staff into a panic, no matter how he felt.

Chapter 12

General Weston felt a certain unease from the depths of his soul. What it was, he couldn't identify. He knew he outmanned this new enemy two to one, but they had superior position, and possibly equal fire power. But that still wasn't it. Sure, anytime you faced an adversary, some apprehension was guaranteed. But not like this; this was downright dread. For only the second time in his life, the general felt that he was being led into a trap.

The first time was when he was a boot lieutenant in Vietnam. His platoon had been cut to ribbons by an enemy laying in wait, who knew he was coming. To this day, he occasionally still had nightmares of the screaming men who fell around him. Men who depended on his leadership to get them out of any situation. He felt that same itching on the back of his neck that he had on that night, so many years before. But he was, and always would be, a Marine. At the very least, he would do whatever it took, no matter what the cost, to take control of that mountain with as few casualties as possible.

"Sir, our recon Marines are only spotting minimal movement on the ridge," Major Bernhard said. The general didn't really like the man, but he was efficient at his job and that was all the general required. "Recon believes they are all hunkered down for the night."

"Or lying in wait."

"Excuse me, sir?" the major asked.

"I'm saying, Major, that they just might be waiting for us."

"Sir, what exactly are we up against? I was under the impression we were just going up there on a reconnaissance mission, and that they were just some rabble with gun licenses."

"That's part of it, Major, but these are well-armed militia that have better defensive position."

"Sir, to be frank, I wouldn't care if they had ten to one odds. These Marines are the finest fighting soldiers on the planet. They'll take one look and probably run home, screaming for mama."

"You might be right, Major. And I hope that you are because I have no desire to ever write another letter to some young Marine's parents again." The major turned away as if to issue orders, but actually because he didn't like the look of concern that obscured the general's face.

"This is no time for self-doubt," the major muttered as he headed towards his junior officers. The general knew he wasn't supposed to hear that last comment, but he felt no hostility toward the major; in fact, he agreed.

Chapter 13

"Hey Becky! Come and look at this," a slight, red-haired, freckle-faced boy said with excitement lilting his voice.

"Oh come on, Bobby Ray, you've been looking through that thing all night. Wouldn't you rather look at this heavenly body?" a sprawled-out, bored blond replied.

Chapter 14

"Hey Dad! I think that one of the planets is exploding."

"No, son. Venus is just particularly bright at this time of the evening."

"Dad, I'm serious. Take a look through the scope."
The father stopped to appease his son with a cursory glance. He then dropped his full can of beer, wondering how he was going to get the number for NASA.

Chapter 15

General Weston's troops crested the mountain and were greeted by sparse and erratic gunfire, which turned out to be decoys, firing blanks.

"Major, what the hell is going on up there?"

"Sir, you might want to come up here."

"Is the area secure, Major?"

"Sir, this area was secured way before we got here. There is nobody up here."

"Then what the hell was all that small arms fire?"

"Sir, they had trip wires rigged to fire some weapons. Sir, one more thing."

"What is it, Major?"

"Sir, they were using blanks. I don't understand it, sir. It seems they knew we were coming and vacated post haste; but they wanted to slow our ascent. It makes no sense; if you're going to leave, why bother with the props?"

The general removed his cap to wipe his now perspiring brow. "I'll tell you why, Major, they're playing with us."

"Sir?"

"Major, they knew we were coming. How? I'm not sure yet, but I'll figure it out. They set up the booby traps just for fun."

"I don't see the humor, General. I've got two wounded Marines, one with a broken collar bone and one a broken wrist. They were diving for cover and hit bad patches of land."

"Well, let's be thankful it wasn't anything more serious than that. I'll be up momentarily." The general turned to his Humvee driver, "Corporal, get me up that mountain, post haste."

"Sir, yes, sir," the corporal said before literally

putting the pedal to the metal. But if you've ever ridden in a military Hummer, you'd agree that's really not saying all that much. The Hummer came up over the ridgeline to an anthill of activity. The majority of the invading Marines had already taken the mountaintop and were checking all of the tents. The major flagged down the general.

"Sir, it appears that they left in an awfully big hurry."

"Why do you say that, Major?"

"Sir, all of their tents and camo netting are here."

"Is any of their gear here, Major? Any weapons?"

"Well, none that we've found sir, except, of course, for the dummies."

"Well, Major, I'm not so sure we scared them out of here. I think they left all the tents and camo netting as a decoy. They didn't want us to know they were leaving."

"Isn't this good news, sir? We took the objective with zero casualties?"

"Not at all, Major. We now have a large, cohesive, armed militia on the move and no idea where they are. At least before, we knew their exact location. We also failed to regain two of our troops, who were reported missing. Major, get on the horn to General Burkhalter and let him know what has happened here. And then tell him to get all the satellite images of this area for the last twenty-four hours. Maybe we'll be able to tell in which direction our 'friends' have evacuated. Major? I'm talking to you. Have you heard a word I've said?" The general followed the major's line of sight. If he hadn't been sitting, he was sure that he would have fallen over. As it was, he had to grab onto the roll bar to keep himself from falling out of the Hummer.

The corporal, who was not paying much attention to the officer's conversation, finally noticed when he realized they weren't talking anymore. He followed their line of sight also.

"What the fuck is that?!" the corporal exclaimed as his cigarette went flying. The noise broke the stunned silence of the general.

"Major!!" He had to yell it twice to break the major out of his stupor. "Major!!"

"Sir!? What the…"

"Major! No time! Rally the troops!! Now! I want defensive positions immediately! Get the tanks up here now!" The general had to give the major credit. He snapped it together in an instant and was belaying orders to the junior officers. Some of the Marines had to be pushed into action, judging ,by their bewildered stares. But the vast majority knew their part; they had trained hard and long for this. Maybe not this particular scenario, but going on the defensive was the same, no matter who the enemy. Marines scurried around, jumping into fighting holes and readying their M-16's or SAW's. The tanks were just beginning to ramble up into the camp.

"Yea, though I walk through the shadow of death…" The corporal had been through a few scrapes with the general but had never before seen him utter the Lord's Prayer. At that moment, the corporal wished he had listened to his mother and stayed in school.

Chapter 16

The world governments knew first, then the major telescopes around the globe, then pretty much anybody who had a scope from Sears. Not until the line of ships was visible, did the planet reach its most heightened state of alertness. Most people didn't have enough time to panic. More than likely, that was a good thing.

Chapter 17

The girls had retired to the front porch and were enjoying some wine in the cool mountain air when they became aware that something was amiss.

"Beth, do you hear anything?"

"No, nothing at all. It's so quiet up here, none of the traffic like back East."

"No, Beth. I'm not talking about traffic I'm talking about anything, bugs, crickets, owls, anything?"

"Now that you mention it, I don't hear anything. I thought it was just me, but I was beginning to feel a little creeped-out."

"Yeah, sort of like when we were on the ship."

Both girls looked up, almost as if on cue. Deb was vaguely aware as she spilled some wine that it was probably going to stain her parents' front deck, but the importance of that completely eluded her.

"Dad!!!" Deb screamed.

Her father came hauling ass after hearing his daughter. "What's going on!" her father said, nearly panicked. "Deb, I thought a mountain lion was attacking you two!" He then noticed the spilled drinks. "Girls, I really think you can handle this mess by yourselves, without all the drama!" he chided. He was beginning to feel a little perturbed that his daughter caused his blood pressure to rise by fifty points for the spilled drink. "You know, if you don't wipe that up soon, it's going to stain."

"Dad, get Mom and Duke and the keys to the root cellar."

"Hon, they don't have tornadoes in the foothills. You know that. A lot of lightning, but no tornadoes."

"Dad, shut up and get Mom."

Deb's quiet steeliness unsettled her father, but he was

still under the impression that this was just one of her many panic attacks since returning from heaven only knows where.

"Dad!" Deb exclaimed as she pointed up into the sky. Recognition finally dawned on his face.

"I'll g-g-go get your mother."

"Good idea, Dad."

Chapter 18

"Hey Paulie! The last of our troops should be arriving within the next five or six hours."

"I don't think they're going to make it, Wags."

"Come on, Paul! You told me yourself you got away from the Marines without them discovering anything."

"You're right, buddy, they have no clue; but I just got off the phone with the observatory in Hawaii and our interplanetary friends are on the way."

"Paul, tell me you're kidding. We've only got about half of our troops 'holed up'."

"No joke, Wags. He says the front running ships will most likely be here in an hour, or two, tops. I want you to issue a Code Red callback on all of our troops Tell them if they're not back in an hour, then don't bother. At one hour exactly, I want the cave gates closed and locked. Then I want everything topside blacked out, and I mean completely out. I don't so much as want a lighter up there. I also want all cellular and satellite transmissions halted immediately. Understood?"

"No problem, consider it done. Paul, I just have one question." Paul knew it was coming and was somewhat surprised that it had taken so long.

"Paul, where is Mike?" Paul thought about lying and saying that Mike had left camp to be with Beth but thought better of it. Historically, he had never been a good liar and Dennis was bound to find out sooner or later.

"Paul, Ron's here. I'm going to have to tell him something. And it's not only him; I want to know and there are others." Dennis suspected Paul might be trying to blow him off by stalling, but he was determined to find out the truth. Something stunk around here and he meant to get to the bottom of it.

"Dennis," Wags didn't like the tone of Paul's voice any time someone used his first name. It usually meant bad news, and this time was no different. "Mike was a spy."

"What do you mean 'spy'? And what do you mean 'was'!"

"Dennis, I don't have time to explain it all right now; but I did what I had to do; I took care of it. I promise to tell you everything and show you the proof as soon as we have some down time."

"Paul, what do I tell Ron?"

"You tell him that you have no idea where Mike is; tell him that you think he's still in Colorado."

"Aw Paul, I don't like this. I don't like this at all."

"I'll explain it later, but for now, get my orders in motion or I won't have to explain myself at all." Dennis understood that completely, but he was still shaking his head in disbelief as he headed out the door.

Chapter 19

The Marines were nothing, if not prepared, General Weston thought to himself. They had completely dug themselves in, thanks, in large part, to the departing army that preceded them. It truly was an amazing maze of trenches and cave systems that criss-crossed the mountain top. They must have worked twenty-four/seven, the general thought to himself. He felt more secure here than at the El Toro base. But would even these defensive measures be enough to stand up to what was coming?

Chapter 20

Militaries around the world braced for the storm. Combatants who, moments earlier, were locked in mortal combat now stood shoulder-to-shoulder waiting for the impending doom to rain down. For the briefest of times in the globe's history, world peace was upon us. Man stood beside his fellow man, regardless of race, creed, color, or any other bogus manifestation of hate created by human discrimination.

For a few hours in the history of man, something that had been prophesized for millennia was taking place. But the why of it had always been conveniently omitted by the ancient prophets. The lucky souls who passed away by natural causes in those last few hours and thereby escaped the coming hell would be forever thankful.

Chapter 21

The gun ships were roughly the size of the tanks they were attacking, but with far more mobility. The general noted no props or detectable engines of any kind. There was no rotor splash or jet exhaust; how they flew was a complete mystery. Their mobility, however, was not as good as he had expected. They appeared to be more designed for spatial combat, not terrestrial. They flew well but not spectacularly well. In reality, they looked more like Volvo station wagons with fins--basically flying bricks. Okay, so they were big bricks with unimaginable weaponry.

The first rounds slammed into the recently vacated and newly repopulated mountaintop above Vail. Rounds? General Weston thought to himself. He didn't really think that they could be classified as rounds.

The bluish light that emanated from the gunships was in sharp contrast to the silvery red that begat the devastation these blasts took when they struck home. The M-1 Abrams tank that was targeting the gunship while awaiting orders to fire had been what? Not vaporized, more like liquefied. All that remained of the fifteen-ton vehicle and its five crew members was something akin to slag. Bright, red-embered slag. Could it be brought down? Visible panic dominated the afterglow for a few seconds of almost every Marine on that mount. But none broke ranks. There would be no running, not that there would have been enough time anyway.

But the Progerians' first strike was all the incentive the Marines needed to open fire. The mountaintop was lit up like a spectacular fireworks display. Red tracers shot upwards as blue fire rained down. The remaining tanks began to move and fire rapidly so as not to make such easy targets. The gunships targeted these behemoth machines first.

General Weston wondered if the aliens were possibly

afraid of them. Then, as if on some cosmic cue, a tank round hit pay dirt. The gunship rocked sideways from the force of the blast, but that was all the general noticed at first with a serious heaping of dismay. If the strongest weapon in their arsenal at this moment couldn't do more than knock the ship off course for a few seconds, then of what use would small arms fire be? The general desperately wanted to sound the call to fall back, but fall back where? The carnage was mounting, the screams of Marines writhing in agony was deafening. He began to flashback to his Vietnam days.

"Oh God, what have I done?" the general asked as he stood up and surveyed all that was happening around him, almost oblivious to it all. What sent him further away was an incredibly loud "POP".

***

He recognized it as the sound that his old cork gun made when he was seven years old. The one his brother had traded for a pack of baseball cards. He had been so mad then, he almost cussed. His mother would have paddled his ass for an hour, had he not thought better of it. But it all worked out in the end. His brother had to buy him a new gun, he got the pack of baseball cards, and he got to watch as his mother paddled his brother's behind.

Days later, his big brother, Mikey, got him back. Mikey was more upset that his little brother saw the tears welling up in his eyes. Mikey made it look like an accident with the swing, but they both knew better. Mikey kept pushing the swing higher and higher, even though Johnny screamed for him to stop, to no avail. Johnny was terrified that the swing would fly off into space. He got so scared, he simply let go. Had Johnny turned around, he would have seen the mortified look on his brother's face. Johnny let go when the swing reached its highest point. Mikey knew no good would come of this and slowly Johnny fell, straight at first, and then a little skewed to the left. Finally, he plunged to the ground with a snap and a crash.

***

"What was that?!" the general snapped back.

"Sir! We got one! We got one!!!" There was a huge, tumultuous "Ooh Rah" and that was the last thing the old man heard before the command post joined the majority of the combatants on the hill. It seemed a pretty fitting ending, the general thought as he watched with indifference. Then, slowly he ascended, failing to understand the imagery below him. The battle waged on; men didn't need leadership when their ass was on the line. Saving one's skin can be incentive enough.

Another gunship was brought down, but this one seemed to be more from mechanical failure than anything the Marines launched. All of the tanks had been taken out early, especially after they proved lethal to the ships. The Marines M-16 fire was about as affective as the charge of the Polish Cavalry against the German Panzer division in World War II, basically nil. Fifteen hundred men were an awfully high price to pay for two gunships, although the Progerians didn't see it that way.

Chapter 22

Aboard the Mother Ship

"The supreme commander is going to be awfully disappointed with your tactics, Kuvlar."

Kuvlar, for lack of a better term, was the interim supreme commander. The Progerians didn't have any sort of fail safes in place like our government; such as, if the president is out of the picture, the vice president steps in, then the House Leader, and so forth. Eleven Progerians had stepped into the Coliseum and performed ritualistic battle. Kuvlar had dominated those games and was now interim supreme commander. But Kuvlar's emotions more closely resembled a human's.

He wasn't proud of it, but he loved this newfound power. He basked in it, wanted it. He hoped that the supreme commander was dead and, if not, maybe he could do something to change that. This was no cold, calculating thought process that we often attribute to crocodiles; this was more like red-hot, human passion. That was why the sub-commander's remarks elicited a loud snarl and gnashing of Kuvlar's jaws.

"Right now, Sub-Commander Tuvok, I am the supreme commander. I have only myself to answer to."

"But sir, we just lost two gunships in our first attack."

"I am fully aware of that. I guess these puny hu-mans really do have a nasty bite." Kuvlar was remembering the blast that had wiped out nearly a quarter of their fleet. He hoped that the fifty thousand ships launched would be enough to conquer this planet. The only other alternative was for him to be forcibly brought back to his home planet to answer for his ineptitude. By then, the meeting would be no more than a formality, after which he would be enslaved and forced to fight in the very games he loved to watch.

Chapter 23

"What the hell is going on?!" Deb shouted in horror as she peeked out the storm cellar door to see five more F-16's scrambling.

"Honey, shut the door," a nervous Mr. Carmody said softly. He wasn't sure if anyone could hear him over the din, but he was afraid to say it any louder.

"It's happening, Beth, isn't it?" Deb asked, turning to Beth. Beth was huddled in the corner. If she had found more room, she would have been in the fetal position. Now Deb appeared to be the stronger of the two. Beth had spent so much time trying to obliterate the memories from her mind that she was now having a difficult time wrapping her thoughts around the present.

"Oh, Beth," Deb said with true concern in her voice as she passed by her shivering father. Shivering? Was it cold? Her dad afraid? Impossible! The man was a rock. He must just be cold, Deb thought to herself as she wrapped her arms around Beth. Deb grabbed her openly weeping mother and pulled her into the fray too. Her dad came willingly enough after that. For two hours, they stayed like that; nobody dared move. Maybe if they stayed still long enough nobody would ever notice that they were there.

Chapter 24
Above Vail

"Con 7? This is Yankee Whiskey 1," Colonel Dodson said from the cockpit of his F-16.

"Go ahead, Yankee Whisky 1, this is Con 7," the control tower at AFB Denver replied.

"Con 7. Vail Mount is burning. I repeat, burning. No signs of life below." The colonel had no idea who was down there but even as high up and fast as he was going, he could tell that the devastation was beyond anything he could ever compare it to. "Please dispatch helo's."

"Confirmed, Yankee Whiskey 1. What of the bogies?"

"We have them on radar, Con 7. They seem to be heading your way."

"We see them. Any sign of them in your area?"

"Negative, Con 7."

"Do you have an intercept YW1?"

"Con 7, at their present speed, we can intercept but it's going to be close. You may want to evacuate."

"Negative, YW1. We have jets scrambling from Colorado Springs."

"How many, Con 7?"

"Two air wings."

"Con 7, even if we make it on time, we're still outnumbered five to one. I must strongly urge you to evacuate."

"Colonel? This is Major General Bastion on the line now. That is a negative on the retreat. We will not abandon our post. We are your eyes and ears and the last line of defense for Denver."

"Roger that, Major General. Squadrons two and four, I want you on full burn with my wing 'til we intercept. Three and five, I want you to maintain present speed. We are going to need fresh fighters with plenty of fuel. Good luck all, today we fight, tomorrow we'll worry about dying." That elicited a chorus of loud "Whoop's over the radio before everyone attended to the business at hand.

Five rescue helicopters from the Forest Rangers department attempted to land and aid. But that was an impossibility right now. The ground itself appeared to be on fire.

"Shit!"

"What is it, Cappy?" Ranger Buckley asked Joe "Cappy" Fremont.

"That ground down there looks like when I used to fly tourists in Hawaii over Kilauea, the active volcano. I thought I would never see that kind of heat again."

"Why did you leave a cushy job like that? Taking tourists on a little cruise flight."

"I'm afraid of fire."

"So you joined the Rangers to fight forest fires?"

"What can I say? I love trees."

"Cappy, that doesn't look like just trees down there."

"Hold on! I'm going to see if I can get us a closer look." Even from five hundred feet, they could feel the heat from the blaze below, but the proximity did allow them to identify some shapes.

"Hey Buck! Are those tanks?" Cappy asked as he pointed down and to the left.

"Cappy, I think you're right but what the hell are tanks doing here? You think this was some sort of firing range accident?"

"I don't think so, Buck, not unless they were firing some low-level nukes. Radio the rest of the helo's. We'll attempt to land closer to the city and confiscate some cars."

"Roger that, Cappy." A fresh bead of sweat rolled off Buck's brow and it had nothing to do with how close they were to the blaze.

***

The F-16's thundered through the sky. For those who were not awake yet, they solved that little problem. Houses shook, knick-knacks flew off shelves. People cried anew. Most really had no clue what was going on; but they saw the invaders come in. One look over at the mountains and you could tell a major battle had been waged and now U.S. fighters were screaming through the air. Most citizens were still under the impression that this was some sort of terrestrial attack, Russia or perhaps, China. But for those unlucky few who knew the truth, there would be no comfort tonight.

***

"Yankee Whiskey 1, this is Yankee Foxtrot 2."

"Go ahead, Foxtrot 2."

"Sir, I have visual confirmation of bogies."

"My radar is scattering, Foxtrot 2. Where are they located?"

"Eleven-thirty, sir."

The colonel turned his head slightly to the left and, by squinting, barely saw the glint of the gunships as they flew over Lakewood.

"Good work, Foxtrot 2. Let's give them hell." Hell might have been a little difficult that night, but they did give them a big heaping of heck.

***

ABC Affiliate KDVR, Denver

"You better get the chief for this one, Malone."

"What's up, Stewart?"

"You have got to see what Fox is reporting!" Bob Stewart shouted over the reporter on the televisions he was monitoring. All the stations did it… Sort of like the big discount stores shopping each other to make sure that the competition doesn't have a leg up on them. While most of the stations were scrambling for the details up in Vail, some had already confirmed that it was either a terrorist-detonated bomb, an industrial accident, or a military jet crashing, depending upon which station reported it. Fox, however, always sensationalized their reports. And it was doing wonders for them. The fledgling station had made dramatic leaps in the ratings war.

"Fox is reporting that we are under attack."

"Attack? From whom?"

"Malone, just get the chief." He meant the editor-in-chief, Warren Sapstein. A severe man who had a disposition and temperament to match his looks. "He's gonna flip."

For such a busy man, Stewart was surprised with the speed at which Sapstein made it down to the monitoring booth, as it was affectionately called. It had, once upon a time, been a fairly large room; but now, with all the monitors stuffed into it, three people could barely fit side-by-side.

"Stewart, this had better be damn important. I have five news vehicles heading up to Vail and another crew headed towards a shooting in Aurora."

"Sir, Fox is reporting that we are under attack."

"Who is under attack, Stewart? This station? An embassy in China? An Army barracks in Germany? Who?"

"Sir, the United States."

"What? What are those assholes doing?" Stewart actually flinched at the severity in the boss' voice. "I love ratings as much as the next guy, but what are they doing? Where, son?"

"Here, sir. Vail. They're saying that Vail is under attack."

"What kind of commie crap is this? Why would the Russians give a rat's ass about a bunch of stuck-up rich socialites and the ski bums that serve them?"

"Sir, they're saying it's not the Russians."

"Spit it out, Stewart, or you're going to be sorting mail on Monday." His wasn't the greatest job in the world, but it beat sorting mail. He was getting paid to watch television, for shit's sake.

"Sir, they are saying that it's an extraterrestrial attack and that they have the video to prove it."

"Like E.T.?"

"I'm thinking more like 'Alien', sir." He was hoping

that the chief had seen the movie; he didn't want to have to explain it. It sounded entirely too strange.

"They have video?" Apparently the connection was made. "Stewart, I want you to find out whoever made that video and double whatever price Fox paid for it."

Stewart meekly answered, "Yes, sir." But he didn't have a clue in the world how he was going to accomplish that. As the chief was about to begin the second part of his tirade, multiple military jets screamed over the station. Everyone who was still at the station ran for the exits to see what the commotion was all about. Luckily for Stewart, the chief was among them.

***

The Mountain in Colorado Springs.

"General Burkhalter we have multiple bogies heading this way."

"How many, Captain?"

"Sir, I can't tell. There are so many of them they are showing up as a blob on the screen."

"Scramble everything we've got."

"Sir?"

"I know, Captain. We sent half our forces to Denver. It's too late for us but let's give our pilots a shot. The captain didn't see the likelihood of good odds. A hundred or so jets against what appeared to be roughly around five hundred of something.

Half of the fighters had been airborne when the first rounds made impact. The mountain shook like a fat man on a treadmill. But she stood. The fighters in the air didn't even have to take aim; if they pulled the trigger, they were bound to hit something. One of the fighter pilots noted that the sky looked like Maine during the black fly season.

"You can't smile without eating some of them." And that was the last transmission Captain David Parker of Bangor, Maine ever made. His jet, moving at more than one and a half times the speed of sound, instantly became a flying molten ball of super-heated metal. Planes were dropping out of the sky at an alarming rate against the onslaught, F-16's, F-15's, Harriers and bombers. There was no discrimination in this slaughter. The jets were able to inflict some damage, although minor. Five gunships found the turf before the melee was through.

The second barrage of rounds that slammed into the mountain made spider fractures along the cavernous roof. Many of the personnel were getting ready to run for the exits when the general belayed that.

"Folks, it has been an honor and a privilege to work with all of you throughout these last tumultuous years. I will remember you all." It began to dawn on everyone that they were doomed. There was nowhere to go. Death would be swift here. A thunderous crack echoed throughout the mountain before an eerie silence that seemed to last for an eternity. Then the roof caved in under the third and final volley from the aliens. The United States command and control center had fallen in less than four minutes.

***

Indian Hill, Walpole, Massachusetts

"Sir, we've been monitoring the news channels. They all have conflicting stories but the gist of it seems to be that Mount Vail is no longer there."

"As in our base and gear, soldier?"

"No sir, as in twenty feet of the mountain literally slid down into the valley below."

"Leave me, Lance Corporal." Paul laid his head in his hands. Mike had been right, he thought to himself. "Did I do the right thing? He did warn us."

"Paul, you couldn't have done anything differently," Colonel Salazar said as he stepped away from the table to put his arms on Paul's shoulders.

"Couldn't I have…"

"Paul, how do you think they knew to hit Vail? From all reports, it's the first place they hit."

"I know. I know. But he was my best friend for so many years. Could you please excuse me, Frank? I'd just like to be alone for a while."

"I understand, sir. But don't beat yourself up over this. You did what you had to do to protect your troops. And there is not a man, woman or child here who doesn't thank God for your decisions."

"What about Ron?"

"Sir?"

"Ron, his brother."

"I'll leave you to your thoughts, sir." The colonel departed. He didn't have the answers; nobody did. War demanded tough orders. The good of the many had to prevail over the good of the individual. Paul understood that; but his decisions up to now had never been so close to the vest.

After the colonel left, Paul began to recall some of the highlights in his and Mike's relationship. The one Paul would never forget was the time he, Mike, and a few of their college buddies decided to climb Mount Elbert, one of the fourteen-thousand-footers that dotted Colorado. A group of six started out that morning before the weather took a seriously nasty turn about a third of the way up. The four others decided to turn back. "No sense in taking any chances," they said, almost as one. Paul could find no reason not to go back down, since it sounded like the right thing to do.

"Fuck that!" Mike yelled. Paul thought he could hear him now. "We came this far; I'm not turning back now."

"Come on, Mike. This is crazy, you can't go it alone."

"There's some pretty serious rope work involved and now you have the weather to contend with," one of the fading friends from school said.

"See you back at the dorms," was all he said as he turned and headed back up the mountain. He wasn't going to argue with anybody or try to persuade them otherwise; but he wasn't going to stop either.

"Come on, guys. He'll go another couple of hundred yards and turn back around."

Paul watched as the group headed down and Mike headed up. He's not even turning around. He's not bluffing.

Well, why not? Paul thought to himself as he raced to catch up to Mike.

"What took you so long?" Mike quipped.

"I had to tie my shoe."

So up they went in the blinding rain and flashing lightning. Mike never wavered. "We're on a mission," he stated more than once, and more to himself than to me, Paul thought. So, for five grueling hours, they climbed, two steps up, one step back in the terra un-firma before they finally crested the summit. The view was unbelievable; they could barely see their hands in front of their faces. They laughed like crazy men while they signed their names on the roster at the top.

"I've got a surprise for you," Mike said as he turned to Paul with a devilish grin. Paul wished he hadn't watched "The Shining" the week before because Mike's grin looked just like Jack Nicholson's as he peered through the bathroom door. Paul half expected Mike to pull out an axe from his backpack. Instead, he was pleasantly surprised when Mike handed him a remarkably cold Moosehead.

"How did you know to carry two beers up here? There's no way you could have forecast the weather up here and our friends' reactions."

"Paul! I brought a six pack for those peckerwoods but none of them are here so I guess we get three each."

And so there they sat in the driving downpour, drinking beer and philosophizing on life and the pursuit of women. Actually, it was mostly women; but there were a few deep thoughts now and then. By the time they got back to the dorms, a full ten hours later, because they also stopped at a local pub, they were loud and raucous. High on life, Paul absently thought. They went to the mountain on a mission and Mike made sure that they accomplished it.

Paul never doubted the story Mike told him about being aboard the ship. He had witnessed his determination first hand as well as his almost blind, single-mindedness. But Paul would always doubt his own actions.

***

The Earth shook for hundreds of miles in all directions as the aliens dropped some sort of charges on Denver. If you've ever gone into one of those novelty shops in the mall with those spheres of electricity that spider out like some low-budget Frankenstein movie, that's exactly what the aliens' charges looked like only they were the size of a VW Bug. However, when these giant special effects balls hit the ground, the charges inside of them were freed and allowed to run rampant. The destruction was devastating. One bomb leveled a neighborhood of ten city blocks.

We've all seen pictures from World War II, featuring the shell of some bombed-out building or the remnants of a house. But this was so much different, it left nothing. Nothing except a three–foot-high wall of debris. It looked like some huge monster's foot came down and flattened everything.

In the days and weeks that followed this initial attack, not one miracle survived. Nobody was found half-starved under a wall. Nothing, not even so much as a dog was seen wandering around, looking for its master. The city of Denver had been halfway to oblivion when the Colorado Springs and Denver air wing defenses caught up. They barely slowed the juggernaut down.

Los Angeles, Seattle, Denver, New York, Miami and Washington D.C. all disappeared that night. Seventy-two million Americans perished in an instant. Heaven, itself, was not prepared for the onslaught of human carnage. Nobody knew at the time, but the rest of the globe was suffering the same fate at nearly the same rate.

Surprisingly, it was the Russians who inflicted the greatest damage on the aliens and, in return, also suffered the greatest wrath. The Russians discovered that by gaining height on the attackers and striking from above, they could inflict more serious casualties. The Russians were actually able to hold their own in the beginning, trading plane for ship at an almost equal swap.

But the bomber ships began to carpet bomb the entire country, knocking out any semblance of radar control or spotters. The Russian fighters began to fight blindly, and subsequently, they fell like everyone else. Russia lost over sixty percent of its populace in one night. Something the Germans once spent four years attempting to do. China fell without so much as a whimper. Europe, especially Germany and England, gave valiant efforts in their losing causes. Australia fell next.

The United States' war effort was hamstringed from the beginning, having made the poor decision to place its armed forces in major cities. All but one regiment, which was stationed in Boston, had been wiped out. The aliens had done their homework thoroughly. Every known and suspected military base around the globe had been targeted with the same deadly efficiency. If anyone had been on the moon that night, they would have been treated to one hell of a fireworks display as the cities burned and anti-aircraft from around the globe sprayed upwards in the slim hopes of finding a mark.

Chapter 25
The Mother Ship

"Supreme Commander Kuvlar, our first wave of gunships and bombers are returning."

"What is the status of Earth and our ships?"

"Sir, Earth's defensive capabilities have been completely neutralized."

"Excellent, Sub-Commander! That's excellent news," he exclaimed as he wrung his hands together.

"Sir, there's more."

"Well, get on with it, Sub-Commander! I want to get to phase two of our invasion as soon as possible."

"Sir, we lost fully sixty percent of our fighter ships in the invasion."

"Sixty percent? That's impossible. That would be over ten thousand of our ships."

"Ten thousand, one hundred and twenty-two, to be exact, sir."

"Did I say I wanted an exact count, Sub-Commander?" At that moment, the ISC wished he could display the capability of humans to sweat, which was less noticeable than dropping open his gaping jaw. As worries of a high court martial swirled inside of his head, he thought he could still salvage his career, as long as the rest of the invasion went according to plan.

He knew sending the fighters in without Battle Master Class ships was risky, but these were puny hu-mans; what could they do? Actually, these hu-mans were something. Never in their long history had the Progerians been dealt such staggering losses. They were much more accustomed to dealing out blows than receiving them. Sure, the majority of the planets they had encountered weren't nearly as technologically advanced. But even the ones that were had fallen with much more ease. Heads were going to roll and he would make certain that his wasn't one of them.

As quickly as they had come, the aliens began to depart. But fully fifty percent of the Earth's population had been destroyed. There was not a soul on the planet who had not in some way been affected by the invasion. Fires raged across the planet, because there was nothing and nobody to put them out. All semblances of infrastructure had been annihilated. Any city that had not been targeted began to send supplies and manpower to whomever was in need, which, at this time, was pretty much everybody.

Although the president survived in an underground bunker in Maryland, nothing that even closely resembled the United States government survived. Most of the Senate and House members had been in Washington debating about how the troops should be dispersed. Few had been outside of the city limits when the barrage began. For days, news stations desperately tried to get back on the air. Radio was first, and the news was not good. The devastation had been as widespread globally as it had been locally. Those with short wave radios contacted every corner of the globe to discover all the grisly facts.

Russia had been the last country to check in, suffering the most damage. Short wave radios had been banned for decades in that country. News that filtered out had been of the nineteenth century type, refugees fleeing on horseback. The bombing of Japan had been particularly crippling. The bombs not only raining their devastation from above, but they also weakened the already unstable tectonic plates that lay beneath Japan's islands. Nationwide earthquakes measuring in the sevens and eights paralyzed any type of rescue effort by what remained of the local authorities.

China had attempted to send some rescue boats over to their ailing neighbor but they were lost in port to one of the many tsunamis that were spawned from the shifting plates. What remained of Oahu after its numerous military bases were permanently disabled was nearly completely obliterated to the incoming walls of water. Most of the islands in the Pacific rim suffered similar fates.

Another ten percent of the global population lost their lives in those chaotic first days after the aerial invasion. Some from shock, especially the elderly and the young who suffered with no one to care for them. A lot died in the ensuing panic that arose from the chaos of not knowing what was happening and not having anybody in charge.

Most people began to look out only for themselves. Altruism was at an all time low. People shot each other for fresh produce. It was the lawless, wild west of the 1800s again, only on a much wider scale. Communities raced to establish some sort of control, before the human condition degenerated any further. National governments had quickly become neighborhood principalities. Governments were established on a street-by-street basis. Each street became responsible for its own borders. Neighbors who lived just one street over were now unwelcome in what had once been their community also. Supermarkets became forts. Whole towns moved into them, sleeping and living in the aisles.

Outsiders who strayed too close were usually welcomed with a warning shot; but if they persisted, they became casualties. There had even been organized attacks by the have-nots on the haves. Previous friends and neighbors savagely fought for Ding Dongs and Rice Krispies. But it was a matter of survival. Those in the store might survive, while those outside would probably starve. Better to die quickly by the bullet, than to slowly starve to death.

Chapter 26

And through it all, the aliens watched and waited. They had witnessed this countless times on all sorts of worlds. The initial collapses of the governments inevitably led to the downward spiral of the entire civilization. The inhabitants would become so disillusioned with life that they almost wept in relief when the conquerors reappeared. At least, these invaders might be able to restore order to their world. It was a tactic that had been employed for millennia with unprecedented results and Supreme Commander Kuvlar saw no reason to change his tactics now.

Just a few more weeks, the ISC thought to himself. He wanted to make sure that these little infestations would be soft and ripe for the picking. He had no desire to have anywhere near the ten percent casualty rate on the ground troops that he had suffered in the air raids. If he continued to lose troops at that rate, he would have to launch his planet-killing agents, which would do his career no good at all. The powers that be did not like having to wait before they could inhabit a planet. Not to mention, rebuilding a planet without slave labor would make colonizing that much more difficult.

Chapter 27

"Girls, we're going to have to leave here soon," Deb's father reiterated. It was something that he had been vocalizing more often over the past few days. They all knew the arguments for leaving, but nobody desired to abandon their safe refuge and check on this brave new world. "We've only got enough food for another week, and even with some serious rationing, we only have enough water for half that."

"Hon, we know that," Deb's mother chimed in. She seemed to be suffering the most from this assault. Always a pleasantly "big-boned" woman, she had nearly lost all of her added padding. Whether it was from the strict rationing or the constant shivering, what Weight Watchers could never attain in ten years, the Progerians had accomplished in a single week.

"Dad, where will we go?" Deb asked meekly. Beth, for once, remained neutral. She also saw the need to leave but had become mighty comfortable in her new confines.

"Well, the supermarket first, and possibly a sporting goods store for some outdoor gear and rifles." With the last word, he looked over at his wife of twenty-three years. She had been anti-gun from the day he met her. Now, however, she didn't so much as bat an eye when he spoke of getting some firearms. "That is, of course, if there is anything left."

Deb was about to ask what he meant by that, and then figured that there probably had been a serious run on all types of commodities. She could even picture looting Best Buy for DVD players. Not that they would do her any good right now. She knew, from poking her head out the hatch from time to time, that nobody had power, at least as far as she could see. If it weren't for her father's generator, they wouldn't even have the single hundred watt bulb in the center of the ceiling lit. It didn't matter to her that the thing flickered like a far-off star. It was still light, and it did wonders to calm her soul. The things we humans take for granted, she thought to herself. More than once she had to remind herself that that her favorite television show wasn't on, and more than likely, never would be again.

Suddenly, Beth rose from the shadows of the far wall. She looked like she had steeled her resolve or at least tin-foiled it.

"Your dad's right, Deb, we have to get out of here; if only to see what is going on with the world. We might be able to help some people. At the very least, we'll be able to help ourselves. I'm with you, Mr. Carmody."

Mr. Carmody smiled. "I don't mean you girls, not right away anyway. I want to go out and get a feel for what is going on." At that, Mrs. Carmody leaped to her feet.

"You can't leave us here alone, James!" Her voice was quavering.

"Hon, I wouldn't feel right taking all of you out. It might be dangerous," he said tenderly.

"All the more reason to take us," she begged. "We could help you." He looked at her, wondering what she could possibly do. She looked like she would faint if a dog farted too close to her.

"I appreciate the sentiment, I really do. But I think it would be best if I went out and checked on things first."

"James, we've been married for twenty-three years. If you go out that hatch, I'm going with you." James had seen that look and stance in his wife only twice. Once, when she wanted to have a baby and he disagreed. The second time was when she told him that she wanted him to start attending church. He had always been adamantly against both, but she stood her ground and ultimately wore him down. Deb and his devout faith in Christianity were proof of that.

He didn't feel it prudent to be worn down this time. She would stick to her guns like a pit-bull on a mailman's genitalia. Who knows? Maybe she could help. He didn't think so but it helped him ease his mind.

"Alright we'll leave in the morning." She looked more like a kid that was promised a trip to the toy store than a woman who may have just signed her own death warrant. Deb had been about to raise her protests at staying when her father threw up one finger.

"Don't even start, Deborah Anne. I'm already risking enough taking your mother along. I have no desire to put your life in danger also." Deb knew better than to argue when her father pulled out the middle name. He rarely used it and when he did, he generally meant business. Fine, she thought to herself, there are ways around that. Beth stood meekly, not really knowing what to say, for one of the rare occasions in her life.

The night went by fairly uneventfully except for the occasional far-off explosion. Deb could see the worry that lined her father's face, but her mother still appeared to be reveling in her recent victory, if that's what you'd call it.

James woke up early just as the sun began its ascent over the horizon. While everyone slept, he had contemplated taking off. But in twenty-three years, he had never backed out of doing something once he told his wife he was going to do it. And the stubborn woman would probably try to follow him anyway. Besides, the idea of her being alone out there sent shivers down his spine. He didn't feel good about this upcoming adventure; it was more out of necessity than desire, and he would do everything in his power to protect his present family, Beth included.

James began to reflect on his father. Oh, how he wished that man were still alive. He was the type of man to tackle problems head on. No indecisiveness, whatsoever. He probably would have stuck the womenfolk in the storm cellar the first night and taken his shotgun to see what all the fuss was about. Yeah, Dad but these aren't some crazy radicals with pistols, he thought before he gently awoke his wife who appeared to be a little confused as to her whereabouts.

"Hon, it's time to go."

"Uh?" his wife responded as she desperately tried to

wipe the sleep from her eyes. "The girls?"

"Still asleep. I want to get out of here before they wake up. Maybe we'll be back with potato chips before they even know we left." James leaned over both girls and gave both of them a small kiss on the tops of their heads. And, as quietly as they could, they left their shelter, their home. James hoped that this wasn't the last time he'd see it, but something in his gut just wasn't sitting right. As soon as the hatch latched shut, Deb's eyes opened.

"Beth, you awake?" she whispered.

"I am now. What time is it?"

"It's time to leave."

"What? Your dad said that we should wait here for them to return."

"Beth, I'll go crazy if I have to sit in here waiting for them."

"But won't he be pissed if we just show up strolling next to him?"

"Yeah, he would. That's why we're going to follow them."

"You're crazy. But I'll do it just to see if we can get some decent shampoo, and

some feminine products."

"I know what you mean. My dad stocked everything in here; but he was severely lacking when it came to women's needs." They laughed a little bit, but it was more of a nervous titter. Deb lifted the hatch door a fraction of an inch. She feared that her father might realize this ploy and wait for them to poke their heads out to chastise them. But her dad wasn't there and neither was the 1979 Vista Cruiser station wagon. Her father preferred his small Toyota, but if he planned to get supplies, he would need something a little bigger.

"The generator must have drowned out the noise," Deb said, a little louder than their previous whispering.

"Must have drowned out what noise?" Beth asked, two steps below Deb, and now starting to feel a little claustrophobic. But that was crazy. Two people had left this small confine so it should now feel more spacious. But the lack of souls was actually having the opposite effect.

"The car, they took the car."

"How are we going to follow them now?" Beth asked. She felt conflicted between being relieved she didn't have to leave; but desperate to escape the ever confining shelter. She would have bowled Deb over to get out, but Deb was already on the move, leaving the sanctity of their hovel. Beth was expecting the air to be immensely fresh when she made her first venture into the outdoors after more than a week. But the opposite was true.

The air seemed stale and dingy. A brown cloud hung over everything. If she hadn't known better, she would have thought she was in downtown L.A. during rush hour. Unbeknownst to the girls at this time, however, the brown cloud hung over the entire planet. Fires still raged in most of the major cities. It would be a long time before the winds of change took away this pollution.

"How are we possibly going to catch them if they are in a car? Do you know where the keys are for your dad's car?" Beth asked as she pointed in the general direction of the blue two-door.

"Yeah, with my dad."

"Doesn't he have an extra set?" When Deb shook her head no, Beth pressed on. "What about your mom? She must have a set."

"No, she never liked that car for some reason; she never drove it."

"So what now?"

"Well, I know most likely where they are going. If we hoof it through some backyards and shortcuts, we shouldn't be too far behind them."

"Where to then?"

"Well, I bet that they'll start at the Safeway down the street. If we stick to the shortcut, we could be there in about ten minutes." Now that the realization of leaving their security began to set in, Beth started to get cold feet.

"Are you sure this is a good idea? What if we run down there and they're on their way back? We'll never beat them, and your dad won't be too happy."

"What's he going to do? Ground me?"

"Good point. But I still don't feel right about this."

"Beth, we can't stay in here forever. One way or the other, we need to go out and see what's happening."

Beth knew she was right, but it didn't make leaving any easier. It wasn't exactly the Taj Mahal but it suited their purposes. Besides, she told herself, her parents must be worried sick about her. If she could find a phone that worked, she'd let them know she was alright.

Mr. Carmody had repeatedly tried Beth's house phone to no avail. It never occurred to her that her parents wouldn't be alright. They were the rocks that her life was anchored to. How could the Earth possibly still be spinning if her parents were no longer here? Beth had no way of knowing if her parents had survived the initial assault. They lived far enough out in the suburbs to avoid the major thrust of the enemy's deadly invasion. Their demise would come more likely from the local variety, looters or opportunists who would take things from people's homes whether they were there or not.

Mr. MacAvoy put up a modest struggle when they had come, but when one of the youth's thirty-two-inch Louisville slugger connected with the back of his head, he crumbled like a sheet of paper on its edge. Mrs. MacAvoy fared even worse. After being repeatedly violated while she stared at the still, lifeless body of her husband, they had simply disemboweled her. They left her to die as she struggled to keep her innards from spilling out. Beth would never know what truly happened to her parents and it was for the best.

The girls walked in silence as they took note of the destruction around them. Multiple forest fires could be seen on the horizon. Countless houses appeared as if micro tornadoes had touched down and ripped them apart. The destruction also seemed random, as if it had been an act of nature instead of just senseless violence. The girls stayed off the roadway but wouldn't have been hindered by traffic anyway. There was no one on the road.

The city was eerily quiet, almost like it was holding its breath, waiting for something to happen. On occasion, the girls noticed a shade being moved to the side or a curtain quickly dropping back into place. If they turned to look at it, nobody came out to greet them or confront them. Deb was perplexed; most of these people had been her neighbors for as long as she could remember.

"What is going on here? Why won't anybody come out?" Beth intoned.

"I think they're scared, Beth." Deb answered warily.

"Of us? Are you kidding? We don't even have so much as a butter knife on us." Beth wanted to laugh out loud but was afraid she might start crying instead.

"Right now, I think that if we were three-year-olds with pails and shovels, they wouldn't even come out," Deb answered miserably.

"How much farther to the grocery store? I don't think I can take too much more of this," Beth said with just an edge of anxiety riddling her voice.

"We just have to cross over two more side streets and then up an embankment, and we'll be there," Deb answered. She had picked up on Beth's nervousness and feared that it might be catching. The girls crested the top of the embankment when Deb yanked Beth down to the ground.

"Ow! What the hell did you do that for?" Beth semi-shouted indignantly. Deb put her finger to her mouth and pointed down into the parking lot of the Safeway. Her parents were talking, no, if she could hear them from this distance, it had to be shouting.

"Who are your parents talking to? And why are they yelling?" Beth asked.

"Well, the guy in front is the manager of the store; the

guy to his left, with the rifle, owns the barbershop next door. I have no idea who the other guy is," Deb answered.

"What are they yelling about?"

"If you'd shut up for a second, maybe we'd find out," Deb answered, a little more snappishly than she meant to.

"Sorry," Beth whispered. Deb nodded her head in acknowledgement.

"You can't come in here, James." The balding, squat manager said.

"Bob, my wife and I have been shopping here for twenty years. I don't want stuff for free. I'll pay for it."

"Your money's no good here, James. Money's pretty much no good anywhere," Bob, the manager, said with sadness in his voice.

"Bob, I've got a family to take care of! Just let me get a few things and we'll leave." Bob shook his head no. It was clear to Beth, however, that had Bob been acting alone, he would have helped the Carmodys.

"James, I can't help you. I, we have got to look out for the people that are already here." James threw what appeared to be money at Bob.

"Fuck this, Bob! I'm going in to get a few things and I'll be out of your way."

Deb gasped.

"What's the matter, Deb?"

"I don't think that I've ever heard my father swear before. That's all."

It was then that Mr. Smythe, the barbershop owner, stepped in front of her dad to bar his way. The man was pushing sixty and thin as a wisp. But his steel-blue eyes burned a cobalt blue, visible even from a distance. He looked menacing, especially since he was carrying a huge, double-barreled shotgun.

"James, I can't let you in."

"Can't? Or won't, Al?" The blue fire in Al's eyes diminished ever so slightly. "Al, I've been getting my hair cut at your place for fifteen years. Hell, we've gone fishing before. You've come over to my house for barbecues."

"James, you don't understand. There's only a finite amount of stuff in there and it's being used up rapidly. What isn't already bad is beginning to rot without refrigeration."

"Alright, Al. Just let me get some of the stuff that's on the fringe and I'll leave." Al and Bob both had their heads bowed, on the verge of acquiescing. They had run off multiple marauders, but not one of their own. Not their neighbor and friend.

"Five minutes, James; that's all."

"Whoa! Just wait a fucking minute!" the stranger shouted out, leveling his weapon at Deb's father.

The man looked to be in his early twenties and, more than likely, had been a bouncer formerly. He was huge and looked bigger with his wife-beater on. "Now, just wait a goddamn minute!" he repeated.

"Son, I don't know who you are, but you had best stop pointing that weapon at me," Deb's father warned with controlled anger.

"I'll point this fucking thing at whomever I please!" he shouted.

"Matt, put the gun down. I've already told him that he could get a few things."

"You might have told him that it was alright, old man, but I never agreed to that. We've only got enough food in there for maybe another two weeks and I have no desire to share it with anybody else."

"Matt, that's the point; we have two weeks' worth, he has none," the manager said as he stepped to James' side in a show of solidarity.

"That's just too bad for him! He should have crept out from his hidey-hole or wherever the hell he was when we ALL agreed that we would not let anybody else in, no matter who they were."

"But this is different, Matt. He's one of my neighbors," Al piped in.

"I don't give a goddamn if he's the Pope's neighbor.

I'm not letting him in."

"Well, sonny," James started. "It appears it is two to one in favor of letting me in. Hon, come on." Mrs. Carmody had been waiting in the car. Her shivering racked her entire body and she had just begun to mobilize herself to get out of the car when the shot rang out. Mr. Carmody slumped over, holding the wound in his belly.

"What are you doing?!" Bob yelled.

"It…it was an accident," Matt fairly wailed. "H-h-he pushed up against me and the gun just went off."

"Guns don't just go off, you idiot! Sarah! Get the first aid kit!" Al yelled inside the store. James was down on his knees. Mrs. Carmody had rushed to his side and was attempting to staunch the flow of blood, but it leaked through her fingers like water through sand at the beach. Deb was beginning to rise in panic to go to the aid of her father when she was violently yanked down by Beth.

"What are you doing, Beth?! That's my father!"

"Yeah, and you're not going to do him any good if you go down there and start yelling at that idiot. He's liable to shoot you too." If that happened, Beth thought to herself, she would be all alone. She knew it was selfish, but that was the first thought that ran through her head. Deb was quaking with rage. If she had any type of weapon, she would have used it without a moment's hesitation on that man.

"Beth! Let me go! I've got to go down there!" Deb nearly shouted. But Beth didn't release her death grip on Deb's waist. "Beth, let me go! I mean it!" Deb struggled a bit before beginning to sob uncontrollably. "What is going on? What is going on?!" she cried into the ground.

Beth watched in horror as the three men began to walk back into the store after just dropping the first aid kit at Deb's mother's feet. That was the catalyst that got Mrs. Carmody moving. She was chasing after the men, screaming.

"So that's it! You bastards shoot my husband and then give me some Band-aids and turn tail!? You fucking cowards!" Deb was too scared and in too much shock to even lift her head to see the macabre scene that was unfolding. Bob, the store manager, tried in vain to calm her mother down.

"Mrs. Carmody, we're all sorry that this happened. It was an accident," he apologized as he turned his steely gaze towards Matt. Matt merely looked down as he, once again, retreated back to the relative refuge of the Safeway.

"Calm down!? My husband's been shot!" she said as she raised her bloodied hands, as if to reaffirm this fact.

"Then you had better go tend to him," Al said as he tried to fend off her pursuit of Matt.

"You animals! You're worse than the aliens attacking us. He's your neighbor, your friend. Help him!" she pleaded. All will had been drained from her body. She plopped to her knees in almost the same position as her dying husband. The three men returned to the store and shut the door behind them. They even pulled the sunshades in an attempt to try and ignore what had happened.

"Come on, Deb. They went into the store. We have to help your folks." Deb tried to focus her eyes, but her tears left her partially blinded. She stumbled forward before Beth grabbed her by the arm to lead her down the other side of the embankment.

Mrs. Carmody had returned to her husband's side and helped him lie down on the hard pavement of the parking lot. She barely registered the fact that the girls had arrived.

"Mom?" Deb cried. "Are you alright?"

"Your dad's been shot," Mrs. Carmody mumbled.

"I know, Mom. Let's try to get him some help."

"It's too late, you know," Mrs. Carmody muttered. Deb thought that perhaps her mom was showing the initial signs of shock. Detached indifference was her first clue.

"No, Mom; he's not dead. He can't be dead." Deb's mom looked up at her daughter as she cradled her husband's head in her lap.

"Hon, he's not bleeding anymore."

"Mom? That's a good thing, right?" Deb cried.

"He's not bleeding, Deborah, because his heart has stopped. Don't you get it?" Mrs. Carmody snapped.

"Mom, he can't be dead. He can't," she said as she dropped to the ground to hug her father. God, he feels cold already, she unconsciously thought to herself.

"He's gone, dear, and you should go too. There's nothing more left for you here," Mrs. Carmody said tenderly.

"Mom, what about you? I can't leave without you." Deb sobbed anew.

"I'm not leaving him. I'll never leave him."

"Mom, please, you're scaring me. You can't stay here, we've got to go. Dad would have wanted that." Deb tried to grab her mother's arm, but her mother pulled away violently, the angelic look on her face quickly diminishing. What was left looked old, haggard and tired.

"Beth, take Deborah and get her out of here. I will not leave James. He was my world."

"No, Mom, please! What about me? You can't leave me alone. We still have each other."

"No, you girls are better off on your own. I'll never survive. I could have never gone through what you did on that ship. I would have just crumpled up and died. There's no place for me now."

"Mom! That's not true!" Deb pleaded. "Please come back with us, we'll go back to the storm shelter."

"NO! I'll never go back there again. That was OUR home. Now there is no OUR; it's just me. I'll never go back there."

"Okay, okay; we'll go somewhere else, we'll start somewhere else."

"Don't you see? I'm too old to start somewhere else. I don't even want to try."

Deb was about to begin her next round of protestations when Bob stuck his head out the door.

"You folks don't want to stay here. There are gangs that run around here, just looking to start trouble."

"What are they going to do, Bob?" Mrs. Carmody

shouted. "Shoot us?!" That stung Bob. He pulled his head back in and relocked the door. Beth was about to say something.

"Deb, please don't start. You need to leave. I will not watch another person in my family get hurt. I may not be worried for myself but I love you deeply; and if anything happens to you, I just won't make it," said Mrs. Carmody, with a voice of resignation.

"Mom, I'm not going to leave you," Deb cried.

"Beth, for the past few days I have considered you family, so please get my daughter out of here. For the sake of you girls' safety."

"I love you, Mrs. Carmody," Beth said as she leaned over and gave her a hug. "Deb, let's go. We're in the wide open here. We can't stay here." Deb realized the truth in the words but still felt bitter that Beth was so willing to leave. Beth reached down and grabbed Deb's shoulder. Deb half-heartedly protested but arose under her own power. Her mother had given up, and she would never forgive her for that, even though she understood why.

She knew she would have given up had Mike died. And again, she felt a pang so deep in her heart, it nearly made her double over in pain. Oh, Mike, where are you? I could use your strength right about now.

Beth led Deb away from her parents' final resting spot. Deb was completely blinded by the salty tears stinging her eyes. The girls had finally stumbled up the embankment and were just about to head down the other way when Deb heard the familiar roar of the Vista Cruiser come to life.

Hope surged; maybe her mother had come to her senses and was returning to pick them up. She ran to the top of the hill to flag down her mother. As she attempted to wipe the tears from her eyes so that she could better see; what she saw confused her. Her mother wasn't coming towards the far edge of the parking lot to pick them up at all. She was barreling full steam ahead right towards the grocery store. That can't be right! she screamed inside of her head.

Shots began to ring out from the grocery store, where the boarded-up plate glass windows had holes cut out for defensive shooting. Deb's vision had begun to clear up from her fervent ministrations. She wished that she hadn't looked. Her mother had been hit by multiple rounds but, like a demon possessed, onwards she drove Faster and faster, until finally her body slumped over the steering wheel and she sealed their fates.

Nothing short of a bulldozer was going to stop the forward momentum of that car. Deb couldn't be sure, but she thought she saw the startled face of Matt as the car crashed through the window and steel frame right into the produce section and over his body. Glass, wood, and twisted metal lay strewn all over the place. Al, the barber, was screaming on the floor with what looked to be a two-foot section of metal impaled through his thigh.

"Oh Mom!!" she wailed. Beth stood next to Deb, in complete and utter shock, her mouth hanging open, unable to express even the simplest thought. The scene had aroused the attention of one of the rogue gangs that patrolled that section of town. This was an opportunistic time for them, and like vultures, they would not let it pass.

Beth noticed the two pickup trucks heading into the parking lot from the opposite side. She also noticed the men in the backs of those trucks who were holding weapons.

"Deb! Come on! We've got to go! We've got to go now!" Deb had begun to stumble back towards the store. Beth smacked Deb as hard as she dared, to try to get her attention. "Deb! Come on! We've got to get out of here. Those guys don't look like the local law enforcement. If we don't get out of here now, we might never get out."

Deb turned and followed Beth, looking more like a stray sheep being led back to the flock than the tough determined girl Beth had come to know. Hopefully, that other girl will return soon, Beth thought to herself, or neither one of us is going to make it.

"Deb, that biker is motioning towards us!" Beth said

with panic rising in her throat. Having been kidnapped once, she had no desire to repeat that performance. And, to be honest, those animals down in the parking lot looked a lot meaner than the Genogerians.

Deb began to get her legs in motion too. Despite her mourning, she recognized danger when she saw it. Before the girls cleared the hill, they noticed two men peel off from the main group and head their way... fast.

"Deb, we'll never make it back to the storm shelter in time if you don't get going. I'm sorry. I know I can't begin to understand what you're going through. But if you want to try and sort all of it out, we need to get moving faster than this," Beth pleaded.

Deb looked more like a marionette being manipulated by a drunken, inexperienced puppet master. Her arms were stiff and her legs didn't look like they had a muscle in them. They looked wooden and unyielding.

"We can't go to the storm shelter," Deb said lethargically as she managed to move her rigid body just a smidgeon faster.

"What do you mean? That's the safest place we can go until we can figure out a better plan," Beth labored out. She was trying to run and pull Deb at the same time.

"Did you see the guys that are coming after us?"

"Of course, I did! That's why I want to get the hell out of here!" Beth wanted to add "duh" but somehow, right now didn't seem the best time to say that.

"The big one on the left with the dirty blond hair? I went to high school with him. He was an asshole then. Doesn't look like he changed much," Deb said sardonically.

"What's that got to do with anything? Come on! Faster!" Beth tugged some more.

"The piece of shit tried to rape me back when I was in the ninth grade," Deb said with almost no inflection in her voice. Beth almost stopped dead in her tracks. "The bastard was a junior and captain of the high school football team. He asked me out on a date. I was so in love with him. I couldn't believe he was asking me out, a mere, unworthy freshman. Come to find out, it was a game among the upper classmen football players to see how many freshmen they could nail. He took me out for a great dinner and then a movie. I might have married him right there and then, the way he was acting so nice. Little did I know, it was just part of some game.

"After the movie, he brought me over to Elm Street, which, at the time, was all new construction and pretty deserted. We were going to park. I was so excited, I was even thinking of letting him get to second base under my shirt. But he had other ideas. When I refused, he became violent. He punched me in the nose. I almost lost consciousness; but I could still feel him ripping off my blouse and pants." Deb almost seemed to be reciting this from a script; such was the lack of feeling that she put into her words.

"He would have 'nailed' me too if it hadn't been for sheer, dumb luck. He had just gotten my pants off and was about to do it when the cops showed up. Apparently, a lot of people were ripping off building supplies, so the cops were patrolling the area fairly regularly.

"The cops pulled up and shined the light in the car. When they saw it was Gary Higgins, star football player, they almost went about their merry way. It was the blood pouring down my nose that gave the idiots a clue that something wasn't quite right. But they still didn't DO anything." That statement seemed to get Deb riled up a little more. "The cops took me home and told Gary to go home and sober up, or something, like it was some big joke. For all I know, those cop bastards probably started the whole 'game' when they were in school."

"So what happened to Gary?" Beth asked as she kept Deb moving.

"Well, my folks put a restraining order on him and pressed charges, but the police cited 'lack of evidence'. Nothing happened to him. But he harassed the hell out of me. He would tape pictures of dicks on my locker. He even taped one on my bedroom window. A week later my cat disappeared. We never found him, but one day there was a piece of fur taped to my locker. The sick fuck killed my cat. It wasn't 'til he graduated that he finally left me alone. He made high school miserable for me."

"Oh Deb, I'm so sorry," Beth said and she truly meant it, but that made her want to speed up even more.

"So you see? That's why we can't go back to the storm shelter," Deb finished.

"He knows where you live. Do you think he recognized you?" Beth worried.

"Even if he didn't, he would have recognized my parents' car." Deb began to cry again.

"You're right. We have got to get out of here."

"What's the point? Where are we going to go? We can't go home. And the supermarket just proved that we can't look for help from others."

"We can't just give up, Deb. There still have to be some decent people out there, and we'll find them. But if we stay here, we'll never see Mike again." Beth hoped that would be the catalyst that got Deb moving, but it had the opposite effect. Deb stopped, just stopped and sobbed.

"Do you think he's still alive?" Deb cried through her hands. It came out muffled, but Beth heard it clear enough.

"You saw him on that ship; I don't think anything could kill him." Deb looked up through her tear-soaked hands.

"Do you really think so?"

"I do. But if we stay here we'll never be able to know for sure." The girls looked back at the hill that led to the supermarket. Their pursuers had just reached the top, and the girls had a mere hundred-yard lead on them, which was fast diminishing. That got both of them in high gear. They knew the shelter wasn't a safe place, but they were running on instinct and they didn't know where else to go.

Beth took a quick assessment of the men following them. The Gary guy was huge. He looked like the prototypical football player. Big shoulders, big arms, and a small waist. She could see why Deb would have been enamored by him. He even reminded Beth of her boyfriend at Pitt State.

The guy with him wasn't quite as big, but still considerably larger than either one of the girls, and he looked mean. Long, black hair in a ponytail, and a goatee that framed a very severe face. He looked like the kind of man that got whatever he wanted by just taking it.

"How much farther?!" Beth puffed. Her lungs were on fire and her legs were beginning to cramp.

"Just through a couple of more backyards," Deb replied. She was equally struggling to catch her breath. "When we get to the house, go upstairs." Beth was about to ask why but that seemed like entirely too much effort.

"How close are they, Beth?"

"I don't know. I'm too scared to turn and look."

The boys had gained some yardage but were frustrated that the girls didn't just fall over like in the movies. "Fuck this!" Gary said as he slowed to a walk, trying to suck in as much air as possible.

"Come on, Vato! The boss says he wants these girls," the dark man said as he pulled up alongside the faster ex-football player.

"Don't worry about it, Jimmy."

"What do you mean, G? If we don't bring these new pussies back, Johnny Ray might make us his new bitches."

"Fuck him, Jimmy! Don't worry about it. I know the girl on the left. I fucked around with her in high school. I know where she lives and that's where she's headed." Jimmy smiled an evil grin. He didn't even need to chase his fresh meat this time; and he would have a nice soft bed to do all the wicked things he was planning.

"Ah, Vato! This is going to be fun," Jimmy said as he grabbed the front of his pants.

"Yes it is, Jimmy. And it's been a long time coming," Gary said with a smile that almost matched Jimmy's evil grin.

"What's that, Vato?"

"Nothing, man. Let's go and get us some." Then they laughed the cruel laugh that only a true bully possesses. "Might makes right" was their credo and they saw no reason to change that now.

***

"Beth, upstairs in my parents' room is a pull-down staircase that leads to the attic. Get up there and shut the trapdoor behind you," Deb puffed as she pushed Beth through the front door.

"Wait! Aren't you coming with me?" Beth asked in horror. The thought of being alone petrified her. "You can't leave me up there alone. And you sure can't take them on yourself."

"I just want to go get some things out of the storm shelter. Hurry! Before they get here!" Deb said forcefully to prevent the argument that was brimming on Beth's lips. "Listen, if we stay here arguing, we're finished. Go and shut the door behind you. I'll tap four quick times on the door to let you know it's me and then you can let me in." That calmed Beth down a bit. Being alone for a little while wasn't so bad as being alone indefinitely, she thought.

"Don't be long."

"Don't worry. Go!" Deb gave Beth one final shove as she headed for the storm shelter. "Oh God! I hope I'm doing the right thing," she said to no one in particular.

***

Jimmy and Gary sauntered up to the front door as if they owned the place. And for all intents and purposes, right now, they did. Gary ripped open the screen door and, for dramatic effect, he kicked open the front door like all those "Cops" shows he used to watch before the aliens cut off the power.

"Lucy! I'm home!" Gary said in his best Desi Arnaz impersonation. Beth heard Gary and Jimmy enter but she found no humor in his impersonation. It was laced with malice and she, too, pictured Jack Nicholson peering through the bathroom door in "The Shining." She shuddered as she drew her legs up to her chest.

"Where are you, bitch?" Beth had stayed near the opening in the hope that when Deb returned, she could open the door quickly. She regretted that decision now. She desperately wanted to retreat into the vast shadows that the attic offered, but she feared any telltale noise now.

***

"Jimmy, stay here by the front door, and keep an eye on the back door, I'm going to check the basement."

"Hey G, you're gonna let me have one of those little puntas, aren't you?"

"Aw, come on, man, you know I'd never leave you out of the loop. You can have the other bitch; I want Deb. Hell, you can have Deb when I'm through with her. That is, if there's anything left."

"Oh, hell no, Vato. I don't want your sloppy seconds, I'll take the other one." Jimmy grabbed the front of his pants again. He loved this brave new world. Having never been a looker or a talker, for that matter, Jimmy always had to rely solely on buying his sex. But the way things were now, he had all that he could handle and then some. Yep, he just took what he wanted whether it was food or women; it made no never-mind to him. He was growing excited at the prospect of their new find.

"Snap out of it, Jimmy. Leave your pecker alone for five minutes and you'll have the real thing soon enough!" Gary snapped. Perspiration was running down his face, but it wasn't from the chase, it was for the upcoming kill. Gary hated to admit it, but he was as excited as Jimmy.

***

Beth shivered as she heard Gary in what sounded like the basement. His voice was muffled but she could still hear him yelling and throwing things around.

"Come out, bitches! We won't hurt you; we just want to talk. No that's a lie. We don't want to talk; we want to hurt you." Then he laughed that same crazed, maniacal laugh that

Beth had heard so many times before when she was on the ship. It amazed her how quickly the worst in humans could be triggered with stress. She could hear Jimmy laughing along with Gary but his laugh was a lot closer, and not moving, she thought.
***
"The fucking cunts aren't down here, Jimmy. Anything up there?"

"No, Vato. Hurry up! My pecker's gonna bust loose soon." That started another round of laughter. Beth was frozen in fear. She desperately wanted to shuffle her way back but fear gripped her harder than she had ever felt it before. She could hear Gary's heavy footfalls on the basement steps. Gary came up to the main level, and she could hear him overturning tables and smashing windows and whatever little knick-knacks Mrs. Carmody had accumulated over the years.

"Fuckin' bitches are going to pay for making me go through all this work!"

"Yeah G; they're going to FUCKING pay." Gary, not being the brightest bulb, still got the pun his friend, Jimmy made.

"Good one, you fuck!"

"No man, we both fuck," Jimmy shouted as he put his hands out in front of his hips and did a pelvic thrust.

"You're on fire!" Gary said as Jimmy laughed and headed upstairs.
***
"He's coming upstairs," Beth moaned, hoping it wasn't loud enough for him to hear.
***
"Hi, Deb. I've dreamed of seeing your room. And now, here I am and it's gonna be just the two of us," Gary sneered.

Did Deb not make it back up here in time? Did she hide in her room? I've got to help her. What am I going to do? Beth thought, quaking in fear. She braced herself to leave the attic and make a run at Gary, when she realized he hadn't seen Deb; he was just trying to bait her.

"Come on, Deb. If you and your little friend come out right now, I promise we won't fuck you up too bad," Gary yelled. Beth could tell his tone was getting more dangerous. Rape, at this point, might be the least of their worries. "Get the fuck out here, you little cunts!!!" he screamed. Beth yelped but she didn't think he heard it over his rant.

"You need any help up there, Vato?" Jimmy yelled from the bottom of the stairs.

"No, you greaser. Now get back to the front door. If they slip out the back while you're at the stairs, I'll fucking cut your throat!!"

"Alright, man; calm down."

"Don't fucking tell me to calm down!!"

"Fucker's loco," Jimmy mumbled to himself; but he went back to the front door like Gary ordered. Meanwhile, Gary ripped through Deb's room, smashing her track trophies and ripping up all the pictures of her friends and her through the years of high school and college.

"What? No fucking pictures of me, you little bitch? Who's this guy?" Gary asked as he picked up a picture of Mike that Deb had gotten from his sister, Lyn. "This dude your boyfriend? He looks like a pussy to me. Where is he now? Probably fucking dead. But don't worry; I'm here now, I'll take care of you." Beth could hear Gary walking around in the upstairs hallway. Sweat was pouring off her.

Gary walked into the master bedroom and stopped dead in his tracks as a huge grin spread over his face. He was looking down when he noticed the little piece of pink fluff. Not a big deal in itself, but when a piece of insulation is directly under an attic trap, it usually means that it's been accessed recently. Nobody leaves that itchy crap just lying around.

"Got you now, bitches," Gary said to himself. He reached up to grab hold of the dangling string and was slowly beginning to put pressure on it. Beth watched in horror from her end as the slackness in the string tightened and daylight started to ooze in. Tears began to form in her eyes. Doom was merely a few feet away and she could do nothing except watch, as if from afar. Light went from a pencil line to a shaft to… A huge crash and yell shut her back into complete darkness.

What was that? It was the first thought that she and Gary shared in common since the whole little scene began to play out. The noise and the sudden darkness threw her into a complete panic again. This time, there was a reaction, she wet herself. She wasn't proud of it, but right now, she didn't give a rat's ass.

***

Deb had raced to the storm shelter and shut the door behind her just as her pursuers ventured into her neighbor's yard. Gary and the other guy smashed through the front door. Deb could hear Gary yelling and he scared the hell out of her. She had more than once been tempted to just hide where she was. But after he was through searching the house, and doing whatever to Beth, he would most surely come down here. And then what? He would finish off what he had started five years ago.

"Screw that!" Deb thought as she steeled herself. She grabbed her father's hand axe off the pegboard of tools he had been so proud of. "Dad, I love you," she muttered as she peeked through the shelter door. She half feared that Gary would be outside waiting for her to pop her head out, like an unsuspecting rabbit. Adrenaline and fear raced through her body as she realized that her worst fears had come true. Her face flushed, she dropped the axe and prepared for the worst.

Only the worst didn't come, unless of course fence posts were going on the rampage these days too. She would have laughed but she was afraid she just might keep laughing and there she'd be, waiting for Gary, with drool coming out of her mouth because she had finally witnessed one too many crazy things.

She reached down blindly and picked up the axe. She

didn't want to take her eyes off the house for a second. By the time she had completely removed herself from the shelter, she could hear Gary tearing up the main floor, smashing everything. Her heart panged as she remembered her mother picking up little souvenirs from wherever. Tacky, little tourist-trap mementos that she just had to have. And her father shaking his head, as if to say, "Don't you have enough of these things?"

"Yeah," she would reply, "but not from here." Then they would laugh and hug like only truly happily married couples can. Could, she thought bitterly. Deb wanted to sprint for the front door but feared that she might trip over her own feet, so she inched her way closer to the house. She got so close, she could hear Gary walking up the stairs to the second floor. Where was the other one? She thought.

She crept closer to the front door when she saw the back of the other one's head. His hair was all matted down with dirt and grease; just the sight of the back of this guy's head disgusted her. She was contemplating what to do when he moved away from the door.

Where's he going? Deb's grip on the axe was tenuous at best, and her sweat kept making the handle slide down her hands. Deb was about to peek through the door when she heard Jimmy's footsteps fast approaching. She ducked her head back around the door but didn't think she was fast enough. What would she do if he came out and confronted her? She figured she'd probably just drop the axe and run, screaming into the street like a crazy woman.

But he never looked out the door; her luck was holding for the present. But now what? Doubt racked her body. She had never killed before. Of course, that didn't include the aliens since they weren't human. But here was a true, red-blooded, breathing, living human. Sure, he meant to physically harm her but that still didn't stop the queasiness in her gut. There he was, with his back to the door; didn't he know she was there? Couldn't he hear her heart thumping? Was he just setting her up? Get her in close, then finish her off? Why is it so quiet in the house?

Suddenly, terror spread across Deb's face. Gary must have found Beth; that could be the only reason for stopping his tirade. Right now, he could be ripping her clothes off, that asshole! She screamed in her head. Anger swelled, adrenaline took over and Deb squared herself to the door, smashing right through the screened plate glass window and 'thunk', right into Jimmy's head. But it hadn't been the killing blow she hoped for. The axe began to slip out of her hands on the downward arc.

Jimmy wouldn't be getting up anytime soon but he was still alive. He started to turn around when he heard Deb's cry but his lack of response to the attack had cost him. Glass lay all around his body and the axe was lodged over his left cheek bone, just below his eye. He had turned suddenly, but not quickly enough to fend off the blow. Blood spewed from the wound. He tried in desperation to pull the foreign object out, but, for some reason, his hands weren't working properly.

He alternated between glaring at Deb with his one good eye and attempting to focus on the protruding axe. He struggled to scream but shock was rapidly beginning to take over his nervous system. Deb began to leave the porch. She could hear Gary racing down the stairs but it did little to keep her from evacuating what little she had for lunch that day. She wanted to run, but all fight and flight had been drained from her body. Jimmy's wrecked eye had frozen her in her tracks.

***

"What the fuck is going?..." Gary had reached the bottom stairs when he noticed his friend lying in an ever-widening pool of his own blood. Now it was Gary's turn to be scared. Bullies don't do well when faced with more might than their own. Was Deb's boyfriend here? Hell, was there more than one? Gary was bolting halfway out the back door when he noticed Deb at the bottom of the front steps, dry heaving. His evil grin reappeared. "Ah, the bitch got in a lucky strike. Well, that won't happen with me," he whispered.

"Hi Deb," he said in his most jovial manner, as if they had been best friends for years. He stepped over the outstretched arms of his friend.

"G! Help me! The frickin' bitch got me." The blood was beginning to fill Jimmy's lungs and his words were beginning to slur.

"Jimmy, you look like shit; you're dead anyway," he said as he made sure not to step in any of his spilled blood. Jimmy laid back down, realizing the inevitable. Deb turned to Gary; her face was an ashen gray, her shirt riddled with vomit. And both of her knees were quaking.

"Geez, Deb, you've looked better. I expected you to be happier to see me than this. You almost look as bad as Jimmy." Deb looked over Gary's shoulder to shudder once more. It had somehow been a little easier, before she knew his name.

"Well, maybe not quite as bad, but you will when I'm through with you. I was going to take you back so everybody could have a piece of you, but I want to be the last person you do. What can I say? I'm selfish like that."

Gary walked down the four steps to Deb and put his arm around her shoulder like lovers sometimes do, before delivering a blow into her stomach that dropped her to her unstable knees. While she was down, he smashed her in the nose. She was on the verge of blacking out. When she awoke, would it still be Prom Night and would her parents still be alive? It wouldn't be such a high price to pay if that were the truth. She could feel Gary literally shredding her pants off her body, but she could do no more than whisper her protests.

"Did you say something, hon? I'm sorry I couldn't quite hear you. You're moaning so loud, it's difficult to hear anything else." Gary was beginning to breathe heavy. He had never been able to perform quite right unless some form of violence was involved, and this was the ultimate high for him. So it was lucky for all concerned that he didn't hear the wet "pop" sound as Beth pulled the axe out of Jimmy's face. Nor did he hear her as she crunched over the shattered glass. Gary was just about to enter Deb when recognition dawned on Deb's face.

"Beth?" she creaked.

"It's not Beth, you little whore, it's me, Gary." You recall that Gary wasn't the brightest bulb on the block. By the time he realized that Deb was looking over his shoulder, it was too late. Gary turned to the right and the axe lodged into the right side of his face, just above the cheek. But Beth's grip had been much more solid than Deb's.

The thwack of the axe and the splintering of the check bone launched his right eye completely out of his skull. Death for this bastard would, unfortunately, be swift. Beth held on to the axe as Gary fell over to the side and she didn't let it go until she was sure he wasn't moving. She rolled his dead mass off Deb's body. Deb had lapsed into unconsciousness.

Beth stayed busy while Deb slept. She threw the bodies down into the basement and bathed and clothed Deb after she brought her into the storm shelter. She had virtually chewed down all of her nails while she waited for her friend to awaken. Hope coursed through her veins when Deb began to stir but it turned icy cold when she awoke screaming and shrieking, wildly throwing punches in the air.

"Deb, it's me, Beth. You're safe," Beth chanted repeatedly. It was around the eighth or ninth time before Deb began to calm down and then she went from uncontrolled shrieking to hysterical crying. But Beth knew this was the cry of loss, the cry of mourning, and all she could do now for her friend was be there for her.

Beth had long ago fallen asleep when Deb's sobs quieted to mini convulsions and finally, blissful, forgetful sleep. It was the following evening before the girls awoke. Beth was stiff and sore from her extended stay in the Lazy-Boy chair.

"What do we do now, Deb?" Beth asked as she

stretched her arms over her head.

"We go East." Deb said as she arose from her bed and began to put her shoes on.

***

"We go West," Paul said to the three men huddled next to him behind a small rise. They were mostly below Indian Hill but they could clearly see the supermarket complex from their vantage point.

"Are you sure you want to go straight through the Stop and Shop parking lot?" Dennis sounded off, a little anxiously. "I can see at least three armed men from here and I'm sure there are more in the front."

"You heard me, didn't you?" Paul sounded a little more than annoyed.

"Dude!" Dennis was about to continue when Paul glared over at him. "General Ginson," Dennis stated more meekly; "there are only three of us. Even if we get in, how are we going to haul all this off without being detected?"

"Ah, my dear friend, in this world of ours there are some things that even you don't know. But when the time is right, I'll let you know," Paul said as he put his arm around Dennis' shoulder. Dennis had been half tempted to shrug it off, but the mad glint in Paul's eyes struck a chord that hinted that might not be the best course of action at this time.

"Corporal Jackson, I want you on point," Paul stated matter-of-factly, as if they were out on nothing more than a Sunday stroll. But in reality, this had been their first venture out of the super bunker since the whole mess began. Dennis didn't understand why Paul hadn't just sent a scout. "The world was far too dangerous a place right now," Paul's response had been. 'If it's my time, then I want to be out, under the sun instead of hiding in a cave." Dennis couldn't argue with that but he would have felt a whole lot better if Paul hadn't been there, all the same.

"Right away, sir," Corporal Jackson snapped. Paul thought that Dewey had made great strides fitting into this new playing field. And that's how Paul thought of it sometimes; that this was just one big game of chess. Unfortunately, there could only be one king but there were a lot of pawns to go around. And if Dennis didn't get with the program soon, he would become one of those pawns. He would bring him down from his mighty loft as a rook in a heartbeat. Paul loved Dennis but he was getting really tired of having his judgment constantly challenged. Well, there it was, Paul thought to himself, that's probably the first sign of becoming a tyrant. An unwillingness to have his "rule" questioned. "Screw it! I'm the one keeping them alive," Paul mumbled.

"Did you say something Paul?" Dennis asked. He was bringing up the rear, making sure some super zealous Stop and Shop guard wasn't on patrol this far out.

"No, nothing, my friend," Paul said as he slowly shook his head.

Whoa, Dennis thought, he almost looked like the old Paul I used to know, for a second anyway. Albeit a tired one, but my old friend nonetheless.

By the time they hit the banks of the Walpole Stream, any chance of surprise had been crushed; not that that had been the plan, anyway. A guard on the roof spotted them, on their old stomping grounds. A sharp pang of longing for the old times almost made Paul's steps falter. The guard appeared to be speaking into a walkie-talkie, most likely warning the guards ahead of their advance. The three crossed the stream in silence. As they started through the dense undergrowth, a voice, amplified through a megaphone, began to speak.

"Go away! Don't bother coming this way! All intruders will be shot!" The voice stopped, as if in anticipation of a response. Dennis had been about to tell Paul that maybe this wasn't such a good idea when Paul finally did respond.

"Don't shoot!" Paul yelled through the bush. "We came here to trade."

"Trade? What do we have to trade?" Dennis mumbled

to himself.

"You have nothing we want! Go away!" the voice boomed.

"I think you'll be mighty interested in this," Paul yelled but not so loudly because they had walked a lot closer to where the dense brush stopped and the back alley of the supermarket began.

"If you come through those bushes, we'll shoot!" the voice threatened, although it also quavered with a little doubt.

"If you shoot us, then you will surely miss out on what I have to offer," Paul said as he stepped out of the brush with both of his hands raised up in the air.

"Get the rest of them out here with you," the supermarket leader said as he leveled his weapon at Paul's chest. Dennis and Dewey stepped out of the undergrowth almost at the same time. Dennis took quick note and noticed at least eight well-armed men with all of their weapons pointed directly at them. Even if they were crappy shots, their numbers and positioning were far superior.

"We're dead men," Dennis said sideways to Dewey. Paul walked directly up to the leader with his right hand outstretched. Dennis wasn't sure if the man would shake his hand or just blow it off. Most of the guns were now trained directly on Paul, as if it were some sort of elaborate trap.

"Don't bother with the handshake, son. They don't mean much these days," the leader said. Paul stopped short, the smile rapidly fading from his face. More guards came, hauling ass from around the corner. There had to be at least fifteen of them now and they all looked pissed off; probably because they had to run to get there.

Old National Guardsmen, Dennis figured. They had some idea of what to do with the weapons but no discipline when it came to personal management. Most of them looked like they were trying their best to clean the store out before the weekend.

"Alright, if you won't take my hand, at least take my

deal," Paul said.

"I'm listening, son, but it doesn't look like you have much to offer."

"What I'm offering is beyond value, sir. I'm offering you your lives," Paul said matter-of-factly.

"Our lives!?" the leader laughed. The rest of the posse followed suit. "What are you? Some kind of religious fruit? Are you one of those born-again fucks? Did you come here to spread the word of God? Have you looked around, you dumb ass? God's nowhere to be found!" the man angrily shouted.

"No, no, nothing like that," Paul said as he put his hands up. "I mean your physical lives."

"I don't know what you're talking about, sonny. So you had better get to the point real quick. From where I stand, I have eighteen or more fully automated weapons pointing at you and your little party. The only reason you're not dead yet is that it's been a little slow around here lately, and we were looking for a little change of pace. So if you want to breathe a little while longer, and keep your body in its present condition, you know, free from bullets and all, then you had better go right back to the bowl you were smoking, or tell me what you want before I say no!" As the man yelled, veins began to form along his brow and his cheeks blazed red. A few more armed guards ran around to see what all the ruckus was about.

"I want the store," Paul stated as if he were asking for fries with his hamburger. The leader began to laugh almost uncontrollably. Dennis figured as soon as he stopped laughing, the bullets would begin flying.

"Well, I've got to thank you, son. That's the funniest thing I've heard in a while," the man said as he wiped some laughter tears from his eyes. "Whaddya think, boys? Should we give him the store?"

One of the guards on the roof yelled down, "Sure, why the hell not? They seem like nice enough kids. Our families don't really need the food and shelter anyway." That got the leader going again. When he stopped, his face became much more grievous.

"See, son? Therein lies our dilemma; our families and friends are in that store. That store is our lives. If we were to just hand it over to you, we'd be sealing our fates and it's not really the type of fate we're looking for. So I'm going to tell you one last time, take your two little friends and go back to the wacky-tabacky you've been smoking and maybe we'll throw you a box of Twinkies."

The same man who spoke earlier stood up and grabbed his belly. "Ah, I'm sorry, sir, I finished those off Monday." That earned another round of chuckles from the men, but the leader was through. Something in this kid's eyes made him nervous and he just wanted him out of here.

"Sir, before I leave," Paul said, "could you tell me how many men guard this fine establishment?" Sweat started to form under the leader's arms; something was wrong but he wasn't quite sure.

"Not that it's any of your goddamn business, but we have around fifty armed guards." That was an embellishment, times two, but he wanted to make this punk kid as nervous as he was.

"Oh! So you have about twenty to twenty-five men back here, which means that you have another twenty-five men up front. Sounds like you've got the situation well in hand." For the first time, the leader took visual inventory of all of his men. And then it dawned on him, this was ALL of his men.

"Lenny, who is guarding the store?" Cold panic settled in the pit of the leader's stomach.

"I-I-I thought Burt was?" Lenny stammered.

"Burt's right next to you! Go check on the store, NOW!!!" the leader screamed. He didn't need a bullhorn anymore.

"Don't worry, sir, they're being well taken care of," Paul chimed in. Ice formed in the leader's stomach as he slowly turned back towards his adversary.

"What do you want?" the leader asked slowly and softly, anger and fear coursing through his veins.

"I told you. I want the store," Paul said matter-of-factly.

"If you harm anybody in there, I'll kill you. If this is some kind of joke, I'll kill you, if…"

"Calm down, Mister. Nobody's hurt and this isn't a joke. Right now, I have about sixty armed militia in your store as we speak. Now, I'm going to only ask you once. If I don't get the right answer, I'm going to press this little button and people in the store will start dying." Paul produced a little, hand-held device, no bigger than an old Atari joystick. It had a large red button on the top with Paul's thumb poised right over it.

"This is a radio-controlled device. Don't worry; it's not attached to a bomb, but the receiver is attached to one of my men in the store. You see, he has a little box with a light on it, if the light goes red, he knows it means something went down out here, and he's to take the store by force. If it doesn't light up, everything's cool. Are you with me so far? Good! So put down your weapons, now!" Paul yelled.

The leader was in shock. He had been in command for so long, he had no clue how to take an order.

"Now! Mister! Or a whole lot of people are going to die, us included," Paul yelled again. That seemed to get the man going. He could tell by looking in Paul's eyes, this was no idle threat. Paul's thumb began to move millimeter-by-millimeter towards its goal.

Katy, I'm sorry I let you down, the man thought to himself. For an instant, Paul thought the man might be suicidal, but the moment passed with no lead flying.

"Put your weapons down!" The man shouted as he bent over to place his M-16 on the ground gingerly. "Sonny, if this is some kind of bluff, then you sure are some kind of poker player."

"Sir," Paul said with calmness overtaking his previous anger, "this is no card game, and I'm not bluffing.

Now tell those two men on the roof to lower their weapons because I am beginning to lose my patience."

The leader couldn't figure it out. Paul's eyes never left his own, yet he was still able to ascertain that the détente wasn't over yet. This kid was dangerous and he had no desire to test him anymore.

"Lenny! Burt! Put down those weapons now! I won't say it again. Or I'll shoot you myself!" the leader shouted.

"Corporal Jackson! Get the troops out here and keep these men company. This fine gentlemen and I are going into the store to talk business," Paul said as he put his arm around the leader and headed towards the front of the store.

Corporal Jackson turned back towards the woods they had departed only moments earlier. "Bravo platoon! Front and center!" he shouted. And, as if by magic, forty or so well-camouflaged and heavily armed men came out from their hiding spots. All of their weapons were fully trained on the slack-jawed Guardsmen. The leader looked up at the roof with disapproval flashing across his face, as if to say, how could you let this force sneak up unnoticed?

Lenny and Burt quickly looked at their feet, as if they were the most important things on the planet. Dennis was in as much amazement as the conquered. He had walked mere paces away from the majority of them and hadn't noticed a thing.

"Paul, how much training did you do up there in Vail?" Dennis asked as he ran to catch up to his leader. Dennis' respect for Paul had just grown by leaps and bounds.

"Enough, Dennis, enough," was Paul's answer. "Corporal Jackson," Paul said as he turned his head around.

"Sir," came the quick reply.

"Safe the weapons and redistribute them back to their former owners."

"Sir, yes, sir!"

The leader was hoping that just maybe they would live to see another day. The three men rounded the corner to the front of the store as if they were long-time friends and not enemies that, only moments earlier, were about to blow each others' heads off. The leader saw that Paul was not bluffing. There were well-armed and well-disciplined men standing guard over the huddled masses in the store. The people were frightened, but otherwise unharmed. The leader's wife looked up from the boy she had huddled in her arms. The leader's heart sank. If he had done anything wrong that would incur harm to his family, he doubted if he could ever forgive himself.

"Sir, I don't even know your name," Paul said as he moved a pace or so away. That broke the leader's locked gaze with his wife.

"Dom… Major Domino of the 12th Brigade, Massachusetts National Guard," the man said as he squared his shoulders to the new usurper.

Dennis was just now catching up, trying to process how in the hell Paul had pulled this little mission off. He knew about the rat-sniffer incident, but this was pure genius.

"As you can see, Major, we have no interest in harming any of you. If that had been our purpose, not one of you would be standing."

"But you don't understand, Paul… Is it Paul?" the major stammered.

"I prefer 'General,' Major. General Ginson of the 1st United Earth Marine Corps."

"I've never heard of them, General." The major had a difficult time labeling this kid as a general, but he sure planted a whammy on him.

"Don't worry, Major. You will," Paul said as he surveyed the survivors who sought refuge in the supermarket. They were mostly old and young, but they all could still serve a purpose. He caught himself doing that more and more; everybody became a pawn in his game. How could he use this or that person to his utmost advantage? And as for sacrificing a pawn now and again, well, that was part of the game too, wasn't it?

"General, surely you are aware that if you take this

store, you will have sealed our fates, aren't you?" The major thought he might be whining a bit and he despised himself for that; but dammit, he was thinking of his family, who depended on him for their safety.

"So, that pretty much leaves you with no options, doesn't it, Major?" Paul replied.

Anger began to flush up through the major's collar, but before he could begin his outburst, Paul interjected, "So that's why I am going to offer you an option, Major."

"I've got a feeling that this really isn't an option."

"Sure it is. You have the option of leaving here like a band of gypsies and hoping that the next supermarket down the road opens its arms to strangers, much like you did for us." Paul quickly gazed at the major's eyes. Shame registered all over them. So much for Sunday school teachings, the major thought. "Or," Paul hesitated to gauge the man's reaction.

"Or? Don't leave me like this. You know you have us over a barrel."

"Or you join us," Paul replied as the man snorted.

"Join you? And your band of merry men? That's pretty funny."

"Good enough," Paul said without a hint of being bothered by the slight. "Your men and families are welcome to all the food you can carry, but no shopping carts." Paul turned to his men. "Get them up! Help them get some food and get them out of here."

His men began to help some of the older people up.

"Wait!" the major shouted, bringing the men to a halt.

"What is it, Major? You've made your choice," Paul said as he turned.

"Ah wait; I may have been a little hasty in my reply." Paul completely turned to face the major. "What are your terms, if we stay with you?"

"Every one of your men, you included, will be demoted one rank. I will assign an officer to take command of your squad. You will obey his every command as if I issued it directly. If you cannot abide by these terms, or you disobey any command, I will cut the lot of you, women and children included, from this place."

"Do you mind if I consult with my men, General?"

"Not at all, Major, but please make it quick. I don't generally like to be out in the open for any extended amount of time. If any of your men do not like this new arrangement, they are free to go, with as much food as they can carry. You have fifteen minutes Major. Sergeant Bolito, please round up the supplies that I requested earlier."

"Sir, right away, sir." The sergeant and a couple of men peeled off from the main group and headed towards the pharmacy for medical supplies. Paul was inspecting the store like a conquering invader, surveying his spoils from the days of yore, when the major came up behind him.

Paul kept his back to the major, as he inspected a can of Dole pineapple. He peered at it intensely, as though if he stared at it long enough, it might yield all the answers he sought. Paul was tense; a lot hinged on the major's decision, but Paul did his best to maintain the cool façade he had adopted since the whole, bloody mess began. Without confronting the major, since he feared that by turning to face him, he might give away his true feelings, Paul asked, "Your decision, Major?"

"Well I can't say it was easy or unanimous, but call me 'Captain'." Paul let out a barely audible sigh of relief.

"And what of the split decision, Captain?"

The newly demoted captain almost rethought his decision. Demoted by this snot-nose, he thought. It was going to take a little time before he got used to this. But he had to look out for his family and friends now; pride be damned. "Uh, there are five of my men who do not wish to stay, General."

"Do they have families, Captain?" Paul still hadn't turned to face him.

"Three of them do, sir. Two just have wives and one has two kids." Paul's face twisted in agony. Had the captain stepped to the side, he would have seen the pain that contorted his features.

"Very good, Captain. See that those departing personnel are allowed to take with them all that they can carry."

"Very good, sir." The captain began to turn to say goodbye to some of his compadres.

"Captain, one more thing."

"Sir?" The captain said as he turned back around.

"Ask them one more time." This time Paul couldn't hide it; pain mingled into his words, nearly strangling him. The captain didn't understand his concern but he vowed to follow all commands.

"Sir, They were pretty adamant in their decision. I don't see any of them changing their minds."

"Captain, please just ask again. Thank you." Paul walked back down the aisle, effectively blocking any more conversation on this topic.

"Very well, sir." The captain turned to obey his order. Alarms began to softly chirp in the back of his mind but the captain could not begin to understand why. He shrugged it off to nerves.

Twenty minutes later, the five men, three crying women and two screaming babies looked like a shoplifter's dream. Cans of food jutted out of every pocket. They looked like walking convenience stores, Dennis wondered where the Slurpee machine was. Even a couple of the younger babies' clothes had beef jerky poking out. One baby was gnawing on the other end. His mother quickly grabbed it, fearing if the baby dropped it, she would be unable to retrieve it without spilling half of the booty she was carrying. The men shook hands with their friends and saluted their major. The women were hugging and crying.

"Sergeant Bolito!" Paul yelled. It wasn't necessary; the sergeant was less than ten feet away, but Paul's emotions were close to the surface at the moment.

"Sir, yes, sir!" the sergeant said as he ran over to

stand in front of the general.

"Sergeant, I want you to get a squad and escort these people to the town line."

"Yes, sir." The sergeant went to call his first squad.

One of the men from the departing party approached Paul. He was a wiry man called Red. Paul thought, he must have received his nickname years ago, because the man was as bald as a cue ball.

"Ah, General." This man had an even tougher time calling Paul by his title than the major did.

"Yes, Sergeant Major," Paul said as he turned to face the man. Paul had respect for this man. He was senior non-com; the men who truly ran the armed forces. Sure, the officers made the decisions, but the senior non-coms were the ones that got down into the muck and mud and blood, and did whatever it took to make sure the task was completed... And correctly. Here was a man who preferred to go out on his own rather than take orders from someone whom, he felt, didn't deserve that respect.

"Sir, we don't need an escort. Most of us have lived all of our lives in this vicinity. We know where the town line is."

"Sergeant Major, if it's all the same to you, the moment you leave this parking lot, you become unfriendlies. This is as much for your safety as it is for my men. If one of my patrols should see you, they could possibly engage you."

"We don't need an escort, General, we can take care of ourselves." The sergeant major's voice began to rise but he caught it before it peaked.

"Like you did in the store, Sergeant Major?"

The sergeant major's jaw closed shut. Anger was beginning to boil over but he had too much military bearing to let this little punk under his skin. At least he hoped so. The captain had been watching this conversation from the start and had to stop himself a couple of times from interjecting. The alarm sound in his head got a little louder and the captain worked a little harder to quell the noise.

"Very well, Sergeant Major," Paul said as he turned to Sergeant Bolito. "Sergeant, I want you to take this group to the Norwood line where you will complete operation 'Raven Claw' and return back to base camp."

The sergeant's face faltered for a fraction of a second, but it was enough to make the captain worry that his head might explode from all the alarm-clanging. Paul looked over at the captain who seemed to be roiling on his feet.

"Captain, are you alright?" Paul asked with genuine concern.

"All of a sudden, I don't f-f-feel so good," the captain stuttered.

"Corporal Dewey, get this man into the store and tell a medic to take a look at him."

Corporal Dewey helped the captain back into the store. Paul turned back to the sergeant major and extended his hand. "Good luck, Sergeant Major." The sergeant major did not so much as glance in Paul's direction.

"Let's go people!" the sergeant major yelled. The seven castaways left, flanked by ten of Sergeant Bolito's best men.

***

When the group passed out of sight, Dennis came up to Paul's side. He leaned in close to Paul's ear. "I can't believe you let them go," he whispered.

"I didn't," Paul replied as he walked towards the store entrance. Dennis stood there for a few moments, trying to decipher Paul's words. When he finally came up with what he thought Paul meant, he just shook his head. Nah, he can't mean that, he thought and tried his best to shrug it off.

Chapter 28
Grid DB-427

"Peter, what are you doing? You know we have strict orders never to open that box."

"Jack; I just wanted to have a peek. It's killing me to play this spy shit and not have any clue what we're spying on."

"Just shut the thing. For all you know, the thing might be filled with plutonium."

"You think so?" Peter asked as he slammed the door back shut, checking twice to make sure the lock was positioned in place and tight. "I don't want my hair to fall out."

"Don't worry, my friend. For you, that would be an improvement."

***

Mother Ship

"Sir, we've got a signal."

Kuvlar, the interim supreme commander, walked up to his sub-commander's station. On the inside, he was almost jumping for joy. "Damn hu-mans!"

"Sir?" the sub-commander said, looking confused.

The commander didn't answer his query. He was too angry at himself for letting the hot-blooded emotions of the hu-man dogs sway his feelings.

"Where is it located, Sub-Commander?"

"Grid DB-427, Supreme Commander," the sub-commander said as he turned back to his station.

"Where is it headed?"

"Impossible to tell, sir. The signal only came through for about ten seconds, then abruptly ended."

"Ended? That makes no difference. I want a ship dispatched immediately with a full complement of troops."

"Right away, Supreme Commander," the sub-commander answered before he barked some orders into his headset and turned his full attention back to the instrument panel in front of him.

Chapter 29
Indian Hill

"I know why your squad is 'escorting' us," the sergeant major said with no hint of menace in his voice.

"I'm not sure of your meaning, Sergeant Major," Sergeant Bolito said, doing his best not to look the sergeant major in the eye.

"Son, you could never play poker. You can't lie worth a shit. I wasn't a hundred percent certain until I just saw your reaction." The sergeant major grabbed the sergeant's arm with a vise-like grip. A couple of the sergeants' men raised their weapons, bracing for a fight. With his free arm, Sergeant Bolito gestured to the men to lower their weapons. The sergeant major semi-pulled the sergeant away from his ragtag bunch of refugees.

"You know, son, you don't have to do this."

"Sergeant Major, I have my orders."

"Fuck your orders!" The sergeant major hissed. The sergeant major had never raised his voice past a whisper, but to Sergeant Bolito, the words echoed in his ears as if blown from a cannon. "I can understand killing the men, but you're going to shoot three women and two children? What kind of madman is your general? Ordering the murders of innocents!"

"Sergeant Major, don't make me do this. Come back with us."

"And take orders from that wet-behind-the-ears-puke who calls himself a general? I'd rather die here in the woods."

"Can you make that choice for those women and children too?" the sergeant asked as he peered over the sergeant major's shoulder at the small group who had now stopped to see what was delaying their newly appointed

159

leader.

    Pain filled the sergeant major's eyes. "Son, I'm asking you as one warrior to another. Don't do this. Don't make me beg for their lives. Even if you were to just kill us soldiers, you're still condemning the women and children. No one will take them in. Altruism flew out the door when the aliens made themselves known."

    "Sergeant Major, what chance do you have now? That snot-nosed kid we call the general took a heavily-fortified spot from hostiles with not one casualty on either side. Does that sound like somebody who doesn't know what he's doing?" Doubt still clouded the sergeant major's face. Sergeant Bolito pressed on.

    "Sergeant Major, that wet-behind-the-ears kid is the smartest and most caring officer I have ever served under. I've seen that man, after a twenty-two-mile forced march, walk around the encampments and check on the condition of each and every man and woman under his command. That man has secured more resources and manpower in the last year to rival a small industrial nation. He has done more to make sure that our species survives this endeavor than our own government."

    Sergeant Bolito felt that the sergeant major's resolve was slipping. He was making headway, and that which he feared most in combat looked like it wasn't going to happen, at least not today. Killing in the heat of combat was one thing, but cold-blooded executions? That was quite another. He fully understood the necessity that the secret of the Indian Hill Fort must remain just that, a secret. But how much could these people actually know? If the sergeant major still refused, Sergeant Bolito thought he would probably just let the man go, despite his orders. More than likely, ironically, that would mean his own execution. But at least he'd be able to die with his head held high and a clear conscience.

    Somehow, the cute, little, towhead baby had gotten hold of the stick of beef jerky and, sure enough, dropped it. One of the sergeant major's men, most likely the infant's father, bent over to pick it up. And then the shit really broke loose.

One of Sergeant Bolito's men, who was distracted by the conversation between the sergeant and the sergeant major, turned back to see the National Guardsman standing up with what appeared to be a firearm. The man, later on even under heavy interrogation, swore incessantly it was a pistol of some sort; and, fearing for his own safety as well as that of his comrades, opened fire.

The world slowed down for Sergeant Bolito as he watched the first bullet rip straight through the young mother's midsection. It entered her back and exited her abdomen, spewing blood onto her shocked husband. Blood and bone flew onto his chest as he caught her collapsing body. Sergeant Bolito began to scream, "NO!" but it was too late.

The lance corporal had his weapon on the "three round burst" setting. By the time the order was issued, the third bullet had already hit home, smashing into the skull of the Guardsman. Shock and betrayal was forever etched upon his features as he fell over backwards with his wife landing on top of him. Two of the remaining Guardsman reacted quickly to this show of force.

The men grabbed the stunned lance corporal, quickly disarming him and turning the weapon on Sergeant Bolito's men. Corporal Joesy literally flew five feet backward as a three round burst smashed into what was left of his midsection. The resounding thuds were deafening.

Then the Guardsman turned the rifle onto the man who had killed their friend and his wife. Lance Corporal Perry, eighteen years old and a virgin, feared the worst: that he was going to DIE a virgin. He eventually did, by the way, but not on this day. Training and discipline took over as the remainder of the squad regained their composure and riddled the two Guardsmen with bullets, before they were ever able to fire another shot.

They were shot so many times they looked like

marionettes on strings the way they danced around. The final Guardsman, a fat little rotund man the sergeant thought was called "Bennett", stood shaking, with his hands straight up in the air. He begged anyone who would listen not to shoot him. The smoke of the battle cleared and still nobody moved. Everybody feared that any unnecessary movement could be construed as a reason to open fire again. Finally, it was the surviving woman who moved over to the body of her fallen friend.

"You bastards!" she screamed as she attempted to roll her friend off her husband. "What have you animals done? Hasn't this world already gone far enough? Or maybe you figured you could make it just a little shittier?!" Sergeant Bolito was taken aback by the sheer ferocity and force that this waif of a woman possessed.

"Bennett! Get over here and help me get Sarah off David!" the woman cried. Bennett first looked over at his sergeant major, then at the four or five rifles that were leveled on him.

"Get over here! We're already dead!" the woman said as she saw Bennett's indecision. Bennett held out his hands, fingers pointing up, palms out, as if to say, don't shoot. He helped the woman roll her friend over. Sergeant Bolito feared the worst. The woman had been carrying her child in a front-carrying papoose. Acid began to form in the sergeant's throat. He didn't think he would be able to take what he knew he would see.

The baby showed the same look of shock and surprise etched on his face. Blood and tissue covered him from head to toe. Sergeant Bolito tried to force down the bile that was creeping up his esophagus, when warm relief flooded through his body--the baby cried. Sergeant Bolito thought he might join the infant; a good cry might feel pretty good right about now. The sergeant major was shaking with rage.

"That girl was all of twenty-four years old, you stupid bastard!" the sergeant major yelled as he advanced on the retreating gunman. "I'm going to rip that stupid little pinhead right off your shoulders!" The gunman stumbled over a branch and fell over backwards. He began to scramble like an overturned turtle. The rest of the squad stood dumbfounded. No one was quite sure what to do.

The sergeant major reached down and grabbed the rifle from one of his private's hands. Every one tensed, and Sergeant Bolito raised his weapon, but quickly lowered it when the sergeant major tossed it aside. The sergeant major began to take out some of his anger and frustration on the private's face. Sergeant Bolito sympathized since he felt that if he were in the sergeant major's shoes, he would have done the same thing. The sergeant allowed it to go on until it appeared that the private was beginning to lose consciousness.

"Sergeant Major! That's enough!" But the sergeant major pressed on. "Sergeant Major! That's quite enough!!" Sergeant Bolito yelled with a little more force. And still, the sergeant major hit the unconscious lance corporal. Blood began to splatter. Sergeant Bolito quickly approached the sergeant major while withdrawing his nine millimeter pistol from its holster.

Not until Sergeant Bolito pressed the cold barrel of the gun to the sergeant major's temple, did the wind seemed to deflate from the sergeant major's sails. He let go of the lance corporal's collar and let him fall on the ground. He exhaled a heavy sigh as he stood back up and wiped the sweat from his brow with the back of his hand. Blood covered his face; some his own, from his split knuckles, but most was from Lance Corporal Perry's face. It would be a week or so before the LC Perry would be able to look into a mirror without scaring himself.

"What now, Sergeant Bolito? Are you going to stand us up against a tree or should we all turn our backs to you?"

"Neither, Sergeant Major. You're all prisoners of war now," the sergeant said without much conviction. This encounter had completely drained him. He suddenly felt tired and weary. The woman who had been kneeling over her slain friend's body began to rise and protest.

"Prisoners of war? What war? You cowards!" she yelled but the ferocity had been drained out of her; what remained was pure, icy anger.

"Shut up, Karen," Bennett tried to whisper in vain. "You're going to get us all killed."

"Fuck you, Bennett. You're almost as big a coward as these other men." Bennett was taken aback by her verbal lashing. "Where were you when Sarah got shot?" Bennett didn't know how to answer that question or whether Karen was really looking for an answer. So Bennett just stood there, mouth gaping like a landed guppy.

"Shut your trap, Bennett, or you're likely to swallow a bug!" the woman said as she turned to face Sergeant Bolito. "And what of your lance corporal, Sergeant? Are you going to give him a medal for his valor in combat today?" she spat.

"Ma'am, there will be a full investigation into the matter," The sergeant answered as calmly as possible.

"An investigation? From you armed boy scouts? What are you going to investigate? The stupid kid shot my best friend and her husband over a piece of beef jerky. Was he afraid they would try to make him eat it? Is that it? He's a vegetarian and he can't stand the sight of meat? And what of the baby? He's an orphan now. There's not already enough suffering?"

"Ma'am, I understand your suffering. I do…" The sergeant interjected.

"You don't understand, Sergeant. You and your little troop can go fuck yourselves. I'm taking this baby and I'm leaving."

"Ma'am, I can't let you do that."

"What are you going to do, shoot me?" Sergeant Bolito had nothing left; all desire for confrontation had been wiped out of him.

"You're free to go, Ma'am. But you're wrong about one thing." She stopped to hear him out. "I do understand your pain. I lost my wife and kid in the first onslaught. And my parents were dragged out of their home and shot for the contents of their refrigerator. So don't stand there and tell me I don't know about suffering."

Her stare softened but she did not apologize. She stiffly turned and began to walk away from the whole scene, with Bennett and the sergeant major in tow. Sergeant Bolito stood stock still as he watched the three fading figures.

"Sergeant, you can't just let them go."

"Well, Corporal Faulk, what would you have me do? Should I run up to them and shoot them down? Tell you what, if you're so motivated, why don't you go do it? Stand back far enough though, that you don't get any blood on you." The corporal quickly broke eye contact and stepped back a few paces. "Does anyone else have any suggestions? I know I had direct orders; and I alone will pay for disobeying them."

The squad headed back to the fort with the bodies of the slain Guardsmen, and the woman. The sergeant would see to it that they all received a proper burial.

***

"Sir!" The excited private exclaimed as he broke into the command tent.

"Yes, private?" A tired Paul looked up from reports that his long range scouts had submitted. And none of them were good. Who feared the aliens when we were doing ourselves in? Wide scale looting and rioting had become the norm in the States. And everywhere else for that matter, at least, based on the reports they heard on the short-wave radios. With the collapse of the infrastructure, people were dying by the millions from the ensuing anarchy.

Super gangs sprang up like wild fire. Paul believed they were already established gangs whose membership was doubling, almost daily. Paul figured, at that rate, they'd have to start attacking themselves soon, because there would be no one left to terrorize.

Most of the police had disbanded to protect and serve their own families. The few wearing the shield that were left mostly holed themselves up in their precinct buildings. If you could get to the station, you could claim sanctuary. But the big "if" was getting to the station. The gangs had become so brazen, they were known to wait outside of the station to ambush some unsuspecting victims. The National Guard were not much better. They were spread so thin as to become wholly ineffective. Most, like the ones at the Stop and Shop, were only concerned with taking care of their friends and families.

"Sir, Sergeant Bolito's party is arriving back."

"Thank you, Private. You're dismissed," Paul said without ever glancing up from his reports. The private, however, didn't leave.

"Uh, sir?" the private said hesitantly. Paul looked up from his papers.

"Well, what is it, Private?"

"Sir, they have casualties with them." Paul rubbed his eyes with his thumb and forefinger.

"Private, when Sergeant Bolito enters into the fort, please have him report to me. Thank you. Dismissed."

"Sir, yes, sir." The private departed as quickly as he had arrived.

Paul, not for the first time, began to wonder if what he had done to Mike had been the right call, but he just couldn't see any other choice in the matter. Thankfully, Sergeant Bolito arrived more quickly than anticipated, preventing any more fruitless thought on the matter. Sergeant Bolito knocked on the outer office door.

"Sir, Sergeant Bolito, reporting as ordered."

"Enter Sergeant, and at ease. Take a seat, Sergeant. I'm sorry about sending you out on this mission, but it was something that had to be done."

"Sir, I let them go." Paul looked over quickly at the sergeant. Disbelief consumed his face for a minute, but he quickly re-composed himself.

"Sergeant, I gave you a direct order. I was very explicit on the results I was expecting." Now Paul's face registered surprise. "So who, Sergeant, are the casualties I was told that you are carrying?" Now it was the sergeant's turn to look tired.

"Sir, there was an accident. One of my men thought the Guardsman had a weapon and he opened fire, killing the Guardsman and his wife. In the ensuing melee, two of the Guardsmen overpowered one of my men, killing him. My men returned fire, killing the two transgressors."

"This gets better and better, Sergeant! You fucked this little mission up royally! And on top of it all, you let them go. Whom, exactly, did you let go?"

Sergeant Bolito had never seen the general quite this riled up. He wondered if a firing squad might not be that far off in his near future.

"Sir, there was a Guardsman named Bennett." Paul remembered him. No one too noteworthy, maybe a little shifty, but not too serious a threat. "The surviving woman," the sergeant continued, "her two kids, and the kid from the deceased parents."

Nothing too serious. Paul doubted they could survive the week out on the streets, especially without any firearms. "And the sergeant major." Paul was seriously pissed now. You don't become a "top" in the military, unless you know your stuff. That man might have made a mistake regarding his store, but he was far from a pushover.

"Of all the people you should have let go, Sergeant, the sergeant major was definitely not among them. How much does he know, Sergeant?"

"Sir?" The sergeant looked perplexed.

"Sergeant! I know you tried to convince him to come back here. How much does he know!" Paul rose and slammed his fists down on his desk, sending several pencils bouncing to the floor. The sergeant jumped a little in his seat at the sudden outburst. He felt the need to answer the general but he couldn't find the right words.

"By your silence, Sergeant, I'm under the impression he knows more now than he did this morning. Private

Cooley! Get in here!" The general's aide, Private Cooley, who was listening to most of their conversation, was only a few steps away from the door when summoned.

"Sir?" the stockily built private replied, trying his best to look like he was completely out of the loop on this one.

"Private, stop looking at me like you don't have a clue what is going on here. I want you to tell Colonel Salazar to assemble twenty-five of his best men, quickly. And when they are ready, have him report to me!" The private turned to obey his orders. "Private?" The private skidded to a stop.

"Sir?"

"I want all of this to happen in the next ten minutes; understood?"

"Sir, yes, sir, ten minutes." Paul could hear his outer office door slam shut as the private raced through.

"Sir, how much of a threat can two men, a woman and three kids be?" the sergeant inquired. His attempt at damage control was, unfortunately, a little too late.

"Sergeant, I'm not even going to begin to tell you how much jeopardy you have put this fort in. The lives of five thousand people were already hinging on the head of a pen; but apparently you felt those odds were too great. You thought that maybe on the head of a pin would be a little more exciting.

"What if they tell somebody? Maybe one of these super gangs? Not that I'm worried about them all that much, but don't you think that somebody else might notice all that gunplay going on? If the aliens get even a hint or a whiff of this place, we're toast. Their main objective is military installations, no matter how big or small. They even destroyed bases that were inactive. Now if that doesn't show thoroughness, I don't know what does.

"Sergeant, I sent you on a shitty mission, but a mission that I trusted you to complete. I expected you to realize the importance of our continued secrecy. I care about each and every member of the UEMC, but even my long range scouts know that this is pretty much the last bastion of human existence. The shit is hitting the fan all across the globe. What the aliens didn't finish off, man is taking care of. My scouts carry implants in their teeth in case they are captured; so they can instantly kill themselves.

"And don't get any illusions that it is not a severely painful way to die. There is no antidote, but each and every one of them, among the finest of my men, has sworn that he would rather die than divulge any information regarding this installation. Sergeant, your mission was a direct order, the sacrifice of the few for the safety of the many."

"Sir, Colonel Salazar reporting as ordered."

"Come on in, Colonel" the general motioned with his hand.

"This had better be good, General. I was right in the middle of my physical fitness routine." The colonel could see that his attempt at levity wasn't warmly accepted. The general dismissed the remark.

"Colonel, Sergeant Bolito here has made a very large error in judgment." The colonel looked sidelong at the sergeant and noticed the fine lines of sweat that were racing down his cheeks.

"Sir?" the colonel asked, looking back towards the general.

"The sergeant let six civvies go," Paul answered.

"Son," the colonel said as he looked down on the still seated sergeant. "What did you do that for?" The sergeant didn't have an answer for the general, nor did he have one for the colonel.

"What do you want me to do, sir?" the colonel asked, looking back towards Paul.

"I want them back, Colonel, alive if, and I stress 'if,' possible; otherwise, dead. There are two men, a woman and three kids."

"Kids, General?"

"Yes, kids, Colonel! I'm not thrilled about this myself. First, try to convince them to come back. But I cannot tolerate them running around out there with any knowledge of this installation."

"Alright, sir. My men are assembled and ready to go."

"Colonel, they have about a half hour lead on you, but as of right now, they are unarmed. Last known contact was approaching the Norwood line by way of the in-town train lines. And one more thing, Colonel, one of the men is a top."

"Son of a bitch! That pretty much means they're not going to roll over and die for us."

"Not only that, but I've got to assume he knows I'm going to send out another detail for them. He has a half hour lead, but with three kids, I don't see them making too much progress."

"Sir, we will do our best to recover them."

"I hope so, Colonel. The fate of our very existence could depend on it." The colonel nodded quickly and headed out the door almost as rapidly as the private.

"Private Cooley! I know you're outside the door. Go get the sergeant-of-arms and have him report here immediately."

"Right away!" came the response from the other side of the door.

Paul sat back down and began reading his scout reports as if the last fifteen minutes never even happened. Rage welled inside of him. He was afraid that if the sergeant-of-arms didn't arrive quickly, he would unholster his sidearm and put a bullet in the sergeant's leg. Or somewhere equally as painful, but not necessarily lethal.

The sergeant sat stock still, afraid the slightest movement might incur the general's wrath once again. The sergeant-of-arms arrived minutes later, wearing his BDU's with campaign cover and duty belt as was customary for all personnel on guard duty. After saluting the general, the sergeant-of-arms spoke.

"Sir, Staff Sergeant Burkett, reporting as ordered."

"Staff Sergeant, I want this man confined to his quarters. I want two guards on watch twenty-four hours a day, until I can figure out what to do with him."

"Sir, as is customary, per Order 22, Article 7b, I must ask what this man has been charged with before I can place him under arrest."

"Staff Sergeant Burkett, Sergeant Bolito is being charged with the crime of treason." Shock registered on the staff sergeant's face since the most serious crime he had seen committed was the occasional fisticuffs. Treason? That was a whole other matter.

The staff sergeant unholstered his weapon and aimed it squarely at the sergeant's back. "Sergeant Bolito, you have been charged with the crime of treason. I want you to stand slowly and remove your holstered weapon. I then want you to turn all of your pockets inside out. And while you are doing this, Sergeant, I want you to realize that I have a fully loaded nine millimeter aimed at you."

The sergeant rose stiffly. His violent shaking hindered his ability to undo his holster. He feared if he didn't hurry, the staff sergeant might think he was attempting to escape. After fumbling with his holster for a few more seconds, the sergeant finally undid it and gingerly placed his weapon on the general's desk. He then proceeded to pull all of his pockets inside out.

When he emptied his left breast pocket, it finally made him lose it. The picture of his girlfriend, Tabitha, dropped out and fell directly on the general's desk. Her sweet face peered up at him as if to say, "What have you done to us? We were to be engaged and married. We were going to make this world right again for our kids." Tears welled up in the sergeant's eyes.

Paul arose and turned his back. "Staff Sergeant, take this man away." Paul was crushed. The sergeant had been one of the fledgling group's first recruits. He had proven himself countless times on and off the field of combat. Paul was even planning to preside over the sergeant's wedding with Tabitha. What was he going to tell Tabby? He knew it was only a matter of time before she came storming through the door.

Paul knew he had to make an example out of the sergeant. He couldn't let a high crime like treason go unpunished. He had no idea what he was going to do. The staff sergeant left with the manacled sergeant in front of him, leading the way.

"Private Cooley, consider yourself off duty. Go back to your barracks," Paul sighed as he gazed at the back wall, which displayed the magnified map of Walpole. He stared longingly at the spot marked by the high school symbol. Oh, to be back then, he sighed.

He turned back around to sit at his desk as he heard the private leave the outer office. He wanted to lock the door and throw away the key, but he knew he wouldn't and couldn't, for that matter. "What I wouldn't do for a few hours of sleep," he mumbled, once again, rubbing his eyes with his thumb and forefinger.

***

Colonel Salazar rallied his troops to the last known point of contact with the fugitives. "Alright, men! We are looking for two men, a woman and a few children. They are to be considered dangerous; but at this time, remain unarmed. I do not want them fired upon unless you are personally threatened. If anybody should spot them, I want to be notified immediately. I want to make first contact. If you fear their imminent escape, I want you to shoot to incapacitate. If that is not possible, I want you to shoot to kill."

That garnered more than a few shocked looks throughout the ranks. "Men, I want you to understand the severity of this mission. These people know about our existence. They threaten everything that we have worked so hard for. Your friends' lives, your sweethearts' lives, even your children's lives are in grave danger.

"If they resist, we have no choice but to extinguish the threat. Believe me, I do not wish for it to come to that, but I will not sacrifice the very essence of mankind for them. If there are any of you who are not up for this mission, I completely understand. No discipline will befall you. If this is something that you cannot stomach, I want you to return back to the fort."

As expected, none of the colonel's men made a move to leave. He knew they wouldn't. Colonel Salazar had purposely chosen men who had strong ties back at the fort. Any and all of these men would die a thousand deaths to ensure the safety of the last bastion.

"Alright, since everyone is in, I want you to break down into groups of three and I want patrols at roughly hundred-yard intervals. Corporal Dewey, make it so."

"Sir, yes, sir! You heard the man; line up and count off in threes."

Colonel Salazar was impressed with the promptness with which his men performed their duties, but he feared that the head start for the Guardsman and the sergeant major's knowledge of military strategy would impede his efforts. What got into Sergeant Bolito's head? If he didn't want to kill them, he should have just dragged them back, kicking and screaming, he thought.

***

The sergeant major tried his best to get his ragtag group hustling. He knew that Sergeant Bolito had only granted the troop a small reprieve. General Ginson was entirely too smart to just let them walk. He had way too much invested to take a chance on this group's ability to stay quiet.

The sergeant major carried one of the bigger kids on his shoulders and the newly orphaned infant in his arms. Karen, who had just witnessed the deaths of her best friends, was carrying the younger of her two children. She was a trooper, he thought to himself. But Bennett, the miserable shit, was the one slowing them down. Bennett wouldn't even carry one of the infants, complaining about a sore back. Of the three men I lost today, why wasn't one of them Bennett? the sergeant major thought sourly.

"Bennett! Come on! Pick it up! We have to put as much distance between us and Walpole as possible," the top shouted over his shoulder. A miserable and testy Bennett was swatting away bugs and had completely stopped his forward momentum right when the top began to speak.

"What's the rush, Top?" Bennett asked with sarcasm in his voice. "The pansy-ass Vato let us go, we're free as birds." The top would have just left Bennett to rot on his own, but he had foolishly confided his plan to go to a food cannery on the outskirts of the Norwood/Dedham line. And the top knew that Bennett, on his own, would be scooped up in minutes. Bennett was ready to call it a day less than a half mile from the conflict.

"Listen, you dumb ass," the sergeant major started. He hated slipping out of military protocol, but this ass was pushing him to the limit. "Do you really think that the general back at that Stop and Shop is just going to let us go? He's probably already put a bullet in that sergeant. Now move!" the sergeant major yelled.

That got Bennett moving again but it was at a grudgingly slow pace. It was just enough that the sergeant major couldn't say anything but not nearly the speed they needed to escape. The top's mind was racing with alternative ideas so that he could just leave the lollygagger behind. But he realized that he couldn't go much further with the children; and they were going to need food. They lost more than seventy percent of the food they took from the grocery store. Every time the top turned around, Bennett was slyly sticking something more in his mouth, despite their agreement to eat nothing until they could ration it out when they stopped for the night.

The cannery was a perfect refuge. Not many people knew about it and it would provide plenty of nutrition for the time being and until they could try to find a way to hook up with another National Guard unit. And then who knows? Maybe they'd go back with a tank and retake that store.

The sergeant major was about to reprimand Bennett again, but when he turned around, he noticed a ridge, maybe a quarter of a mile away, and two or three Marines on it. He didn't think they had been spotted yet, at least, judging by their movements. The sergeant major put his fist up into the air to halt his small troop. Karen immediately froze as fear spread across her face. Bennett walked right into her, still smelling of the Kit Kat bar he had just stuffed into his mouth.

"Hey what the…" he said as he oomphed into her back. He finally looked up to see the top's "no movement" signal and nearly choked on his candy bar, much to the top's delight. The top studied the patrol a little longer, satisfied that they had not seen them yet. They were still coming in their general direction but they were looking in every other direction as well. If they had been spotted, the scouts would be double timing to their location.

"All right, we're going to have to split up," the sergeant major began and Karen began to protest.

"We can't split up; they haven't even seen us. Let's just hide in this underbrush until they pass," she argued.

"Karen, we can't be sure the kids will stay quiet. And I'm positive they have more than one patrol out there. No, our odds are horrible if we stay together. I will get as far away from you, Bennett, and the kids as possible; and I will draw them away from your location." Karen was about to double her protests. No way did she trust Bennett with her life. But the top looked at her harshly as if to say he didn't want any of his orders questioned.

"I will meet up with you and Bennett when I am sure that I have lost them. Keep on this path and don't stop for anything, no matter what! You hear!" he stressed. The top pulled Bennett to the side while Karen did her best to comfort the infant who was beginning to realize that not all was right in its tiny, little world.

"Bennett! You fuck this up and I'll fillet you! Do you understand? For once in your life, I want you to think about somebody besides yourself, do you hear me, soldier?" Bennett nodded in agreement, but internally, he was already trying to figure out how he could save his own skin.

"Karen, Bennett, good luck. I will meet up with you

two later tonight at the rendezvous point. Wait until I am spotted before you begin to move. That will focus all their attention on me and you should have pretty fair sailing from that point on."

"What about you, Red? You're really not intending on meeting us tonight," Karen said solemnly. The top never answered. He started to move away from them at a fairly good clip, he wanted to be at least a few hundred or so yards away before he began the ruse. Karen turned to Bennett.

"You're going to have to carry one of these kids, Bennett. I can't do it on my own. And don't pull that injured back crap with me. Remember! I was a nurse on the base; I saw your chart. You had more than twice the sick calls logged than your nearest competitor. Why they didn't kick you out, I'll never know."

Bennett wanted to tell her to fuck off, but he figured that the top was still too close and, although he might not be afraid of Karen, the top scared him. "Oh, and don't think I don't know what's going on in that shifty little head of yours. If you try to leave me here with all these kids, I'll scream my bloody head off until those Marines find us." She watched as the sneer on Bennett's face disappeared. She nailed that one. "Spineless little bitch," she mumbled under her breath.

Bennett's options began to run out on him. Damn top, he thought to himself. If I hadn't been so scared of him, I would have just stayed there at the Stop and Shop. At least, then I'd be safe. What do I give a care who's in charge. They're all assholes to me. "Go ahead, scream. I'd rather give up anyway. I'll go back to the Stop and Shop and let them guard me and I won't have to listen to the top anymore."

"What makes you think they are looking for prisoners, dumbass? They're here to finish off what that Sergeant Bolito couldn't."

"Do you think so?" Bennett was scrambling; he hadn't thought about that. There was no way they'd be able to get away with all these kids. "Damn top."

"What? That man's out there risking his life for us."

"Well, if he hadn't cornered us into leaving in the first place, he wouldn't have to try and save us now, would he?"

"I don't know about you, Bennett, but nobody cajoled me into leaving. I have principles, I wasn't going to let some gang leader make us call him 'boss.' He's just a thug with a uniform."

"Yeah? Well, I'd rather be alive and well, calling him whatever he wanted to be called, then dead and full of principles."

"Well, I guess that's the difference between you and me then, isn't it?"

"What about your kids, Karen? What do they have to say about your principles? And what about Little Orphan Bobby over there? What does he have to say about your principles?" Bennett spat. Karen looked away, tears welling up in her eyes. Her upright principles had gotten her into jams before but never had the lives of her kids been jeopardized because of it.

"We'll be fine. The top won't let anything happen to us."

"Yep, I'm sure that's exactly what Garrity, McHenry and his wife were thinking too."

"You bastard, Bennett! Why are you doing this?"

Bennett knew a better man would not torment a woman like this, in their darkest hour, but he wasn't that man. He wholly believed in the old axiom "misery loves company" and he was taking her with him. Bennett was about to reply when they heard the alarm being sounded. They could see the patrol looking in the direction the top had gone.

One of the Marines was on the radio, more than likely identifying their position; the other two were yelling. It appeared like they were ordering the top to halt, but from their viewpoint, it was impossible to tell. The warning shots, however, sent shudders down Bennett's spine.

He could tell from the way the Marines were aiming that these were only warning shots, but he didn't figure that it would be too long before they lowered their muzzles. And, even from this distance, he could tell that they meant business. Bennett and Karen both squatted down, adrenaline racing through their veins. The movement made Bennett acutely aware of a lump in his pocket that made it extremely uncomfortable to remain in that position. Bennett reached into his pocket and pulled out the annoying culprit, a sixteen ounce can of creamed corn.

What made me grab this? Bennett wondered, I hate corn. Bennett hefted it in his hand. This sucker's pretty heavy; maybe I should just get rid of the damn thing. And then, there it was--the back of Karen's head. Maybe some options were still open, Bennett thought.

The top's plan was nearly working to perfection. The three Marines on the ridge were quickly advancing to his position. They weren't looking left or right, just straight ahead. They'd catch that bastard in the next twenty minutes or so. How far could the five of us really get? They'd have us half an hour after that.

"Fuck that!" Bennett said out loud, though he hadn't meant to. Karen started to turn around to see what Bennett was bitching about now, when her world suddenly went black. Bennett had slammed the can so hard into the back of Karen's head, that the can split in two.

Blood poured from her skull, bone shards mingled with the creamed corn. Bennett stared in fascination as the dark red mixed with the yellow and ran down her neck in a pinkish mixture. It seemed much more Hollywood-driven than real life. Bennett still held onto the can as Karen's body fell away into the scrub brush. He was frozen for only a moment as Karen's oldest shrieked out in protest.

"Brat!" Bennett was going to brain the kid also when he realized that his weapon of choice had been reduced to a useless, bent piece of tin. Bennett turned and ran, not really sure in which direction he was heading, nor caring. But he made sure he wasn't headed back to the Stop and Shop, nor forward to the cannery. It would be just his luck if the top made it through and found him there alone. No sir, he'd have none of that. He'd do just fine though, he figured. Rats always find a way to survive.

Bennett heard a three round burst. He thought they were shooting his way, but when he didn't fall over bleeding, he deduced the top must've been found. He finally crossed through the scrub brush and into some thicker woods and felt it was safe enough to stop and take a look. He peered out from the trees and saw five or six Marines standing over something. He wasn't a hundred percent sure what it was, but it didn't take a rocket scientist to figure out that the top was in that general area.

"About time somebody put that bastard out of my misery," Bennett half smiled. He wanted to do a dance, he was so excited. He probably would have if he hadn't noticed a dozen or so more Marines rising over the crest. Apparently, the ruse hadn't worked as well as the top expected. It had delayed the Marines, but definitely not stopped them. They were still fanned out and the ones that weren't looking down at the top were most assuredly looking for the rest of the party.

Bennett quickly glanced over to where Karen was. If the bitch got up now, he was as good as dead. Sure, he was in the National Guard, but every time it was physical fitness time, Bennett had his ass parked down at the hospital. He had about spent all of his energy running into the woods. He could see that someone was stirring in their little enclosure. His heart started hammering in his chest. He didn't want to go out like this, especially not running.

He contemplated emerging from the woods with his hands raised above his head. Maybe they would show leniency. They might even let him join his unit if he told them that the top forced him to go along. But what about Karen? She's going to tell everyone that I tried to kill her.

"Bitch!" Bennett said angrily, as if Karen had willed

Bennett to crush her skull with a can of corn. Even if she were dead, they'd find the body eventually, 'cause of the kids, Bennett thought. He continued to weigh his options. Could he get back to his original hiding area and dispose of Karen and the kids before the Marines arrived?

"Dammit!" he screamed. Rage and frustration coursed through him. The top had started the slice along his neck and Bennett had finished making the cut. I cut my own throat! He turned and ran; there was no other way out for him. Alone and without enough food to make it any longer than through the night, Bennett was filled with remorse. He had eaten most of the food he was carrying, and figured he'd live off what the others had hauled until they found more. "Fucking top! I'd kill you myself if they hadn't already done it for me," he grumbled. It was false bravado, and Bennett knew that even as he said it, but it still made him feel good nonetheless.

***

"Colonel Salazar, you're going to want to come over here and see this," the excited corporal said as he looked down on the body of Karen Fogarty. The kids had been huddled around their mother, trying to make her get up, but nothing short of the hand of God was going to do that. And God seemed to be on short supply right now. The colonel walked over to where the corporal was and noticed immediately that the children's pleading for their mom to wake up was falling on deaf ears.

"Corporal! You and your team get these children out of here." The corporal leaned over to scoop up the kid closest to him and literally had to pry the kid's fingers from his mother's lifeless body.

"Sir, what do you want us to do with them?" The corporal held the kid out in front of him like somebody might hold a skunk, unsure of its intentions.

"Bring them back to base camp. Get them cleaned up and fed, Corporal." The corporal and his detachment left the colonel to his own devices. The colonel really wasn't sure what this Bennett fellow looked like, but he was a monster all the same. The colonel knew what happened here. The top had set up a diversion so that these five could get away; Bennett figured his chances were a lot better if he loosened the load.

"What kind of a monster kills a mother in front of her kids? Corporal Hanraddy, get over here with that radio." The colonel got on the horn to relay his orders.

"Alright, gold, silver, red and blue teams: we have one fugitive left. I want no warning shots, I repeat, NO warning shots. This man is to be considered armed and dangerous. If you have a clear shot, take it and ask questions later." He might only be armed with canned goods, but the result was still the same, the colonel thought to himself.

***

"Sir, there's a Corporal to see you, sir, and he has some guests, sir."

"Send them in," Paul said. Guests? he wondered.

"Sir, we found Mrs. Fogarty dead. Her kids and the baby were with her."

"Dead, Corporal? How?" Paul prayed it wasn't by the hand of any of the platoon he sent out.

"Sir, by a can of corn." Paul looked perplexed and the corporal plowed on. "Sir, it looks like that Bennett fellow killed her and then took off."

"Has he been found yet, Corporal?"

"Not yet, sir. We've been monitoring radio traffic and we've heard no word yet."

"Where was the top during all of this?"

"Sir, the top was spotted about a click away from the woman.

He seemed to be leading us away from their location."

"Where is he now?"

"Sir, he refused surrender, and was shot attempting to escape."

"What am I going to do with these kids?"

"Sir?"

"I can't give them back to the National Guard's families. They'll never believe that we had nothing to do with their mother's death. I really hoped she would be alive and could take care of them. This could start an uprising among them. Corporal, get on the horn and tell the colonel that I want Bennett alive. I'm going to let that man stand trial for her murder. That's the only chance we have to appease the Guardsmen and their families."

"Yes, sir; right away, sir."

***

"Paul, I've had my team out for four hours. We can't find a trace of Bennett," a bone-tired looking Colonel Salazar said from right inside Paul's office.

"Come on in, Frank. Have a seat," Paul said as he stood up and reached over to his file cabinet, pulling out a brandy snifter. "I always thought this stuff was for people my grandfather's age and now I find myself looking forward to the end of the day when I can have a glass," the general said as he handed Frank a snifter.

"Thank you, sir, but I don't think that the day is quite over yet. I have sent out another team to replace my men, but with Bennett having such a great lead now, I don't see how they could have any luck finding him. And then there is the other thing."

"The other thing?" Paul asked as he looked up from his glass of brandy.

"Sir, we've had two skirmishes with gang elements in Norwood."

"Any casualties, Colonel?" Paul asked with genuine concern.

"Only on their side, sir. But I'm concerned with how much attention we may be drawing towards ourselves. We made short order of those gang members, but there's no telling how many eyewitnesses saw the whole thing."

"I understand, Colonel. I've been weighing out the lesser of the two evils, myself. Bennett knows we're up here but whether or not that information is of any use to him remains to be seen. Hopefully, most of the people that saw us today will think that we are some sort of rogue unit. I don't want any more active pursuit for Bennett. I want your men to set up listening posts. Chances are, we passed right over him while he was in some hidey-hole. With any luck, he'll come to us."

"Alright, sir. I'll let my men know immediately," the colonel said as he rose to his feet. "Thank you for the drink, sir."

"Colonel?"

"Yes, sir."

"You didn't drink any of it."

"Sorry, sir. I'm more of a Corona type of guy."

***

Bennett couldn't believe his luck when he saw the patrol that had been on a course straight for him suddenly stop. Sure, they were still a hundred yards off, but from Bennett's position, there was nowhere to go. He decided to hide in a small thicket with one large oak that dominated the center. The thicket, however, was smack dab in the middle of a clearing. Bennett hadn't fully realized the stupidity of his hiding choice until he spotted the patrol. If he got up to run, they would see him before he ran ten feet. But none of that mattered now; he saw them stop.

Were they taking a break? That would be no good. It would just delay his capture or, worse yet, his demise. Bennett's heart was racing. And then a huge smile spread across his face. He saw one of the men standing watch while the other dug a foxhole. They're setting up a listening post. I've got the whole night to get out of here, he thought. Bennett couldn't believe his luck; he even planned on getting a couple of hours of shut-eye before he made his great escape.

Chapter 30

"Wake up sleepy head!" Beth said as she lightly shook Deb.

"Where exactly are we?" Deb mumbled, stretching and wiping her mouth with the back of her hand.

"Well, while you were asleep, my princess, we entered Pennsylvania," Beth said with a smile on her face.

"How long was I asleep?"

"At least five, maybe six hours; I can't really remember. I'm so tired I can't even see the instrument panel clearly."

"Why don't we stop for a while and take a break?" Deb said.

"Are you not awake yet? Do you not remember what happened the last time we tried to catch some sleep?" Deb hadn't forgotten but she wished she had. The girls had stopped to get some sleep at a rest area outside of Nebraska. They both dozed off only to be awakened by two guys who had been quietly attempting to snake their hands through the partially open windows to unlock the doors.

It was Deb who woke up first, when the man on the passenger side accidentally brushed against her hair. Deb thought that a fly had entered the truck and absently attempted to wave it away. When her hand came in contact with the stranger's arm, she nearly froze. Her leg had kicked out in convulsion, waking Beth.

"Deb, I'm trying to sleep," Beth murmured, her eyes half opening. When suddenly, her eyes grew as big as saucers as she realized what was going on. Deb thanked Beth every moment she could for Beth's fast action. Without blinking, Beth hit the power windows, pinning the would-be intruders' arms inside. Deb couldn't believe the howling that ensued; it was purely animalistic.

They began to beat on the windows in rage, but that quickly turned to fright as Beth immediately started the car and took off, with each of them hanging by their arms. At first, they were calling the girls every imaginable word that they could think of; then they began to plead for their lives.

"Come on, we weren't going to hurt you. We just wanted to have a little fun." Beth sped up as cold shivers chilled her body.

"Their idea of fun, I'm sure, is a lot different than ours," Beth said as she turned to Deb with a wicked smile. Deb noticed that Beth increased the acceleration.

"Are you going to let them go?" Deb asked. She was scared and just wanted them gone. The idea of removing a bloody stump from her window was making her feel a little queasy inside.

"Screw them, Deb. What do you think they planned to do once they got inside? Play dominos? I don't think so," Beth stated as sweat poured off her body; her adrenaline was surging. "If we let them go now, they'll be on our ass in five minutes."

That was true, Deb figured. They would come after them for revenge and then what?

"Deb, get me the gun."

"The gun? What do you want the gun for?"

"I want to do my nails; what do you think?! Get the gun, please," Beth snapped.

"I don't like this, Beth. We can't just kill them. We don't know for sure what they were going to do," Deb pleaded.

"I can't believe you, Deb! After all we've seen and all we've been through? You still have faith that these two fine gentlemen are upstanding citizens?' Beth said sarcastically.

"I'm just saying that they haven't done anything, yet. They don't deserve to die."

"Okay, Deb, what did Gary and his friend do when we killed them? Break a little furniture? Did that deserve the death penalty?"

"That's not fair, Beth. We both knew what their intentions were."

"My point exactly, Deb."

"We can't just shoot them! I don't want anything to do with this."

"Little late now, my friend," Beth said as she punched the accelerator again. The two men were desperately trying to cling to anything they could get a hand or foothold on, with little success. The men's legs began to drag on the pavement. Their begging turned to screams of pain.

"Well, then shoot them! You can't just drag them to their deaths!' Deb screamed. Beth picked up the gun and pointed it right at the man on the driver's side. He could do little more than flinch; there was nowhere for him to go. Beth's arm began to shake from fear. She wasn't sure if she could pull the trigger looking straight into someone's eyes.

"Is your seatbelt on, Deb?"

"Yes, but wh…" Deb never finished her question as she felt herself being flung towards the front of the car while the seatbelt dug deep into her shoulder and waist. She was about to complain of the pain to Beth when she heard the splintering of bones from both sides of the truck.

At first, Deb thought Beth had pulled the trigger, so loud was the snapping of bone and the tearing of cartilage. Deb thought it sounded like dry twigs being broken to start a campfire. The men had no restraints as the girls did, and were quickly thrown towards the front of the truck. Their arms had been wrenched free but at a savage price. Both men's arms had been torn completely from their sockets. Smashing onto the front quarter panels hadn't done them any good either.

"Well, I didn't kill them but they'll be out of commission for a while," Beth whispered. Deb wasn't sure if she should respond, but she really didn't know what to say anyway. Beth lingered for a few more seconds to make sure that neither one of the men was faking before she took off. Deb couldn't figure out how they could possibly be. They looked like a pair of mismatched freaks. The man on the driver's side's shoulder, or what was left of it, appeared to be hanging down somewhere in the middle of his chest.

The man on her side he was even more grotesque. His arm was bent two more ways than it was ever designed to be. The man's wrist had been broken in such a way that the back of his fingers were touching his forearm; and, below his elbow, his arm jutted out at a ninety degree angle. Deb thought she might become physically ill if she kept looking at it. But human nature dictates differently. Deb didn't stop looking until he became nothing more than a small speck in her vision, albeit a small distorted speck, but a speck nonetheless.

"Yeah, I guess stopping wouldn't be such a good idea," Deb said with a far off look in her eyes. "Are we going to have enough gas?"

"Well, we've got four more five-gallon jugs of gas in the back, but this truck is a pig on fuel. I don't think so. We're going to have to try to find a place to get some more. But I don't think that we're going to get as lucky as we did the last time." The girls had taken Deb's neighbors' truck. It had been her neighbors' baby. He only drove it on weekends, when he was going camping, fishing or hunting, hence the gun. It had been locked up in his shed in the backyard. Otherwise, it would have been taken or destroyed a long time ago by marauders or gangs or whatever the hell you wanted to call them.

Deb couldn't understand it, for the most part, these people had been good citizens their entire lives, speeding tickets mainly their biggest run-ins with the law. And now, these same people didn't think twice about looting, or raping or worst of all, just flat out murder..

"I always considered <u>Lord of the Flies</u> a piece of fiction," Deb said reflectively.

"What are you talking about, Deb? Have you been breathing in too many gas fumes?" Beth snorted.

"No, I just mean I never really thought that what happened on that island could ever really happen in real life.

That's all. People have gone completely nuts."

"Well, you got a taste of that on the ship, didn't you? Look at what some of those animals became. I hate to call them animals because even animals wouldn't do that to their own kind."

"And then there's Mike, cutting through the gloom like a knight in shining armor." Both girls stopped talking for the moment as they reflected on their lost love. Then they both realized why they were making this journey in the first place: to see him, and find out which one he loved more. Deb broke the silence first.

"I'd rather have only a piece of him than nothing at all. I don't know if I would have anything worth living for if he rejected me." Beth sympathized with Deb. She felt that pit lodged in her stomach too. If Mike picked Deb, what would she do? Where would she go? She couldn't stay there; she'd be on her own, the thing she dreaded most.

"I feel the same way, Deb. I don't think I could handle losing him. I'd rather have a piece of him too than to lose you or him."

"Oh Beth," Deb said as she leaned over to give Beth a hug and wipe away the tears that were beginning to form in her eyes.

Chapter 31

"Sir?" There was a quiet rap on the general's door. It was soft enough but it echoed deeply through his migraine. "Sir, are you still awake?"

"What is it, Corporal?" Paul asked as he raised his head up from the cradle of his hands.

"Sir, there is someone here to see you, and he is very adamant."

"Corporal, I've had a very long day at it doesn't appear that it is going to get any shorter, can this wait until tomorrow?"

"No, Paul! It can't wait until tomorrow!" Ron said as he pushed by the stunned corporal.

"Sir, you just can't barge in here, you'll have to make…"

"It's alright, Corporal," Paul said as he dismissed the man. "Ron, it's good to see you."

"Is it Paul? If it's so good, why has it taken two weeks for you to do so?"

"Ron, you must realize what kind of endeavor this is. It takes everything I have to run this place."

"Cut the crap, Paul. I've known you for a long time. I was the first person that found you lying in a pool of puke after your first run-in with Michelob." Paul was visibly uncomfortable with Ron's barrage. Leadership was a fragile existence; he didn't need any stories like this leaking out and undermining his authority.

"Paul I cleaned you up and got you sober enough so that you didn't spend the majority of your freshman year grounded."

"What do you want, Ron?"

"I want the truth, Paul. Where is my brother? Dennis

has been giving me nothing but stall tactics. Every time I corner him on the subject, he turns tail and runs. What is going on, Paul? You owe me that much."

"Do I, Ron? Do I owe you that much? What have I given you so far? Let's see, the safety and well being of your family in this completely turned on its ear world. Is that not enough?!" Paul shouted. The weight of the day was beginning to collapse around him.

Now it was Ron's turn to go on the defensive. "You know, Paul, that I'll never be able to repay you for the sanctity you have provided for my family. I just want to know what has happened to my brother, your best friend."

The fury drained out of Paul as fast as it had accumulated. "He was a spy," Paul muttered.

"I... I can't believe that, I won't believe that," Ron stammered as he backed up. Perhaps he was thinking that maybe, if he distanced himself from Paul's words, it would make them less unbelievable.

"I couldn't believe it either, Ron. If it makes it any easier, he wasn't a spy in the traditional sense."

"I... I don't understand. What do you mean 'in the traditional sense'.?" Ron's face had turned ashen with the realization of Paul's words. Ron knew the fragility in which this encampment was set up. Extreme measures were constantly required to ensure the safety of the enclave.

"He didn't know he was a spy." Ron's face took on the look of a freshman trying to undertake his first trig problem.

"What does that mean, Paul? How could he not know he was a spy?"

"The aliens compromised him." Ron was about to ask more questions when Paul silenced him with the wave of his hand. "Ron, no one was happier to see your brother than I was, no one. He saved my life once, and I loved him like the brother that I never had. When he showed up in Colorado, I almost fell over, we talked for hours when he got back.

"He told me everything that happened on that ship.

And I told him about all the things that were going on around the mountaintop. But not everything, something just didn't feel right. Call it a hunch, sixth sense, whatever, it doesn't really matter. But something deep inside me kept telling me to not let him know about this place, the real reason for the training in the mountains. I was holding back from my best friend, from my brother.

"I concealed the true designs of what we started in his name's sake. His story was fantastic, almost unbelievable; and then it hit me, maybe it was unbelievable." Words began to form in Ron's mouth again. "Please, Ron, let me finish. If I haven't answered any of your questions when I am through, I will at the end." That seemed to appease Ron for the time being.

"Sure, Mike took their supreme commander hostage and sure, their mother ship had been temporarily disabled, but I was beginning to think that perhaps those aliens let them go."

"Let them go?" Ron interjected. "You just answered your own doubts! Mike had their leader and their ship was crippled."

"No, Ron. Their ship was disabled, not crippled. I have high res scans of that ship straight from the now defunct DOD. That ship had a whole other side of bay doors. Thousands upon thousands of more ships could have launched within minutes of Mike's departure."

"Why would they hold off?" Ron questioned.

"With Mike's knowledge of that ship, Ron, who do you think would want to see him?"

"Almost every military and governmental agency on the planet. So they sent him down as a plant? But you saw him! Paul, you can't believe that he would turn on us. He hated those things more than I've ever seen anybody hate anything."

"There's no doubt in my mind, Ron, that he was on our side, but he was a spy nonetheless. He had been implanted with at least three different devices. We weren't quite sure of their purposes, but it doesn't take too much logic to figure that they were some sort of homing devices and or audio/video type.

"Ron, one was hooked up to his optic nerve and the other to his left eardrum. My guess is they heard and saw everything he did and had his exact location at all times. My suspicions were completely confirmed with the initial phase of the invasion."

Ron's ears perked up. "How so?"

"Ron, the first installations hit were the ones that Mike had visited, almost without exception. The aliens blew up every critical governmental agency we had within the first few hours of the attack. It's not a coincidence that they knew where to go."

"Come on, Paul, those aliens had been watching us for months. Of course, they would know the most critical sites to hit; that doesn't prove anything." Ron now was beginning to look pissed off.

"Sure, Ron, I could see why they'd hit the Pentagon and the 'Fortress'. But why would they bother with Area 51 or, for that matter, Camp Talbot? Come on! A bunch of rebels playing commando on a mountaintop? Of what significance could that have been to their master plan? They hit it because Mike was there. To a tee, they hit every military and government location where he stepped foot."

"They set him up?"

"I'm not sure if they truly meant to set him up. I think that every slave on that ship was outfitted with the same devices he had. Talk about being inside the competitor's head. They probably sold tickets to the viewings from the gladiators' perspective. I feel confident that they had no desire to have a hole the size of Rhode Island blown into their hull or their leader taken hostage. But when the opportunity presented itself, I think they felt it would be better to let them go than to endanger their Commander in open space.

"I'm sure they don't feel that we are a viable threat to

them, but then again, why take the chance? Learn your enemies' innermost secrets and then use it to your advantage."

"I don't like where this conversation is going, Paul. You still have yet to tell me where my brother is." Paul hesitated for a moment, studying Ron's face. Paul was unsure of whether or not he should get some guards to protect him before he told Ron the truth. But ultimately, he felt that it would be better if he told him one on one, no matter what the outcome. Paul took in a heavy breath and almost immediately sighed. Age beyond years began to show on the surface of his face.

"Ron..."

"Sir!! We're under attack!" Paul swiveled in his chair, almost ready to rip off the lance corporal's head for interrupting him at that moment, when his words sunk in. Paul's initial thought was that the aliens had discovered the base and all was lost. The last bastion of human safety had been compromised.

"Sir, the Stop and Shop is being assaulted!"

Why would the aliens bother with the store when they could have the whole mother lode? "Sir, they have about fifty fully armed men. What should we do?" the lance corporal nearly shouted. The look of confusion on his commander's face was doing little to allay his adrenaline rush. Men?

Men? "How many of our men are there?"

"Sir, we have a small squad of about fifteen men."

"Who's in charge of the squad?"

"Sir, Colonel Wagner." Paul aged almost ten years in ten seconds. He easily had the manpower to squash the attack but compromising the Hill was not an option. A force that big was sure to have some scouts out there. And it would only take one error for this place to be discovered. But the alternative seemed far worse to him. Could he leave one of his best friends out to dry?

"Has Colonel Wagner's squad radioed in their situation?"

"Sir, yes, sir. He said that four of his men were killed instantly when they were outside on their cigarette break. And another two were injured, one critically. He thought he could hold them off for another ten minutes or so but that he would greatly appreciate some reinforcements. And…"

"And what? Lance Corporal?" The lance corporal looked like he wanted to go and hide.

"And then the radio went dead."

Paul's heart fell. "Do we have any patrols out?"

"Sir, we have the silver and black patrols out, but they're almost up on the east side of town. Even at full tilt, they wouldn't be here for another fifteen minutes."

"What are you doing, Paul? Dennis is down there in the fight of his life and you're being indecisive!" Ron burst out. Paul was visibly upset. He wasn't sure if it was because Ron was right or that he had pointed it out in front of one of his enlisted men.

"Ron, I'd appreciate if you kept your opinions to yourself. You don't understand the situation."

"What's not to understand, Paul? The repeated fact that you don't have a problem with disposing of those closest to you?"

"Ron, get the fuck out now or I'll have you physically removed," Paul said with icy cold seriousness.

"Don't worry, Paul, I was leaving anyway. Unlike you, I'm going to get a firearm and whoever will come with me and go help Dennis and those men."

"Ron, I will not let you fuck this up. Lance Corporal, escort this man out and make sure he is detained. He is not to leave this compound. If he so much as sees daylight today, your ass will be in front of a firing squad tonight." Ron stood as if he were about to bull rush the lance corporal. But the lance corporal heeded the general's warning, as well he should. The lance corporal pulled out his pistol and leveled it squarely on Ron's chest. Ron was heaving with frustration and rage.

"Sir, what about the colonel?"

"I'll take care of that."

"I'm sure you will, Paul," Ron sputtered.

"Make sure he is detained! Get him out of here!" The lance corporal waved Ron out of the room with his free hand. Paul got on his radio as soon as the lance corporal left.

"Sergeant McCabe! What's the status on tunnel two?"

"Sir, I briefed you on that last week."

"What's the status NOW, goddammit?" The sergeant on the other end was taken aback by the force of the voice.

"Sir, we've advanced a few more feet through the collapse but it will be another two weeks or so before we break through." The sergeant heard the audible pop of the radio clicking off and wondered to himself what he had done to spark such fury in the general. He ordered two more details to finish digging out the collapse.

'I set this shit up to save my loved ones. I'll be damned if I let another one die.' Paul thought to himself.

"Colonel Salazar! Sound the Type I alarm," Paul ordered. He could tell that the colonel was lying down by the disorientation in his voice, but he recovered extremely fast.

"Uh.. sir? Type I alarm? Yes, sir." More conviction rang in his voice as the realization of the general's words sunk in. "Are we under attack, sir?"

"Yes," came the succinct reply. Paul knew that his own suspicions were now going through the colonel's head. "Relax Frank. It's not the aliens. Not yet, anyway. The Stop and Shop is under attack and our men are outnumbered nearly five to one."

"Sir, the tunnel is collapsed. How do you propose an assault?"

"Colonel, I know the tunnel is not serviceable."

"Sir, we talked about this exact scenario. We're supposed to let the Stop and Shop fall if this is the case and get it back at our discretion. If we fly out of our hidey-hole like pissed-off ants, somebody is sure to notice."

"Frank, Dennis is in command down there." Frank paused and sighed.

195

"What do you want to do, sir?"

"I want twenty of your alpha platoon to head out of emergency hatch three and go as stealthily and quickly as possible. I then want twenty civilian-looking personnel to head out hatch four and round up any potential scouts. Are we clear, Frank? I want everybody rounded up within one square mile of this facility."

"We're clear, sir, but I don't agree with the risk that you are taking here."

"That's why I like you, Frank. You've never been a yes man. Now get it done."

"Right away, sir."

***

"Have you gotten that damned thing to work yet?" Dennis yelled after his last burst found pay dirt in the scumbag who had come through the produce aisle. The remaining seven UEMC were now pinned behind the deli counter. Glass shards flew everywhere as bullets exploded all around them. Dennis hoped the rebels didn't have any hand grenades or the battle would come to a quick and nasty conclusion.

"Sergeant, did headquarters get the last message?"

"Colonel, I don't know. The radio operator was shot at almost the same time the radio was." Damn, Dennis thought to himself. It's another fifteen minutes 'til the next check in. This little skirmish would be long over before the Hill even realized it had started.

"Sir, I don't think it will matter even if they got the message. You know the protocol as well as I do. With the supply tunnel temporarily down, the standing order is to let this place fall, if necessary."

"I know the orders, Sergeant. I just have no desire to die next to cured meats. How are we doing on ammo?"

"We've got enough to take them out. I just don't think we have the manpower to do it."

"I appreciate the candor, Sergeant, but is this really the time for sarcasm?" Dennis said as he sat down hard on his ass to change his magazine out.

"Sir, they are coming up aisle eight," an over exuberant private yelled.

Well, it seems that the fat lady is beginning to warm up. Shortly, they would be completely flanked and it was only a matter of time. Well, at least I'll go out with a bang, Dennis thought. He stood up to fire off his newest cartridge when a bullet ripped his helmet clean off. Blood flew from the side of his head as he spun downwards, smashing his head on a…"What? A ham?" And the world went black for Dennis.

"Colonel's down, men," the sergeant shouted over the volley of rounds. "I say we go out in style." The five remaining soldiers didn't completely concur with the sergeant's point of view but they saw the writing on the wall. Better to go out fighting than sitting here huddled together. With that, the six remaining men stood up and shoulder-to-shoulder, momentarily caught the usurpers off guard.

Many of them fell before they gathered their wits; and then numbers and strategic location began to take its toll. One by one, the defenders fell, most of them with multiple wounds, but still they pressed on. When their clips had been emptied, only two survived to rearm--the sergeant and the private who warned about the approach on aisle eight.

"Well, son, it's just you and me now. No sense in keeping God waiting," the sergeant said, pride swelling up in his chest. The private really didn't mind though if God waited, say another fifty or sixty years, but no way was he going to let the sergeant die alone.

The attackers had momentarily ceased their onslaught. They knew what was coming, and they had no desire to be caught off guard again. Let the poor bastards show themselves again; they'd be more than happy to end the day from where they waited. The sergeant was milliseconds away from standing and opening fire when he heard gunfire from outside the store.

"Sergeant! What is that? Are they celebrating their

victory before we're dead?" The private asked. The sergeant didn't think so.

"Naw! Nobody would waste ammo like that anymore. We've got help."

"Help? From where? No one would come from the Hill."

"Private, I don't know, but do you really care from where? Who knows? Maybe it's one of our patrols." The sergeant didn't really believe that because the patrols were usually only four or five people and this sounded like a hell of a lot more gunfire. "I hope it's not the Hill."

"Sergeant? Are you crazy? We're being saved."

"I'll never live this down if we survive. I let my commanding officer fall in battle. I didn't hold our position and then I had to be saved by headquarters. It's over… No way I'm going out like this."

The sergeant jumped over what remained of the deli counter and began advancing on the enemy, whose attention had been drawn to the front of the store, to engage in a new battle. The sergeant's gun began to glow a dull red as he fired away at anyone who retreated from his near suicidal advance and maniacal laugh.

***

The crack alpha squads caught the potential Stop and Shop usurpers completely unaware, so wrapped up were they in the battle being waged at the back of the store. The rescue effort was nearly completed before it was started. The rogue gang did not have the foresight to post a rear guard for such an event. Colonel Salazar was convinced that these were merely desperate people who had armed themselves, and not a truly organized force.

A few of the more desperate individuals made for the side doors to try and salvage what little of their existence still remained. Under normal conditions, Colonel Salazar would have allowed their retreat, but too much was at stake now. "Lieutenant Braverly, I do not want any prisoners," the colonel shouted over the finale of shots being fired.

Lieutenant Braverly, a slender man of Australian descent, saluted and motioned for his squad to peel off from the main assault. He had been a career soldier in the Australian Royal Guard and knew exactly what the colonel ordered him to do. He dispatched his men with not so much as a flicker of disobedience in his eyes.

Colonel Salazar had seen his fair share of bloodshed but had never come across someone with such a predisposition for warfare as Lieutenant Braverly. The man struck a chord of fear deep within Salazar's soul. It was something he couldn't quite grasp, but possibly stemmed from the man's penchant for cold and calculating precision. He seemed more robot than human, at times.

Colonel Salazar had known this man for something close to a year and, for the life of him, never remembered ever seeing the man crack a smile. The colonel watched in detachment as Lieutenant Braverly's men closed in on and dispatched the enemy, as if sweeping up a dirty floor. Lieutenant Braverly had hand-picked his men most likely because they, for the most part, matched his persona. Colonel Salazar thought these men might need some further investigation, but thus far, their record of accomplishment had been second to none.

"If it's not broken, don't fix it. That's what my dad used to say," the colonel muttered as he headed towards the back of the store where he hoped to find Colonel Wagner safe and sound. What the colonel saw, however, both shocked and amazed him. His good friend and one of his commander's best friends was lying in a pool of blood. You'd be hard pressed to call that a pool; it looked like a small pond. So much blood was lost, but he still saw Colonel Wagner attempt to move. Colonel Salazar was in momentary shock. There was no way somebody could lose that much blood and still be trying to hold on to life.

"Relax, Frank, it's not mine, at least not most of it," Dennis said as he sat up with great effort. His head was ringing like Big Ben. "Could you please stop letting flies land in your mouth and get over here and help me up?" Frank walked over, extending his hand, valiantly trying to retain a good footing on the slick, blood-stained tile. Dennis grabbed his helmet as Frank hefted him up. Both men gaped at the helmet wondering how anyone could survive from that bullet hole. The slug had entered the helmet dead square in the center of Dennis' forehead, but was deflected by the sturdy Kevlar armor. The bullet veered hard right instead and scraped the side of Dennis' skull. He bled out like a stuck pig but, beyond not getting haircuts for a while, he was no worse for the wear.

"You might just be the luckiest man on the planet, Dennis!" Frank said as he slapped Dennis on the shoulder. That rattled Dennis' brain almost more than the bullet. He winced some, but not enough to ruin Frank's exuberance.

"I don't know if losing almost all of my squad would fall under luck, Frank." Frank nodded and held his tongue for a respectful moment of silence before he spoke.

"Part of that might be true, Dennis, but you held your post against a force five times your size and they ambushed you."

"Well, I appreciate that, Frank, but now the matter becomes, why did they surprise us? There's no way that this many guys should have been able to just waltz on up here. I want to know where every listening post was assigned today and I want to know who was manning them," Dennis said. His heart was beginning to beat more rapidly at the thought of betrayal from within, and his heart's hammering did nothing to quell the throbbing in his head. Dennis paled for a moment and caught Frank's shoulder.

"I'll get that for you, Dennis, but right now I'm taking you to the infirmary."

"I wish I had the strength to tell you to go fuck yourself, but that sounds like a pretty good idea to me," Frank snorted as he put his arm around his comrade and walked him out. He made sure to make it look more like they were coming out as brothers-in-arms, instead of acting as a physical support, he felt that Dennis needed. He could tell Dennis' knees were wobbly at best, but still he threw on the brave front.

"Only you could be shot in the head and walk away from it," Frank said as he smiled.

"Well, I was always told there wasn't much in there anyway. I guess this just proves it. By the way, how did you guys get down here? I thought the tunnel wasn't going to be ready for another couple of weeks."

"We didn't use the tunnel." Dennis looked perplexed for a moment before the realization hit.

"Don't tell me you used the escape hatches? You and I both know that could jeopardize this whole operation."

"I let him know that; and we do have a contingency plan in effect as we speak."

"What is it?" Dennis queried.

"Don't worry about that now, we have more serious threats to our immediate safety."

"Such as?"

"We have reason to believe that the cave-in was deliberately orchestrated."

"Who would do that and why?"

"Probably the same person or persons who let our little rogue unit slip through the cracks."

"You mean you think we have saboteurs in our midst too?" Dennis asked.

"That would seem to be the case."

"Is it the National Guardsmen?"

"That would have been our first option; but we keep pretty good tabs on them and they are always assigned to our men when out on patrol or other such missions."

"Oh this is just beautiful! I lost my men here to some renegade within our ranks! That poor bastard had better hope that I'm not the one that finds him."

"Don't worry, Dennis; we'll flush him out eventually." Both men reflected on the word "eventually." Sure, odds were that they'd find the betrayer or betrayers, but would it be too late by then? Would whatever damage they intended to inflict already be done?

Chapter 32 – Mike Journal Entry Five

"Where am I!" I yelled. At least, I thought I yelled but what really came out was a small, shallow, dry rasp. Adrenaline surged in my veins as I struggled to recall where I was, but orientation was nearly impossible. I couldn't even see my hand in front of my face. I wasn't even sure if I had moved my hand to that position.

My brain was so addled and cloudy, the first thoughts that raced through my head were that I'd been on an all night bender with Paul. Whoa! His name sounded a small alarm in the back of my head; but why? Did he drink my last beer the night before? Why would I be mad at Paul? And then the queasiness hit; first my head, and then my stomach as I evacuated whatever was in there. I felt so hungry, how could I possibly throw something back up?

The clouds began to part in my head as I realized I was on the alien ship. I'd never gotten off it. This had been all some elaborate stress-induced dream! I was on the ship and there was nothing I could do, nor anybody to save me. I was going to be facing Durgan soon and he would finish off what little of me was left.

But I felt all right with myself and with God. I felt I had made peace with those who mattered most to me even if it were only in a dream. I said goodbye to my sister, my father, my brothers, Dennis and Paul.

"Bong!" There it went again. What the hell was that? Tiny electrical currents rippled through my brain as it racked itself, looking for the connection between my alarm and Paul's name. As the synopsis struck home, I was slapped with the brutal reality that my best friend had shot me… Shot me? Shot me!!!

"He shot me!" I rattled again. And then my brain transferred its thought from that staggering blow to the next. So where were we then? it asked, oh, so softly.

This was hell. This was my just reward for killing those people. How long was one relegated to purgatory?' Fear was my constant companion. Would I forever be alone and never again see the light? I meant that figuratively and literally. Was there emotion in hell? I guess there must be. What would be the purpose of pain and suffering if you didn't care? Would Lucifer himself address me? That thought terrified me more than facing the entire population of the alien ship with an air rifle. They could only kill you once; but Lucifer could do it for all eternity and in an infinite number of ways.

Was hell supposed to be cold? My back burned from the frozen surface that I was making contact with. Not having complete control over my extremities, I forcibly moved my hand to gain a sensory perspective on my surroundings. The surface was cool to the touch and damp.

Was their moisture in hell? Who knows? I scratched the surface of the material with my fingernail. I could feel a sliver of it work its way under my nail, but it wasn't a sharp pain like you would expect from a splinter. It was more like the aggravation you get when you are working on a car and grease gets under your nails. It was more of a mild irritation.

My head throbbed in pain but I was unsure whether or not I would be able to raise my hands high enough to rub my sore temples. Even with the iciness of the surface I was on, sweat began to break out all over my body as I struggled to regain control of my body. Did Paul paralyze me? Or blind me? Was anything I was doing now reality? Or was I trapped in my mind? Like a comatose patient, was I struggling in the dark to find my way back to reality? Yup, I was definitely back to the point where I wished that I was facing the aliens again. I didn't care if I had no more than a slingshot either.

My hand eventually found its way to my skull, where it encountered spiders. Oh God! Spiders! Spiders were crawling on my head and I didn't even have enough strength to wipe them away. They were eating me! I was trapped in a web and they were eating me! My body spastically jerked as a bolt of synaptic energy found its way to a nerve receptor in my shoulder. I was able to jerk one of the "spiders" away when I realized that perhaps it wasn't a spider at all.

I did not yet have enough control of my hand to grasp the new puzzle I was holding. Intuition told me that it was some sort of wire, a lead of some sort. Alright, so that effectively ruled out hell and/or purgatory. I didn't really think that the devil needed to monitor my brain waves.

That, however, steered me back into the direction of being back on the alien vessel. Did Paul shoot me, then deliver me to the aliens? Or did I sustain such grievous wounds in the arena that I was on some sort of life support? Could everything else just be a dream?' But I remembered the pain in my father's eyes when he told me about Mom. And I remembered the feeling when I left Beth and Debbie in Maine... That couldn't have been just a dream. And I could never forget my feelings about Paul when I realized he shot me.

The betrayal cut deeper than any enemy sword ever could. If he'd really shot me, there would have to be sensory proof. No matter how long I'd been lying here, there would have to be a scar. The question now became, would I be able to reach it? It would have been a difficult spot to touch even in the best of times and I was far from optimal at the moment.

Control of my body seemed to be coming back in spurts. I made a stab at rolling onto my side, but that was fairly ineffectual. What do turtles on their backs do? Oh yeah, they use their arms and legs to help topple them over. Neither leg seemed to be responding to the call for arms. Right now, I couldn't be sure if I had them or not. Would my right arm, which I was guessing I had about fifty percent control of, be strong enough to get me on my side?

My next big hurdle was to make sure that I didn't roll completely over onto my face, because I felt certain I did not have the strength to roll back over. My left leg began to twitch while I debated my rolling strategy. Energy was flooding back into my legs... Okay, maybe "flooding" was a bit of a stretch, but it was most assuredly trickling in, and right now, that was fine. Slowly but surely, I was reaffirming my humanity. The blindness was disturbing but if I was starting to feel my legs, maybe my sight wasn't too far behind.

I burned with the desire to find out the truth of my location. Control or not, I was going to find out, to the best of my ability, where I was. I placed my right hand to the side of me and pressed for all I was worth. My muscles squealed in protest; my shoulder popped like it was trying to snap through the rust of disuse.

And, like a rocket that just seems to hang there at lift-off, I was stuck; having raised my shoulder barely two inches. Then, like that rocket that finally gains enough momentum, I broke free. Everything gave at once and I almost did what I feared--rolling myself completely over. But, like the cavalry, my left hand came to the rescue and stabilized me, albeit precariously, on my side.

Now the question, became would I be able to reach where I presumed Paul shot me? And if so, would my less than tactile digits be able to discern a scar from the rest of me? Pain coursed through me as I attempted to reach Paul, the betrayer's, wound. Slowly, my hand inched its way to the hole, sweat pooling under my arms from the strain and pain.

Had this been the version of me two years ago, I would have just given up and let the chips fall where they may. But this was the new and improved Mike. I was version 2.0 now.

I gritted my teeth through the fire that flowed like lava in my veins. Centimeter by centimeter, I urged my hand forward, sheer determination winning out over the protests of my unused shoulder. My back popped as I strained to arch it in an attempt to help it meet my outstretched hand. But I finally struck home. My hand touched the spot where my best friend shot me, only there was nothing there, not so much as a pimple.

"What the hell!?" I mumbled. Without warning, lights blazed from all directions. Well, this is it, I thought to myself. I'm having an aneurism. I'm going to die after lapsing into a coma and having one of the most delusional nightmares ever conceived.

Only I didn't fade into black. My eyes hurt like hell while they tried to adjust to the searing white light. I couldn't be dead if my eyes still hurt, could I? I looked up from my precarious position to notice someone had entered the room. It was a Progerian. My lungs collapsed as I screamed and screamed myself back into oblivion, back to a place with no alien usurpers. Sweet, sweet bliss… I passed out.

"Mike, wake up." I sensed the voice from afar, along with a gentle nudging. "Come on, Mike. I know you can hear me." I searched the data banks of my mind to try and put a face or a name with the voice, but I kept coming up blank. I dared not open my eyes. My chest felt like it might heave right through my rib cage. I didn't want to open my eyes, I had no desire to know where I was. It was so much easier while I was asleep. Nothing was life or death in my dreams, it just was. I didn't have to save anyone and there were no best friends who shot you in the back, either.

"Mike! I know you're awake; I'm looking at your vitals."

Who was that? Maybe if I pretended long enough, she would just go away. She? Was she one of my "spoils?" If so, recognition was still not forthcoming. She shook me again although this time, not quite so gently. I guess she wasn't going to go away. I might as well see what form of purgatory I'm in now. I slowly opened my eyes, trying my best to gradually adjust to the fluorescent lighting that hung from the ceiling.

"Fluorescent lighting, huh?"

"What's that?" the mystery woman's voice asked.

"Fluorescent lighting," I said, more than a little perplexed.

"That's right, fluorescent lighting," she answered condescendingly, like an impatient adult would to a slow child.

"I guess I'm not on an alien vessel then?" I asked, half expecting her to say I was crazy, that there were no such things as aliens. I more than half hoped that would be what she answered. I was wrong.

She looked up at the lights, suddenly realizing my thought process. "No, Mike. You're not on a mother ship." My heart sank when I realized I wasn't going to be waking up from my nightmare any time soon.

"Where, am I?" My voice was gravelly. It felt like I had swallowed dirt and then tried to wash it down with cotton.

"Here have some water," the woman said as she tilted my head back; "and then I'll answer all of your questions, that I can."

What did she mean by that? I wondered as the cool water moved down my throat and into my belly. Does she mean what she knows? Or what she's allowed to tell me? "Alright," I said as I sat up on my, what, medical gurney? "Let's start with the basics, where am I?"

"Paris," she answered with a small smile on her face. She was probably amused at the shocked look on my mug. All of a sudden, the water wasn't sitting too well. Was it tainted?

"Paris? As in France?" I asked but I already knew the answer from her accent. It was the type of accent that let you know she could speak English well, but was too contemptuous to ever let her nationality slip.

"Actually Paris, as in the Bastille." I could tell she was loving this, watching my face drop even more.

"I'm in prison? For what?"

"Not technically prison, Mike. More of a sanctuary, if you will."

"Can I leave this sanctuary?" But I, once again, already knew the answer to this question too.

"Not yet." She said. I must be psychic.

"Alright, I could probably ask you a thousand questions and get a thousand one word answers and still be no closer to what is going on. Is there any chance you, or possibly your superior, could come in here and give me the Readers Digest version of what is going on here?"

"Readers Digest?"

Now it was my turn to act like the impatient adult talking to a slow child, and I don't think that she liked the turn-around. "You know, the condensed version."

"Mike, try to stay calm." I blinked once because I heard the words but they weren't coming from this lady's mouth. Then I looked over my left shoulder to see the video camera and speaker box from which the voice was emanating.

"I'd be a whole lot calmer if I knew what was going on!" I screamed, ripping off all of the leads that were attached to my body, including the IV that was in the back of my hand. Blood splattered everywhere from the violent withdrawal of the needle.

"Stay still, Mike," the woman beside me beckoned as she tentatively reached out to restrain me. "Or you are going to pull out your sutures."

"I knew it! He did shoot me! Where are the sutures?" The woman looked helplessly at the video monitor, desperately looking for assistance. It was then that the door on the far end of the room opened up.

"In your head," the man said as he walked into the room, holding what appeared to be a large needle.

"Listen, Doc, you come any closer with that thing and I'm going to take it from you and stick it right into your Adam's apple!" He must have seen something in my eyes that told him this was the truth, because he stopped dead in his tracks.

"It's a mild sedative," he gestured as he pointed to the bottle that the syringe was imbedded in.

"Listen, Doc, first off, I don't read French. Secondly, I don't care if it's Labatts beer in that thing, you come any closer and, I promise, you'll regret it." I kept my eyes on him as I attempted to stand up for the first time in…! I had no clue how long. But my legs did; they buckled the second I put any pressure on them. Luckily, my arms held out as I caught the edge of the gurney. The nurse? At least, that's what I figured she was, tried to help me get back into the bed but I shrugged her off.

"Listen," I glared at her, "it's been a long time since a woman has touched me. If you do it again though, you are liable to get a broken finger or hand."

She snorted. "Theze Americanz! They all theenk that they are Rambo!" I thought it was funny that her grasp on English slipped when she got upset. I chuckled a little, but the doc didn't see the humor. If anything, it looked like he was going to back out of that room and run. I must have been a sight: all bug-eyed with blood covering the front of me, half grinning and holding onto the bed. I'm not sure I could have done much more than raise my arm in protest if he had approached me. But it didn't matter; he wasn't coming any closer anyway.

"You are in the Bastille," he said as he exaggeratedly laid the syringe down on a table near the entrance to the room.

"Yeah, I got that much," I replied.

"May I approach?" he asked as he splayed his hands open to show that he had nothing hidden. I nodded my ascent and attempted to stand myself upright, to give him the impression that a butterfly landing on my shoulder wouldn't knock me over.

"The Bastille hospital. You are in the Bastille hospital."

"Because Paul shot me." Even as mad and scared as I

was, the hurt still bled through my eyes, and the doctor must have seen it.

"Yes, Paul shot you, but not for the reasons you believe or even in the manner that you believe."

"Huh?" was all I could muster. Did this frog slip into French 'cause I couldn't, for the life of me, understand what he was saying? "In English," I said and I didn't even mean it as a cliché.

"It was a dart gun, Mike. It was a tranquilizer. He used probably a little more than he needed, but he didn't try to kill you." I now thought back to that day and I remembered marveling, at the time, how quiet the bullet that finally does you in could sound. Most people who had ever been shot during war said they never heard the one that hit them.

"Then why?" I bemoaned; the stress on my legs and arms was beginning to take its toll.

"You were a spy," he answered straightforwardly. That was it. My body gave out and I crumpled to the ground like a Coke can under the weight of a large boot. The doctor and the nurse both rushed forward, only this time I didn't care. It was tough to maintain your dignity while licking the linoleum floor.

After some agonizing moments, we were all able to wrestle my body back into the bed. By that time, I actually hoped maybe he would give me that shot after all. It sure would beat the alternative of staying awake and having to wrap my mind around being a spy. But the shot was not forthcoming, at least not in the foreseeable future anyway. The doctor anxiously took my pulse as his nurse examined my body for any possible fractures.

"I'm fine," I said as I tried in vain to shoo them off me. "What do you mean I was a spy? Am I not anymore?"

"No, not anymore," he said in exasperation. Then he tried to, once again, get the pulse count I had interrupted. When he was done, he elaborated without any prodding.

"When you came back from that ship, you brought

extra baggage." Bewilderment spread across my face.

"Baggage?"

"You were bugged."

"Bugged?"

"Listen! If you're going to interrupt me every time I finish a sentence, we're never going to get out of here, and I won't be able to go home to my wife."

"Alright, I'm sorry. I'll wait 'til you finish."

"The aliens had pretty much tuned into you." I was about to ask another question when the doctor held up his finger. I halted, mid-breath. "They had attachments to your optic nerve and your eardrum, but the kicker was the homing signal. They had that one buried in your spine. We weren't sure that we would be able to operate on it without crippling you." I couldn't resist; I had to interrupt him.

"Is that why my legs don't work so good?" Instead of getting perturbed, he let out a small chortle.

"Oh, heavens no. We never even operated on your spine." The doctor saw my look of terror. "Relax, relax. We neutralized the signal; they can't track you anymore."

"How? Alright, no more interruptions, I promise."

"We realized that there could be no way to remove the device without damaging the host; the host being you, of course, so we had to come up with an alternate plan. We shook the little bugger to death, we compartmentalized a high intensity beam of sonic waves and literally blew the thing into a million little pieces. Most of which have already passed through your system. There was some damage to the tissue immediately surrounding the device but it's nothing that a little time, therapy, and cortisone won't cure.

"We couldn't, however, take the same measures with your eyes and ears. We were afraid that any type of explosion in your head would cause an embolism. Or, at the very least, permanent loss of eyesight and/or hearing.

"For those, we had to operate in a more traditional manner. They were tricky to remove because they were of an organic nature. As opposed to being a foreign object, your body accepted these devices as part of itself and did nothing to reject it.

"We've been studying this new technology for weeks. It's fascinating. It seems that the material is organic but is neither alive nor inanimate."

The doctor looked over at me, realizing that this was not the tangent I was hoping to travel down. He abruptly stopped his diatribe. I noticed that he let go of the string a bit hesitantly and I can't say I blame him. He was exploring a brand new form of technology and it wasn't even from this world. Scientists could spend their whole lives searching for something one tenth of this magnitude, and this guy had it dropped in his lap.

"Have those senses been hindered in any way?" I asked, somewhat concerned.

"No, if anything, they've been enhanced. Apparently, the aliens didn't want poor reception on their hosts, so these little 'bugs' actually fixed any inherent flaws that most humans have in their eyes and ears. Can you imagine what this could do for the medical community? We could cure blindness and deafness in the world forever."

"Yeah, I'll have to thank the Progerians the next time I see them."

"Um hmm." The doctor cleared his throat, just now possibly realizing where this "wonderful" technology had come from.

"How long have I been down and out?" I asked as I lay back down.

"Close to two weeks," the doctor answered almost absently, still thinking of the applications that could arise from this new device. He was even daydreaming about what he would say when he accepted the Nobel Prize for medicine.

"Two weeks?!" I bolted back up. "It took two weeks to get rid of those things? How have we not been discovered?"

"No, it took about ten hours to get the 'bugs' out of you. The rest was either your transit here or your post op recovery."

"Transit? Speaking of which, why was I shipped across the ocean for this operation? You can't tell me that there wasn't somebody stateside who couldn't have taken care of my situation," I said, exasperated. The doctor looked a little perturbed.

"I am one of the top surgeons in the field. I have a vast knowledge of the entire human body. I have virtually operated on every major organ with, I might add, unparalleled success."

"Alright! Alright already! I'm sorry I asked." The doctor seemed to relax a bit, letting some of his defensive posture slough away.

"Besides, I don't think Paul likes France much. He figured if they leveled this whole country looking for you, who would care?" He said it so absently, I wasn't sure if he was pulling my leg or not. I let discretion win out and decided I would have a long laugh about this one later when nobody was around.

"Doc, how long am I going to feel like a sick kitten? If you had so much as blown hard on me, I would have fallen over."

"Well, it truly is amazing that you were able to stand at all. I had about three to four weeks pegged for your recovery time, but you just might halve that."

"Doc! I can't be shelved for another two weeks! I've got to get back to Paul, to the Marines, to everybody." Everybody being who? Deb? Beth? Even now I wasn't sure.

"Mike, I'm glad you're lying down for what I am about to tell you." The grave look on his face had me concerned. Had my father died? I wasn't so sure I could take that news right now. But what he told me far outweighed any losses I may have suffered.

The planet as I knew it was gone. Chaos ruled and it didn't appear that it was going away anytime soon.

The severity and scope of the event was too much for me to grasp. I had to bring it down on a much smaller level and then the true pain settled over me like a death shroud. My concern for my family, friends, Deb and Beth made it a constant struggle just to breathe correctly. I felt like bands of steel had been fastened around my chest and were, ever so slightly, constricting.

"Did Paul make it off the mountain?" It was all I could think to ask, that he might possibly have some answers.

"He did, but barely. He wanted to give you some information that he thought would be useful to you, when you were ready."

"Am I ready? 'Cause if you have some more bad stuff for me, Doc, I'm liable to just go in the corner and cover up."

"I'll be honest, Mike, I have absolutely no clue what it means, but he said you'd understand."

"Lay it on me," I waited in anticipation.

"He said he was sorry for the shot and hoped that it hadn't hurt too much and that the Hobbit Tree awaits your triumphant return." The doctor noticed the shine in my eyes. "Apparently, that's good news?"

"Fuckin' A! Right! That son of a bitch did it!" I yelled.

"Did what, Mike?" the doc said with a quizzical expression.

"Doc, as the old cliché goes, I could tell you, but then I'd have to kill you."

"What does that mean? I've never heard that cliché before."

"Doc, you've given me a ton of news, the vast majority bad, but you laced it with some silver flocking and I just kind of want to hash it over for awhile." The doctor understood he wasn't going to get any answers and began to rise with almost a pouty expression.

"Besides, Doc, I'm dead tired. All the excitement of the day has kind of worn me out." That was an answer he could live with, and it almost seemed to wipe the pout off his face. "And doc?" The doctor turned, his lower lip still jutting out, just a tad. "I just wanted to say thank you for everything

215

you did for me." The lip retracted and the doctor seemed to gain a small hop in his step as he sauntered out.

Great, I thought to myself, I just had a grown kid with sharp tools operate on my head. And even though I wanted to sit and think through everything the doctor had told me, I fell asleep. I fell asleep to a world full of Hobbit trees. At first, I was apprehensive. If there were this many trees, how would I ever find the one I was looking for?

"Hello there, my friend." I turned, in my dream, to see a young version of Paul leaning against a tree, baseball glove in one hand and what was he tossing up in the air? A grenade? I steadily walked toward him. At least, my legs were working correctly here. Paul smiled that sly grin I'd come to know so well during college. Usually, it meant he was up to something, not necessarily for the benefit of mankind. Or he was about to bag Susie something or other. I couldn't wait to just go over and give him a huge hug or maybe a punch; I wasn't sure just yet. I noticed Paul toss the grenade up into the air with his right hand.

He let his left hand stay where it was, almost in a cradling position with the glove and, like the athlete he was, he knew he'd catch it. But a glint of something caught my eye as the grenade started its downward plunge. What was that? It looked like a pin.

"Paul! The pin!" I tried to run, but my legs failed me miserably. Paul just sat there, still looking at me with that devil-may-care grin. The grenade/ball landed in his glove just like we both knew it would. And for a horrible second, nothing happened.

I couldn't move and Paul wouldn't. And then everything went white as I watched the grenade detonate. Paul was literally cut in half, I could feel the heat from the shrapnel as it blazed by. Blood was everywhere; the Hobbit Tree was covered with it. It seemed that the tree itself had suffered grievous wounds. Now the world was pitching, no, it was the tree, it began to creak and moan its protests. I watched as it slowly began to fall over. It started to gain momentum and then came to a thunderous crash which momentarily lifted me off my feet. The demise of the tree hurt me on so many levels, I wasn't sure where to begin. But my dream self wasn't ready to let me off the hook quite yet.

"Mike! Help me! Help me!" It was Paul, but we weren't by the tree anymore, he was in my car, stuck, like he was the first time. The only difference was that I couldn't move. I pulled at my legs with my arms, but nothing happened. The little man who controls those buttons had quit moments earlier. The request was in, there just wasn't anybody to punch the card. So I stood there helplessly as I watched my best friend slowly burn.

He screamed repeatedly at me, "Why won't you help me? Please don't let me burn!" I could do nothing. I couldn't even lift my arms to wipe away the tears that were free-flowing from my eyes. He stretched out his hand and I began to scream for all I was worth. Black flesh dangled off his arm, sizzling like pan-fried bacon. I screamed as I watched my friend melt. I screamed and then what? Fell asleep? I don't know. Everything just stopped happening and the world went black. Was I awake and the lights were out? Or were they on and I was blind, courtesy of Doctor Dooday?

"Where am I?" I yelled. No echo, so I sure wasn't in my room. As my eyes adjusted, I was able to distinguish small pinholes of lights. There were dozens, no hundreds, millions and they were all around me. They were stars, so now I must be floating out in space. Whatever the doc gave me, I'm going to have to remember to ask for more. I was really starting to enjoy this little mind journey when a small, disconcerted feeling began to form in my belly.

It was then that I noted that some of the stars were beginning to blot out. Suddenly, I began to hurtle through space. I'm not a scientist but I'm pretty sure I was approaching the speed of light, and yet the star-blotting effect was getting larger and still larger, in pace with the churning in my stomach. The object in front of me began to take shape. My view, including peripherally, was completely engulfed. It was the mother ship.

I awoke, purging nearly everything in my system. I fell off the hospital bed from the convulsions. Blood began to spew through my fingers as I attempted to stem the tide. Alarms were going off in my head. Nope, I thought, as I watched tissue worm its way through my interlaced fingers. Those alarms were coming from the machines hooked up to me. People came rushing from what seemed like all directions, but that could possibly be because I was spinning down, towards the ground. Hands grabbed me from everywhere.

I remembered hearing something about "blue carts and crashing" but those things seemed so distant, so foreign. I began to drift slowly. I arose, looking down at the throng of people. I was trying my best to figure out what all the hubbub was about but, to be honest, it didn't really seem all that important anymore.

Blood was everywhere; I knew that wasn't a good sign, and I felt a small pang of pity for the person who had spilled it. But that truly was the most emotion I could muster. The weight of the world was literally being torn and shredded from my shoulders. And it felt great, no, not great, magnificent, stupendous, miraculous! I didn't have a care in the world. But the world of the living wasn't quite through with me yet. My physical body still had a say, albeit a short one, from the looks of things.

"What about Deb and Beth?" The slab of meat down there suddenly brought up.

"Who?" And honestly, for a tenth of a second, I didn't have the slightest clue who they were nor who had spoken.

"Deb and Beth!" That thing down there tried to yell the last part but I could tell that it was losing the struggle because the yell was barely above a whisper pitch. But the whisper struck home. A distant thought started to form and take shape. but I wasn't thinking it. Then I saw them in all their grace and beauty. Were they angels?

"Deb and Beth," the pink thing on the floor rattled off. And then the angels grabbed me. Sweet grace of God! I was off to heaven and eternal bliss. Their grip was severe, how could an ethereal being feel pain? What were they squeezing? And why aren't we going up?

They were pulling me down, I tried to kick their hands away, but, unlike them, I could find no purchase, their arms would dissolve as I passed through them. "This isn't fair. I'm done! Let me be done!" I protested, but they just smiled their angelic smiles and continued to drag me down, closer and closer to that THING that lay on the floor. I redoubled my efforts. "No! I don't want to touch that thing. That's not me! This is me!' I was pleading to die. How often does that happen?

I began to feel the pull from the body, from my body, like a magnet I was being drawn into it. Deb and Beth had finally released their grasp, but it was no use. It was like trying to pull away from a black hole, it wasn't gonna happen.

"Doctor!" an excited nurse yelled. "We've got a pulse!"

"Quick! Get him on the gurney," Doctor Dooday said calmly. Wow, I noted as the last vestiges of my spiritual being returned. He sure doesn't act like a kid when he's under the gun.

"Get him up to the O.R. We've got to get blood into him; he's lost too much. Way too much", the doctor said as he looked around the floor of the room. "You don't lose this much blood supply and keep on living. What is driving this kid on?"

"Doctor?" the excited nurse looked up.

"Nothing, nothing. Get this kid going!" The doctor lost a little composure. He wasn't prone to believing in miracles, but even he knew enough to recognize one when he saw it. And he wasn't about to just let it slip through his fingers.

Chapter 33 - Massachusetts Line – Mass Pike

Deb had been driving for about two hours, now cruising at a comfortable seventy-five miles per hour. She was amazed at how little traffic there was; especially as she began to cross over the New York line. It was almost as if people were avoiding this highway, she thought to herself. Sure, traffic had been light almost their entire trip but now it was almost eerie. Then, the reason why became evidently clear as she crested a rise. Down the slope of the highway, no more than a quarter of a mile away, was a roadblock It appeared to be a military checkpoint with at least two tanks and a five-ton troop transport.

"Uh, Beth? You might want to wake up for this one," Deb said as she nudged her companion. Beth stirred and awoke relatively fast. She had barely fallen asleep more than ten minutes before.

"What's up?" were her only words as she wiped her eyes. Deb had brought the car to a near standstill in the middle of the roadway.

A huge lit-up construction sign glowed to their left: **Massachusetts is in a state of emergency. All personnel not on official military business will be detained and their property seized. Proceed Forward Cautiously!**

"What now, Beth?" Deb asked with the slightest bit of panic interlaced in her voice.

"Well, we can't just sit in the middle of the road. They'll either get suspicious and shoot at us, or somebody is going to plow into the back of us. Either way, we're in a world of hurt."

"What about turning around?"

"That would be a great idea, except for the median divider."

"Dammit!" Deb said as she slammed her fist down on

the steering wheel and then placed her head on it.

"One of the Jeeps is moving, Deb. It's coming towards us," Beth said as she pushed on Deb's shoulder to get her head up off the wheel.

"Beth, get the guns ready."

"Deb, you think that's such a good idea?"

"Right now, I don't think anything is a good idea, but we have no way of knowing if these guys are military at all. Maybe they ransacked a military post or maybe they are just a rogue unit acting on their own. But you and I both know the military, as we once knew it, no longer exists. So, best case scenario, is that they are a National Guard unit that still adheres to their credo. But I'd still like to be prepared."

"I sure hope they don't know how to use that tank," Beth said, more under her breath as she reached around to the back of the cab and pulled out a .357 Smith and Wesson revolver for Deb. She grabbed the Remington 30-06. She hated the kick it gave but right now, it was all about making a statement. She wasn't going to give up without a fight. The Jeep approached cautiously; the gunner manned at his mounted machine gun was expecting the worst.

"Do you think they're scared?." Deb asked to no one in particular.

"As scared as us?" Beth replied as Deb gave her a sideways glance. Beth began to heft the rifle up in preparation to put the muzzle out of the window.

"Beth, I wouldn't do that. As soon as he sees that barrel, he's likely to fire. And scared or not, with that many rounds coming in our direction, we'd be sitting ducks."

"Deb, spin this around and let's get out of here!"

The Jeep was about three hundred yards away when Deb made her choice. She threw the truck in reverse and let the tires squeal as she began to back up. Beth was caught unawares by the blue smoke that rose from one of the tanks. She had little time to wonder what it meant as she watched a dozen or so trees splinter into toothpicks not more than fifty yards to their left.

"I guess that answers the question as to whether or not they know how to use the tanks! I would imagine that was their version of a warning shot!" Beth said excitedly. Deb's driving had been something less than perfect and going backwards was not improving her skills. The Jeep was rapidly making progress; it was a mere hundred yards away now.

"Deb, you should probably turn this thing around!" Beth yelled as she watched the gunner cock back on his weapon. "Uh, now! Deb! Please!"

"Stop screaming at me!" Deb yelled as the muscles in her neck began to throb from the quandary they were in. Deb wanted more than anything to spin the truck around like she had seen in so many action movies, but she was afraid she would, more than likely, lay the top-heavy truck on its side, or worse yet, flip it over completely. Neither she nor Beth were wearing their seatbelts and they'd be flung out the doors like rag dolls.

But this wasn't going to work either; the Jeep would be up on them in moments. The tank fired once more but this shot was well clear, more likely so they wouldn't suffer any friendly fire casualties as opposed to not knowing how to aim the mighty gun.

"Beth, put my seatbelt on and then get yours on!" Deb screamed over the fracturing of trees. Beth looked like she had been slapped, stunned and red-faced. "Now Beth!" That got Beth moving. She reached over Deb's waist and fumbled with the shoulder harness. Trying desperately to put slot A in receptacle B.

"Hurry Beth!"

"I am hurrying!" Beth yelled as she desperately tried to make the two ends meet amidst the bouncing and swerving of the truck. "Click!" the audible noise was unmistakable, Deb was harnessed in.

"Now you, Beth. Move!" Beth had much more ease getting her belt on in this more familiar fashion.

"Are you ready!"

"Ready for what, Beth?"

Their Dodge Ram had just climbed over the hill as Deb slammed on the brakes. The tires howled in protest. Beth nearly suffered whiplash from the severity of the stop. As it was, she knew she was going to be sore for days to come. Deb threw the truck into drive without completely coming to a stop. The transmission made an audible clunking as it did what it was told, but not without severe complaining.

"Deb, what are you doing?" Beth said as she grabbed hold of the dashboard. The truck first inched over the hill and then began to gain momentum. All of the passengers in the Jeep had been caught unawares as the bigger Dodge truck now began to descend upon them and fast.

The driver reacted instinctually as he slammed on the brakes with both feet. The gunner also did what was instinctual and opened fire. The first few rounds came dangerously close to the front end of the girls' truck, but then the laws of gravity began to take hold. As the nose of the Jeep descended from the inertia of the brakes, so also did the barrel of the M-60 mounted on it.

The gunner's fingers were completely squeezed on the trigger and, as he held on for his life, he was unable to let go as the barrel fell even more, cutting into the front end of the Jeep. First the radiator popped with an audible swish. Then the fan was next to go as bullets blazed through the blades. The engine block came next as hot lead split the head. Piston parts shot up through the hood almost as hard as the bullets had slammed down.

The gunner most likely would have put a bullet or two through the dashboard if he himself hadn't been knocked against the gunstock and rendered dazed and confused. Blood trickled from his left ear. The Jeep came to an abrupt stop as the disc brakes and the bullets finally did their job. Hisses and pops were all that could be heard through the ensuing silence as the Jeep's engine died out.

"Deb, did you plan this!" an excited Beth said as she positioned the barrel of her gun out the window.

"Hell no! I was planning to ram them." Beth looked over at Deb to see if she was telling the truth or not. It appeared she was, Beth thanked her lucky stars it had turned out this way. Deb brought the truck to a stop not more than two feet from the destroyed grill of the Jeep.

Deb stepped out of the truck and rapidly approached the passenger as she saw him attempting to gain access to something around his shoulder. It had to be a gun, but the still stunned soldier was having a difficult time undoing the snaps. His seatbelt, which restrained him was also restraining the weapon. The precious few seconds he needed to process this information, however, were not his for the taking. Deb ran right up to the passenger side.

"Put your hands on the dashboard now!" she screamed. At first, neither man moved but when Deb cocked the trigger, they both acquiesced. Beth ran out to join her friend, loosely aiming the rifle at the driver.

"Deb, it looks like we're going to have company soon." Beth motioned to the roadblock. Two troop transport trucks were now on their way and most likely, filled to the hilt with armed personnel.

"Call them off!" Deb screamed. Neither man moved. Deb put the gun up against the temple of the man closest to her. "Listen, Mister, we might die in the next few minutes, but if you don't call them off you're going to die in the next few seconds." That was more than enough incentive for the lieutenant.

"Sergeant, get on the horn and call those trucks off, now!" he shouted as if he needed to reiterate. The sergeant noted that on his side, the woman had leveled the large bore weapon right on his face. He didn't need urging from anybody to call those trucks off.

"Fortress One, Fortress One, this is Interceptor Three. I say again, this is Interceptor Three."

"Go ahead, Interceptor Three, this is Fortress One."

"Call off the dogs, Fortress One. I say again, call off the dogs."

"Interceptor Three, dogs one and two are coming to your aid," the voice crackled over the airwaves.

"Fortress One, if dogs one and two come any closer, they will only have mop-up duty. I say again, call off the dogs!" the sergeant said with some edge to his voice. The trucks were getting dangerously close and these women looked scared. Scared led to unpredictable, and the sergeant wasn't having anything unpredictable today. The sergeant watched in the rear view mirror as the trucks first slowed and then came to a complete stop, not more than two hundred yards away from them. Men began to pour out of the trucks. Not advancing, but definitely taking an aggressive posture.

"Sergeant O'Bannon," Deb said as she looked at the sergeant's nameplate. "Get on the radio and get those trucks out of here!" Deb yelled, panic beginning to rise up in her throat.

"They won't listen to me. You got them to stop; they won't retreat," the sergeant muttered back. He wished, like his best friend, Barry Watson, that he left his unit when their captain said "Any men who want to be with their families in this time of need, will be granted full immunity. And let no man or woman here think any less of that person if they should decide to go."

Barry was one of three who decided to turn in their gear to be with their respective families. Most of the men had called them cowards and deserters, Barry had been near to tears over leaving this extended family to protect what was left of his immediate family. Barry's wife Amelia, and daughter, Andrea, had been shopping in downtown Boston for Andrea's seventeenth birthday, when the first wave of alien attacks had struck. Barry was left with a fourteen-year-old son and a seven-year-old girl who still had not spoken a word since that fateful day.

At the time, he felt that Barry was betraying his country and worse, his unit, by leaving. He knew that Barry had no one to care for his kids but that didn't make it any easier on him. Now with a 30-06 pointed at his head, he wondered if he had done the right thing. His family was still intact, but how would they survive if he died today? His boy was only eight and although he was of hardy stock, he was still only eight. His wife, Meg and son were with his mother and father since the invasion had started. He was going to die today and for what? Border patrol? Brilliant!

"Sergeant! Get those men back on the truck!" Deb screamed in near hysterics. The sergeant looked at his captors for the first time with clear eyes. They were only kids themselves, not some desperados. How hard of a journey have they had? Two women alone in this brave new frontier, and all the way from where? Colorado! he thought as he scanned the license plate on the front of the truck.

"Girls, they are not going to leave and right now you are both being painted by snipers."

"Girls!" the Sergeant shouted. "Get us out of the Jeep and use us as shields."

"Sergeant!" the lieutenant nearly shrieked. "I'll have your stripes for this!"

"You can have them if we get out of here. I'm through," the sergeant replied, almost casually.

"Get up, lieutenant," Deb motioned with her gun. The sergeant didn't need prodding, he got up and walked straight in front of Beth.

***

"Sir, I've lost target B. I say again, I've lost target B."

"Sir, target A is still hot, target A is still hot. Should I paint the target sir?"

"No, repeat no, do not fire until both targets are reacquired, then fire at will. If we only take one out, the other will surely waste my men and I won't let that happen." The Captain said.

"What about him, Deb?" Beth asked as she pointed back at the gunner who was still lying on the back seat.

"Oh, I don't think he'll be too much trouble before this thing is over with." Deb answered.

"Move, Lieutenant!" Deb yelled as she suddenly felt

herself entirely too exposed on the pavement. A chill ran right up the center of her spine along with her grandmother's voice. "That's the dead, come to visit dearie." And that had always scared the bejesus out of Deb from the time she was six.

***

"Sir, they are retreating to the back of the pickup truck," the sniper's spotter relayed.

"Do you have a shot?" the captain inquired.

"Sir, target A is still hot. But target B well…"

"What is it, Perkins?"

"Well sir, it's almost like the sergeant is intentionally getting in the way."

"Come again?"

"Sir, he has to realize that we have a bead on these assailants, but he has completely cut off any shot." The captain couldn't, for the life of him, figure out why the sergeant was protecting his assailants, but he must have had a good reason. The captain got back on the radio.

"Recons One and Two, I want you to stand down from my previous order. Keep the targets acquired but do not, I say again, do not fire unless directly ordered, do you copy?"

"This is Recon One, we copy five by five."

"This is Recon Two we also copy five by five." Thank the gods, the spotter thought to himself. He wasn't even sure if he could shoot a madman threatening babies, much less two young females.

***

"So what now, girls? How long do you think they are going to let you hold us hostage? They'll just wait until nightfall and put on their night-vision goggles; what then? You won't even know which way it's coming from," the lieutenant sneered. Deb's "Rambo" impression was beginning to erode through. She actually had no idea what they should do now. The sergeant looked over at the lieutenant and just shook his head.

"Boot," he muttered under his breath.

"Did you say something, Sergeant?" the lieutenant asked as he looked over. "If it weren't for you, Sergeant O'Bannon, this whole unpleasant mess would already be over."

"And what, sir? We'd have two dead young women on our hands? Would you be satisfied then? Would that make you a war hero?" The lieutenant looked like he wanted to say something, but he didn't want to give the sergeant the satisfaction.

"What's the plan, Deb?" Beth asked cautiously. She was afraid that Deb just might take off screaming into the woods, because she was beginning to get that "deer in the headlights" stare.

"I…I don't know, Beth. We can't all fit in the cab of the truck and if we try to take off without hostages, that tank is sure to open fire."

"Yeah, and that tank commander is one of the best shooters in the tri-state region," the lieutenant interjected.

"Give it a rest, lieutenant," the sergeant said forcefully. "Girls, I'd say to take me hostage and let the lieutenant go, but I'm afraid he'd have them open fire on all of us."

"Damn right," the lieutenant snarled.

"That means you're going to have to take the lieutenant."

"Wha…what?! You can't be serious? I'll have you court-martialed for this!" the lieutenant protested.

"He's right, Deb. We'll put our friend, the lieutenant, in between us and we'll top the hill and drop him off, out of the tank's range or at least, sight."

"And I'll delay any pursuit. I'll tell the captain that if you saw anybody chasing you, that you were going to kill the lieutenant," the sergeant said. The lieutenant looked over at the sergeant, pure hatred in his eyes.

"You know, when I get back, my report of the unfolding of events is going to be a lot different from yours,

Sergeant."

"What makes you think you're coming back?" Beth threw in. The lieutenant couldn't tell from her tone if she meant it or not and at this point in time, he had no desire to try her.

"Alright, that's the plan. We'll take the lieutenant," Deb said, as she motioned to the cab of the truck with her gun.

***

"Sir, this is Recon One. The lieutenant is getting into the truck. I repeat, the lieutenant is getting into the truck."

"Crap," the captain muttered. This was going from a hostage situation to a kidnapping. He couldn't let them go; what would he tell their families?

"Recons One and Two, do you have a shot?" the captain asked, not really sure which answer he was hoping for.

"Sir, this is Recon One. Target is hot."

"Sir, Recon Two. Target is a no go; say again, target is a no go." Just then, four strange and very related things happened almost simultaneously. The captain lost a little of his military bearing and swore while still holding down the talk button on his radio.

"Dammit!" the captain yelled. Recon Force One, spotter Corporal Eddington, already hopped up on adrenaline, thought he heard the order to fire and relayed that to his sniper, Corporal Harris. Corporal Harris had a beautiful shot, dead center chest, just like he was trained to do.

And then the third event unfolded, the lieutenant, upon opening the door to the truck, had unwittingly sun-blinded the sniper with the truck's side view mirror just as Corporal Harris was pulling the trigger. His rifle moved only a fraction of an inch, but now his shot went from a confirmed kill to a shoulder wound.

Deb spun from the force of the lead smashing into her shoulder. Her hand spasmed around the grip of her pistol, sending one round through the truck's windshield and right between the lieutenant's eyes.

"Get down, the both of you!" the sergeant shouted as Beth could only look on in horror at where Deb's bullet had flown. Deb was cussing and screaming from the fire burning in her shoulder. The sergeant scrambled over to her and pulled her down to the ground with her good arm. Blood flowed down her wounded arm in rivulets. Beth sort of slumped down on the front grill, still in shock. Sergeant O'Bannon was busy taking off Deb's jacket trying to staunch the flow of blood from her arm.

"What happened?!" the captain yelled into the radio.

"Sir, this is Recon One. We have a confirmed hit, say again, confirmed hit!" the corporal said excitedly.

"Listen, you little piss-ant! I never gave the order to fire!" the captain yelled, sending the corporal's elation plummeting.

"But... but sir, I heard the order," the corporal swallowed hard.

"I gave no such order! You had better hope that neither of our men are hurt, Corporal, or I'm going to make you personally responsible. I'm going to make you tell their families that your screw-up cost them their husbands' and daddies' lives!"

The corporal could think of no worse fate. He knew both of those men's families; he had eaten dinner at both of their houses on more than one occasion. He even played with all the kids. There was no way he could do what the captain had threatened. The corporal threw off his headset and stood up, as he pulled his Colt .45 out of his holster and began to run towards the truck.

"Sir! This is Corporal Eddington. Corporal Harris has taken off towards the truck."

"I can see that, Corporal! I want you to stop him now!"

"How sir? I'm not going to shoot him."

"Get up and tackle him if you have to."

"Sir, you know about Corporal Harris."

The captain knew alright. Corporal Harris was the fastest man in their unit, in the whole region. Twice a year, the various National Guard units got together and put on their version of the Olympics. Mostly, it was an excuse to get away from their spouses and drink a little, but it was also for pride of unit. Corporal Harris had proven three times over that he was the fastest hundred-meter, two-hundred-meter and six-hundred-meter runner for two years and counting.

Corporal Harris was halving the distance to the truck while the sergeant was trying to decide how critical a hit Deb's shoulder had taken. The noise around the truck was deafeningly quiet. Deb's curses had died down to small whimpers as the beginnings of shock began to take over. Beth stared, glassy-eyed into space. The vision of the lieutenant's brains splattered all over the front of the truck was a sight she didn't think that she'd forget any time soon.

The sergeant was applying pressure to Deb's wound when he heard the unmistakable sound of combat boots on pavement. The thunk-thunk-thunking was coming, and coming fast. How many of them were there? the sergeant thought. They'll never give these girls a chance. They'll see the dead lieutenant and want revenge. What am I about to get myself into?

The sergeant grabbed the rifle out of Beth's hands. She didn't protest in the least. On the contrary, she seemed relieved to let the thing go. The sergeant moved over to the passenger side door of the truck and rested the barrel of the 30-06 on it.

"God forgive me," the sergeant spoke before he pulled the trigger and watched as his shot hit true. Corporal Harris went down with a shot to his thigh. His femur was neatly cut in two from the force of the shot. His running days were over.

And if he ever got to live out a long and fruitful life, he would complain about the pain in his right leg every time the weather was about to change. Corporal Eddington had been in pursuit of his friend when he saw the sergeant take aim and his friend go down. Eddington fell to the pavement almost as fast as his friend.

He stayed in prone position, almost frozen with fear. But Harris was his friend and he'd be damned if he remained there and let him bleed out. Harris was howling in rage and pain, his leg splayed out before him in grotesque form. Eddington rose up and began to lumber over to his friend.

Sergeant O'Bannon once again took aim, but the corporal didn't seem concerned in the least about him. Eddington grabbed Harris and hefted him up onto his shoulders in the familiar fireman rescue maneuver. Eddington stared at the sergeant for a split second that seemed to stretch for all eternity. The sergeant watched everything he valued go flushing down the drain. Sergeant O'Bannon thought for a millisecond about killing them both and destroying any witnesses but he dismissed that thought almost as quickly as he thought it. It did, however, disturb him that the thought had even arisen from the deepest, darkest corners of his mind.

Sergeant O'Bannon knew that they didn't have much time; as soon as Corporal Eddington got back to the troop transports and got his wind, his unit would come at them full on. Sergeant O'Bannon had crossed the line and he would be dealt with as swiftly as these girls.

"Time to roll! Let's go girls!" the sergeant yelled. Neither one moved. The girl on the right sat slack-jawed against the grill of the truck and the other one was showing the first signs of shock. Her complexion was rapidly paling and her breathing was getting shallow. He did what he had to--he open-slapped Beth across the face. Beth's face immediately reddened with anger.

"You bastard! What do you think that you are doing!?" she yelled as she began to rise to give this man a dose of what for.

"Saving your lives!" he shouted back. "Get your friend up. I'll get the truck ready to travel." She knew immediately what he meant and she thanked God he did it.

"Deb, come on. Get up," Beth said as she gently tugged on Deb's sleeve. Beth did not like the hue of Deb's skin. Her lips were turning a bluish-white, almost like the color of fish. Beth shuddered as she heard the thud of a body hitting the pavement.

"Come on Deb!" I don't want to look like that, she thought to herself. "Come on!" she fairly wailed. That got some response out of Deb, but not enough. The sergeant had finished moving the lieutenant's body out of the truck and most of the gray matter. He looked up and noted that Corporal Eddington was back at the troop transport, pointing towards them.

"Lady, get your friend up and moving or I'm gonna toss her in here!"

"Deb! Get up! If you ever want to see Mike again, get up!" Beth screamed. Deb finally showed some signs of life. She didn't rise completely on her own but with Beth's help, she did manage to get into the truck, just as Sergeant O'Bannon was putting it in gear.

The troop transport was rolling now and it would only be a matter of seconds before the tanks began to open fire; and this time they wouldn't be warning shots. The sergeant was glad that those tanks hadn't been retrofitted with the latest optical laser-guiding system. They wouldn't have made it twenty feet before a round would find them. As it was, the men manning those tanks took their jobs seriously and were ranked among the best in the Massachusetts National Guard. But hitting a moving target was still difficult and the sergeant wasn't going to make it any easier for them by driving in a straight line.

"You had better get you and you friend buckled up. We're going to be in for a bumpy ride," the sergeant said as he belted himself in.

"I really am getting sick of putting my seatbelt on. Every time I do, something bad happens," Beth said as she leaned over to get Deb's seatbelt on. Deb offered no resistance; in fact, she didn't offer much of anything. My

God, she looks pale, Beth thought as she brushed past Deb's hand. She noted how cold she felt too. But she didn't have too much time to dwell on this, as she heard the first volley of shots heading in their direction. It was deafening. Is this how death sounds? At least you, my friend, won't feel it, Beth thought as she leaned over to embrace Deb.

Chapter 34 - Mike Journal Entry Six

"Doc, just for a couple of minutes?" I whined. France must be rubbing off on me, I bemused.

"Listen, Mike. I know you look good, you feel good, and your tests all say you're doing good. But it's only been two days since you hemorrhaged and I'm not taking any chances," the doctor said as he wrote copious notes on the chart he had taken from the foot of the bed.

"I just want to see the sun for a few minutes. I feel like I'm back…on the ship." I think the doctor caught my hesitation and the look I got in my eye because he finally acquiesced.

"Oh alright!" he said in exasperation. "But Nurse Hitchins will be with you the entire time and you are not to leave the wheelchair."

"Wheelchair?"

"Wheelchair! Or you're not going. And that's it, Mr. Talbot, whether you're a super hero or not. Apparently, even super heroes can die."

"Almost."

"Almost?" the doc asked.

"Almost die," I said whimsically.

"The wheelchair or nothing!" he answered as he headed back to his office, mumbling something or other about kids these days and how ungrateful they were.

Nurse Hitchins showed up ten minutes later, pushing a wheelchair that I think came from the Industrial Age. The thing had more steel on it than my last car.

"You don't have anything a little flashier do you?" I

asked sarcastically. Nurse Hitchins didn't see the humor or more likely didn't appreciate it. She pulled my covers back. I was feeling really exposed in the hospital gown and expressed my dissatisfaction.

"Don't you have anything I could wear that might be a bit more appropriate than this smock?" I said as I pulled at the sides of the material.

"Oh honey, you don't have anything I haven't seen before," she answered condescendingly.

"Nothing?" I asked, a little embarrassed.

"Listen, you might be a super hero but you aren't Superman," she said as she looked at my crotch for a fleeting second.

My cheeks blazed. "Fine," I said as I let her assist me into the chair. And thankful for the help I was. For all the bravado I had displayed to the doctor, I don't think that I could have made it up the first flight of stairs out of this place. Lucky for me, I had a chauffeur and an elevator.

My heart began to pound unexpectedly as we began our ascent. I blamed it on my first real view of this brave new world that our history was now recording. But deep down inside, I knew better. My senses had increased tenfold during my stay on the alien mother ship. I had come to rely on these newfound instincts, however hard I tried to quash them, and the uneasiness kept seeping in around the corners. I turned to my nurse, my face feeling like most of the color had drained out of it, and more than likely, it had, at least, from the nurse's perspective.

"You all right, son?" she said cautiously, not sure if I was having some sort of relapse, again.

"I'm fine. But are you sure this is such a good idea? I mean, is it safe up there?"

"Honey," she snorted, "this might just be the safest place on the planet. Not many people these days trying to break into prisons." That did little to ease my concern. Then she added, "And this place has at least twenty to twenty-five good men guarding it." I felt a little better but my gut said otherwise. I had learned early on in my combats that my gut was something well worth the effort to heed.

"Listen," I said without much conviction. "I think maybe I should just go and lie back down."

"Nonsense, it's a beautiful day out and you look like you could use some sun." I mumbled a few obscenities under my breath but I went meekly. What was I supposed to do? I was in a wheelchair. What did I know? Maybe the sun would do me some good. Then the elevator door beeped onto level one. The doors opened up, and my nightmare came into full vision.

Paul was standing there with a Colt .45 aimed squarely at my chest. Bastard was going to finish me off. I cringed, trying my best to melt into the back of the chair. And then…nothing, I opened my eyes to notice one of the orderlies getting onto the elevator we were vacating with what appeared to be an ice cold Coke.

"Huh?" I said as a bead of sweat rolled down my forehead.

Nurse Hitchins either did not notice or did not speculate on my odd behavior. She rolled my wheelchair out of the lobby towards two huge glass doors, guarded by two heavily armed, what I can only describe as, freaks of nature.

The one on the right was the smaller of the two. He looked to be about six foot, five inches, two hundred and fifty or maybe two hundred and seventy-five pounds. The guy on the left was of approximately the same height but he had to be over three hundred pounds, and not an ounce of it looked like fat.

Both took a good long glance at me, and then dismissed me. Probably thinking that I hadn't done a hundredth of what the stories circulating said I had done. Can you blame them? I was pale as warmed-over death, sitting in a wheelchair and wearing a stupid backless contraption that should have been outlawed years ago.

The men turned away from me and began speaking in French and laughing, never looking back at me, which gave me the distinct impression that they were talking about me. "Tsk tsk! That'll be enough of that, Jean-Paul and Freire!" my nurse spoke up. Oh great. Not only did I look feeble, but now my guide was defending my honor. What next? Should I just wet myself and get it over with?

"Jess, we were just playing," the guys said almost in unison. They weren't sorry about teasing me but they definitely didn't want to cross swords with the nurse. She had, on more than one occasion, sewn both of them up. She had actually saved Jean-Paul's life a couple of years back when he got into a street brawl. The man's buddy, who Jean-Paul had literally been beating the snot out of, came up behind him and stuck a six-inch knife, almost to the hilt, into his spleen. It was Nurse Hitchins' quick thinking and medical expertise that saved him from bleeding out. She was known around the place as being completely fearless and everybody respected her.

At first glance, I thought perhaps that I was having another one of my grand illusions. Surely that's a bird, a big bird perhaps, do they have pelicans here? Naw, too big for a bird; it must be a plane. But I was told that most aviation had come to a screeching halt since the attacks. Maybe it's a private plane. It's a little big for a private plane, but hey, Trump has his own jumbo jet, maybe it's him. The plane-bird seemed to be flying straight at us.

I hadn't noticed earlier; I had been too distracted by the banter next to me, but my gut was screaming in agony. Something was wrong. Terribly, wrong. And then it happened. Piss streamed out of me in long hot rivulets. I still had no clue what was going on but my body sure did. I looked down at the spreading wetness in my lap, trying to figure out how I was going to explain this to Hulks One and Two. Luckily, or rather unluckily, that wasn't going to be necessary.

Nurse Hitchins paused in her reprimanding as she noticed my distress, which was now clearly visible on my lap. Then she looked up and over Hulk One's head. I'll tell you what, that lady sure had a head on her shoulders. She didn't say a word as she wheeled my chair around and, straight out, ran for the elevators.

Jean-Paul and Freire had seen the stark terror in her face but couldn't, for the lives of them, figure out what was going on. They had seen Hitchins in combat situations with body parts flying but she never batted an eye. Freire turned around first and quickly grabbed his friend's shoulder, pulling him down to the ground with him.

Jean-Paul said something in French, which I can only assume from the tone and emphasis were swear words. He had just begun to finish off the last of his obscenities when the rumbling began. It started as a belly grumble and quickly rose to the crescendo of a freight train, barreling full speed and out of control on a steep mountain pass. The doors to the elevator were just closing as the first of three alien scout ships flew overhead. Dust shook down from the high ceiling in the lobby while the elevator began its hasty descent.

The door opened to a clamor of doctors, nurses and aides who wanted to go up to see what all the fuss was about. Most quickly began to rethink their position when they saw the ashen faces of my guide and me.

"What's going on?" a concerned Dr. Fenoir said as he positioned himself at the front of the cacophony. "Our air raid alarms are going off!"

"They're back!" was all Nurse Hitchins was able to mutter as she quickly headed back towards my room.

I think that you could have probably heard a pin drop in that room, except, of course, for the incessant wailing of the air raid sirens overhead. A few ventured onto the elevator, but most headed to the phone banks to make sure that their loved ones weren't in any direct harm. But, I thought to myself, I'm pretty sure that everybody right now is in direct harm.

My gut was still roiling. Was this the second phase of the invasion? The occupation? Were these three ships just a small sample of what the rest of the world was seeing?

Somehow I just didn't think so, but thoughts alone weren't going to allay my fears. Nurse Hitchins had diligently wheeled me into my room before she headed off to where, I can only assume, she was making her phone calls.

So there I sat. Tired and weak but pumped up with adrenaline, I wheeled myself out of the room, looking for I wasn't sure what, but if I stumbled across it, I'd know. People were running around in hysterics and the place was complete bedlam. Nobody paid me the least amount of attention as I circled around some of the more robust revelers.

I rolled up to the telephone bank, only to find people three deep in line, waiting. I grabbed the arm of the man nearest to me. At first, he either ignored me or truly couldn't acknowledge my existence.

"Excuse me!" I said as I yanked a little harder on his cuff.

"Pardonez-moi?"

Damn! No luck there; I didn't know French and something told me I wasn't going to have enough time to learn it, even if I wanted to. I gathered what little strength I had left and blurted out in one long breath: "Does anyone here speak English?" Over the din, most of the people chose to ignore me. Finally, one little girl of about ten or eleven popped out from underneath the arm of her mother who was next in line for the phone.

"Oui, Monsieur. I speak Eengleesh."

It wasn't great but it sounded oh, so sweet right now. I caught a few breaths before I began hoping that this little girl would have at least some sort of clue about what I was asking. I wanted to be as clear and concise as possible because there wasn't much left in the reserve tanks.

"Thank you!" I shouted over the noise. I wanted to hug this little girl just for acknowledging me. She looked at me with her large brown eyes, probably wondering if I was going to ask her something or not. She was beginning to look a little bored with the whole procedure. I pressed on. "Is there a radio room here?" I exaggerated the word radio so it came out more as Ray-Dee-Oh. I don't know what I was thinking. She was French, not stupid.

"Monsieur?" She cocked her head a little bit to the side.

"Radio," I repeated again as I held an invisible microphone to my mouth."

"Oui, sir, le telephone."

"No, no, munchkin! I'm looking for a way to get in touch with the United States, specifically, one place."

"Oui, oui, you want a telephone!" she said excitedly.

"No," I said as I shook my head slowly from side to side. I was attempting to turn my chair around in the crowd when she yelled out again.

"Oui, sir. You wish to contact your friends at the Fortress on the Hill?" I stopped dead in my tracks, or at least my wheelchair did.

"You know about Indian Hill?" I asked incredulously.

"Everybody does, sir. My mama, my brother, and I are going there next month." I was having a hard time swallowing the fact that Paul would let so many people in on his secret after all the security measures he had in place.

"Have you been there?"

"No, silly," she laughed. "None of us have been there. We don't even know exactly where in your country it is. But my mama told my brother and me that it is a safe place for us to live away from the bad crocodiles."

"You have no idea how bad they are," I muttered under my breath.

"Sir?"

"Nothing. So where is this radio?"

"Telephone, sir. It is, I believe, a direct line to the Fortress on the Hill. At least, that is what my mama has told me."

"Could you show me where it is?"

The girl turned back to her mother who was frantically dialing her home number. When the girl decided that she could make it back before her mother even noted her absence, she nodded in ascent. I put my hands on the wheels of the chair and began, or at least, tried to begin, to get my chair moving. I wasn't sure if it was because my arms felt like spaghetti or the wheels were glued to the ground. But I couldn't get the thing to move. The little girl, Suzanne, (I found out later), saw my dilemma and never said a word as she got behind my chair and started to push it towards our destination.

    Weeks later, I was so happy to run into her back at Indian Hill. I feared that she had died in France along with the countless other millions when the aliens decided to level the countryside in an attempt to find what they had come for.

Chapter 35
Indian Hill

"Sir, I've got a Captain Talbot on the direct line from Paris," the radio operator said hesitantly. The static coming over the line made the communication nearly impossible.

"Sir, he says it's an emergency, something about them being back. Is it true, sir?" The radio officer turned to look at his commanding officer, hoping that whoever was on the other end was mistaken.

"Well, Private, nobody has said anything to me about 'them' being back. Let's just hope he's some crackpot who broke into the radio room. In the meantime, you find out more information and I'm going to get Colonel Salazar."

"Yes, sir," the private said as a fresh bead of sweat broke out across his brow.

***

"Yes, sir; he says his name is Captain Talbot" Colonel Salazar had been busy preparing the duty roster and guard duty for the tunnels when the lieutenant stepped into his office. The colonel's hand froze when he heard that name.

"Did you say Captain Talbot, Lieutenant?" the colonel said as he slowly raised his head up from the paperwork crowding his desk.

"Yes sir, it's not a great connection. There is a lot of discharge over the lines today. We've been running all sorts of tests but we can't seem…"

"That's enough, Lieutenant. Is the captain still on the line?"

"Sir, he was when I left the com room about five minutes ago."

"Lieutenant! Get General Ginson and have him meet me in the com room," the colonel said as he breezed past the semi-stunned lieutenant.

"Ah, yes, sir," the lieutenant said to the receding back of the colonel.

***

"Captain Talbot? Captain Talbot? Is that you?!" the colonel shouted into the static-laced headset. "This is Colonel Salazar!"

"Colonel Salazar? Frank? This is Captain Talbot. Can you hear me?" I shouted with what was left of my strength.

"Barely," the colonel answered.

"Same here, Colonel. Listen! I might not have much time, but they're back!!"

Goosebumps rose up on the colonel's arms.

"Is there any activity over there?"

"That's a negative, Captain; say again that's a negative. The skies over the States are four by four clear." Why are they there? the colonel was thinking. Even when the world was in a full-on assault, the French had done little to prove the effectiveness of their fighting. They almost rolled over as easily against the aliens as they had against the Germans in World War II. If it hadn't been for the presence of some NATO troops, the colonel was sure it would have fallen even more quickly. So why now? What are they doing?

"Are you being fired upon, Captain?" the colonel shouted over the incessant static.

"Not yet, sir. Early indications seem to have them circling the skies." Almost like vultures looking for rotten meat popped into my head, and I quickly did my best to suppress the idea, but there it was. It's like trying not to think of a pink elephant. Go ahead. I dare you.

"Circling? What are they looki…" And then the line went dead.

"Private! Reconnect me NOW!" the colonel said, rather calmly but the private was under the impression that the stony calmness was just a ruse. He thought if he didn't reestablish communication instantly, he would be bucked down even further in rank than he already was. Almost as if on cue, General Ginson walked in. The private now began to have images of firing squads flashing before his eyes.

"What's going on, Frank? The lieutenant here was a little too out of breath to get anything more than someone was on the phone and you wanted to see me here."

"Sir," the colonel responded, "Captain Talbot just called."

"Great! I was hoping he'd be up and about by now. How's he doing?" the general asked almost jovially. The private relaxed a little bit, thinking perhaps that maybe he would just make it through this whole thing intact. But the general's smile quickly faded as he saw the grave expression on the colonel's face. The private redoubled his efforts with a renewed vigor, doing his best to try to ignore the two most senior officers on the base.

"General, he said the aliens were back." Paul reacted as if he'd been sucker-punched in the abdomen. Frank noted his distress. "Yes, sir; that's exactly how I felt when I heard," Frank answered solemnly.

"Have our scouts reported anything?" the general asked.

"Nothing, sir," Frank answered.

"What about any of the other encampments?"

"Nothing, Paul. From the lack of news coming in from any parts of the world, I have to assume that this is a fairly isolated incident."

"Did he say what they were doing?"

"Circling, sir."

"Circling? For what?" And then the truth hit him. He didn't know why he knew; he just knew that he knew. "They're looking for him."

"Him, sir? How could they possibly know he's there?" the colonel asked perplexedly.

"I don't know how they know. Maybe someone dropped the box and it opened. It doesn't really matter now how they know. The point is that they do know. And I've got a feeling that they're not going to stop until they find him."

The general stopped to think for a moment. "Colonel, as soon as the communications come back up, I want you to begin evacuation of key personnel at the Bastille. Have them lay low in Europe until it's safe to bring them here. For now though, I want all of our people out of Paris," the general said as he whirled back towards his office, and undoubtedly, a few days without sleep.

The colonel turned back towards the private. "Anything yet, Private?"

"Nothing yet, sir."

"Very well, let me know the instant you have reestablished communications."

"Sir, yes, sir," the private answered as the first of many sweat beads fell to his desk.

Chapter 36 - Mike Journal Entry Seven
The Bastille

The first impact, for what else could it be? Shook the ancient prison to its very foundation. We would later learn that the blast struck southern Paris, more than fifty miles away. But at the time, I would have sworn that it was a fifty-thousand-pound-bomb smacking dead center on one of the many turrets that occupied this place. It was almost comical the way that everyone, including myself, went stock still after the first blast. I guess at the time, we were just waiting for the other shoe to drop. It did drop and in a big way, just not within the seemingly endless span of our collective breaths.

It was after a minute of standing stock still that people began to realize another impact wasn't imminent, and again there was a huge rush for the phone banks. But this time, there would be no sweet solace in hearing a loved one on the other end. All circuits were busy according to the automated voice. But we knew better, all circuits were destroyed.

Nothing happened that day or even the next, for that matter. But Southern Paris was burning. All efforts to stifle the flames had been ineffectual. Whatever the aliens dropped had made the city a molten pit. Fire crews couldn't even get close enough to attempt to quench the insatiable blaze.

One water plane had been dispatched to the area but never got within twenty miles of the fire. An alien vessel had swooped down and literally obliterated the tanker. The massive water carrier had simply been there one second and then vanished into a mist of water vapor as the aliens discharged a seemingly smaller version of their city killer.

In the ensuing two days, people had begun to travel out of their homes or shelters or hidey-holes or wherever else they had sought refuge. Life still had to go on, even if three huge alien ships were parked a mere twenty-five miles above in the atmosphere. And for another two days, after the tanker had been downed, still nothing happened.

People tried to do what was necessary to survive, but it's hard to get anything accomplished when the executioner's axe is poised above your head and you can see its shadow. Southern Paris was still ablaze but it was significantly less than it had been. Crews were now actually making progress against the inferno, and still nothing happened.

It was on the brink of dawn on the seventh day when the aliens made another move, this one seeming even more inexplicable than the last. They began to broadcast a message over the radio waves. What frequency you ask? Every one of them. Their message was going to be heard, of that there was no question.

I spent most of the seven days in my room or down at the rec center on the treadmill trying to get some wind back into my sails. I had no desire to venture outside in the least. I wanted to blame it on my recuperation, but I was actually beginning to feel like my old self again. Of course, I mean the "new" old self, but that's beside the point.

Every time I even considered going topside, I had to resist the urge to throw up. My knees would quake, my muscles would spasm and my friggin' bowels would loosen. My knocking knees and weakening bowels had almost cost me a serious mishap on more than one occasion. I would get physically ill at just the mention of getting fresh air. Nurse Hitchins was all over me to go outside and get some color back in my cheeks, but I would have none of it. I had just finished my five-mile run, okay jog, okay trot, on the treadmill when I returned to my room to cool off. I was preparing to take a shower when my door was thrown open.

"Anyone ever hear of knocking?!" I yelled as I pulled

my shorts back up.
"Honey, we've already been through this." Nurse Hitchins dismissed my modesty with a wave of her hand. "Come on, you've got to hear this for yourself," she said. After entering the room, she half dragged me through the door while I tried in vain to put my sneakers back on. We were halfway out the door when I saw two armed, uniformed men running towards us. They had their weapons at the ready and looked like they meant business. I was hoping they would run on by but the reaction of the man in the lead when he saw me made me think otherwise.
"Captain Talbot?" the lead man asked.
I really didn't feel like a captain at the moment, half naked, all sweaty, and being pulled by a nurse half my size. I stopped short and, by default, so did my nurse. She nearly teetered over but I was quickly able to stop her momentum and prevent her from toppling over. But the sudden movement had caused some pain deep within me. I winced but did my best to not let anyone know.
"Yeah, that's me." I said as I slowly stood straight up. The second man had overtaken his comrade and stopped about three feet further down the hallway. So there we were, the first man who asked my name, Nurse Hitchins, myself and the second man who seemed not very thrilled with whatever orders had been bestowed upon him.
"Nurse, I am going to have to ask you to step away from that man," the first man said as he lowered his weapon onto her midsection.
"Who are you miscreants?!" she yelled. "How dare you point that thing at me! I will not step away from this man!"
"Ma'am, step away or we will have to physically remove you!" the second man chimed in.
What was going on? Would I be able to take two armed men in this confined space? Would I have enough in me to do the job?
"I will not!" she said defiantly. "I have spent weeks

healing this man and I will not see it undone here and now!" she said as she placed her hands on her hips.

The second man did as he warned her he would do. He picked her up by the waist and deposited her five feet away from the little ordeal. Nurse Hitchins started to run back into the fray when the first man placed the barrel of his weapon directly in her midsection. Instantly, she froze.

"Whoa!" I said with my hands up in the air. "That's enough! Your beef is with me. Let the nurse go." Nurse Hitchins looked into my eyes, pleading for help. "Let her go," I said more forcefully. "And I will do what you want of me." The man's eyes unglazed a bit more as he started to regain his composure.

"Come on, man! Let her go." I half begged. The man, ever so slowly, eased his finger off of the trigger.

"Go," he said to her.

"What about you?" Nurse Hitchins asked.

"Go," I answered. "Don't make this any worse than it has to be." She turned and began to run. When she had put a comfortable distance between us, she turned and yelled.

"I'm getting help. I'll be right back!" Tears were rolling out of her eyes.

The first man who approached turned towards me after making sure that Nurse Hitchins wouldn't be making a surprise return.

"Captain Talbot, I need you to come with us." He may have made it sound like a request, but I doubted that I had any choice in the matter.

"Whatever you two are going to do, just it do it now and be done with it," I shot back. I was in no mood to spar with them. And I sure wasn't going to make it any easier on them by acquiescing to what I felt was the inevitable.

"Sir?" was his only response.

"I do not plan on going with you two voluntarily to be a patsy in whatever agenda you and your superiors have." I spat. If I had been a snake, venom surely would have shot out; but that not being the case, saliva would have to do.

"Sir?" Now he even cocked his head. "I think that you have a misunderstanding of our 'agenda'." He smiled slightly. Now it was my turn to look confused.

"Listen, I'm not up much for games. Why don't you just tell me who you are and what is going on here?"

"Sir, my name is Vice Sergeant Roy and my compadre over there is Corporal Michaud." The second man merely nodded in my direction as he kept a vigilant watch on anybody that was coming in our general direction. "Sir, we are from the French Foreign Legion and we've be sent here to protect you."

I was now completely lost, I felt like a six-year-old in the woods of Maine. "The French Foreign Legion? Who sent you and who are you protecting me from?"

"Sir, I would feel much more comfortable if you would let me answer all of your questions in a more secure location."

"Listen, Vice Sergeant, I already told you, I'm not going voluntarily, not unless you give me some answers and some damn good ones at that."

The corporal turned to his sergeant. "Let me just knock him in the head and let's get out of here."

"You're more than welcome to try, Corporal, but I can almost guarantee you'll end up with a 5.56 millimeter enema," I answered back. The corporal, who probably outweighed me by fifty pounds, sneered and began to close in on me.

"Corporal!" the sergeant shouted. "That's enough! You so much as misplace a hair on his head and I'll deal with you personally!" The corporal stopped but he was using every muscle in his body to restrain himself.

"You aren't worth it," he said calmly as he took his place five feet away and once again began his scan of the surrounding area.

"Alright, Captain, can I at least explain while we're moving?" the sergeant almost pleaded. as I merely folded my arms.

"Alright, you friggin' Americans are so obstinate. We were sent here by General Ginson." My interest was piqued. "He wants to get you out of here before the locals get to you and throw you to the wolves," he continued.

"Why would the locals be after me? What have I done to them?"

"You truly don't know?" he asked.

"Do I look like I know?" I answered curtly.

"Have you been near a radio in the last hour?"

"No, I've been on the treadmill. What's so interesting about the radio? First Nurse Hitchins, and now you."

"The aliens are broadcasting across the radio wave spectrum. They somehow know that you're here, and they want you back."

My face instantly paled if it hadn't already although I didn't want to show any weakness to the corporal. If not for that, I most likely would have just collapsed. Now my mind was racing. Did the doctor forget some deeply buried tracer? No, that couldn't be it. They would have just stormed the building and be done with it. Why all the drama of flying overhead and destroying the southern part of the city? I had been so engrossed in my own thoughts, I didn't even notice when the sergeant began to talk again.

"… And if we don't give you up, they'll take out another chunk of the city."

"What..what did you say?" The sergeant was beginning to look a bit agitated. Loud voices began to rise from the lobby area.

"Let's just get him, so they'll go." And a different voice, it sounded female,

"I will not lose any more of my family."

"Captain, the aliens are ordering the people of Paris to turn you over. If they don't comply, they will take out another section of the city until there is nothing left." This time I did falter, but I shot my hand out fast enough to make it look more like I had slipped than fallen. But I don't think either one of them bought it. "Listen, Captain, the natives are getting restless; you can hear them as well as I can. We move now or we might not make it."

"I...I can't be responsible for the lives of these people, if I run, they'll die," I answered meekly.

"Listen, Captain, my orders aren't to protect these people, they're to protect you. Let's go!" he shouted as a group of five or six turned the corner and began to approach.

"There he is!" one of the men said as he pointed right at me. He was one of the orderlies whom I had been joking with on almost a daily basis. They began to advance faster when they saw me, but Corporal Michaud intervened, leveling his weapon squarely on their leader.

"Any one of you takes one step closer and I'll level all of you!" he said menacingly. Their steps faltered, looking down the barrel of the rifle he held and also by his tone of voice. The group felt confident that this wasn't an idle threat. And yet, that almost didn't stop them. The orderly put his hands out to halt the progress of his little group. He whispered into the ear of the man nearest him, who looked surprisingly like the head janitor of the place, but I sure never remembered that scowl on his face. The men departed, reluctantly.

"Captain Talbot, they're leaving now, but believe me they are coming back most likely with more people and weapons. We need to move now."

"But what about the rest of the city?" I resisted, but not too convincingly.

"We can work that all out later, but right now we need to move."

"Why don't I just let them take me to the aliens and stop this madness now?" I didn't really feel that I wanted to go to the aliens but it seemed like the right thing to say under the conditions.

"Captain you'll never make it alive. The aliens never said in what condition they wanted you, just that they wanted you. If you give these people even half a chance, they'll drop off what's left of your body. If you decide to go to the aliens, they will more than likely not allow you to go on your own terms. Those five people are going to be back, and it will be a mob by then. Do you really want to chance your well being to a mob mentality?"

"Which way, Sergeant?"

"Finally," the corporal muttered, just loud enough to make sure I heard.

Chapter 37

New York / Massachusetts State Line

Beth literally felt her fillings shake loose, partly from the G-force of the truck as the now rogue sergeant gunned it for all it was worth, but mainly from the concussion shock from the tank's rounds.

"Oh my God!" Beth screamed. "I think my head is going to explode!"

"Well let's just be glad it's only your head and not this truck," Sergeant O'Bannon said as he realized they were finally out of danger from the tank rounds. Deb roused her head for a fraction of a second after the last volley, but managed only a sigh, as if she couldn't be bothered with the events of the day.

The sergeant glanced over at Deb. "Is she going to make it?" he asked Beth in what he hoped was an appropriate tone, but under the circumstances, it came out more as a shout.

"Make it? She has to make it. She's the only friend I've got," Beth started to sob. In the excitement of their escape, she really hadn't had enough time to dwell on the subject. But as the truck began to descend over the crest of the freeway, realization began to set in.

Deb already looked dead. Her eyes were sunken, and her skin was cool, cold to the touch. Beth couldn't even be sure if Deb's chest was still rising. And now she just wanted to be out of the truck and as far away from this whole scene as was entirely possible. The final volley of shots ringing out from the vanishing roadblock shocked her back into the here and now.

"We need to get her to a hospital!" Beth said as she turned to look at their rescuer. "Fast!" she added needlessly. The sergeant had already made up his mind by looking at

Deb that she wasn't going to make it.

"There isn't a hospital in working order on this side of the state line for fifty miles," the sergeant said with concern in his voice. "And the way she looks, she won't make it another ten."

"I can't let her die," Beth sobbed, covering her face with her hands. "We've been through too much. She can't just up and die, not this way. Not at least until she sees Mike again. She'll…she'll never forgive me," Beth wailed on.

"Do you have a first aid kit in this truck?" the sergeant asked, trying to make Beth get a handle on her emotions. Beth kept crying.

"Listen!" the sergeant said as he grabbed Beth's arm. "Do you have a first aid kit in this truck?" he asked a little louder. Beth was only able to nod her head in ascent as cries kept bubbling up out of her throat.

"Do you have a knife or something sharp like that?" the sergeant asked, seeing that Beth was once again beginning to slip back into panic mode.

"T-t-t-two of them," Beth stammered out, holding two fingers in the air to reiterate her point.

"There's a rest stop not more than five miles. Get all the supplies you can find ready for when we get there!" the sergeant barked.

"For… for what?" Beth managed to stammer out.

"We're going to operate," the sergeant said matter-of-factly.

"Operate!? Can't we just take her to a hospital? Or something?"

"'Or something' would be great right now," the sergeant said sarcastically. "Unfortunately, right now, 'or something' is us." Beth redoubled her sobbing. "You had better get moving!" the sergeant said as he once again shook Beth's arm. "If you want any chance of saving your friend's life." Beth calmed down a little with the task at hand, but the thought of operating on Deb, in a parking lot no less, was making her seriously uneasy, to say the least.

Beth had finished putting together what she hoped would be sufficient supplies for the impending operation. The truck was equipped with a fishing tackle box that contained a beautiful steel-finished Gerber fishing knife. Beth dragged the blade across the top of her finger to see if it was sharp, and was painfully answered in the affirmative by some droplets of blood. Also, the box, for whatever reason, contained both needle and thread. Beth couldn't imagine for what, but she could not help feeling that it was a good sign.

In addition, crammed way under the seat, was a bag of rags. They appeared to be unused from the condition of the Auto Zone bag. Again, Beth was immensely thankful to the powers that be. They even found a pair of tweezers in the tackle box, but would this be enough? There were no bags of blood lying around to make this a truly miraculous find. Would it be enough? Then Beth found herself doing something she had not done since she was a little girl at the foot of her bed--she prayed. Only this time, it wasn't for a pony or a new Barbie or even an Easy Bake oven.

No, she was praying for the life of the woman that sat next to her. A woman whom she once detested but who was now, far and away, her best friend, irrespective of Mike. A sharp pang hit her chest as she thought of his name but she quickly disregarded it. There would be time later to think of him. Right now, she had to focus everything on Deb.

The truck screeched into the rest area, however, they were not entirely alone. Beth saw at the far end of the lot what appeared to be a mini convoy of white panel vans. Trepidation rose in her heart. Since this brave new world had started, strangers only meant one thing--danger.

"We have to find somewhere else to do this!" she said as she grabbed the sergeant's arm.

"There is no place else," he answered as he witnessed Beth's distress. He was under the same notion; those four vans most likely, didn't mean good news, but right now they were out of options. He planned to set Beth up to stand guard while he put his rudimentary first aid skills to use on Deb. He wasn't sure what upset him more, the sight of those sterile white panel vans or the impending surgery.

He'd done some basic first aid in the field, even once going so far as to splint a man's leg that fractured during a weekend excursion in the White Mountains. But nothing he had ever done before even remotely prepared him for this. Not to mention, those damned vans. Uneasiness oozed out of them. No, he thought to himself, that's just my imagination. I'm just nerved up, he thought as he walked up to the restrooms.

Well, at least he wouldn't have to worry about the doors being locked. Someone had kicked the door off its hinges, and it looked fairly recent. They hadn't been kicked in; the wood was splintered in a hundred different places. Someone had driven their car up here and let it do the leg work for them, so to speak.

Beth was cradling Deb in her arms and stroking her hair. She felt that it was more for her comfort than Deb's. Deb had stirred once or twice, but it looked like any effort was draining for her. Beth looked over towards the vans and through the darkly tinted windows she saw the glowing ember of a cigarette that was pointed directly at her. She felt somewhat uneasy with just the prospect of what or who were in the vans and now that she was certain somebody, or some bodies, were there just staring at her, her distress increased tenfold.

"You had better lighten up on your friend's head."

Beth screamed out in surprise. The sergeant came up the other side of the truck and she never even noticed. Meanwhile, her silent caresses had become more like delousing procedures.

"I'm sorry. I didn't mean to startle you," the sergeant said apologetically.

"There's somebody in that second van," Beth said trying her best to not look over, but failing miserably.

"Well, I've spotted at least five people in three of the vans, and they haven't said or done anything yet; so let's just try to put them out of our minds and concentrate on your friend." Even the sergeant thought his words sounded hollow, but the girl seemed to swallow it. "By the way, my name is Sergeant O'Bannon… Grady." he said, extending his hand. "Oh, huh? Yeah. I'm sorry. I feel like I've known you for years and I never even knew your name until now. I'm Beth and I can't ever express how grateful my friend and I are for your help," Beth said as she took the sergeant's hand.

"Well, how grateful your friend is largely depends on how well I do right now," the sergeant said, gesturing towards Deb.

"Her name is Deborah," Beth said as she looked back down at her friend.

"Well, Beth, let's get started," the sergeant said as he glanced over at the vans once more before he began to put on the rubber gloves he found in the first aid kit.

***

"The girl looks shot. Should we help?" The gravel faced man with the cigarette said. His passenger barely raised his eyes above the page that he was reading.

"What's she to me?" he stated matter-of-factly.

"Nothing, I suppose," the gravel faced man answered. 'But seeing as you ARE a doctor, you arrogant little prick.' He thought.

"Let's go. This little drama is beginning to bore me," the doctor said. The gravel faced man knew what side his bread was buttered on. He felt for the injured girl but he was nowhere as altruistic as the sergeant. He said a little prayer and put his van in drive. The rest of the team followed.

***

Indian Hill

"What was that?" Paul said as he grabbed the edge of his desk to keep from falling over. Dust rained from the ceiling as the walls groaned from the shock. "I asked," Paul yelled to his clerk, "what was that!" The corporal was about to answer that he didn't know, when he realized that wasn't the answer his general was looking for. The corporal immediately got on the radio, calling all of the duty officers.

"Sir!" the excited corporal said as he stepped into the general's office.

"Go ahead, Corporal," Paul said nervously. He heard the corporal's switchboard buzzing and lighting up and knew that this wasn't going to be good news. But, he was learning, there were degrees of bad news he could tolerate, although definitely not enjoy. But, at least, he could keep marching forward. He hoped this was the case. He knew about the aliens in France. Had they somehow found out about this place?

"Sir?" the corporal said again, realizing, quite possibly, that his general wasn't all there at the moment.

"Uh yeah. Go ahead," Paul said as he mentally shook his head to get the nightmarish images out of his skull.

"Tunnel two has collapsed." Paul stood up like he was shot out of a cannon.

"Again? What happened? Is anybody hurt?"

"That's the thing, sir, it seems that some sort of charge was planted and detonated." Paul started to head out the door, and the corporal figured that the general was going to chew some serious ass. He was glad his last guard shift was over a week ago.

"Sir, there's more." Paul turned to look, anxious to get out and learn the details for himself.

"Sir, Colonel Salazar and a few of his men were in the tunnel." Paul wished he had never left his seat, because he suddenly needed to sit down.

"Are they dead?" Paul crossed his fingers, if only mentally.

"Nobody knows for sure, but rescue efforts have already started." The general's back was already fading away as the corporal finished his sentence.

Chapter 38 - Mike Journal Entry Eight

"Is the hood necessary?" I managed to garble out.

"I'm sorry, Captain, but if you are captured, we do not want the whereabouts of our unit discovered."

"You might be sorry, but I think that your friend over there doesn't mind at all."

Michaud merely snorted, most likely in agreement. "How much further then? This thing smells like Frenchy's feet over there and it's itchy." Michaud got up and made a move to cuff my head but he was diplomatically stopped by Roy.

"About ten more minutes, Captain. And just for your safety, some of the time we have been driving has not been necessary."

"You've driven a more circuitous route so that I won't be able to timeline my way back. I get it, I get it. You don't trust me. Fine, but if we don't get there soon, I'm taking this thing off."

"I would advise against that, Captain." I heard the ominous sound of Michaud's pistol being cocked. I prudently decided to remain quiet and still for the remainder of the journey, much to the chagrin of Michaud. From the way the van lurched back and forth, I'm pretty sure I wouldn't have been able to tell where we were going without the hood. But if they wanted to play this game, I guess I was all right with it. Not like there was much choice in the matter anyway.

My internal clock timed the remainder of the ride at about twenty more minutes. And you know how they say when one of your senses is handicapped, the other ones perk up and try to compensate for the discrepancy? Well, even with my super sensitive hearing, I never heard Michaud uncock his pistol. That gave me goose bumps, thinking that he had that thing pointed at my head. While the van screeched left and right over the pock-marked roads that dotted the landscape! And my brief knowledge of him, he was most likely smiling the whole time. He might have had seventy-five pounds on me, or thirty friggin' stone, like they said out here, but when I got my chance, I'd get even.

The thought helped ameliorate the smell of feet over my head, if only for a minute. The van stopped and I hoped that would bring the salvation of fresh air, but no such luck. I was unceremoniously pushed out of the back of the van. I stood up, wiping the small stones that had embedded themselves in my kneecaps and tried to orient myself. I wasn't even sure now in which direction the van was.

A low vibratory hum seemed to pass over my head. My first impression was that it was the alien ship and these bastards had baited me right into a trap. I was on the verge of ripping my hood off and giving anyone within my striking distance, some good old what for. Then I realized that the hum seemed more all around and not just directly above. More like a power station, I reasoned. I wasn't sure if it was information I needed, or could eventually use, but I filed it away anyway. Sometimes you just never know.

"Let's go, Captain," Roy said as he grabbed me just above the elbow and kind of steered me in the general direction. I heard Michaud walk off in the opposite direction. He was talking to someone else in what sounded like French, saying something about licking a frog's ass, or maybe it was just that he wanted a beer. Either way made no never mind to me.

The gravel gave way to concrete and for a few more feet, I shuffled on, half expecting to slam my nose into a door. The temperature of the air changed; it was warmer. I was being led inside, to what? I didn't know. It was just safe to say it was inside. The door behind me slammed shut and I jumped a little.

The hood was pulled off almost immediately, I sucked in the new air as if I had been under water for a week. I squinted out of reflex, thinking that I was about to be light blinded. But it was hardly necessary, the room I was in wasn't much better lit than the hood I was wearing. Even so, my eyes still needed to adjust to something that wasn't an inch away.

When my eyes finally did adjust, it didn't look anything like a power station of any kind. It looked more like a huge warehouse. Crates were piled high. In the distance, I could even see a forklift getting one of the crates down.

"Where are we?" I asked as I tried to wipe the smell from my nose.

"Where we are, Captain, is of no importance to you," Roy answered. "At least not right now," he added. "Colonel Brintley wishes to see you, and after he is through briefing you, I will show you to your quarters."

"Any chance I could make a pit stop? The springs in your van aren't so good, and I just finished a quart of Gatorade when this whole little adventure began."

"I'd say yes, but Colonel Brintley expected you seven minutes ago and I'm already going to catch hell," he snorted.

"Seven minutes ago?"

"Let's go," he said as he once again grabbed me above the elbow, but this had more of a death grip to it. I was going in the same direction he was, no matter what the consequences. Bladder be damned, full speed ahead.

***

"Oh my God!" Beth shrieked. "Is there supposed to be that much blood?"

"Just wipe my damn forehead!" Sergeant O'Bannon said as he tried to blink away the sweat that was accumulating at the top of his brow. Deb had begun to turn ash white as the sergeant dug around in her shoulder, attempting to retrieve the bullet without doing any more damage than was necessary.

He was feeling like a bull in a china shop, routing around in this girl. He tried in vain to not look at her face. He could tell even in this extreme situation that she was a beautiful girl, and so young. He noticed himself speaking in the past tense and did his best to correct it, but the facts were right there in front of him. Blood, which he had no means of replacing, was pouring out of Deb at an alarming rate. He finally found the bullet lodged squarely in Deb's shoulder blade. If she lived, he figured she had at least six months of painful physical therapy ahead of her before she would be able to move this arm correctly. Her days of beach volleyball were over for sure. Hope sprang forward as he pulled the fragment out of the wound with an audible pop.

"Is that it?" Beth asked incredulously.

"Well, it's either the bullet or I reached up too far and pulled out a filling." Beth smiled slightly at that. She figured that Deb was out of the woods now that the bullet was out. Naïve sure, but she still felt better. Deb stirred a little as the sergeant dropped the piece of lead into the top of the tackle box.

"Keep her steady, Beth. I've got to sew her up as fast as possible." Beth laid her head down on Deb's right shoulder and spoke comforting words into her friend's ear. She didn't know if Deb could hear her at all, but it made her feel good anyway. The sergeant worked fast, stitching her wound. This was more his speed anyway.

"I'm done," he said to no one in particular. He would have high-fived somebody if he hadn't thought that was totally uncalled for. Beth's head sprang up from Deb's shoulder to congratulate the sergeant on a job well done, but as the sergeant's eyes turned towards Beth, his face fell.

"What? What's the matter?" Beth's eyes grew as wide as saucers. The first thing that came into her mind was that the men in the vans were approaching. But that couldn't be it, she was looking in the direction of where the vans were and they were gone. They left sometime during the operation; and quietly too, because neither she nor the sergeant heard their departure.

Beth felt more than saw something land on her shirt. She tore her eyes off the sergeant momentarily to look down. Her shirt had multiple blood splatters on it. Then her mind began to race. Had she been hit in all the excitement and hadn't even realized it? She had heard about things like that, but was it possible? She didn't have any unexplained pain. She didn't feel woozy. Where was the blood coming from?

Both she and the sergeant looked down at Deb in the same instance. Crimson red blood was streaming out of the corners of her mouth. She looked the part of some B-movie actress with crappy special effects. But this wasn't a movie and this was no B-movie actress. This was Beth's friend. Deb began to cough up what little blood she had left began to fill her lungs. The coughs became more violent as the sergeant tried to prop her up. The wound on Deb's shoulder began to pucker and then blistered open, fresh blood spilling from the gunshot caused by Deb's violent hacking.

"Put pressure on her wound!" the sergeant said in a near panic.

"Oh God!" Beth wailed.

Chapter 39 – Mike Journal Entry Nine

"Deb? Is that you?" I couldn't tell if I was hallucinating or not. Deb was standing before me, but she was shimmering in an almost soft golden light. I thought for sure I had finally been driven over the edge, but if that were the case, I was bringing Roy with me.

His first reaction was to unshoulder his weapon. But it was dawning on him that weapons would be ineffectual. I think he had begun to mutter prayers. Swears or prayers, I couldn't truly be sure but a lot of the time they are one in the same. He kept muttering something about spirits or ghosts. But it couldn't be a ghost; it was Debbie, my companion for so many nights. My heart panged for her at the sight. Her arms were outstretched and she was walking in my direction; although walking might not be quite accurate, she seemed to be hovering two or so inches above the ground.

Roy grabbed me by the shoulder. "Come on, Captain let's go! No good can come from this," he said as he uttered another prayer and crossed the trinity on each shoulder and then his forehead.

"I know her!" I said as I shrugged my shoulder away from his grip.

"You KNOW this spirit!?" he said, backing away.

"She was on the ship with me she..she ..." Was what? Not my girlfriend, not just a companion... What was she? I felt pathetic. I loved this girl and I didn't even know what she was to me.

"Deb, how did you get here?" I was still blinded by the sight of her. "Are you crying?" And still she advanced. A slow dawning began in the depths of my brain. Tiny dots of fear began to shimmer and then shine. At this rate, they would be ablaze soon. But reason began to take over, why would I be afraid of Deb? "I love you," I said weakly.

It looked to me like she was mouthing she loved me back, but no sound emanated from her mouth. Still, I heard it ring out, loud and clear. She finally reached me and the touch of her hand was oh, so warm (freezing); her embrace was so inviting (disenchanting); and her kiss was sweet (bittersweet). And then she was gone.

***

New York – Massachusetts State Line

"She's gone," Sergeant O'Bannon said sadly as he stood up and walked away from the truck.

"She's not gone! She can't be gone!" Beth protested as she began to pound on Deb's chest, hoping that somehow, some way she would be able to beat the life back into her. After a minute or so of trying this unorthodox method, she gave up and laid her head on Deb's chest. Then she just sobbed and sobbed, and then sobbed some more until there was nothing left. When she thought she was all wrung out, she would begin anew. Finally, the sergeant came back and wrapped his arms around Beth's shoulders.

"I'm so sorry, I did everything I could." Beth turned and buried her head in the sergeant's shoulder. "We can't stay here, Beth. Those vans might come back, or worse, my unit might send out scouts. We've got to go before it gets dark."

"We… We can't just leave Deb here." Beth started crying again.

"Beth we're alive, and we've got to keep it that way. I know a back way to get you into Massachusetts, if that's what you want to do. But if we stay here, there's no telling what might happen to us. My unit would be more than happy to finish off what they started here today."

"I will not leave Deb at a rest stop, for hungry pigeons to feast on."

"Beth, you're not being reasonable. We've got to get going while we still can."

"Go! I'm not stopping you."

"Listen! You and your friend are the reason I'm here! If I leave without you, what was the point of it all?" the sergeant asked as he threw his hands up in the air.

"Well then, we have a dilemma because I'm not leaving her like this."

"Start getting some wood."

Beth didn't understand at first, but she followed the sergeant's gaze towards the picnic tables. Picnic tables that were slated for removal next year to be replaced with the new and improved Lucite models. That would never happen now, the tables and benches were still the good, old, garden variety wooden ones.

The sergeant picked up Deb's limp, lifeless body and gently placed her on the nearest table. Beth tried not to focus on the reason why as she continued picking up the wood dutifully. The sergeant gathered some brush and wood also. When he felt they had accumulated enough combustibles, he headed back to the truck and grabbed one of the spare gas cans.

Beth couldn't help but let out a whimper, "Won't that hurt her?" She, once again, started to cry, not because her friend had died, but because her friend never got to finish what she started. She would never get to be in Mike's arms again. She'd never get to kiss him or touch him.

The fire blazed in the oncoming twilight, and the sergeant merely stood there with his cap in hand, and head bowed, absently trying to rub the blood off his fingers. Beth, for one of the few times in her life, was speechless, but she managed.

"Deb, I haven't known you for all that long, and for most of the time I ever knew you existed, I hated you." The sergeant looked sideways at her, but she pressed on. "In a time when I wanted nothing more than to be in the arms of my boyfriend, you were the one that found solace there. And although I knew he loved me and still does, I hope," she added softly, "he also loved you. You were there to pick him up every time he fell. You kept him strong so that we could all escape that ship."

Now the sergeant took a long hard stare at this girl. He thought he recognized them back at the checkpoint but he had no clue from where. They were the ones that escaped from the alien vessel! He suddenly had so many questions to ask her, he didn't know where to begin, but he didn't think that now was a good time to do the asking.

"Mike said that everything he did on that ship was for me, but that's not entirely true. I watched him on our return flight from that godforsaken ship. He was a man torn, torn in two. He loved you at least as much as he loved me, maybe, and probably even more. You two had been through so much. And then we began this journey together, both of us hoping that we would find Mike again. Both of us secretly hoping he would pick one of us. Of course, at least I was the one hoping for that. But even if we had to share, I think we would have been able to do it.

"And then you saved my life back at your house. You had the strength to rescue me even after you watched your parents die. I would have just fallen over into a blob of Jell-o, but you kept going. I saw what Mike saw in you, you ARE..." (And she made sure to emphasize "are.") "... a beautiful person both inside and out. I consider it a privilege to have known you for the time I did. Mike loves you and so do I. Godspeed Deborah Anne Carmody, may the angels praise you with their songs." Beth wiped a tear away from her eye before she headed to the truck. The sergeant was quickly on her heels.

The sergeant had been driving for two hours before he felt it appropriate to break the silence. Beth was staring out her window the entire time. She had ceased crying, and speaking as well.

"You were on the ship?" the sergeant started cautiously. It was a long moment before Beth answered. The sergeant wasn't sure whether she heard him or just didn't feel like responding at the time. The sergeant was about to let his attempt at a conversation die when she began.

"We had gone to a concert, Mike and I, that is," she began slowly.

"Mike Talbot? The one who brought the alien commander back?"

"The very same."

"You know, a lot of people blame him for bringing this destruction upon us. They say if he hadn't abducted their commander, they would have never come and wrought this devastation."

"What do you think, Sergeant?" Beth turned to look squarely at the sergeant to gauge his response.

"I think they were coming no matter what. They weren't parked out there to catch some rays."

"Well, you're definitely right, Sergeant. They were coming no matter what. If anything, Mike's actions may have actually bought Earth a few more precious days. The aliens are very full of themselves. They would constantly tell me about their plans to conquer the universe; and how they had done this to countless planets before our little dot in the Milky Way was targeted."

"You used to talk to them?" Beth had to remind the sergeant to keep his eyes on the road as he glanced over at her.

"Yes," she said as a shiver ran up her spine. The mere thought of being so close to those creatures, so foreign and strange had, at the very least, been unsettling. "Unlike Mike and Deb." She had to pause momentarily as the mention of Deb made her voice crack. The sergeant reached over and gave her shoulder a comforting squeeze. Beth flinched a little, but it wasn't altogether unwelcome.

"Like I was saying," she began again as she cleared her throat. "Unlike Mike, Deb and the thousands of other people on that ship, I was more like a guest than a prisoner." And for the next three hours, she told her experiences to the sergeant. The sergeant was familiar with Mike's side, at least most of it. The military had been briefed on his narrative.

But Beth's part had been, for the most part, ignored. And the military's version had been sanitized until it was very antiseptic and fact-based only. Beth's account had been full of emotion and pain. As an eyewitness account it was fascinating.

It was approaching the wee hours of the morning before the sergeant even remotely began to feel the effects of the preceding day. Fortunately, their destination was quickly approaching. Beth had begun to wrap up her saga when she noticed the signs.

"We're going to the Kangamangus?"

"Yeah, it's the safest place around this area. No one will bother us here… At least not military. We'll regroup and head into Massachusetts a different way, a way that shouldn't be guarded." The sergeant contemplated telling Beth how he planned to approach the state, but a quick glance at Beth convinced him it would fall on deaf ears. She was fast asleep.

The sergeant's mind had been wavering all day on whether he had taken the right course, or could have done anything differently to save Deb. He saw the pain in Beth's eyes and knew it would be a long time before she ever let the memories of the day slip on by. The sergeant hoped that she didn't hold him responsible for the death of her friend. But he knew he would always be a constant reminder. So now what? Was the big question.

Even if he could get Beth into Massachusetts safely, and that was a big if because his unit also knew the unguarded routes back into the state; more than likely, they would have to cover quite a few of them in the days to come. He couldn't go back to his family since they were probably being watched and who knows? His commander had, more than likely, already visited his house and told his wife and parents what happened.

There were, most likely, two versions. Either the colonel told Mr. & Mrs. O'Bannon that he was a hero and had died in the line of duty or that he was a traitor to his men. Either way, it wasn't good news. The colonel could have spared his family the shock of being a traitor, he thought. But there was always the chance he could slip by the defenses and get to his family. Then what? If he were still alive, he obviously didn't die a hero's death.

Furthermore, the colonel knew that his father came from a long line of military career men. He would never tolerate traitorous behavior. If the colonel even suggested that, O'Bannon would be in more danger from his parents than from his men.

"Oh, what a tangled web we weave." It was the only cliché he could think of but it fit. He pulled the truck over into one of the most remote camping locations that the state park had to offer. He wanted to ponder his multiple dilemmas a little more but sleep now had a firm hold and it wasn't about to let it go.

Beth, meanwhile, dreamt a thousand dreams but they all revolved around one theme. She dreamed she had finally made it back to Mike's open arms, but he wasn't waiting for her. No matter how fast she tried to reach him, Deb kept beating her to his warm embrace. Her heart swelled when she realized Deb was okay, only to be deflated again as soon as she realized Mike wanted Deb and not her. A thousand times, in a thousand dreams, she ran and every time was beaten out by her friend.

Beth woke with a start when, on the last embrace between Mike and Deb, Mike had pulled away with blood on his hands. "It's not mine," he said as horror began to contort his expression. Deb dropped to the ground as Mike pointed his finger, dripping with blood, squarely at Beth's chest. "You did this!" he screamed.

Sweat gleamed on her forehead, and she quickly wiped it away as she noticed the sheen of frost on the windows. The sergeant's head was against the driver's side window. It didn't appear that he would be waking up anytime soon. Beth took the opportunity to check out her surroundings and find a suitable place to relieve herself.

After having taken care of nature's call, Beth decided to explore her surroundings. She had been cramped in the truck for the better part of ten hours and had no desire to get back in it right away. Besides, it continually reminded her of Deb, who was someone she didn't want to think about, at least not right now.

She meandered down to the river and marveled at its beauty. The water shone in the morning sun and the sound was beyond soothing; she found it hypnotic. She thought Deb would have loved this place and that was all it took to snap her out of her reverie.

"Beautiful isn't it?" the sergeant said as he approached from behind. Beth turned in surprise, ready to bolt, before she realized who it was.

"Yes it is," was all she managed to answer. Beth's suspicions piqued as she wondered if the sergeant had tracked her to this place, until she noticed the plates, dishes and pans he was carrying.

"These dishes don't look like they've been washed in days," the sergeant said as he noticed where Beth's gaze had landed.

"They haven't," she said coolly as she brushed by him and headed back to the truck. The sergeant didn't understand her distance, but then, he often admitted to his friends, he had no clue what made the female mind tick.

He took in the breathtaking scenery for a moment and proceeded to wash the dishes. Freezing water or not, he was starving. He hadn't eaten a bite before his shift yesterday and that seemed like a lifetime ago. Well, the more he contemplated it, it definitely was a different lifetime ago.

When the sergeant returned, he noticed Beth had rummaged through the back of the truck and started preparing food for breakfast. He didn't say so, but he was grateful.

"Here, put the pans over here. I'm going to make pancakes and bacon," Beth announced as she looked up into his eyes warmly. The distance she exhibited before seemed to evaporate. The sergeant mentally shook his head; she only reaffirmed his theory.

"I didn't mean for you to cook breakfast," he commented.

"I know. I just wanted to do something nice for you, for all you've done for us. I mean, me," she added quickly. He noticed her tone soften as she caught her slip. He quickly spoke before she had too much time to dwell on all the tragic events that had transpired.

"I can take care of breakfast. I was a cook for a local diner before I enlisted in the National Guard."

"No that's fine, I'll take care of it," she said weakly as a tear welled up in her eye. The sergeant knew he was in trouble from that point on; his heart was melting. Beth was one of the most achingly beautiful women he had ever seen and she was in distress. It was almost like a fairy tale, but he reminded himself, in this tale, he wasn't the prince. And for only the second or third time in his life that he could remember, he felt envious of another person. He stooped down to wipe the tear away from her cheek and Beth flinched, as if she were expecting a slap.

The sergeant stood up quickly. "I...I'm sorry I...I just wanted to...ah... I just thought..." Beth just looked at him questioningly, the tear still rolling down her face but now her eyes took on the look of anger. And pissed off, the sergeant thought, only added another aspect to her beauty.

"I like my bacon crispy," he said as he walked away. He had no clue what else to say. He felt like Beth's eyes were boring a hole through his back, but she quickly turned to the task at hand. She lit the small gas grill that she and Deb had acquired a thousand miles ago at a local Ace Hardware Store.

She was shocked by the sergeant's move, but she couldn't deny the electrifying sensation it created on the surface of her skin. Her cheeks were on fire and she thanked her lucky stars that the sergeant had turned tail and ran. She knew from past experience her cheeks were blazing red. The sergeant made a triumphant return an hour or so later, carrying a couple of fish he had snared out of the river with a makeshift net.

"I caught us a couple of trout for lunch. I hope you're not a vegetarian." He winced inside as the words came out. How could he be so thick? They had just eaten bacon and pancakes for breakfast. Beth stared at him like he had gone out of his mind, but she thought it was cute anyway.

"Yeah, I'll eat fish," she stated. "But I'm not cleaning them."

"Not a problem" he said as he sat down on the cooler next to her. "I did that down by the river; I didn't want to gross you out."

"I've seen a lot worse."

"Uh yeah, I guess you have." Dumb! Dumb! Dumb! He mentally slapped his head with his fist. "Listen," he started hesitantly. She looked over at him with her beautiful, hazel green eyes. He hesitated. He wasn't sure if he should keep going or not. She kept staring at him, waiting for him to continue, another millisecond and he thought he might lose his nerve. Thank God, he thought, as she saved him the trouble.

"Don't worry about it," she said as she held his gaze. "I know you were just trying to show some kindness. I guess this new world has me kind of shell-shocked. I don't really expect any sort of warmth from people, at least not right now. You just took me by surprise, that's all."

"Thanks for letting me off the hook. So much has happened in the last twenty-four hours, I'm not sure which way is up." Then, for the first time, she truly realized what this man had given up for her and Deb. Emotions that were long buried and reserved for another welled up inside her. Before she knew what she was doing, she leaned over and kissed him.

Now it was his turn to be shocked. But he didn't pull away. The kiss lingered for a few seconds. Beth slowly eased her head back, before she leaned in full tilt, grabbing the back of the sergeant's head, pulling him close. Any closer, he figured, and he'd be on the other side.

The sergeant felt a brief moment of remorse for this act of infidelity, but it was inexplicable; he was drawn to this woman like a moth to the flame. And, knowing her penchant for getting in trouble, he figured that would be the way he went out. But right now, however, that was okay.

They made love for hours on a musty, old blanket. The snap in the air only electrified their exposed skin. And for the briefest of times, Beth never thought once of Mike.

Chapter 40
Indian Hill

"How bad is the cave-in?" Paul slammed his hand on top of his desk so hard that the private in the outer office jumped.

"Sir, we're not sure. It's impossible to get close because of the small arms fire." Paul looked at the man with murderous intention.

"Small arms fire from whom?" Paul demanded.

"We aren't sure, sir. And..."

"I want answers."

"Sir, I have no answers. The only thing I know for sure is that Colonel Salazar and his team were in the tunnel when she blew." Paul's stomach turned; he couldn't afford to lose his second in command. He relied on Salazar's expertise and handling of the troops immeasurably. The captain noticed the change in Paul's demeanor. He pressed on.

"Sir, for good or bad, we have to believe that the colonel or at least some of his men are alive." Paul looked on questioningly.

"Sir, there is a small battle going on down there. I've got to believe it's Colonel Salazar and his men against whoever detonated that bomb."

"What about getting some men down there and helping out?"

"Two things, sir. First off, that whole tunnel is now structurally unsound. Do you want to risk any more men down there? And the other is that you can't see two feet in front of you in there. It would be impossible to know who you were shooting at. We could cut our own men to ribbons and not even realize it."

"Captain, I want full guard details on both sides of

that tunnel. I want each and every man that comes through that tunnel unarmed and restrained until we sort this mess out."

"And Colonel Salazar? Should he come through?" Paul couldn't believe that his friend and second-in-command had anything to do with this whole affair. Sure, they had their differences, but nothing that would accommodate treason.

"Bring him here immediately, unless he requires medical attention."

"Unarmed sir?"

"Everyone, Captain. Get to it, now!" The captain saluted and headed out the door. Paul was left to reflect on the events that led up to this whole scenario.

The National Guardsmen had assimilated very well into Paul's unit. Sure, there was still some suspicion regarding them, but Paul had done his best to alleviate the worst of it. He made sure that these men were evenly distributed throughout the unit and none of them had too much in the way of high security positions, although he allowed for that to change.

Some of these men had very skilled positions previously when the Earth still made sense. It made no sense at all to waste that talent. Sure, some of them despised what Paul had done, and still others fell easily into the routine. Military was military after all, and that's what some people needed--the attention to detail and the discipline that was inherent with that philosophy.

***

When Mrs. Fogarty's children came back parentless, many grumblings had
surfaced and not all from the Guard unit. Some had not liked the dogma associated with it. There was no easy way out of that one. The events of that day had spread like wild fire throughout the Hill. The fact that Paul had intended to kill those people in cold blood was not lost on anybody.

Most realized the wisdom of the decision, and had to, even if with great difficulty, accept the reality of it. To let those people go, was tantamount to suicide. Secrecy was security. But still others would never come to terms with their leader's actions. To them, there was no justification for murder, not even self-preservation.

In these people, Paul felt the trouble began, although that wasn't the only front he was battling. Rumors also spread, "from God knows where," Paul muttered. One was that the aliens were providing amnesty to those who gave themselves up. These acquiescent ones would be given wonderful places to live out their lives, safe from the wrath that would be brought to bear against those that bore arms against them.

Where this information came from, Paul had no idea. Every conceivable area of bandwidth was scanned by Paul's highly-skilled radio men. If they received a peep about anything like this, he would have most certainly heard about it. But to those few bad seeds who began this rumor, the rot had already taken hold and started to infect.

Sure, who wouldn't want to get out from living underground and safe from the highly trained and dangerous enemy? Yeah, it sounded like a great deal. Problem was, it wasn't true. The people that gave up were far more likely to end up on the dinner table than be set up in some seaside resort. Most knew the fallacy of these rumors and the damage they could inflict. Information was the key to dispelling these myths and Paul had made sure to disseminate as much of this as possible without making it look like propaganda.

But still it persisted and apparently festered, judging by the day's sabotage. What did they hope to accomplish? Sure, blowing the tunnel would be harmful but not to any extreme. Most of the food had long since been removed from the grocery store. In fact, plans had been laid to close that tunnel to prevent anybody from finding the entrance to the Hill and to relieve the guard details who monitored the site twenty-four/seven. Guard duty was important but there were still other very valuable jobs that could be performed here. So what was the reason? What was the point?

It was nothing more than a hastening of the plans already in effect. Paul sat at his desk with his elbows resting on the surface, his hands folded over each other. He slowly lowered his head down when suddenly, his head shot back up with the dawning of a thought. Diversion, it was a diversion!

"Damn it!" Paul exclaimed. "Private! Get in here!" It was an amazingly quick response, but the private was already on the move when his general began to shout.

"Get Colonel Sal.." and then he corrected himself. "Get Captain Baker up here, fast. And on the way out, sound the general alarm." The private nodded at all the right times, but understanding did not come so quickly. He knew about the tunnel and the measures the general had taken to contain the situation, so why the alarm? The alarm only meant bad things. Right now, the private wished he hadn't eaten that second bowl of oatmeal this morning. It was sitting in his belly like a lead weight.

Red lights blazed along the hallways and in each room occupying the Hill. A controlled pandemonium broke loose as the alarm rang three times and silenced itself, lest it be discovered from above. But the effect was instantaneous. Men and women ran to their posts in various stages of disarray. This was not a drill, that was understood. The alarm would only be sounded under the gravest of matters. Were they under attack? No one knew. They could only hope they had prepared well enough to thwart off whatever threat came their way.

The second explosion, although not close enough to do any physical damage, still had enough power to throw Paul to the ground.

Chapter 41 - Mike Journal Entry Ten
Paris

Many moments passed before I could shake the dread of the encounter with Deb. She had been here. But what did it mean? Roy had completely retreated down the hallway, crucifix in hand and Hail Mary's flying. He didn't approach me until a full five minutes had passed and he was somewhat assured that the vision wasn't coming back. Thankfully, he didn't say anything about the whole affair. I'm not sure I would have known what to say anyway.

He quietly escorted me to the colonel's office, and I noticed that his grip on his crucifix was much tighter than that of his weapon. If I had any notion of escaping, this would have been the time.

My concern for Deb was, so far, outweighing all the events that were unfolding before me. What I saw left me with an ominous feeling. One which I hoped I would not carry for the rest of my days.

Colonel Brintley's office wasn't lit much better than the rest of the warehouse. Apparently, the aliens succeeded in severing one of the main power grids to this region. Battery-operated backup lights were the only source of energy in this place. How long would they last? Candle power next. The aliens were doing their very best to throw us full tilt back into the Stone Age. A few more days of this type of barrage and they would succeed.

Colonel Brintley was a big man somewhere in the neighborhood of six foot and two hundred pounds and he looked dangerous. The salt and pepper crew cut did little to

The colonel looked like he had fought his
temper that...rs lined his left cheek, as well as a wound
way to the t... below his neck line and looked like it would
that disapp... about anyone else except this man. He stood
have kille... hand extended.
to greet ... ptain Talbot! It is so good to see you. I hope that
my me... were not too rough with you," he said as he looked
sever... y at Roy. The act was for my benefit. The colonel
didn... look like he gave a rat's ass about my welfare or abuse
... the hands of his men. Roy completely dismissed the
glance.

"Not at all; we even stopped for croissants. Although, I have to admit, I like the ones at McDonalds better." The colonel's face tightened for a moment and then softened as he regained control. And then it came out.

"You can see, Captain, why we are not all that thrilled to be in your company at the moment." I can't say I was expecting that but at least he was honest; and for that I could respect him.

"How long until the next attack, Colonel?"

"They have given us another twenty-four hours to deliver you," he stated flatly.

"Then could you please have Roy here direct me to my quarters. I have some things I'd like to take care of." The Vice Sergeant looked pissed. I think he thought I didn't give a care about the country, but the colonel understood. Well, now I knew he had brains to go with the brawn.

"Vice, please take the captain to my quarters." Roy was now more puzzled than ever. He knew some sort of information had been passed between these two but he'd be damned if he knew what it was.

"Right away," Roy said as he snapped to attention and saluted.

I made my decision almost immediately. I knew that ultimately, every one's fate on Earth was predetermined. But I'd be damned if I was going to be labeled as the man who destroyed France. Who was I anyway, to decide their fate? I was not the judge and jury. My life, in comparison, was nothing. The good of the many far outweighed myself. Although when you are put in that spot, the rhetoric isn't quite as easy to swallow. It's a lot easier to hold up mighty ideals when you're not the crux of the morality.

My encounter with Deb had been taking up the majority of my thoughts. I was now more convinced than ever that she had departed this earth. I could only hope she found a better place, as I found myself desperately wanting to join her. That made my decision that much better. I hoped Beth would understand.

I tried twice to catch some sleep before my departure, but no sooner did my eyes close, when a myriad of visions would reawaken me. The bulk of them were not pleasant by any stretch of the imagination. For the better part of the past two months, I had been trying to forget what the aliens looked like. Now I was going to them, almost willingly.

The colonel sent me a meal fit for a king. "So this is what last supper's look like," I quipped to the delivery man.

"Pardonez-moi, monsieur?" the private asked.

"Nothing, nothing. Thank you. Gracias." I just said "thank you" to the man in two languages he didn't understand. He merely handed me the tray and left. I wanted to savor my last few moments of life, or at least freedom, but I was afraid that the aliens might have itchy trigger fingers, so to speak. I didn't want any more innocent lives pinned on me.

At four hours to the deadline, I contacted the colonel and told him I would be ready to go in another fifteen minutes. I was not one for prayers, even having been raised a strict Roman Catholic, but this seemed as good a time as any. I knelt at the edge of the colonel's bed and did the "Our Father" like I had done so many times with my father, oh, so many years ago.

I finished up and headed towards the door. The sight I encountered when I opened it almost sent me back into the room. Men and women, all military, were lined on both sides of the hallway. When they saw me step out, they all stepped up to attention; and as I walked down the long corridor to where the colonel was, they each snapped off a salute as I passed. I was both honored and embarrassed by this display. Little did they know that to me, mine was more an act of cowardice than courage. I didn't want to be blamed for anymore mass murders and, more importantly, I wanted to be reunited with Deb. I guess I could call it "suicide by alien."

"I hope you enjoyed the meal," the colonel said as he led me to the waiting Jeep.

"Yeah, everything was great," I lied. The only thing I didn't sniff at and put back on the plate was the cheesecake. The colonel said little else throughout the journey except an occasional direction to the driver. There really wasn't much to say, not much sense in talking about the weather anyway right now.

"Where are we heading, Colonel?" I asked not so much because I cared, but because the silence was driving me nuts. There were about a half dozen times I wanted to jump out and take my chances with the locals.

"Ground Zero."

"Ground Zero?"

"Where the Eiffel Tower once stood. There's a huge crater there, and that's where they want you."

"I always wanted to see the Eiffel Tower," I said.

"Well, then today's not your lucky day."

"Not at all," I added.

And that was it. Not another word was uttered as we approached the complete destruction of Paris. Buildings that once stood mighty and proud now barely reached the height of an average man's knee. It looked like the work of a spoiled giant child who had taken his hand and completely leveled his Lego structures. That was, of course, until the crater began to loom.

It was vast. It looked like the fist of a great god had slammed down into the soft ground. It was a mile across, if it were a foot. Earth had surged up out of the expanse and dripped down the sides. Where the rest of the landscape was flat, the lip of the crater had risen to almost a hundred feet. I was about to ask the colonel how he planned to navigate it when I noticed a makeshift tunnel that had been drilled through the ledge.

The Jeep plunged into the darkness; it was nearly as dark as my heart was feeling. And then we came out on the other side. The same engineers who made the tunnel had constructed a roadway of sorts. By the looks of it, the donkey trail at the Grand Canyon would have been the Autobahn in comparison. The vastness of the crater struck home, once inside. It had to have been at least a half mile deep and there was nothing manmade anywhere. How could anything have survived this blast?

But there was something, dead center in the middle of the crater. It glinted in the sun as we approached, and by the way my nerves were reacting, I could tell it wasn't of human origin.

"Here we go again," I said to no one in particular. The colonel took note of my words but said nothing. The men in the Jeep tensed; they didn't want to be any closer to this than I. As we approached, the ship began to take form. It was of the fighter class that had been described to me not so long ago. The hull appeared to be scorched in places, whether from the bomb that was detonated inside the mother ship, or from fighting on this planet was not clear.

The Jeep abruptly stopped about five hundred yards from the vessel. I knew that this was as far as my ride was going. The colonel stepped out. First, he surveyed the ship in the distance and then turned to salute me as I also stepped out. Military protocol was the furthest thing from my mind at the moment but I returned the salute, half-heartedly before I headed towards the ship.

I had no sooner gone five or six steps when I heard the Jeep roar into life and begin its ascent back up the alien-created mount. I had never felt quite so alone in my entire life. Every step was an effort, my breathing, laborious. My legs felt like tree trunks. After what seemed like an hour and five miles crossed, a voice emanated from the hull.

"Halt! State your business." The language was English, but the speaker was not. From the rasp of the voice, I knew it to be of alien origin. The hammering in my chest made it difficult to breathe, much less speak. From this distance, I would have to yell in order to be heard, lest they vaporize me on the spot. Who knows? Maybe that wouldn't be such a bad idea.

"My name is Mike Talbot!" I yelled.

Immediately, the fighter's outer door hummed and opened. Two Genogerian guards, armed to the teeth, and I guessed their teeth were also a weapon, I thought sardonically, ran out. They approached me with their weapons at the ready. It didn't much matter though. They could have come with fly swatters and beaten me, I was already defeated. My head was bowed, my spirit was shot. The guard who arrived first wanted to make sure, unnecessarily, I might add, that I was no threat.

He thrust the butt of his rifle squarely into my solar plexus region. What little breath I still possessed was expelled from me in a loud and resounding "Ummph." I toppled over, not even having the presence of mind to break my fall. I was astounded at how bad French soil tasted. I was then unceremoniously hoisted to my knees and dragged towards the ship.

But I was wholly unprepared for what happened next. Standing at the top of the ramp way was Durgan and he looked more pissed off than either of the two guards. At this point, the thought of fighting and taking my chances seemed the better of the options presented to me. I tried to find the strength to get one of my legs back into a position that would allow me to stand on my own accord, when I felt, what can only be described as a huge horsefly, biting the back of my neck.

Before the world completely blacked out on me, I noticed Durgan with his hands on his hips, laughing that maniacal laugh I had heard so many times before on the ship. "This isn't good," was the only verbiage I could muster before the pinhole of my vision completely disappeared. Sweet black nothingness. I slept the sleep of the dead. If only I had been so lucky.

Chapter 42

The ride back to the Massachusetts border was a quiet one. Both Beth and the sergeant weren't sure on what grounds they stood. The sergeant was solemn. He had crossed a line from which there was no return.

Beth was almost inconsolable. She felt, in a word, dirty. Even worse, tarnished. She had no idea if she would ever see Mike again, and if she did, how could she ever face him? It was tearing her up inside, and yet she had given herself willingly. Who was she kidding? She threw herself at this man. The companionship was something lacking in her life of late. She liked the feel of his powerful arms wrapped around her. It made her feel warm inside. She was rapidly developing feelings for this man and it scared her to the depths of her soul. Yet, she still had a strong urge to continue going to Massachusetts. But to what end? Would she run into Mike's arms and beg forgiveness? Would he accept? And what of the sergeant? Was she just using him as a means to an end? By sleeping with him had she solidified his help? At times like these, even she felt it difficult being a woman.

"We're going to have to ditch this ride."

"Huh?" Beth shook her head trying to orient herself back into the here and now.

"I said we are going to have to get rid of this truck before we go into Massachusetts." He really wanted to ask her what she was thinking about, but he had a good idea what it was and he wasn't so sure right now that he wanted to know.

"Do you mean that we should steal another before we get to the border or are you saying we should abandon the car thing completely?" She wanted to tell him what she was feeling right now, but she wasn't sure if she was ready to hear what she had to say.

"Abandon it. At least until we get a few miles in. Any road access is going to be completely covered. If I know the colonel, he'll stretch his forces to the limit to make sure he finds us. We'll ditch the truck in the woods and then hike for five or ten miles until we'll find some alternate transportation." The sergeant didn't let Beth in on the fact that this was probably going to be the most difficult hike she had ever endured. Massachusetts' forest is among the thickest in the country. Briar patches are more common than squirrels in this part of the world.

"We're only going to be able to take a few things, so pack lightly. Just enough food to get us through the next day or two and the medical supplies." 'Why was he acting so distant?' Beth was looking for some sort of signal that the events of the morning hadn't been an anomaly or was she? Maybe she should just leave it alone. Maybe that was the best solution for the situation.

"Beth, I wanted to talk to you this morning," the sergeant began. Or maybe it wasn't, she reasoned.

"Go on," she said hesitantly.

"Beth, I'm married."

"Is that what that ring on your finger means?" she said jokingly to try and ease the tension that was building in the truck's cab.

"No, I'm serious. I'm married and I love my wife. I've known her most of my life; we grew up on the same street. And this is the first time that I've ever been with anybody else."

"Ever?" she asked incredulously.

He turned a shade or two of red but regained control. "There were a couple of times in high school when I made out with one or two different girls but, besides my wife, you are the only other person I have ever slept with." Beth was caught a little off guard, this was not the turn of events she was expecting.

"What are you trying to say, Grady?" She hoped beyond hope that he wasn't going to tell her that he loved her. She didn't think she could take it right now. It would just open up too many doors she was not prepared to venture beyond, much less look into.

"I'm just saying…" he started hesitantly. "I don't know what I'm saying, I just thought that you should know that. I'm not this stud that just goes around and sleeps with anybody. I mean I guess that it was special for me, and I think it was special for you too."

"Stop. Just stop there. Don't go any further." She put her finger over his mouth as he turned to look at her, an injured expression spreading across his face. "It was special for me too, Grady, but I'm not ready for this, I'm not ready at all. The death of Debbie still has me all confused. I just don't know what to think right now. And frankly, I don't want to at the moment." The sergeant turned his face forward. "Please don't be hurt. We've both been through some pretty dramatic things in the last forty-eight hours. Let's just try to see how things develop from here."

"That's fair enough," the sergeant said through clenched jaws. Beth wanted to try and smooth things out, but she just didn't have anything emotional left inside of her right now.

"How far 'til we have to start walking?" she asked.

"About an hour," he answered. Beth hunched down in her jacket and propped her knees up on the dashboard to try and get some much needed sleep.

Chapter 43
Indian Hill

"What do you mean, 'the aliens have Mike'? I knew I couldn't trust them. I'm going to send a battalion and wipe their asses off the planet once and for all! I'll finish off what the Germans couldn't." Paul was pissed, to say the least. His office looked as if a cyclone had passed through it, and in a sense, one had. One truly pissed-off cyclone.

"Sir, they didn't hand him over; he went voluntarily." Corporal Jackson said, trying his best to calm the general down.

"There's no goddamn way he went voluntarily. I saw his eyes. Those aliens scared him."

"Well, sir, apparently, the thought of more innocent lives dying for him scared him more." Paul stopped to think about that one for a moment, but it did little to slow down his tirade.

"But there's one thing you're forgetting, Corporal Jackson. He knows about this place." Corporal Jackson's face literally paled. "Yeah, do you see the dilemma now, Corporal?"

"Well, wha…What do we do now, sir, evacuate? Do you really think he'd give them this location?"

"No, I don't think he'd willingly give this place up, but he might not have a choice. He might not even know he's doing it. We have no way of knowing what type of interrogation tactics the aliens have. And no, we don't evacuate. We have nowhere else to go. If they come, we stand and we fight. There is no choice in this matter. This is our best hope and this is where we'll stand, or fall." he added softly.

Paul sat when the corporal left to think out the events of the past couple of days. Colonel Salazar and some of his men came out of the tunnel and all sustained injuries of one sort or another. Two of the more severely injured were still in the hospital with gunshot wounds and a couple of broken bones. The rest had varying degrees that would classify them as "walking wounded," injured but not badly enough to be taken off active duty.

Colonel Salazar had taken a small detail down the tunnel to figure out if shutting the tunnel would have been the best overall plan for the Hill; and, if so, how would they go about it safely. They were studying some of the blueprints for this leg of the tunnel when a small band of five men came running in their direction. Even from a hundred yards off, Colonel Salazar saw the trepidation in those men's eyes. They hadn't been expecting company. The colonel immediately withdrew his side arm. Most of the rest of the small detail followed suit. The two that were shot had not been so quick to react, and thus, Darwin's theory of evolution is wrought forward.

The approaching men stopped and started firing on the colonel's position while the colonel's men returned fire, killing one of the saboteurs instantly. Then they did something that took the colonel completely by surprise; they got up and started running towards him. This was like target practice, the colonel thought. Two of the men didn't made it twenty yards before they were riddled with bullets. Another man fell when the bomb blast hit. Debris rained down and the colonel heard sharp cries from his men. Some had been hit by falling rocks and beams. The choking dust was thoroughly blinding. The colonel wanted to get his men out of there but was unsure which way that was.

Then the nearby sound of an M-16 report followed by the entirely too close sound of a high-velocity projectile slamming off to the right of the colonel's head caused him to hasten his decision. The colonel and two of his men who hadn't succumbed to injury fired suppression shots to keep the attacker at bay. But it was like shooting in the dark. "There's no way he can see better than us, can he?" one of them asked. The shots were coming dangerously closer.

"Keep firing." The colonel shouted over their protestations.

"Colonel, I can't see anything," one of his men replied.

"Neither can that bastard, but he's still getting pretty close."

The opposition shots had ceased, and the colonel told his men to stop shooting for fear that the noise would muffle the others' true intentions of just slipping by through the cloak of dust. An eerie silence broke out. The support timbers groaned under the new weight load, and the colonel feared that if he didn't get his men out soon, they would be added to the victims of the day's roster. With four men severely injured and only three relatively healthy, getting them out of there in one try while watching their six was going to be extremely difficult. But difficult times call for extreme measures. So slowly but surely, the injured men extracted themselves from the damage, breathing a little easier as they went, but remaining vigilant.

Nothing was ever seen of the lone gunman again. He never surfaced at either end, and when the tunnel collapsed two hours later, he never would. The colonel was just emerging from the tunnel when the second blast hit. From what he could tell, the blast was more than halfway across the compound.

"Colonel!" came a very disoriented voice. "I request that you and your men drop your firearms."

"Don't you see I have wounded here!" the colonel barked.

"Sir, my orders are to disarm everyone that comes through the entrance." The colonel seethed but fighting with these guards could cost him the lives of more of his men, and his swollen pride was not that big.

"Fine. Get my men to the infirmary and take me to the general." The guard's stance softened a bit when he realized there would be no fighting.

"And, Sergeant," he added as he turned around. "There's at least one more man still alive in there and he's armed; the difference is, he's also dangerous." The sergeant stiffened, realizing that maybe his day was becoming a little more eventful than it already was. The second explosion came dangerously close to the Hill's ammunition banks. If that had ignited, the aliens would have had to award the rebels a gold star for helping them. As it was, the ammunition bunker was a closely guarded area with armory troops hand-picked by Paul. They had been there since the beginning and comprised the elite of this military force.

The renegades assumed a charge placed close enough would do the trick but Paul had planned well. The bunker was re-bar, reinforced concrete. It was the type of concrete-reinforced structure that military units throughout the world used; and no small C-4 explosive device was going to penetrate that tough skin.

Two men, who were seen running from the vicinity moments before the blast were rounded up and persuaded to talk. It was amazing what an unanesthetized tooth extraction can do to a grown man's philosophy on life. They sang like freed canaries.

Within minutes, twenty or so dissidents were rounded up who were also convinced to talk, albeit with less brute force. One look at their comrades' bloody mouths and they gave up everything. All in all, they captured somewhere in the neighborhood of fifty hardcore rebels.

The majority of them started running for their freedom with the initial bomb blast. Most of those, however, had also been taken captive while some died in the ensuing gun battles. But at least five survived to escape. Paul had troops out looking for them, but he had to admit, if only to himself, that if they hadn't been found by now, the likelihood of them being caught later was next to nil.

Chapter 44
Somewhere in Space

Most semblances of broadcast radio, and television, especially, were in shambles. An occasional local station was still up and running. Most of them were only on to broadcast the safest places to go for shelter or where there was a possibility of getting fresh bread. These stations, that were still operational, were guarded like fortresses.

During the early days of the invasion, a great many of these stations had been overrun with doomsayers and throngs of people who wanted to have their fifteen minutes of fame. Who could blame them when they only thought they had an hour left? Why not be a celebrity for one quarter of it? But on this fateful night, ratings were about to take a huge leap. The aliens had beamed a signal to each and every functioning station on the planet, radio and television alike.

"Hu-mans!" the alien voice began. "We have an event unlike any other ever viewed in your lifetimes. One week from tonight, your champion, Mike Talbot." At this point in my illustrious career, the vast majority of the planet's population had no clue whom I was. The aliens must have assumed I had paraded around the world, telling everyone of my exploits. Nothing, however, could have been further from the truth.

The military, from the beginning, wanted to keep this story as quiet as possible. Even if they hadn't, I had no desire whatsoever to keep reliving the events of those eighteen months. The droning voice continued.

"...will face another of your own, Durgan O'Shea, in a fight to the death. The winner will be crowned champion of the Earth gladiator games. He will then have the honor and privilege to fight, also to the death, the Genogerian champion, Slook Vademux."

At this point, all of our faces were shown on the screen. Although I wasn't actually there to witness it, I can tell you that every person who saw that broadcast had all the color drain out of their faces in an instant. Sure, Durgan looked insane and I looked scared, but it was Slook's mug that had everyone captivated. Most people had yet to see the species that was wreaking so much havoc on the planet, but here he was.

He wasn't skinny with big black eyes and long slender fingers like most of the earlier "abductees" claimed. He was immense, intelligent and fucking scary looking. The snout was smaller than today's traditional crocodile, but the teeth looked every bit as nasty.

"The winner of this match, if human…" The pause on "if human" was purposeful. The aliens had no illusions that their champion would lose. Only once, on the hundreds of planets they ransacked, had the local champion beaten the Genogerian champion. That was the Stryver's, Andible Louter. The Progerians hadn't taken too kindly to that loss and retaliated by wiping out the entire bloodline of the offending Genogerian, making future losses that much less, palatable.

"…will simply be set free." The message was repeated that way for two hours every day, basically just a recording that played over and over. Eventually, anyone who had not heard about it electronically learned by word of mouth. It could have been the biggest pay per view event ever in human history, but Don King was already presumed dead and now there wasn't a promoter big enough to take on the event.

***

Beth had actually dozed off when fate, divine intervention, coincidence, whatever you want to call it stepped in. The truck hit an enormous pothole, shaking the cab to its core. Beth was startled to alertness, but the swaying of the cab knocked her knee into the old Delco stock radio, roaring it into life. Beth's first instinct was to hit the power button before the obnoxious blare of static came on. She and Deb had tried unsuccessfully throughout their ride across the states to find something on the airwaves, but each and every time, they were only rewarded with the sound of the crackling paper, as they came to affectionately call it. They simply quit trying when they hit Pennsylvania and hadn't turned it on since. But before Beth could get to the dial, she caught something about being "set free."

"Did you hear that?" She sat up straight and looked over at the sergeant trying to gauge whether or not she had just hallucinated or actually heard right.

"Yeah, I heard something. I didn't really catch it though." The sergeant was excited also. His unit had been monitoring everything since the attacks began. The most they ever got was the occasional ham operator fishing to see if anybody else was still out there.

"This message will repeat in five minutes," the radio blared as Beth cranked the volume to maximum in an attempt to wring out more from it. She hastily turned it back down, but not too far; she didn't want to miss a word. She was almost giddy with excitement and had no idea how she was going to make the next five minutes pass, she thought conversation might help.

"Do you think it's a message from the government telling us the aliens have left? That would be so wonderful," she continued as she clasped her hands together. "I mean, could it be true? Could we all be free?"

"Hold on, Beth! What exactly did you hear?" The sergeant asked cautiously.

"All I heard was something about being 'set free'." The excitement in her voice was palpable. The sergeant wanted to catch the fever also, but he was a little more skeptical, but not because he didn't want to believe. He just didn't want to believe before he was sure it was true. Utter disappointment was a little more pain than he was prepared to deal with at the moment. What if everything he had done in the last few days was unnecessary? How could he tell his wife and child? His parents? What would he tell his men?

"Pull over!" Beth moaned.

"What is it? What's the matter?" The sergeant was concerned. He thought Beth saw something. Something potentially dangerous.

"I think I'm going to be sick. Please pull over." She labored, her cupped hands at the ready in case the truck didn't get into the soft shoulder fast enough. The sergeant did his best to bring the truck to a safe and controlled stop. Beth had barely enough time to fumble with the door handle before her breakfast made its triumphant resurgence.

The sergeant waited the obligatory few minutes until he heard her innards calm down. And then he climbed out of the truck. "Are you alright? Was it something you ate? I hope not 'cause I ate the same things you did."

"No," she said as she stood up, wiping the corner of her mouth with her jacket sleeve. "It was something I heard."

"Was it something I said? Oh… Wait. The radio? What about it?"

"The man they were talking about."

"Yeah, Mike Turtle, or something like that."

"No, Mike Talbot," she said, a little exasperated. "That's my Mike."

Recognition dawned on the sergeant's face. A pang of jealousy ripped through his belly. Where did that come from? He mused. "That's THE Mike Talbot? I thought he was safe and sound in a protected bunker somewhere."

"So did I." Concern laced Beth's face. "We've got to get to Walpole as fast as we can. I've got to find out what's going on." And the jealousy was back. The sergeant, for the life of him, couldn't figure out why he was having such strong feelings for this girl. But he found it terribly distracting.

"Say something, Grady!" Beth pouted. She looked like a spoiled child who wasn't getting the attention she felt she deserved. The sergeant was half expecting her to stomp her foot on the ground and cross her arms and then what?

Pout her bottom lip out? Yeah, that would complete the picture, he figured.

"Well, with any luck, we should be able to get to Walpole in two days. Three tops." Now her lip did begin to protrude.

"That's too long. I want to be there tonight."

"We can't do it, Beth. We've got to be extremely careful crossing over. Every access road is going to be covered. I told you we are going to have to ditch the truck and cross over by foot. And once we hit the woods, it's going to be some difficult traversing.

"And IF, (he emphasized "if") we get through without any serious problems, we've still got to secure some sort of transportation, which in itself isn't going to be easy. The Massachusetts National Guard, confiscated nearly all the cars and trucks that weren't being used by their owners. And in some cases, they took those too. So you kind of see the dilemma." Beth clearly saw it, but that didn't mean she liked it.

"Fine! Let's get going," she said as she hopped back in the cab of the truck.

Chapter 45 – Mike Journal Entry Eleven

"Where am I?" I said somewhat dazed. I attempted to sit up, but to no avail. I was not sure whether I was sedated into paralysis or wearing restraints. When my head cleared up a little later on, I realized it was both. The room was lit but, much to my chagrin I realized, it was the ever present, all-surrounding luminescence of the alien variety.

"Damn! I hoped that part was a dream," I muttered out loud, more to calm my nerves than for any particular audience.

"Not a dream, you turd. A bad dream possibly. A nightmare, most definitely." That voice alone snapped me back from la-la land. My eyes probably bugged halfway out of my head.

"Yeah! I'd be scared if I had to face me too," he laughed, that grating, familiar, maniacal laugh.

"Well, I see the extra time on this ship hasn't done much for your personality, Durgan." I nearly cursed out his name.

"Oh, it's done plenty, you little pansy. While you were down with your little girly-friends, I was training and fantasizing about this very day. And to be honest, looking at you now, I'm a little disappointed. I have to admit that, at one point, you had me somewhat concerned. Not scared per se, but a little concerned. You looked like a wily and crafty adversary, one that was due a small measure of my admiration. The way you dispatched some of your foes was brilliant. Sheer brilliance. But now I'm not sure you're even worthy of my attention, even with one prosthetic leg."

Indian Hill 2: Reckoning

Durgan spat the last part out as he hiked up his jeans to show me what appeared to be something more out of 'The Terminator' than anything else.

"But I still do owe you for this little beauty, even if it is stronger than the original. Maybe when I'm done with you, the aliens will piece back together whatever is left and I can keep you as a pet." He laughed again.

"Listen, you ape…" I wasn't sure if this was the right approach, especially considering I was drugged and tied down, but the dude was started to piss me off. Anyway he didn't seem too concerned. "I have no clue what you are even talking about. And to be honest, I'm not sure that even you know what you're talking about."

Durgan was leaning against what appeared to be a desk but from my limited vantage point, this was not clearly discernible. What was clear was Durgan cleaning his fingernails with a six-inch curved blade. That appeared to be much more important to him than anything I said. He looked up after he finished his task. A deranged grin spread from ear to ear.

"Well, I'm here to tell you, old buddy." As he stood up and began walking over to me. I involuntarily tensed up. "Oooh, you are the nervous one, aren't you." He started to toss the knife back and forth between hands. I struggled to keep up with the movement, but it was impossible. Either he was just too fast or my doped-up perception was for shit. Then he folded the blade up and placed it in his pocket.

"You see, my friend…" he continued as he leaned on me, his hot breath scraping the inside of my nostrils. "One week from tonight you and me are going to dance. Only this dance is going to be unlike any other. Me and you are going to have the largest audience of all time. So you had better make this last. If you go and die on me in the first minute or two, I'm going to be really pissed."

"Yeah? How do you think that's going to make me feel?" He stood up, and this time, true laughter came out. Perhaps it was something closer to who the original Durgan had once been. But it was short-lived.

"You're a funny man, Talbot, and I'm going to enjoy ripping that funny right out of your neck," he said as calmly as if he were telling me about the weather forecast. "Don't embarrass me out there! If you fall to your knees and just start begging for your life, I guarantee I'll take my sweet ass time slicing and dicing you in front of your adoring fans."

"You're a sick bastard, Durgan, and don't worry about me. I should have kicked your ass when I had the chance." Durgan snarled at me as he walked out the door. I was hoping that my false bravado held up. Good thing for the restraints though; they kept me from shaking right off the friggin' table. I fell back to sleep sometime, since there was really not a whole bunch to do when you're strapped down. I was awakened later, by one of the Progerians whom I recognized, as crazy as that sounds. I definitely spent too much time on this ship.

"I know you, you helped me once."

"Yes, yes I did. That might not have been the most prudent move, considering the outcome. But the fact remains you have made me rich. And although you destroyed a bunch of our ships and kidnapped our supreme commander, (may the great one live forever), my cousin was out on that dock! Did you know that?" His head bobbed up and down in an exaggerated tempo. It was something I noticed often happened when the Progerians got a little too agitated.

I wanted to tell him that I had nothing to do with the destruction of the ships, but it didn't seem like it would have mattered, so why bother?

"I thought about killing you myself... Maybe just coming in here and shooting you with some poison. And I most likely would have, but when they posted the odds of your upcoming event, I couldn't help but ponder the possibilities. You see, you are a hundred to one shot against beating Durgan and still the drakkar keeps pouring in on his side. The odds will just keep rising and that's when I'm going to make my bet, when they are at their peak. I don't know what it is about you, hu-man, but you seem to always 'pull it out in the clutch,' as your species says. No matter how bad it looks, you just win. And right now, from where I stand, it looks pretty bad. So instead of killing you, I'm going to give you some of my special concoction and free you up here so that you can begin your training."

"I guess I don't have any say in this?" I inquired as he raised up my shirt sleeve and revealed a hypodermic.

"Silly hu-man, you'll never have another choice in your life." I grimaced as he seemed to deliberately jab me with the needle. I guess I couldn't blame him. But he was wrong if he thought I was going to be his little lap dog from here on. My blood began to boil; sweat came out of every pore. I thought I might combust on the spot.

"What did you give me?" I was concerned maybe he had changed his mind and decided to go with the poison.

"Just a little something to get you on your way. You look a little lighter than I remember; you had better start bulking up. A week is not that much time." The Progerian left but not before he had completely freed me from my confines.

I sat up rubbing my wrists where the straps had been. I glanced around my room. It was my original room. A pang stirred in my belly. It was the same room all right, but there were none of the previous occupants. Images of Deb and Beth flashed before my eyes. I wanted to cry, right there and then. But what would that solve? If I ever wanted to see them again I was going to have to take care of business first.

I walked over to the weight bench. I felt like I could lift ten men, but in reality only if those ten men weighed twenty-seven pounds each. Right now, I wasn't much weaker than when I left the ship, but how long would this doping last? That, however, wasn't going to be a problem.

My greedy Progerian friend showed up every day to feed me food and my daily supply of "vitamins," as he liked to call them. What this was doing to me internally, I had no clue. Physically though, it was unbelievable. Stamina, strength and sheer muscle mass, which had been lacking since my "surgery", were now coming back in leaps in bounds. Progress that should have taken months was being reduced to days. It was almost hour-by-hour. I knew it couldn't be good for me, but what was the alternative? Die at the hands of a madman?

Durgan also came to visit me on occasion. I felt like a toy to him, one which he had been waiting for some special holiday to unwrap. Somehow, I never got the feeling that I'd be one of those toys that stayed on a shelf as a souvenir. He meant to play hard and if he broke his "toy"? Oops.

Chapter 46

Beth and Sergeant Grady O'Bannon made it across the state line, completely undetected. The going had been rough and slow, but for the most part uneventful. Beth's surliness had only exasperated the sheer silence of their crossing. Had Grady known about his previous unit's condition, they could have easily driven the truck across the border and into Walpole. A large group of bikers and hot rodders had tried to plunder the Guardsmen's bounty.

The ensuing battle had nearly crippled Barracks Twenty-Seven. The commanding officer recalled all units that were patrolling other ports of entry into the state. The Guard unit lost nearly a third of its men and just about half their equipment and munitions before thwarting the attempted takeover. The colonel was busy meeting with the wives of the newly departed while O'Bannon and Beth made their crossing.

Getting new wheels proved difficult but not nearly as dour as O'Bannon first speculated. While the National Guard had "acquired" a great many vehicles, the bulk of them had been pickup trucks or SUVs, things that were more suitable to carting around a lot of gear. When the two travelers came upon a Jeep, sitting by the side of the road, they could hardly believe their luck.

"Do you think it runs?" Beth asked as she pulled the briars out of her jacket sleeves. Whoa! She spoke, was his first reaction, but Grady knew that wouldn't get him anywhere.

"A better question to ask is, whose is it and are they close by?" She gave him a sideways glance and then looked up from her sleeves as they both approached the Jeep cautiously. Most of the people they encountered didn't take kindly to strangers, especially those that were trying to take stuff from them.

"Shhhh," the sergeant said as he held out an arm to Beth to hold her back. Beth's eyes grew wide.

"What? What is it?" she asked as she looked around nervously.

"Stay here. I think I see somebody in the passenger seat."

Beth stopped short as she squinted her eyes to see what he saw. The glare coming off the hood made it nearly impossible, but she thought that she also saw a figure. And it didn't look like it was moving. Beth could almost sense that she was staring down the barrel of a gun.

The sergeant moved up the side of the Jeep while Beth stood like a statue in the middle of the street. The sergeant made it to the driver's side window and peered in, his stomach muscles tensed. The passenger's throat had literally been slit from ear to ear. The sergeant turned away as fast as he could; but the image of the maggots spilling out of the man's jugular would be something that he would carry with him for the rest of his life. He felt that his baggage was becoming more cumbersome.

"What is it?" Beth asked as she saw Grady's reaction. She started to run up to the Jeep. The sergeant caught her right before she made it.

"Wait! Wait! There's nothing in there you need to see." Her curiosity was piqued but if what was in that car turned him so pale, she thought, that was all the reason she needed not to argue.

"Well, what about the car?" she asked, trying to change the subject. Grady pointed to the gas tank. The top had been popped and was loosely hanging from its restraining cord.

"My guess is that's it's as dry as a bone. And I don't think I could get in that thing anyway." Unlike Lot's wife in Sodom, Beth decided against turning back to take a quick look. For if she had, she might also have been turned to a pillar of salt.

The sun was temporarily obscured by a thick mass of clouds, leaving the dead stranger to gape, sightlessly, as the two rapidly departed. The pair preferred to walk down the center lane of the roadway except when they occasionally chanced to hear an oncoming vehicle. Then they would plunge into the woods like ten-year-olds playing war games. Both times had been false alarms, but that wasn't going to stop them from diving into the brush, no matter how many thorns had to be removed. The alternative could be much worse.

They had been walking for close to an hour when the sergeant finally felt that his stomach had calmed down enough. He was thinking about Beth and him for the better part of the morning. Now he had built up enough courage to broach the matter. He hoped this wouldn't re-upset his churning gut, but not knowing seemed infinitely worse.

"Beth, I wanted to talk to you." Beth turned to face him, knowing full well which way this conversation was headed. She knew it was coming. But knowing and preparing are two different things entirely. She nodded as if to say, "Go ahead." Grady took her lack of communication as a bad sign but he plodded forward anyway.

"Beth, I just need to know what yesterday morning meant to you. I mean, I feel…"

"Stop!" she exclaimed as she turned to face him. Her face blushed a few shades of red. "Please don't go there. Can't yesterday just be about yesterday? I was scared and lonely and you were there. I love another man, Grady." Grady's gut was not going to be let off the hook so easily, just yet.

"Listen, I was there too. You can't be implying that I was just an available body. I may not be a genius when it comes to figuring out women, but I know you felt something too." Beth shied away from his insinuations. She knew he was right; she just didn't want him to be. How could she do this to Mike? She should have died in that firefight. Debbie was much more worthy to be with him. Beth began to cry at the thought of her friend.

"Please," she sobbed. "I did feel something, but I'm in love with Mike, and you're married. What we did was beautiful and it meant a lot to me, but… but it was a mistake. Please, for my sake, just let it be what it was--a one night affair. Something we can cherish but something that can never happen again."

Grady wanted to say something, no, he was dying to say something, but nothing made any sense. They stood there looking at each other long after they heard the dull roar of an approaching engine. Both had been so lost in their own thoughts that they nearly became road kill before they bolted for opposite sides of the roadway.

The sergeant kept his head bowed and listened to the car come to a stop, approximately right where they were standing moments before. He was angry at himself for letting Beth down like this. Maybe he could distract them long enough so that Beth could get away. His plan was cut short by a voice.

"You can come out now. We won't bite," the voice coaxed. The sergeant tried to place the voice with someone in his unit but no matches were being made. The voice sounded a little too frail.

"Hello?"

Beth? What was she doing? Could she make it any easier for them? The sergeant stood up to try and urge Beth to make a run for it, but the military two-tonner he expected to see was actually a '56 or '57 DeSoto with an occupant that appeared to be double the age of the car he was driving. The man's companion, who, they were soon to find out, was his wife, looked directly at the sergeant and waved.

Her gapped-toothed smile completely disarmed the sergeant, who found himself smiling right along with her. But her smile quickly faded as she produced a sawed-off shotgun from her lap. The sergeant was caught totally unawares. He stood frozen.

"Never can be too sure, sonny," the old woman

cackled. "Now, I want you to carefully open up your jacket and slowly remove anything that I might perceive as a threat to me or my husband." As the sergeant slowly began to unzip his jacket, the woman continued.

"Now I want you to remember, son. That I have a twenty gauge shotgun leveled on your chest, and the barrel has been reduced, so as to increase my pellet spread. Now, I would imagine even if I hadn't been last year's senior Discus Downrange champion, I would still have a difficult time missing at this range with this weapon." The sergeant nodded to her that he understood her perfectly.

"Ma'am, don't go getting any thoughts. I've got a nine millimeter pistol that I am going to remove from my shoulder holster." The old coot didn't so much as flinch but he noticed she may have put an extra ounce or two of pressure on her trigger. *My life is hanging by a thread with this old lady! I sure hope she doesn't have palsy*, and that was the only thought he could muster. He placed the weapon gingerly on the pavement, so as to rid himself of his potential demise.

"What else you got in those pockets, dearie?" the lady whistled through her missing teeth. The sergeant noticed that Beth was also woodenly going through the same routine as he. He felt angry at himself for being duped so thoroughly and putting Beth's life in danger like this. Rage mounted in him as he stared at the rifle pointed at Beth.

"Sonny!" the lady shouted. "I said, what else you got in them pockets?"

"Just a small fishing knife," he answered, not really paying her much attention. The old woman followed his gaze to see what was keeping him so transfixed.

"Listen, boy. Don't go getting your dander in an uproar! As soon as you do as I tell you, this will go a lot smoother." The sergeant finally pulled himself away from the drama on the other side of the car long enough to listen to the lady.

"I said, get the knife out and be quick about it," she

repeated as she hefted the shotgun up for emphasis. The sergeant did as he was told and placed it next to his sidearm.

"Careful," she said as she watched him hesitate for a millisecond near the pistol. "I don't want to shoot you, but believe me, I will." And he believed her as he pulled his hand back in. The sergeant heard, rather than saw, the sound of a metallic clanking before he heard the old man speak.

"Alright, Miss, you look like you know what these are and what they're for. Now put them on."

'What is going on?' The sergeant thought, but before he was able to come to a conclusion, the answer was quite literally thrown at him. Handcuffs twirled through the air, catching a glint of sunlight as they hit the ground and skidded to a stop a few inches from his feet. She even had a good arm to go with her marksmanship skills, thought the sergeant.

"We've done nothing to you. Why are you doing this to us?" the sergeant asked.

"You haven't done anything to us, because we're not going to let you. How's that for an answer? Now put on them bracelets, or I'm going to make sure that you don't need them." He watched her finger tense ever so slightly. He thought to himself, there can't be much more play in the trigger.

He grabbed the handcuffs, hoping she would ease off, but she never did, at least not until he had them on and she was shown that they were good and tight. Once the old lady felt it was safe to do so, she opened he car door, never taking her eyes off the sergeant. She opened up the rear of the car and motioned for the sergeant to get in. The handcuffs were one thing, but the sergeant had no desire whatsoever to get into the car.

"Boy, you had better stop stalling. I'm already an hour late for my afternoon tea and when that happens, I get cranky."

"You had better listen, son. I've been married to her for the better part of fifty years and, without her tea, she can be rather difficult." The old man ducked his head down so that he had a clear path of vision to the sergeant and flashed his matching, gap-toothed smile. "And plus, if you don't hurry up, I'll take out the Mrs.' crankiness on your girlfriend, here." Maliciousness oozed out of the old man. Grady didn't doubt his intentions for a moment.

"It'll be alright, Beth."

"Yes, it will, Beth," the old lady impersonated. Beth had flight written all over her face. Fear poured out of her body. He knew he had to calm her down before something truly bad happened.

"Beth! Look at me!" Grady shouted, trying his best to dissuade her suicidal thoughts. She recoiled at the intrusion but seemed to somewhat recover her senses. "Beth, get in the car. Everything will be alright," he said in his most sincere tone. He hoped it was sufficient because it didn't sound very convincing from his end. Beth moved hesitantly, almost jerkily, like a defective robot.

"That's a good girl," the old man said. But his voice didn't sound sincere at all, it was full of malevolence. For what? The sergeant didn't know. Beth got into the car. The old man got out and fumbled with something in the back seat. The sergeant wasn't sure what it was but he could hear the quiet sobbing of Beth. That asshole! What did he do? the sergeant thought.

"Hold your hosses there, boy! Your turn is coming," the crone said as she halted the sergeant with her weapon.

"You done in there, Lloyd?" the old lady asked without turning her head, keeping her full attention on the sergeant.

"Yeah, I'm done, Mary Helen."

"Well then, get on over here! I don't like the look this one has in his eyes."

"I'll be right there lickety-split, Mary Helen," the man said as he began his shuffle to the other side of the car.

"That damned fool," the lady said, almost kindly to the sergeant. "That man hasn't been anywhere lickety-split in over twenty-five years." Then she cackled.

The sergeant exhaled a precursory breath from his mouth. He couldn't believe the mess they were in and he had no way of knowing how bad it might get. The old man stood on the other side of the open door, waving for the sergeant to get in.

"Well, let's go, boy. I already told you the Mrs. gets a little edgy without her tea and you, standing there lookin' all slack-jawed, isn't helping the matter none." The sergeant approached the car slowly, not wanting to give either of these geriatric lunatics a reason to cut his existence any shorter. Then he noticed what made Beth cry.

Bolted to the floor, in the back of the car was a chain, with three pairs of cuffs attached to it. One pair of links had been attached to the cuffs already around Beth's wrists, thus restricting her movement. It was an ingenious technique. But why three? And not two or four? The back seat was definitely big enough to accommodate that many and easily. It was almost as if they were purposely looking for three people.

Maybe us three, thought the sergeant as he heard the floor restraints being attached to him. When the old man felt confident that Beth and the sergeant were adequately restrained, he stood up and cracked his back with an audible "pop." He shaded his eyes as he looked up at the sun.

"Looks like we've got plenty o' time to make it back, 'fore it gets dark, Mary Helen."

"Goodness gracious! I hope so. I don't want to be outside when the dark falls. That's when all the loons come out," the old woman added. The sergeant stifled an audible snort at that. If nothing else, these two were the unappointed king and queen of lunacy. Well, at the very least, ideal emissaries, anyway.

"Where's the other girl?" the man asked without ever turning around to face his new captives. The sergeant was right; they had been looking for them. He tried to think on his feet, so to speak, as fast as he could.

"Listen! If it's money, I've got some stashed!" he said

excitedly, hoping for a possible escape from this dilemma.

"Hush, son, I never said nothing 'bout no money. I asked you a direct question. I expect a direct answer. The sergeant's hope quickly deflated.

"She didn't make it," he said with grim resignation.

"Pity," the old man said as he began the long, drawn-out process of constricting his brittle body into the confines of the ancient vehicle.

***

"Five of them, Frank! They're going to blow the lid off this place!" Colonel Salazar sat across from Paul, far removed from the dirt and dust that choked his lungs and sullied his skin. He had cuts scrapes and bruises covering most of his body, but if anything hurt, he didn't show it.

"I take it, then, we haven't heard anything from our long range scouts?"

"Nothing." Paul sat back down, a dejected look on his face. "All that we've gained here is going to be lost in a matter of days." Colonel Salazar could only nod his head; he didn't have any answers either.

***

Bennett had fully prepared to surrender when he looked up from his pillaged sleeping bag to see the five uniformed men looking down on him. "I was just getting ready to come back to face my justice," he sniveled. The expressions on the men's faces changed to bewilderment. Bennett smelled hope.

"You're n-n-n-not looking for me?"

"We don't even know who you are," one of the dirtier fellows answered. "We just need a place to stay for a day or two and some food, if you have any extra."

Bennett was so relieved that, for a moment, he actually forgot how small and greedy he was. He showed his guests to the enormous pantry of wares he had been stealing from anywhere and everywhere.

Chapter 47 – Mike Journal Entry Twelve

The days melted away as I prepared for the upcoming bout. I was now running ten miles in the morning before I even began my daily workout. Durgan had not come to visit me in over two days. I think my rapid improvement was unnerving him somewhat, probably not enough for him to physically register, but on a subconscious level. Or maybe I never took enough psych classes and he really just didn't give a shit about me. But I chose to believe the former as opposed to the latter. It felt better.

The sheer hatred I felt for the man bubbled to the surface with every waking moment. I relived every murder I'd seen him commit. Along with the "vitamins," this was what impelled me to win. I once vowed to avenge those women's murders and now it was time to pay up.

There was only a day and a half 'til D-Day and the three hundred and seventy-five pounds wasn't going to lift itself. I had nearly wrapped up my routine when I heard the familiar sound of the shield to my abode being lowered. Durgan walked in, as if he owned the place.

"Did you know I stayed here while you were gone?" he said conversationally. I didn't know how to respond and he wasn't looking for that anyway. "I wanted to see how the great champion lived," he added mockingly as he spread out his arms and twirled once around.

I sat up from my workout bench, keeping a wary eye on him. The man was psychotic; and I couldn't afford a sucker-punch right now. That would hinder any abilities I would need. He advanced a step or two; but, when he realized I wasn't going to let him approach unnoticed, he seemed to lose interest in that endeavor.

"Did you know that I had a 4.0 GPA in Chemical Engineering at Amherst College when I went to that concert? Did you?" I guess now he was looking for some sort of answer from me.

"I...I didn't know that." This great ape was almost a rocket scientist! I guess that made sense. They say that the most brilliant geniuses are a hair's breadth away from insanity. This ship had been the catalyst that triggered his lunacy.

I thought that maybe if I kept talking to him, quite possibly, he might open up to me. Who knows? Crazier things have happened. "Chemical Engineering, huh?" I sounded lame but I didn't know how else to approach this guy. He had, thus far, never shown a human side. I didn't think he was even capable. "What made you decide on that major?"

"Listen, Mike, I'm not trying to get all touchy-feely with you. I just wanted to let you know that I have an incredible brain to go with this near perfect body, that's all. So don't go trying to psychoanalyze me. I was always an outcast on Earth. Let's just say my people skills were for shit. I found my true calling up here." A light began to shine in his eyes as he began to recount all his victories.

"This place was made for me. When I killed my first opponent, it was the first time I ever truly felt alive. It was nothing like the cats I used to kill when I was a kid. Sure, that was enjoyable and all, but nothing compared to the rush of my blade hitting home. That shudder of the knife as it scraped against his bones... The way his eyes first bulged in shock and terror and then began to dim with the realization of the inevitable. I thought I was going to burst out in tears with the sheer joy of it all."

"Durgan I knew you were sick before you opened your mouth, but I had no idea of the depth to which your insanity has plunged," I answered. Horror invaded me like no other time before in my life. The men in the ring were, for the most part maniacal but that was probably because of the situation they found themselves in. This bastard actually relished the idea of the competitions. My words did little, if anything, to curb his rant; he continued as if I weren't even there. I think his speech was more for his own benefit than mine, anyway. He was, without a doubt, an egomaniac.

"I think my parents suspected something about me, after our third cat 'disappeared.' We stopped getting animals. We did get a couple of fish but they weren't nearly as fun to fillet live. Their mouths would just gape open for a few seconds and that was about it. No screaming or howling. I don't even think they knew they were dying, not like the cats anyway. The cats would put up one hell of a struggle." He snorted.

"This one time I had to keep my stomach covered for a full week. Our second cat, Bonanza, scratched me real good. I've still got the scar." He proceeded to raise his shirt to show me a razor thin mark that started a few inches below his right nipple, crossed over his belly button and dropped down another inch. "Yeah, that got me good."

"I think you got him a little better."

"Yeah, you're right!" He laughed as he smacked my back. "Good one." Apparently this brainiac wasn't accustomed to sarcasm. "I'm glad to see that you're looking a little bit more competitive-ready. I want my Earthly debut to be a grand event. I'll be a star back home."

"What makes you think that killing me on global television is going to make you a hero?" I intoned.

"Mike, don't you get it? People love this crap. Why do you think that the news was so popular? Nobody wants to hear about the good Samaritan that helped some homeless man. Which, by the way, they always run at the very end of the newscast, if at all. They want to hear about the lead story. You know the one, where some sicko is stalking college girls and disposing of their used-up bodies by the side of the road. That's what people tune in for. Sure, they'll be shaking their heads when our event starts and lying to each other about how wrong and terrible it is. But nobody will turn it off. Oh no, my friend," he said as he clasped my shoulder.

His eyes were focused a thousand yards down range. "Once the first drop of blood from you shoots out, they'll be animals. Their heart rates will increase and their chests will rise and fall as adrenaline pumps through their muscles. More than likely, they'll start rooting for you to kill that 'bastard'. It will be amazing! I'll bet they have odds going just like our friends here do. There may be a few 'tree-huggers' out there, who truly think this is an archaic display of barbarism. But I can guarantee you one thing, they will be few and far between."

"And when the cameras close in on your twitching and near lifeless body, people will almost be foaming at the mouth from the sheer thrill of it all. They'll want more and more and I'll promise them that. And for delivering that promise, they will hold parades for me. They'll give me keys to cities. They'll probably give me cities."

"Durgan, you have lost it. They're not going to love you for killing me. They are going to loathe you."

"Loathe, love. They are almost interchangeable. Don't you know that some of the biggest villains are the most revered people? Look at J.R. Ewing. People loved to hate him. Mike, look at Hitler. He slaughtered millions of people and they still write books about him. Countless people are still trying to start the Fourth Reich. Does that sound like lunacy? Think on that for a while but don't dwell too long," Durgan said as he stood up and headed for the door. "You really shouldn't spend too much of what little time you have left pondering." He laughed a small chuckle. He was almost through the beamed door when I yelled out to him.

"Durgan!" He turned. "I am going to kill you," I stated as surely as if I told him the sky was blue. His face faltered for a millisecond, if that. I might have even imagined it.

"Yeah, right," he answered as he passed through the

door and the familiar humming of the force field around the door resumed.

Chapter 48

"Where are you taking us?" Beth wailed. Fear had reddened her eyes.

"Oh dearie," the old crone said as she turned around. "Do be quiet, I think that your sergeant friend here already knows the answer. Beth turned towards Grady. She had been so busy wallowing in her own terror that she had not spared the occasion to look over at him. Meanwhile, he had paled to an ashen gray. All his life tones had bled out of his skin. He looked as terrified as she felt.

"Where are they taking us?" Beth said more quietly, trying not to panic and/or possibly push the sergeant over the edge.

"I think these are Corporal Mike Harris' parents. They're taking us back to the National Guard Post. That's my guess," the sergeant said listlessly.

"I'd kill ya' myself, laddie," the old man grumbled as he spared a glance through his rearview mirror. "But luckily for you, I don't believe much in the vigilante way of life. I figure you'll get a fair trial and then you'll get shot for treason."

The old lady looked back with venom in her eyes. Beth could never imagine this lady baking apple pies for, much less winning, the Belchertown Blue Ribbon twice. Right now, she looked as mean as a rattlesnake on meth and probably twice as venomous.

"We've lost two sons, Sergeant, before you shot our Mikey in the leg. He's all the reason we have to live, except of course, for catching the man that maimed him. We figured you'd be too smart to come back into the state the regular ways and we were right, weren't we, Mary Helen?"

He grinned a wide, mostly toothless smile, but it was humorless. His eyes narrowed as his grin grew. Beth was unsure whether they would make it to their destination or not. Mary Helen cackled at his grin. Beth thought that perhaps Mary Helen was in the early stages of Alzheimer's. She didn't seem to be altogether with it; but perhaps it was the death of two of her sons sending her over the edge. She wouldn't be the first, nor the last to watch the last shredded remnants of their sanity float off into the breeze like ragweed on a hot summer day.

"Mrs. Harris, I know that I should be tried for my treasonous acts, but the girl had nothing to do with this. Just let her go, and I'll go peacefully back," the sergeant pleaded in desperation. A sparkle flashed across Mary Helen's eyes, like somebody had turned on the lights or at least walked by with a strong flashlight, Beth thought. Mary Helen looked Beth up and down and turned to the sergeant.

"You're wrong in that aspect, dearie. I think that she had everything to do with it. Would you have risked everything if she was perhaps thirty years older or maybe sixty pounds heavier? Or a man? I doubt it." She cackled as she looked back at Beth with a knowing smile. "What would your wife be thinking right about now, Sergeant? I can smell it all over you both. It reeks of adultery and lust and sin." Beth bowed her head in silent shame. Was it that noticeable?

They drove in silence for another hour while the old car rumbled along at an unimpressive thirty-eight miles per hour. Mary Helen began to clap in glee when the old, underused barracks, up until recently anyway, came into view. The small two-story building, in addition to being an armory, at one time, served as the state police barracks. But that was another lifetime ago.

Now, the men housed there weren't so much taxed with the burden of serving and protecting the people as they were with serving and protecting themselves. Sure, to some degree, they felt they were still working toward the common good, but like many people throughout the ages, absolute power, and all that… And the colonel, for all intents and purposes, was the ultimate power, at least in these parts. He ruled his realm like any good overlord would have in medieval England, with an iron fist.

The sergeant was forcibly removed from the car. It seemed that everyone wanted a piece of him as they dragged him out. Beth was treated with a little more civility, but not much. If not for the appearance of the colonel, the sergeant thought that his life might have ended on the pavement. But after what ensued, he looked back and wished it had.

"Ah! So our not-so-triumphant treasoner returns," the colonel said as he spat and looked down on the kneeling sergeant. The sergeant swiveled his head to look up at the colonel but the sun was right behind the colonel's head, making it difficult to see anything but his silhouette.

"I have someone here that's very eager to see you, O'Bannon," the colonel half-laughed. The colonel moved to the side a few inches to let the mystery person enter his field of vision. He still couldn't see, but recognized the halo of hair from a mile away. The sergeant began to openly weep when he realized that his wife was here.

"Why?" she asked softly as she placed her hand on his cheek.

"I'm so sorry, Meg," he cried as he placed his handcuffed hands over hers. His contact, however, made her withdraw almost as if she'd been snake-bitten and, to a degree, she had been.

They were high school sweethearts. Neither of them, to her knowledge, had ever been in a serious relationship other than the one they shared. Through the ups and downs of their lives, they managed to build something decent together. Wasn't their son testament to that fact?

"They fucked!" The old woman yelled from the car before she began to howl with laughter, rocking back and forth, like a hyena on speed. "They fucked!" she repeated, a little more softly, but still the majority of those present heard it. The hustle and bustle only moments before came to a standstill as the men in the troop watched to see what would happen next.

"Is that true?" Meg cried. The sergeant stared, helplessness etched on his face. "Is that true?" she yelled.

"Meg, I'm so sorry," he stammered between tears.

Meg brought her hand back up, but this time it wasn't for a soft caress. Her slap stung the sergeant harder than any bullet ever could. She turned her back and returned to the barracks to gather her belongings and head back home, where her boy would wait for a daddy who would never return.

The colonel waited until Meg had completely vanished into the building. "I always knew you weren't quite an exact fit for our outfit, Sergeant, but I would never have guessed how far you could have strayed from your country and your family." The colonel turned on one heel and headed back from whence he came. "Throw them both in the brig," the colonel added as he stepped through the door.

The sergeant felt a pair of rough hands pick him up off the pavement. Tears streaked his face, giving it a ruddy appearance. Any swagger that the sergeant might have once possessed was now completely drained from him. He walked the walk of a thoroughly defeated man, head bowed while his feet barely rose above the level of the ground.

Beth stumbled as she was shoved in the direction of the barracks. She turned to glare at the man who pushed her. He was a brutish man, not overly large, but he looked powerful.

"Turn around, bitch, and get moving," he said as he shoved her again. She nearly lost her footing. The cuffs made it difficult to walk in the first place, much worse with someone shoving her. The door to the station began to close as Beth heard the old woman yell out her favorite comment.

"He fucked her!" she yelled again as the wild cackle began anew. The sound of the cell doors closing behind Beth awoke something both primitive and dark from deep within her. It was a fear that mushroomed from her toes to the top of her head. She had never, not even while on the alien ship, felt so completely trapped.

There was no outside light source and the

illumination in the cell was supplied by one sixty-watt bulb that hung in the center of the small corridor she had just crossed. From the lighting, she couldn't even tell if she had the cell to herself; the far end was completely bathed in shadow. The brutish man with the pock-marked face had already closed the door and was headed back up the corridor when Beth called out to him.

"What...What about the cuffs?" she asked as she raised her hands, as if showing him her problem might make it better.

"Eat me, bitch," he answered without ever turning around.

"Oh, great," Beth mumbled to herself. "I really have to pee too." Beth recognized her quandary and it made her smile for a brief moment, but it was a smile nonetheless.

The sergeant found his way into his cell after sustaining some moderate punishment. Nothing had been broken, but that thought did little to ease his mind. These men, for the most part, had once been his good friends and to see the brutality and hatred that formed on their faces as they took out their frustration on him was almost more than he could bear.

He had worked through many a natural disaster with the bulk of them, risking their lives together, and now he had betrayed them. He had betrayed the only family he had and for what? A pretty face? Was that it? No! It was more than that! It had to be, right? He had a wife and a son that he knew he would never see again, but still the treachery that these men, HIS men, felt that he had created was the knife that twisted in his side. And what pushed the knife even deeper were the results he had achieved.

The two women whose aid he had galloped toward were in no better shape than if he had done nothing at all. Deb died and Beth would soon. At this point, he only hoped it would be quick for her. There was no telling what the colonel had in mind, for either of them. Colonel Masterson showed up almost as if he knew he was the subject of the sergeant's thoughts.

"How are you doing, soldier? I hope the accommodations are up to snuff," the colonel said as he lit his pipe. The pungent smell of sweet hickory wafted through the cell. The sergeant never cared for the smell of that tobacco and right now was no exception.

"I know you didn't come down here to see how I was doing," the sergeant said as he righted himself, doing his best not to let the colonel see him wince as he attempted to stand amidst all the bruising and beating that his body had been through.

"I hope my men, haven't treated you too unfairly," the colonel added as he watched his pipe smoke drift away. "Why'd you do it, Grady? And please don't tell me that you threw away everything for a piece of tail." The colonel had yet to look over at him. The sergeant wrestled with his thoughts, unsure if he should answer the colonel or not; but at this point, he figured why not? *He couldn't do anything worse to me than what I've already done to myself.*

"They needed help," he said bleakly.

"So you wanted to play the knight in shining armor, eh?"

What was going through the sergeant's mind. Is the bastard reading my thoughts? "I guess maybe it was something like that, sir."

Now the colonel did look in his direction, almost as if to say, "How dare you call me that. You don't have enough rank to call me that anymore." But no words were exchanged.

"I had a split second to think, sir." There it was again, but this time, the colonel put his poker face on and completely ignored the affront. "They were in trouble and, at the time, it just seemed like the right thing to do. I've been thinking about all that has happened in the last few days, Colonel, and I can't say that if it happened again, I would not do the same thing. But I honestly think, that I would. Maybe it's a character flaw on my part. I don't know, but there was something about those girls that compelled me to help them."

"And what of the second girl?" the colonel interjected.

"She died from her wounds."

The colonel merely nodded. "And so, what have you gained, Sergeant?" The sergeant could now see why the colonel had risen so far and fast in the officer's ranks. This man was intuitive to a fault.

"Nothing sir, I have gained nothing. And I have lost everything," the sergeant said with his head bowed low.

"Your execution will occur two days from now, at dawn," the colonel stated. The sergeant's head shot back up. He knew it was coming but it still surprised him.

"Why no trial, sir? We both know the outcome of that avenue, but I still deserve that."

"You lost your right to that the moment you pulled the trigger, Sergeant. You WILL have your say, but your words, by and large, will fall on deaf ears." The colonel took one last puff of his pipe and turned to head out.

"Sir, I'm sorry." The sergeant said as the colonel stopped briefly.

"So am I, Sergeant, so am I," the colonel said as he resumed his exit.

***

Beth, for the most part, was left alone that day and much of the next. Her only contact with the outside world was the occasional tray of food that was slid under her door. The colonel never bothered to stop in and tell Beth that her fate was to be determined or predetermined in forty-eight hours. He saw no need to waste his time on the civilian woman who cost the lives of two of his men. When Beth's dinner arrived the second night, she shouted to her delivery person.

"Please let me talk to Sergeant O'Bannon." She sounded so pathetic, even to herself; but this was no act, this was how she felt. Private Monroe had been warned to do nothing with this woman except drop off her meals, but he hated to see anything suffer, much less her.

As a child, Monroe set up a pretty good facility for dealing with strays throughout his neighborhood. If anyone had a bird with a broken wing or a lost cat, Monroe was sure to nurse it back to health or find the previous owner. In a great many cases, much to his mother's chagrin, he would keep the animal for himself. He intended to go to veterinarian assistance school after graduation, but never succeeded. Without a father and with his mother barely making ends meet by slinging hash at the local greasy spoon, the money was just not there. The National Guard promised him a GI bill to pay for his schooling. They even offered tuition reimbursement.

But he never, ever signed up for the crap that was going down here. Having personally killed at least three people in the last raid against the unit, he'd been deeply affected. He always thought he'd been put on the earth for a loftier purpose, to save animals. Actually, to save anything that needed saving. He was not so altruistic that he would risk his life for anybody else's, but that didn't mean he couldn't at least somehow try to console this girl.

"Ma'am I can't do that." Beth was taken aback that somebody, anybody had addressed her. "I can get you a paper and pen, if you want to send him a letter." Beth nodded her head in ascent.

"What's going to happen to us?" she asked, pleading. The private thought she needed a little more help.

"I'm not sure," he lied. Beth saw it in his eyes.

"You can't let them kill us. We did nothing wrong." The private's face drained as he realized she had read one of his thoughts as if he had verbalized it. When Beth saw his face change, she knew the truth beyond a doubt. Tears silently streamed down her face. Private Monroe had seen that look a hundred times in the faces of the animals he tried to protect. It was shock, plain and simple.

"Listen, there is going to be a trial tomorrow for you. You'll have the opportunity to have your side heard. And who knows?" he shrugged. But they both knew tacitly that she had a better chance of playing with rabid dogs and not getting bit than she did of getting any semblance of a fair trial.

"For me?" The implication was clear; there would be no trial for Sergeant O'Bannon. Beth could hardly believe what was happening.

"I'll go get the paper and pen," Private Monroe said as he moved as quickly away from this unsettling conversation as possible. He returned moments later, but Beth had curled herself up on her cot with her back to the bars.

"Ma'am? Do you want the paper?" The private said as he put his hand through the cell. Beth didn't so much as stir. The private wanted to leave the paper there but that could land him in hot water and he had no desire to get on the wrong side of the colonel, especially right now. He turned to go back to his station. Two more hours of guard duty and one more long, sleepless night, he lamented to himself.

Beth didn't touch her dinner that night and her dreams seemed to reflect the emptiness inside her. During her fits of sleep, which weren't interrupted by cold sweats, she dreamed of Deb and Mike. They both had a very ethereal quality. They were bathed in bright white light and seemed so happy together. Love reigned all around them. Deb was smiling like a kid on Christmas morning.

It panged Beth that Mike also seemed so happy. She looked for some sign in his mannerisms that something was missing, or rather, someone. But he kept smiling and laughing and stroking Deb's long, brunette hair. Then it happened; she got the sign she had eagerly been anticipating, Mike looked squarely at Beth's face and told Deb how much he loved her.

Beth woke with a start. The sun was beginning its rise, but it would offer no warmth to her, not today.

The day dragged on for the sergeant. Just sitting idly, waiting for the inevitable, was brutal. He tried repeatedly to come up with some sort of defense to save his skin. Every avenue he pursued came up for naught. He knew he had let his men down. Even if what they were doing was wrong, he was still under orders and had disobeyed those orders. Worse yet, he had ultimately got his Lieutenant killed. It didn't matter that, almost to a man, nobody liked the LT. He was still a National Guardsman and needed to be cared for as much as the next soldier.

The sergeant wished that the trial was today, so that the firing squad would be greeting him tomorrow morning instead of the next. But this was, more than likely, all planned out by the colonel also. Just letting him sit there, contemplating his abbreviated future, was infinitely worse than execution. Sergeant O'Bannon had always wondered what death row inmates thought about while they awaited their executions. "Bad choice of words," he mouthed.

Did they regret the choices they made that landed them in their particular predicament? Did they long for simpler times? Did they dream about stays of execution? None of those things, however, occupied his mind now. Mostly, he thought about his wife and his son, and how were they going to get along now, without him. Even when he had been on the run with Beth, he figured, at some time, he would be able to steal away to his suburban home and see them again. And then what?

He knew Meg was raised a military brat, her father traipsing around the world with his family. And Meg loved every minute of it. She loved the fact that her father protected "the American Way of Life", as he liked to call it. Meg herself would have joined up if not for a broken condom in the back of the sergeant's 1974 Buick Century. That put a real damper on her dreams, but when the sergeant decided to enlist, her whole world brightened up.

She was going to be in the service of the "Service," if only by proxy. But that mattered little to her. Sergeant O'Bannon was never really sure if she loved him or the uniform more. But now all of that mattered little, she turned her back on him. And rightfully so, he added. He WAS a traitor, and he had brought shame onto her and his family.

She would do her best to distance herself as much as possible from him. She would not come to see him in his final hours and for that, and that alone, he wept. His decision at the time had been the right one.

Beth alternated between pacing her cell floor and curling up on her cot. She knew if this dragged on too long, she would more than likely go insane. "Not much chance of that, though," she whispered. With each ticking of the clock, she was one second closer to death; and, not for a moment, did she think that Mike would be coming on a white steed to save her. He was literally hundreds of thousands of miles away and had his own problems.

At that same moment, however, Mike was on his bed, thinking about her. She knew it in her heart; she could feel it, even from all this distance. And she was right.

The day passed quickly, though the clock never seemed to move. As the shadows lengthened, so did the blackness that inhabited the sergeant's heart. The night ended much like it had on every U.S. installation for the better part of two centuries. The mournful wail of Taps was played over the loud speakers and everyone caught outdoors stood at the position of attention while they waited for the colors to be ceremoniously unfurled and folded.

But then something unexplained happened before the final note of Taps had been blown. Men scattered in various directions as the base alarm blared. Well, that wasn't on the itinerary, the sergeant thought, bemusedly. Maybe it's the cavalry, although they were a little early.

Sirens wailed on but the sergeant had no idea what was happening. Still, his interest was piqued; what else was there to do but wait for a bullet with his name on it? The sirens grew blisteringly loud, but louder still was the low thunderous sound of what? Engines? What kind? And how many? It was impossible to distinguish anything, but it was safe to say there were plenty.

"Private Monroe!" the sergeant yelled, after the sirens had finally stopped their wailing. The sound of the engines was almost as deafening and the building shook from the cumulative effect. "Private Monroe!" he yelled again. A disheveled private ran into the holding area, desperately attempting to place a loaded magazine into his M-16.

"I'm a little busy right now, Sergeant; what do you need?" he said without actually looking up from his rifle.

"What is going on?" The sergeant asked with more than a little angst.

"We're under attack. It seems that the same group that tried to take us over a couple of days ago is back, and with reinforcements," the private answered anxiously. Now the sergeant was nervous. It was one thing to be under attack; but it was an altogether different beast when you were completely defenseless.

"How many more, Private?" the sergeant asked with a morbid curiosity. He figured, at the best of times, the unit could hold off two to three hundred armed attackers. But the unit was down by more than a third of its personnel and the morale had fallen a lot further than that. Monroe didn't answer; he was now fumbling with his utility belt, which kept finding its way to the floor.

"Private, put down the weapon and then buckle up your belt," the sergeant said in as soothing a tone as possible to try and calm the private down. It worked to some degree, but the sergeant noticed how badly the private's hands were shaking.

"Private, how many men are headed this way?" he asked again. The private looked up with fear in his eyes.

"About a thousand," came the tortured reply.

"Wow!" the sergeant said as he slapped his forehead.

"Yeah, I agree," the private said as he finally managed to get his belt squared away.

"Give me a weapon."

The private swiveled his head to look straight at the sergeant, as if maybe he hadn't heard him right. "Did you just say, give you a weapon?"

"Come on, Monroe, you know this unit isn't capable of thwarting that size an enemy. I hate to tell you this, but we're all dead and I would much rather be out fighting than shot like a fish in a barrel. Let me regain a measure of my honor! Let me help to defend this place."

"Sergeant, I can sympathize with you but there is no way that I have the authority to let you out, especially with a weapon." Shots began to ring out from all around. The impact of small arms fire against the building sounded like hail, lead-based hail. The private ducked instinctually, as glass and wood debris flew around the room. Thank God for brick, the private thought, or the end would already be here.

Return fire from the barracks was a welcome sound. The staccato of the M-16's, although a lot closer, did not drown out the enemy fire.

"Oh, fudge this!" the private announced. The sergeant almost laughed out loud at that. Here they were in the middle of a death match and the worst profanity the private could manage was "fudge."

But the mood turned serious when an errant bullet struck the wall, not more than four inches from where the private's head was. Monroe headed back to his desk on all fours and reached his hand into the top drawer, pulling out his Colt .45, before he scurried back to the sergeant's cell.

"Here! Take it, Sergeant," the private said, holding out the weapon. He wished the sergeant would hurry up and take it so he could pull his exposed arm back.

"Monroe! Let me out of here! By the time I have an opportunity to use this thing, it'll be too late."

"Mother fracker!" the private yelled. Sergeant O'Bannon couldn't help himself; he loudly snorted at the private's second attempt at profanity. "I don't see the humor, Sergeant," Monroe said as he fumbled with his key ring. With the door unlocked, the sergeant bolted from the cell as if he'd been shot from a cannon.

"Where you going, Sergeant?"

"I'm letting Beth out. Throw me your keys," he said with his hand outstretched.

"Oh crap, I'm dead now," the private said as he handed over the keys.

"Don't worry, Monroe, you won't be alone," the sergeant added wryly.

"Oh, that makes me feel tons better," the private yelled to the sergeant's retreating back. The sergeant reached Beth's cell and panicked; he couldn't find her.

"What the hell?" And then movement. "Beth?"

"Grady, is that you?" she said as she uncurled her body from the shadows of her cell. "What is going on?" she cried as she ran to his arms. Glass exploded and Beth wrapped her arms around the sergeant, holding on for dear life. The sergeant pulled Beth off him and told her to get down, which she dutifully obeyed. The sergeant crawled over to a window to see what was happening on the outside. But what he saw completely disheartened him.

From his vantage point, it appeared that the insurgents had the place completely surrounded. They were well-armed and seemed to have some semblance of structure. They weren't advancing yet, but that would only be a matter of time. The sergeant low-crawled his way back to Beth.

"Beth, I'm going to have you do a few things. They may not make much sense, but you're going to have to trust me on this." Beth looked up at him with her huge, sad eyes. The sergeant's heart never felt more vulnerable than it did at this moment. If he had to, he could have withstood a hundred bullets to get her out safely. But that wasn't going to happen, and although this plan was risky, it was all he had.

"Beth, you need to get your cot made up and get your tray out of here." She looked at him as if he'd gone nuts. Now was not the time for good housekeeping skills, her eyes conveyed. "Beth, I know it sounds crazy, but nobody is getting out of here. You are going to have to hide."

"Hide where? Here?" Beth asked as she shook her head. "I'd rather fight."

"I know you would, but that's not what I want from you. I want you to live. I want you to go find Mike and tell him how much you love him. And I want you to remember me, but don't ever tell him about us. I know it meant much more to me than to you, but I can't help myself, Beth. I've fallen in love with you. And I'm going to do everything that I possibly can to protect you." Beth moved over to where he was and kissed him like she had never kissed anyone, Mike included. She didn't want to let go, ever.

"Sergeant!" Monroe yelled from across the room. "Sergeant, they're coming!"

The sergeant peeled himself away from Beth's embrace. "Move, woman! Get this place squared away, and leave the door open."

"Leave the door open?" she asked, confusion tinged in her voice.

"No sense in locking a door if nothing is in there, right?" the sergeant said with a small, sad smile on his face. He lingered for a second more, before the private yelled his warning one last time. "Move!" he mouthed wordlessly as he took up his position next to the window. Beth moved but almost as if a marionette on a string. Her arms and legs felt wooden as she did her best to clean up the room while chunks of wood and brick flew past her. She pushed her tray out into the hallway when Private Monroe was hit. He screamed in pain as the bullet pierced his lung. A slow, strained, sucking sound came from his chest as air rushed to escape.

"Aw frick," he wheezed. Beth made her way over to him to aid as best she could. Sergeant O'Bannon yelled at her to get back.

"I'll get him, Beth. Get back and hide." She hesitated for a moment, but as the volley of bullets began anew, she retreated into the darkness of her cavern. She half closed the door and hid under her cot.

The sergeant made it over to the private and lifted his shirt to check the wound. Blood and air blistered out of the

333

large caliber gash. There was not enough time or medical expertise in the room to save the private, and they both knew it. Monroe was rapidly falling into a state of shock as the sergeant did his best to place a pressure bandage on his chest.

The sergeant had almost completed his task when a gunman showed up at the window who placed a hasty round into the sergeant's arm. The sergeant spun around from the force as Beth shrieked in fright. The gunman looked to see where the sound had come from, giving the sergeant enough time to recover from the assault. He placed a well-aimed shot dead center in the bastard's forehead.

"Are you alright?" Beth asked as she began to emerge from her hidey-hole.

"I'm fine," he snarled. "If you say anything else or move again, I'll shoot you myself. Do you understand?" Silence came from the depths of her confines. "Good," he said as he turned his attention back to the private. But poor Monroe wouldn't be needing any more assistance, at least, not in this world.

The gunfire from the barracks began to get more and more intermittent as the enemy fire increasingly found its mark. The National Guard was inflicting heavy damage on the usurpers but, like the Alamo, it was all about numbers now. And the advantage favored the "away" team. Roars began to thrum through the mob outside. They smelled blood, which wasn't all that hard, considering that the floors were covered in it.

Sergeant O'Bannon had, long ago, grabbed Monroe's discarded weapon. He moved away from the window he had been occupying. He wanted to get as far away from Beth as possible for two reasons. First, he didn't want her to see him die; and second, the further he was from her, the less likely it would appear he was trying to defend someone. The sergeant could hear boots as they ran down the corridor towards him.

So this is it, he thought. He never really figured it would end like this. But then, how did he really think it was going to end? Not many people put much effort into that endeavor, I guess, What would be the purpose? the sergeant mused. He hid himself behind the bulk of the private's desk. He didn't think it would actually stop a round but it gave him the illusion of safety. His finger poised on the trigger, he hoped to get at least ten of the sons-of-bitches before this was over.

    Surprise overcame suspense as the colonel and two other men that the sergeant only knew by rank ran into the room. The colonel stopped short; looking down the barrel of an M-16 can be very intimidating especially when you don't know the intentions of the one wielding it.

    "Get in here, Colonel. You're gonna get shot with your ass hanging out in the breeze that way."

    "Monroe?" was the colonel's reply as he attempted to regain his composure.

    "Dead," the sergeant answered as he motioned his head in the direction of the private. From the look on the colonel's face, the sergeant added, "I didn't do it." The colonel didn't think that he had but it was still good to get verbal confirmation.

    "What about the girl?" the colonel asked.

    "I let her go before they got here," he lied.

    The colonel eyed him suspiciously but he didn't have a better theory and besides, there were more pressing matters at hand. They all heard footfalls in the corridor and this time, there was no doubt, they weren't military, at least not in the traditional manner.

    The door burst open. The men, who were not really expecting any resistance, sauntered into a hail of gunfire. Three men crumpled to the floor before they knew what hit them. The men in the hallway stopped their advance. Sure, they wanted in, but none of them were suicidal.

    The sergeant sprinted up from his hiding place and ran towards the door. The colonel put a bead on him with his rifle, figuring he was going to desert once again. But the sergeant was interested in only one thing, well actually, three things--the weapons the men dropped when they were shot.

The sergeant and the colonel weren't quite out of ammunition yet, but why take the chance? The sergeant dragged the weapons back into the room as the disapproving rebels opened fire.

"Colonel, you had better get your men on the windows. Now that they know they don't have free entry, they'll try to take us out through them. The colonel nodded his agreement.

"Jenkins, take the window on the east." The sergeant's heart fluttered; that was close to Beth, hopefully not too close. "Adams, you take the other side." The men had no sooner manned their stations when trouble erupted on all fronts. Although the men attacking might not have been military, there were a few of them that definitely had prior military expertise. The attack was fast, precise, and, for a third of them, deadly. Jenkins had barely made it to the window when he was met by two men. The bars on the window had hindered their angle to shoot but not enough to spare Jenkins' life.

Sergeant O'Bannon spun and fired. At least one of the men had gone down; the second had just plain dropped out of the line of fire. The door to the holding area was littered with men who had unsuccessfully tried a frontal assault. Adams, on the west window, had repelled more than his fair share of gunmen. The attempt ceased for the moment but the situation was far from improving. There were only three men still capable of fighting and they were in this room.

The sergeant, the colonel and Adams could only bear witness to the occasional shot that rang out throughout the building, signifying the end of one of their not-so-lucky comrades. Those that were injured were being murdered ruthlessly, most to the cries of mercy, some just relegated to crying.

Beth shivered with every shot. That these men could be so callous frightened her; they were of the same stock that killed Deb's parents. They cared for no one but themselves. And Beth knew very well that this was exactly what the aliens wanted. Divide and conquer was not something known only on Earth; it was a universal truism.

She didn't believe she would be so lucky as to receive a bullet to the head, at least not right away. And that would just not do. She wanted to go out on her own terms. She began to uncurl her body and ease her way out from under the cot.

Her objective was clear, Jenkins' gun; but how to get it was a different matter. She crossed halfway through her cell when a shadow passed across the window. She nearly froze in place and jumped up running in the same instant. Sergeant O'Bannon caught the movement out of the corner of his eye and rose to meet the threat. What he was least expecting to find was Beth, prone on the floor like a discarded toy.

"What are you doing?" he mouthed, never really taking his eyes off the window. Beth's adrenaline was so hopped up, she felt that if she spoke she would start screaming. She did the next best thing; she pointed at Jenkins' sidearm which was still holstered. The sergeant saw her objective and understood it. He would have done the same thing if he had been in that particular situation. It looked grave for everyone and she should also have been able to go out on her own terms. He hoped that it wouldn't be necessary for her, but she might as well have been prepared.

The sergeant pumped a round through the window to let whoever was out there know that this might not be the best path to take if one was still enamored with life. This move, he figured, bought him a little time. He bent over to undo the strap that held the pistol in place. Once it was free, he pulled it from its constraints and left it on the floor. He stood up as the passing shadow came into view and placed a well-aimed three round burst squarely in the eye of the would-be assailant. Then he kicked Jenkins' unneeded, at least to him, pistol to Beth's outstretched fingers.

She clasped the gun and quickly retreated back into the darkness. She hoped she would be able to use the gun when the time came and its heft gave her a small measure of safety. The colonel watched the entire transfer happen, unbeknownst to the sergeant. But what was the difference? In a matter of minutes, they would all be dead.

"Hey! You in there!" a voice said that was obviously behind cover judging by its muffled quality. "Come out now and we'll treat you fairly."

"I'd love to know which dictionary they use to define fair," Adams said from his defensive point at the west window. Sergeant O'Bannon laughed a bit at that, but the colonel didn't. Being originally from North Carolina, he had never truly been comfortable when dealing with sarcasm anyway. He never understood the use for it.

"Hey! I'm still waiting for a response!" the muffled voice urged.

"Here's your reply!" Sergeant O'Bannon yelled as he placed a round aimed as closely to the voice as possible.

"Come on, guys! If you give us the combination to the armory, we'll let you all go free." Everybody in that room knew it was a lie, but it still sparked a little hope in each of them. The vault, as it was known, housed over five hundred small arms, mainly M-16s and some Colt .45s. There were more than a few shotguns and even some of the local Guardsmen's weapons who, for whatever reason, were not allowed or chose not to keep them at their homes.

There were also two rocket launchers, although only one of them worked. The men once tried it out on a old combat Jeep many years previous, when they could get away with bending the rules and not having the code book shoved up their asses. In addition, there was a crateful of hand grenades and some sticks of dynamite. For what reason those were there, the sergeant never knew. He attempted, at one time, to send it back from whence it came, Army Surplus. But the paperwork involved in that endeavor made the outcome not worth the effort.

On occasion, some of the lazier or more curious Guardsmen had taken a few sticks over the years to blow one thing or another to smithereens, usually after several six packs of beer had been swallowed. A staff sergeant was partially deafened a few years prior by a stick that he was holding for far too long. It nearly burst in his hand before his friends drunkenly warned him to throw the damned thing. After that mishap, the colonel placed better security over the volatile material.

He requisitioned and received one of the best armory vaults in the New England region. It was near bank quality. How the colonel pulled it off, only a handful knew. The colonel had, once upon a time as a young captain in the National Guards' version of the military police, caught Lieutenant General Healey's oldest son, Lyle, in a very compromising situation in the back bed of a Ford pickup with a corporal from the captain's command.

The corporal was quietly expelled from the service with an "Other than Honorable" discharge. Formal charges had never been filed, due to the damage that it could inflict on the general's career, and for which the general had been eternally grateful. So, when the request went up the chain of command to the now four-star general, it was a no-brainer. He would pay off his dept in full and be done with the whole mess.

Lyle, meanwhile, had moved away right after being dragged out of the closet. The relationship with his father also changed dramatically. Although never loving nor nurturing, Lyle's father had always been cordial but stiff towards his son. When the truth emerged, it seeded open hostility in the Healey household. The elder Healey would not so much as stay in the same room when Lyle entered.

Genna Healey had, on more than one occasion, tried to mend the rift that was ever expanding between her son and husband. But bridging that gulf was equivalent to Evel Knievel crossing the Snake River on his rocket bike, doomed to failure. More than likely, the backlash would strike from almost every angle. The one that hurt the most was when Jud, her husband, blamed Lyle's "fagginess" on her, "for bringing the boy up like a momma's boy." She contemplated leaving his stubborn ass after that fight. But three days of heartfelt apologies and the glimmer of a tear from his tough, old hide of a face, Genna relented.

Lyle loved both of his parents. He didn't always understand his father but he vowed he would not be the reason for their marriage's demise. That would just be one more reason for his father to hate him. So, to a tearful mother, he said his goodbyes. His dad, for some reason, decided to go to work early that day.

And off to Paris Lyle headed and happily too because he became an up-and-coming fashion designer for one of the bigger firms over there. That was, of course, until his life was cut short by the aliens who leveled the Eiffel Tower. He hadn't actually been on the tower but was enjoying a nice cup of coffee at a café not two blocks from Ground Zero.

The thugs who surrounded the building would not stop until they blew up the vault and all of its contents because they had no clue how else to get into it. Of the three surviving members of the Guard unit, only two of them knew the code, the colonel and Sergeant O'Bannon. The colonel intended to change the code after the sergeant's defection but was sidelined by the group's initial attack.

The colonel looked over at the sergeant. "Looks like we have them right where we want them," the colonel said with a laugh. Sergeant O'Bannon smiled in amusement at the rare display of sarcasm offered by the colonel. The sergeant shook his head before turning back to keep a vigilant watch at his window. The windows in the room, both barely wide enough to let a small child squeeze through sideways, were only about eighteen inches in height. They were used more for the ambient lighting than for anything else, but right now they posed the biggest threat to the trio and the hidden solo.

Sergeant O'Bannon feared a rocket attack or even a grenade floating through the defensive bars. He prayed if that were to happen, it would have already done so by now. While all was relatively quiet and the usurpers plotted some sort of plan to unseat the defenders without killing them, (at least not yet), the sergeant wanted to try and shore up their defenses.

"Colonel, can you keep an eye on the window for me?" The sergeant asked as the colonel eyed him wryly.

"Why? You going to get coffee?"

"Wow sir! Twice in two minutes! I don't think I've heard you joke the whole time you've been here."

"It must be the stress," answered the colonel. But for the life of him, the sergeant couldn't see any sign of distress from the colonel. Sure, he looked tired, but definitely not afraid. He didn't even look like he was sweating. The sergeant shook his head briefly in bewilderment and briskly walked over to the heavy filing cabinet.

He strained until kinetic energy won out over potential energy and the cabinet creaked and groaned its way towards the window. The room plunged into darkness, Beth equated the feeling to a full solar eclipse, with almost as much anxiety as the ancient peoples had during such an event.

He braced it with Private Monroe's favorite chair. Jamming the chair between the bars of Beth's cell and the filing cabinet, it would take nothing short of a rocket attack to dislodge the cabinet. Beth felt a little less exposed but no safer. She attributed the effect of the darkness on her mood, that was dampening even further.

"What do you think they're going to do, sir?" Sergeant O'Bannon said as he sat down heavily next to the colonel.

"Well, I would imagine…" the colonel began as he paused to pull out a cigar form his breast pocket. The sergeant couldn't believe it, but the thing was in perfect condition. The colonel bit off the end and lit it, taking a long puff and restarting his commentary. "Well, to begin with, they'll try coaxing us out by promising to spare our lives and all that nonsense. Then they will try and root us out of here, preferably alive and kicking. And when that fails, they will just gang rush us until their objective is secured. Then they will take their chances with the vault, again, at which they will ultimately fail."

"You seem pretty calm about the whole thing, sir."

"Well, unlike you, Sergeant, my significant other passed away four long years ago. I'm more than ready to meet up with her again. Now, if she were here," the colonel said as he turned his head to look in the direction of Beth's cell. "My innards would be flapping around like a sunfish on a dirt lane on a hot summer day."

"Yeah, I guess that's exactly how they feel." The sergeant said, the colonel nodded as he took another long drag off his cigar.

"You know, Sergeant, I never could stand that pencil dicked Lieutenant I can't say I was sorry to see him go. But what you did still wasn't right. I will say that I'm glad you're going to be going out as a soldier instead of as a traitor." The sergeant wasn't quite ready to throw in the towel just yet, but he nodded in agreement, nonetheless. If the end did come, this was infinitely better than the alternative.

Rounds pinged into the sergeant's makeshift window dressing, bowing out the sidewalls closest to Beth. But they held and the remaining survivors quickly learned this was more of a diversionary tactic than an actual attack.

Adams had taken his eyes off his station for no more than five seconds to watch the filing cabinet dance to the riddle of bullets. That was all the opportunity the attackers needed. A single shotgun blast to the chest literally ripped his ribs off his exposed left side.

For a moment, Adams realized the dire state he was in as he attempted to hold his lung into place. But sanity and life are fragile things; both slipped quickly away as his damaged lung plopped to the floor with an audible splat. Adams hadn't even hit the floor before the frontal assault began. The first two never made it through the door, but managed to shield it long enough to let three of their team through. Now it was a full out dogfight in the holding area.

Two of the men jumped off to the right and had Sergeant O'Bannon pinned down. The sergeant was sure that he had winged one of them, but it obviously wasn't a mission impeding injury, because the man still fired back. The colonel dispatched the man who jumped to the left, where there wasn't a stick of furniture anywhere in sight. The man's eyes grew to the size of saucers when he came to the realization that he would never get a shot off.

He, however, was quickly replaced by three reinforcements and the colonel found himself completely outgunned. The men began slowly advancing, each taking turns firing covering rounds. The sergeant and the colonel could not even get a single shot off now as bullets buzzed all around them. The sergeant did find humor in the fact that Private Monroe's desk top was actually bulletproof, not that it was going to matter much soon, but it still provided some humor for him.

"What are you smiling at, Sergeant?" the colonel said as he placed another clip in his weapon. The colonel did find that the sergeant's grin was infectious and soon he was grinning at the corners of his mouth also. Stress can do funny things to a man, it can make him weep like a child or make him laugh like a loon. This duo leaned closer to the latter than the former.

"Are you ready, Sergeant?" the colonel asked. Although the question was never clearly stated, it did not hinder the sergeant's understanding. He knew without further clarification what the colonel had in mind.

"On three, Colonel?" the sergeant replied as the colonel's grin threatened to wrap around his head.

"One," the sergeant started.

"Two," the colonel added.

Wordlessly, they counted to three in unison and popped up like Jack-in-the-boxes on crack. Sergeant O'Bannon was dimly aware of how close the attackers crept in. He had to adjust his aim as the men, mere feet away, froze in fear at how exposed they suddenly were. The sergeant's senses were in overdrive as he watched, yes, watched the bullets come out of his barrel, like a high-speed camera.

His first round made contact with the man closest to his proximity. The sergeant was amazed with the damage the bullet made upon impact. The man's chest first collapsed around the bullet as it began its penetration through his chest bone. Then the super-heated blood and bone began to expand and the chest literally blew out towards the front. As the sheer force of the impact hurtled the man backwards, the wound once again collapsed in on itself. The sergeant watched as blood droplets arced downwards from the entry wound. He was a little astonished at how little blood came from the wound, but what the sergeant didn't have time to contemplate was that the super-heated round almost completely cauterized the wound upon impact.

The sergeant turned to fire at anyone in his scope of view. A ray of hope surged in the sergeant's chest as he realized just how completely they had caught the attackers unawares. They knew that they had been caught with their pants down, and there wasn't a thing they could do.

The colonel was laughing like a madman. The barrel of his M-16 was blazing as rounds burst through it. Four men fell by the time the colonel had exhausted his thirty round clip. Sanity did lapse for a split second when he realized he was dry firing his weapon.

As he reached down for his next magazine, the first round struck home. The colonel turned towards the sergeant as the bullet tore through his heart. Pumping blood soared through the air as the sergeant realized the colonel's aorta had been shredded. Death came quickly and honor followed.

The sergeant also had unloaded his clip and with agonizing slowness, he reached down to replace his rounds. With his hand down by his belt, the sergeant attempted to pull the clip up from its resting place when he got shot in his left hand. It caught him in the index finger and ripped right through to his middle finger. Both fingers hung from his now useless hand by no more than the seven layers of skin we all possess.

The sergeant could think of nothing left to do than heave his weapon at the men advancing on him. Rounds hit from seemingly everywhere. The sergeant collapsed in a heap on top of the colonel. As he fell, he hoped that his son would never see him like this. Then darkness folded in upon his senses.

Three more men came into the room. One appeared to be the leader judging by his mannerisms and the way the men were deferential to him than by any insignia or obvious sign of rank. The sergeant gained varying degrees of alertness. He was bothered by something which he failed to complete, but for the life of him, or lack thereof, he could not remember what it was.

Between the incessant buzzing in his head from things he had not yet completed and the pain in his side from who knows what? The sergeant knew that right now would not be the end. He slightly shifted his weight to alleviate the pain from what was poking him, but to no avail. His broken body could not respond to his commands. He slowly moved his arm and was happy when it did. He moved it under his side just as he closed his hand upon the source of half his problems.

The colonel's gun, still in its holster, was sticking straight up when the sergeant's body fell on him. The sergeant reveled in his luck that he might just be able to satisfy some of his desires in this life before he moved on.

"Check the cells," the leader said as the smoke settled in the room. An eerie silence crept over the floor while Death smiled at its handiwork.

Beth's heart was slamming against her chest wall. How could they not hear it? she thought. At any second, she felt like her rib cage would begin to break under the thudding.

The men advanced, but this was a more cautious advance, lest they get caught unawares again. Beth could hear the men's boots as they came towards her cell. She listened in horror as the metallic sounds of bunk beds being turned over rang in her ears.

She kept her pistol pointed straight up in the air so that when her bunk was upturned, she would at least get some measure of satisfaction as she watched one of her assailants die before she became their next victim.

The men had gotten down to her cell and hesitated. The frightfully poor lighting was affecting them. The two men envisioned their worst fears as they stumbled into the dead zone at the far corner of the cell.

The first man said a small prayer and did the sign of the holy trinity upon his chest as he took his first tentative step forward. A single shot broke through the silence and Beth wondered if she had done it. No, she realized, her finger wasn't even on the trigger.

The man who was approaching suffered the bullet as it passed right through the back of his knee. But the bulk of the damage was inflicted as the bullet found its way out. The man's kneecap exploded when the round exited. His bone fragments littered the floor as he fell, face first, into Beth's cell.

Beth panicked when the man looked right at her, and tense milliseconds passed before she realized that nothing cognitive flashed through his eyes. Shock had begun its slow demise and soon Death would have another party-goer. More bullets tore through the sergeant, but he had already left this world the moment his final shot exited the colonel's handgun.

"Detrick! Get Feyonovich out of here. Take him to the doctor," the leader shouted. Detrick couldn't be more pleased to get out of that hallway. Something sinister awaited him in that cell, he was sure of it, and he had no desire to find out first hand. Detrick hefted Feyonovich onto his shoulder and never spared a look back to see if anybody or anything was following.

Death sat upon Beth's bunk. A deep scowl lined his face; two lives had been taken off his roster. No matter, he thought, they'll be mine soon enough. He left with his bundle of souls, some to be delivered heavenwards, but the bulk of today's would be headed down below. But again, this did not bother him, it was just another facet of his being. He, by definition, was neither good nor bad; he just was. As integral to the universe as air, fire and water and older than the cosmos itself, Death wandered the great vastness of time and space long before God and Satan began to play out their games.

Death had always known that the souls of the dead could never truly be owned, he was merely the way station upon which these souls made their transformation. But God had petitioned Death. "These are my creations and when their life runs dry, I wish to have their essences remain here with me." Death acquiesced more out of curiosity than from deference. For not even God had power over the eternal one. Man had only to realize that no one nor anything could control his soul. But first God and then Lucifer requested this and Death had obliged. It made no difference to him. All the souls he had collected over the millennia would be free again someday anyway.

Everyone had an expiration date, everyone. And when their time came they, like everyone else, would once again be reunited with the column of life force that pervaded the cosmos from one end to the other. Of all that Death had seen created and destroyed and recreated again, this life force column had always been there too, pre-dating even him.

Where it came from, he never knew. It was there when he came into consciousness and, as far as he knew, would always be there. After all this time, one thing he was sure of was that he never would know. It was just another part of the grand scheme of things he had to accept and expect. Death pondered for a moment more, but he did not have the luxury of time to dwell on such matters, his slate was full and growing.

Beth listened as the rest of the men went around the room looking for anything of value. None came down Beth's corridor and for that, she was thankful. For two full days, Beth kept herself cramped under the cot. During the majority of that time, she lapsed into fitful bouts of sleep, only to wake up twitching with her muscles spasming.

On more than one occasion, she had tossed her cot into the air, the clanging of which lingered for what seemed a small eternity. She had lain there, silently waiting for the approach of men that was sure to ensue from such a foreign noise. But, fortunately, the men moved on to a different part of the building where their prize waited.

It had taken nearly a whole case of explosives and a bulldozer, but the men finally gained entry into their coveted possession. Beth listened to them for nearly four hours as they celebrated their victory. She had been in sheer agony those last few hours, needing to partake of the most basic of bodily functions, elimination. She cramped in pain as her bowels and bladder writhed in agony.

She contemplated just merely relaxing and doing the deed where she lay, but she feared that the smell would give her away if the men came around for one more sweep. So it was, when she heard the trucks, cars and motorcycles start up, that she began her exit from her cavern. It was a mighty effort for her to even get to her knees. Standing fully erect was not a possibility. The cramping kept her crouched over like someone more than triple her age.

She waddled past the carnage that littered the jail floor, never stopping to look at the man who had briefly stolen her heart. Her eyesight was a pinholed focus. She knew if she didn't make her destination soon, she would pass out and do what she was so valiantly trying not to do. Beth made her way out the door and took an immediate left. The rest rooms were mere miles away, at least her body thought so.

Oh great! The ladies' room is further down the hallway, was the first notion that passed into her mind. "God! What am I thinking?" she mumbled as she opened the men's bathroom door. She had nary a second to spare as she

fumbled with her jeans buttons.
"Damn button fly!" she cursed. Beth rested her sweating head against the stall walls as she alternated between relief and cramping. She was sure she had not done her body any good by its long stint of abstinence. Even long after she had finished, she stayed put, reveling in the normalcy that had been reinstated. Peace and tranquility overcame her, at least until she heard the whistle.

The sweat on her forehead instantly turned to ice. Beth moved as quickly and silently as she could to stand back up and refasten her pants. 'Oh my God, my gun!' Beth panicked. She was defenseless. At least she was until she looked at the floor of her stall and realized she had brought the treasure with her.

In her agony, she had neither the will nor the strength to unclutch her hands, and one of those hands had been holding onto the pistol. She counted her lucky stars as she picked up the pistol and stood upon the seat of the toilet, lest someone look under the partitions and see her shoes.

"Boady!" The mystery voice yelled. "Come on, Boady! The rest of the guys are leaving, man. Let's go!" The man got closer, opening every door he passed to search for his friend. The man pushed open the door to the bathroom. "Boady! You in here?" No response. "Oh my gawd!" the man said from an obviously pinched nose. "Boady? Did you kill a skunk in here?" Beth blushed in embarrassment. "Can't....get...my...breath," the man stuttered, obviously thinking he was making fun of his friend. But what Beth wasn't prepared for was what the man did next. He approached her stall, the man's face turned instantly ashen as he pushed the door open. Beth sat on her haunches with the pistol aimed squarely at his head, while his weapon had been placed on his back for comfort. He had not seen the reason to keep it at the ready, at least, not until this very moment. As the initial shock wore off, the man attempted to pull the rifle to the front. Beth fired, more out of instinct than knowledge.

The noise was deafening in the small enclosure. Her

hearing was toast and the only sound she heard were the bells that clanged in her head. Smoke filled the small cubicle. The recoil of the weapon pushed her off her haunches and thudded her back onto the seat of the toilet. The bullet had not pushed this stranger away.

She feared that she had completely missed. With the disorientation that she felt, she didn't think she would be able to get another shot off. And then she looked up to realize that the top half of his skull had given way to a gray and red, fleshy matter, which held no obvious shape she could recognize. The man seemed to slide down more than collapse, but the outcome was the same. She stared at his head as it pulsated out its remaining contents.

The wheels spun in her head. She could not stand to look at this man but neither could she tear her eyes away from the macabre event. His head took on the appearance of a soft boiled egg in a teacup. Shards of bone protruded all around his crown. His thoughts or, at least, his thought container was spread open for all to see.

"Hammie?" she heard faintly. "Hamster! Where are you? Stop screwing around!" That was a little louder and sufficient to begin the sweeping process in the dusty regions of her brain.

"Oh shit," She intoned. Her reasoning took over. If she had been temporarily deafened by the shot, than this "faint" voice was a lot closer than she wished. Beth sprang over the folded body and nearly lost her balance as she slipped on the wet tiles. Tiles slickened by the material that once made this man whole.

She looked down long enough to make her footing sure, but the sight was a nightmare to be revisited on another occasion. Beth opened the door and took a precursory glance out to see how close the man was. Thankfully, he had not rounded her corner, at least, not yet.

She debated with the thought of going back and hiding in her cell, but she vowed to herself to never go back there. Anyway, she didn't think that she would be able to handle the sight of the bloated and now blue body of her sergeant. She ran down the corridor towards the exit, heedless of the fact that the blood and brain on her shoes was leaving a telltale trail for someone to follow.

***

Kuvlar, the interim supreme commander sat huddled in his chair, or throne, as he liked to think of it. But had he been wearing a crown, it would have weighed heavily right now. All was not going well in this planetary invasion. The ship, HIS ship, he reminded himself, had suffered a grievous wound, the likes of which had not been inflicted since the intergalactic war with the Stryvers.

During that time long, long ago, all of the Progerian ships had been fitted with distress beacons. Whenever a ship came under attack, a signal was emitted. For fighters, the signal went to the mother ship that launched it. In the case of the much bigger and thus more valuable mother ship, the signal traveled through sub-space folds back to the Progerian home planet. The ship had transmitted for no more than three minutes before Kuvlar had the foresight to shut it off.

But three minutes was two minutes and fifty nine seconds too long. The signal had not yet reached his home planet but it would, soon. And after that, at least one mother ship would be dispatched to see what the problem was. And then, Kuvlar feared, all hell would break loose. He was not responsible for the hu-mans' attack on this ship, but in the eyes of his superiors, he would be blamed. This was a philosophy that killed more than one officer in the ranks. When one officer had the buck passed onto his desk, he would, more often than not, relinquish such responsibility to his immediate subordinate. Most times by a rifle blast to the underside of the jaw.

Kuvlar, however, would not go down, not that way. He was much too resourceful and ambitious, he thought to himself. True, they had lost a much larger percentage of fighters than anticipated, and also true, the hu-man civilization had not yet completely crumbled under the stress of anarchy. He was determined to have this planet under his control and being productive by the time his so-called "help" arrived.

It was only a matter of time before his Genogerian troops were ready for a ground war. He had only to wait for enough transports to send them to the planet's surface so as to be effective as a fighting unit. 'Those hu-mans will run for their lives when they see my army marching towards them', the ISC mused. He knew that hu-manity was tough, but with no military left, his troops would have nothing more than mop-up duty to complete.

Kuvlar would be held more accountable for the loss of fighters and their pilots than for the Genogerian troops and with this fact, he made a decision that could ultimately determine the fate of this third stone from the small sun. He was sending in his troops without air support. This was usually the case, since by the time ground troops went in, there was little or no resistance left in the locals. So this reasoning gave him a foothold, should there be a hearing on his actions.

He would not, however, risk anymore of his ships. He had more than enough Genogerians, somewhere in the neighborhood of ten million. It was tough to tell; the brutes were always fighting and breeding so getting an accurate count was difficult at best and he felt he really only needed a third that many to do the job.

The most ever sent onto a planet at one time was half a million, and that had proved an enormous strain on their supply line. The food and supplies required for that undertaking had also been a strain on his pilots. "No, two hundred and fifty thousand will be plenty. I will start in their greatest country and let the rest of the world watch and learn what happens should they resist our rule." He laughed to himself or showed something as close to a laugh as his species possessed.

Yes, he would have everything under control, when the other "rescue" mother ship came. He would fix the mistakes of his predecessor, fool that he was, and become a hero on his home planet. Once this gem of a planet became a viable mining facility and colony, he would have a great city erected here called by his name.

Yes, it would be a beautiful place, and hu-mans would be in their proper place. The ones who acquiesced would be serving their masters and the ones who didn't, they'd also be serving their masters, as the main course, he daydreamed. He would wait for the outcome of the "games" when his champion, Slook, killed the remaining hu-man. Then, he would hit the planet while its morale was at its lowest. He slammed the great mitt of his hand into his palm and licked his front teeth. The crown didn't weigh so much now.

Chapter 49 – Mike Journal Entry Twelve
The Fight

It was D-Day or rather, my personal D-Day. I wasn't nervous, which actually surprised me. Concerned, but almost from a distant vantage point. I thought I should be nervous but I couldn't seem to muster it up. I guess I had come to some sort of peace with the whole thing. The inevitable conclusion was here, but how it played out was still to be determined.

The guards came in, four of them. They didn't exactly exude their feelings, but I almost got a sense of the respect that they had for me. If anything gave it away, it was their postures. All four of them were at the ready if I so much as sneezed. Chances were, I wouldn't make it to the arena, at least, not in one piece.

Two guards walked ahead of me, regularly turning their heads to make sure that I wasn't creeping up on them and the two in the rear were even more vigilant, if that was possible. It was kind of comical, twelve hundred pounds of ferocious, man-eating, planet-conquering, croc-aliens being afraid of me. I didn't think that I'd make a good snack for just one of them.

My heart sank a bit upon entering into the arena. There was nothing, except, of course, for the thunderous crowds and the dozen or so cameras. If my eyes weren't fooling me, it looked like they had been raided from some local Boston television studios, one of the cameras had a WBZ sticker emblazoned on it.

But beyond that, nothing. The arena floor was just

that--a floor. And from the sight of it, a concrete floor. I touched it to be sure, and without a doubt, that's what it was or at least a passable facsimile of that material. The walls were also barren. There wasn't so much as a slingshot. How was David supposed to take down Goliath in this adventure without a slingshot? Now my nerves began to show themselves. Great timing, I cursed. The guards took that as their cue to get out.

The announcer began my introduction. The hissing at the pronouncement of my name let me know what they thought of me. I guess I couldn't blame them. I was the equivalent of a New York Yankee coming into Fenway Park. They hated me, and not just for being a "hu-man." Rightfully or not, I had been blamed for the nuclear strike that crippled the ship. But then again, I had also kidnapped their supreme commander and shot some of the guards down. So, apparently they had good reason to hate me.

Well, screw them! I hated them too as I gesticulated wildly with my middle finger. The nuance might be lost on this crowd, but I'm sure the people back home liked it. It kind of reminded me of a poster that a friend of mine once had when we were kids. It showed a small mouse holding up his middle finger to an eagle that was bearing down on him. It was called "the last act of defiance," or something along those lines.

But now that I thought about it, I really didn't want to be the mouse. He may have gotten off a great gesture, but he still ended up as lunchmeat. A small quiver shook through my body. I hope nobody just walked over my grave.

***

At that moment, Paul touched the old Hobbit Tree to say a small prayer for my well being, before heading inside to watch.

***

Lost in my thoughts, I looked up when the crowd began to roar; Durgan had entered. Like most of his bouts, he had no shirt on and he looked chiseled, literally. He looked like he could have been cut from stone. He flexed and brought his arms up to egg the crowd on, and it worked. They truly loved him.

I wondered for a moment if they would cheer this loud for him when it came time to fight "their champion." I quickly brushed that thought aside since it would mean he had won this battle. I was not quite ready to meet my maker, not just yet anyway.

The buzzer sounded and an eerie silence came over the throngs; the game was afloat. My legs felt wooden as I approached the center of the arena, for truly, there was nowhere else to go. Durgan's approach was much more relaxed and casual than my plodding. As we drew nearer to each other, I got into a readied position. We circled each other a couple of times, sizing up the competition, but I was as familiar with his style as he was with mine. I seemed to rely more on luck whereas Durgan relied on a maniacal brute strength; advantage Durgan.

Waiting for the tiger to strike seemed the prudent approach, but prudence was never my forte. I sprang, thinking that perhaps Durgan's nonchalance would be his undoing. But, for all his acting, he was ready.

With lightning bolt speed, he landed a blow to my cheek that sent me sprawling; but more dangerously, had me seeing spots. Unconsciousness was a heartbeat away. Durgan lunged after me. He was in motion right after his initial contact and he almost made it to the ground before I did. Dazed as I was, I couldn't believe how fast this madman was. Does insanity make you faster?

Durgan landed on my chest and the air rushed out of my lungs as if expelled through a cannon. But I never had any chance to attempt damage control. Punch after punch rained down on me. The spots in my eyes begin to darken and my vision started to narrow.

***

Paul and the rest of his officers sat glued to the television set. How I was going to get out of this totally eluded them. Paul stood up, getting ready to leave the room before he watched his best friend in life become another casualty in this brutal war.

***

Mercifully, Durgan switched his weight to get a better angle for his punches. Sweet air rushed into my lungs as the tunnel vision widened ever so slightly. But it was a short-lived victory as he renewed his assault.

Durgan was in heaven as he watched my eye swell almost completely shut. Even he couldn't believe his good fortune. The fight was going way better than he ever anticipated. The stage was set and he wanted to claim the title of victor that I stole from him for so long. My hands fell to my sides. I was not even able to defend myself, I hoped that his signature move of breaking my neck wouldn't hurt too much. It couldn't hurt more than what he was doing now.

***

Paul turned and headed towards his outer office. Nobody noticed his departure.

***

Durgan was right; people were eating this up. It was macabre and they knew it, but it didn't make any difference. It was like a car accident, everyone HAD to slow down and take a look; it was human nature, hardwired into our instincts, for better or worse.

I had one card left to play. It wasn't a great card, not an ace, more like a nine, but it was the only thing I had left; besides it worked on my sister, at least, sometimes. Especially when she wasn't expecting it, and I couldn't believe that Timmons thought I had anything left.

I purposefully pulled my legs up and, with one quick thrust, I pushed up on my pelvis with everything that I had left. Durgan lost his balance. His center of gravity had been shifted and, with his arms being used as human hammers, he had nothing with which to stabilize himself. He fell to the right as his right hand came smashing down dangerously close to my already bruised and battered face.

His hand came into full contact with the concrete. I heard an audible cracking even over the electric buzzing of the spectators. He howled in rage, his face turning ten shades of red as he pulled back his wounded, mangled hand. Ragged pieces of flesh dangled from his misshapen fingers and blood poured out. The bright white of bone was in stark contrast to the much darker brew that flowed freely.
***
The officers at the Hill yelled in amazement. Paul rushed in to see what the din was about.
***
Durgan was enraged, with what would amount to a small hiccup in his plans. He began to use the still very functional and lethal left hand to deliver still more face-smashing punches. And if I called these hammer blows before, Durgan had since grabbed a sledge; he wanted to end this thing now.

I tried to thwart off his attack but it was like using toilet paper to sop up the ocean. I changed tactics, I stopped my defense and began my own offensive. By the time Durgan figured it out, it was entirely too late. I snatched after his completely unprotected and wounded hand. I grabbed his hand like a pit-bull. He attempted to pull me away but I hung on, constantly squeezing and pulling, prodding his sore wound. My stomach involuntarily convulsed as I heard the bones in his hand grind together.

Durgan's punches stopped all together. He was screaming in pain and agony as he cursed me to let go of his hand. I tried for all I was worth to rip his ring finger and pinkie from his body. I lost my grip from the slickness of the blood that cascaded from his hand. His last two fingers hung uselessly from his hand as he spun away from me.

He bounded up and walked away from me, hunched over, cradling his wounded extremity as he left. I lay on the ground, not knowing if I could muster the strength to get up off the tarmac. My face had puffed up to nearly double its size. Blood oozed from a half a dozen spots on my oh, so sore face.

***

"Get up!" Paul screamed. "Get the fuck up!" He was yelling at the screen.

***

My chance was now, Durgan's back was to me, but just keeping my eyes focused seemed about the most intense thing I could accomplish right now. The clouding gray around me ever so slowly began its recession; but not to worry, pain filled the gap. Ultimately, pain meant life; I was still alive, at least, but Durgan would not let me rest long. I marshaled everything I had to roll over and began the monstrous task of standing up.

Upon regaining my stance, I had to reorientate myself to a still recoiling Durgan. His back was completely turned as I made my not so stealthy approach. He knew I was coming and I knew that he knew. One hand or not, the man was still three times as dangerous as any other man I had ever fought.

I had not completely covered the distance between us when Durgan stood up and whirled my way. His teeth were gritted in determination. I stopped in my tracks, so much for the element of surprise.

"You know, I'm going to have to kill you for this!" He yelled as he held up his twisted, useless hand for me to see.

"I was under the impression you were going to kill me anyway," I answered. My sarcasm angered him even more, if that was possible.

He rose with a vengeance. He came at me slow and steady, but advancing nonetheless. Images of Arnold Schwarzenegger as the Terminator flitted across my brain. He was coming and, useless hand or not, I could see in his eyes that he meant to finish what he had started.

My face ached from the swelling. Although I couldn't see it, I could feel the bruising. Rocky had nothing on me. My vision was suffering, some from the puffiness but mostly from the blood that kept oozing in. The sting of it was, in a word, excruciating, but I feared rubbing it away because I thought I might completely lose my vision. Like a car that gets oil on the windshield, more times than not, if you try to wipe it away, it merely smears all over the place making your drive just a little more interesting. My depth perception was taking a serious hit. I was beyond wary of Durgan, I was hyper-sensitive.

He was planning to end this; no softening me up, no playing to the crowds, this was just pure murderous intention in its most unadulterated form. He grinned as he moved in. Any confidence I had built up was rapidly flowing away, like water from a burst dam. I made a feign for his wounded hand, and Durgan's advance did falter. He didn't exactly stop, but he did hitch a bit. Well, at least it was nice to know he was still human, to a degree.

"I know what you're thinking, you little turd," he growled. Spittle flowed freely from his mouth. "And you had better stop. I'm still twice the man you'll ever be, or were," he sneered. "Today's your lucky day, bitch." Durgan kept moving forward slowly as he spoke. Maybe he was hoping I was distracted by his eloquent prose. "I was going to mess you up a little more before I snapped your little twig neck. But now I've changed my mind, I'm just gonna twist the thing off now."

I couldn't take it anymore, the blood in my eye was stinging, I had to try and clear it away. He took that opportunity to lunge at me. Even as the impact of his left fist registered throughout my body, my mind tried to gauge how fast this brute was. My right temple throbbed from the abusive fist. My sight pinholed immediately. The only thing that saved me was pure, dumb luck.

As I became gravitationally challenged, I unconsciously reached out to break my fall. It just so happened that it was Durgan's shattered hand that I reached for. He groaned with the agony. His instinctive impulse to pull away caused me to land chin first on the concrete. From a far off, remote place in the recesses of my mind, I took note of the hard crunchy things in my mouth. Somewhere in the confused grasp of consciousness, the thought of teeth came into being. And then I finally put it all together. Son of a bitch! He broke my teeth!

If I lived long enough, I was going to be truly pissed. Uttering that thought might have been an issue because I had a good hunch or rather, a bad one that, along with my teeth, my jaw had also been broken. Durgan was moaning about something.

I could barely register any cognizant thoughts; but at least, I wasn't in any pain, not this far down the consciousness ladder. But like a determined fireman, I began to advance up that ladder rung by rung. The pain, the excruciating pain was the first thing that struck my senses. I was in agony, my jaw was ablaze. I tried to move my jaw, which was, most likely, the worst thing I could've attempted today.

Alarms went off in my head, stars swam before my eyes. The pain brought me quickly to full alertness, but it was impossible to think clearly. Pain ruled all. I swallowed my splintered teeth; opening my jaw to spit them out was not an option. I pulled myself up off the ground, and standing, took a monumental effort. I swayed like corn in a Kansas tornado.

Durgan was hunched over a few feet away from me. It was difficult to decipher his actions, but he appeared to be trying to splint his hand up with some material from his pants. I staggered over in his general direction, but it definitely wasn't as a crow flies.

He didn't pay me much attention; he was lost, I supposed, in his own agony. If he even looked in my direction, I would probably have fallen over. But he did look up and I didn't fall, not yet anyway. His eyes narrowed as I made my circuitous charge.

With every possible ounce of energy I had left, I kicked my leg up. If I had missed, I would have fallen to the ground and never gotten up. There simply would have been nothing left with which to do it. But I did not miss. My shin came into full contact with Durgan's Adam's apple. I felt, rather than heard, it crack. I hoped to God it was him and not my leg. The contact sent shivers of pain up my spine. He teetered and then toppled over, his hands rushing to his now crushed larynx.

***

"Ahhhh!" Paul shouted. "He did it!" he exclaimed as he raised his arm up in the air.

***

Durgan reached out his bad hand towards me as if pleading for my help. Did he think I'd forgotten what had just been happening? I knew I didn't have the best short term memory in the world, but it wasn't that bad.

I wanted to let him slowly suffocate there on the ground. A quick death was entirely too good for the prick. But I was now drifting in and out of complete awareness. I knew if I passed out without finishing the job, there would be a high probability of the aliens fixing both of us up for round two, and luck or no, I'd never make it to a round three. Durgan's eyes pleaded with me as I came in close. But there was no remorse in those eyes, only self-preservation.

"Fuck you!" I mouthed silently as I brought the heel of my boot down on the bridge of his nose. The cartilage snapped like branches in an ice storm. I ground my heel in, caving in his face as best I could. Bones shattered as I brought my heel down three more times.

"Do something with that!" I yelled as I pointed towards Durgan' now ruined face, my ruined jaw grated with every word. The crowd was completely silent. A lot of drakkar had been lost that night. I was not going to be a fan favorite this time.

I stood there in the silence, not knowing what to do. Nothing happened as the crowd watched in shock and denial. And then the first sign of anything decent from these animals took place. The Genogerian champion that I was to fight next stood up and began clapping.

Now it was my turn to look on in stunned silence. No

one joined in his ovation, but the gesture was enough. Two guards came my way. Movement from the ground caught my attention. Durgan's hand twitched and grasped as I waited for my escort out of there. I stepped on his hand as I went to meet the guards.

Check out these other titles by Mark Tufo

Zombie Fallout

It was a flu season like no other. With fears of contracting the H1N1 virus running rampant through the country, people lined up in droves to try and obtain one of the coveted vaccines. What was not known, was the effect this largely untested, rushed to market, inoculation was to have on the unsuspecting throngs.

Within days, feverish folk throughout the country, convulsed, collapsed and died, only to be re-born. With a taste for brains, blood and bodies, these modern day zombies scoured the lands for their next meal. Overnight the country became a killing ground for the hordes of zombies that ravaged the land.

This is the story of Michael Talbot, his family and his friends. When disaster strikes, Mike a self-proclaimed survivalist, does his best to ensure the safety and security of those he cares for. Can brains beat brain eaters? It's a battle for survival, winner take all!

Zombie Fallout 2: A Plague Upon Your Family
Zombies have destroyed Little Turtle, the Talbot's find themselves on the run from a ruthless enemy that will stop at nothing to end their lineage. Here are the journal entries of Michael Talbot, his wife Tracy, their three kids Nicole, Justin and Travis. With them are Brendon, Nicole's fiancée and Tommy previously a Wal-Mart door greeter who may be more than he seems. Together they struggle against a relentless enemy that has singled them out above all others. As they travel across the war-torn country side they soon learn that there are more than just zombies to be fearful of, with law and order a long distant memory some humans have decided to take any and all matters into their own hands. Can the Talbots come through unscathed or will they suffer the fate of so many countless millions before them. It's not just brains versus brain-eaters anymore. And the stakes may be higher than merely life and death with eternal souls on the line.

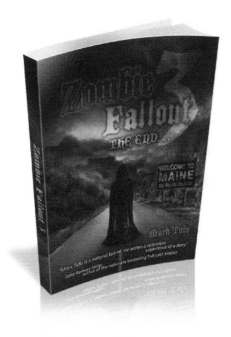

Zombie Fallout 3: The End…

Continues Michael Talbot's quest to be rid of the evil named Eliza that hunts him and his family across the country. As the world spirals even further down into the abyss of apocalypse one man struggles to keep those around him safe. Side by side Michael stands with his wife, their children, his friends and the wonder Bulldog Henry along with the Wal-Mart greeter Tommy who is infinitely more than he appears and whether he is leading them to salvation or death is only a measure of degrees.

As Justin continues to slip further into the abyss he receives help from an unexpected ally all of which leads up to the biggest battle thus far.

Dr. Hugh Mann – A Zombie Fallout Prequel 3.5
Dr Hugh Mann delves deeper into what caused the zombie invasion. Early in the 1900's Dr. Mann discovers a parasite that brings man to the brink of an early extinction. Come along on the journey with Jonathan Talbot is bride to be Marissa and the occasional visitations from the boy with the incredible baklava. Could there be a cure somewhere here and what part does the blood locket play?

Zombie Fallout IV: The End…Has Come and Gone

The End…has come and gone. This is the new beginning, the new world order and it sucks. The end for humanity came the moment the U.S. government sent out the infected flu shots. My name is Michael Talbot and this is my journal. I'm writing this because no one's tomorrow is guaranteed, and I have to leave something behind to those who may follow.

So continues Mike's journey, will he give up all that he is in a desperate bid to save his family and friends? Eliza is coming, can anyone be prepared?

Indian Hill

This first story is about an ordinary boy, who grows up in relatively normal times to find himself thrust into an extra-ordinary position. Growing up in suburban Boston he enjoys the trials and tribulations that all adolescents go through. From the seemingly tyrannical mother, to girl problems to run-ins with the law. From there he escapes to college out in Colorado with his best friend, Paul, where they begin to forge new relationships with those around them. It is one girl in particular that has caught the eye of Michael and he alternately pines for her and then laments ever meeting her.

It is on their true 'first' date that things go strangely askew. Mike soon finds himself captive aboard an alien vessel, fighting for his very survival. The aliens have devised gladiator type games. The games are of two-fold importance for the aliens. One reason, being for the entertainment value, the other reason being that they want to see how combative humans are, what our weaknesses and strengths are.

Follow Mike as he battles for his life and Paul as he battles to try and keep main stream US safe.

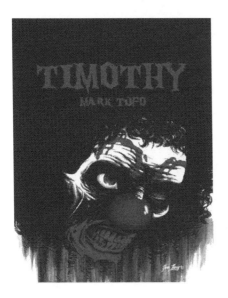

Timothy

Timothy was not a good man in life being undead did little to improve his disposition. Find out what a man trapped in his own mind will do to survive when he wakes up to find himself a zombie controlled by a self-aware virus.

Please look also for:
the story '**My Name is Riley**' published in the Undead Tales Anthology by Rymfire books!

Follow Riley an American Bulldog as she struggles to keep what remains of her pack/family safe from a zombie invasion.

Printed in Great Britain
by Amazon.co.uk, Ltd.,
Marston Gate.